Also by Hannah Fielding

Burning Embers
The Echoes of Love

Book 1 of the Andalucían Nights Trilogy:
Indiscretion

Praise for *Indiscretion*:

'A captivating tale of love, jealousy and scandal.' ***The Lady***

Praise for *The Echoes of Love* (winner of the Gold Medal for Romance at the 2014 Independent Publisher Book Awards):

'One of the most romantic works of fiction ever written ... an epic love story beautifully told.' ***The Sun***

'Fans of romance will devour it in one sitting.' ***The Lady***

'All the elements of a rollicking good piece of indulgent romantic fiction.' ***BM Magazine***

'This book will make you wish you lived in Italy.'

Fabulous **magazine**

'The book is the perfect read for anyone with a passion for love, life and travel.' *Love it!* **magazine**

'Romance and suspense, with a heavy dose of Italian culture.'

Press Association

'A plot-twisting story of drama, love and tragedy.'

Italia! **magazine**

'There are many beautifully crafted passages, in particular those relating to the scenery and architecture of Tuscany and Venice … It was easy to visualise oneself in these magical locations.'

Julian Froment blog

'Fielding encapsulates the overwhelming experience of falling deeply, completely, utterly in love, beautifully.'

Books with Bunny

'Hannah Fielding writes in a beautifully elegant style, full of atmosphere and the sights, sounds and smells of Italy. I was transported to a Venice in winter for the Carnival, to the Italian coast, and to Tuscany.'

Lindsay Townsend, historical romance author

MASQUERADE

HANNAH FIELDING

LONDON
WALL
PUBLISHING

First published in hardback and paperback in the UK in 2015 by
London Wall Publishing Ltd (LWP)

First published in eBook edition in the UK in 2015 by
London Wall Publishing Ltd (LWP)

A CIP catalogue record for this book is
available from the British Library.

PB ISBN 978-0-9929943-6-5
EB ISBN 978-0-9929943-7-2

1 3 5 7 9 10 8 6 4 2

Print and production managed by
Jellyfish Solutions Ltd

London Wall Publishing Ltd (LWP)
24 Chiswell Street, London EC1Y 4YX

And, after all, what is a lie?
'Tis but the truth in masquerade.

LORD BYRON

CHAPTER 1

Cádiz, 1976

Luz set eyes on him for the first time from her seat on Zeyna's back as the fine white Arab mare stepped down the narrow path from the cliff that led to the beach. He was sitting on the edge of the track, leaning nonchalantly against a wild carob tree, watching her while chewing on a sprig of heather. As she drew nearer, she met his steady gaze, spirited and wild. At that moment she had no idea this man would have the power to change her world and create such havoc in her heart, that she would emerge from the experience a different person. Fate had not yet lit up the winding pathway of her life nor the echoes of history along it, but now, in front of this stranger, a disturbing awareness leapt into flame deep inside her and began to flicker intensely. Without thinking, she tugged on Zeyna's reins to slow the mare down.

For a moment they stared at each other. He was clearly a *gitano*, one of those people that Luz's family had always warned her to steer clear of. The frayed, cut-down denims sat low on his hips, revealing deeply tanned, muscular long legs, and his feet were bare as though he had just walked straight from the beach. Unruly chestnut hair, bleached golden in parts by the sun, tumbled to his shoulders; his smooth copper skin glowed more than that of any gypsy she had ever seen. As she allowed her gaze to flick back to his face, Luz caught the flash of amused, provocative arrogance in those bright, burning eyes, mixed with something deeper that she didn't understand. She swallowed. The overwhelming masculinity of the *gitano* unsettled her. Luz lifted her chin resolutely but felt the pull of his magnetism reaching out and gripping her, beguiling and dangerous, so that instinctively she nudged her mount and they broke into a smooth canter. The thumping of her heart sounded loud in her ears. She could sense his eyes on her, as a palpable touch, even as she rode away, trembling, and the feeling remained with her until she knew she was out of sight.

Had Zeyna picked up her mistress's inner turmoil? Luz was pulling on her bridle as the mare tossed her head this way and that, snorting. Surprised by the horse's unusual behaviour, Luz looked down at her hands and realized that she was clutching the reins much too tightly. She relaxed her hold. 'I'm sorry, old girl. My fault,' she whispered, leaning forward to pat the mare's neck. Feeling free, the handsome creature surged forth without hesitation.

The wind blew warm and salty; it touched Luz's long black hair like a caress, threatening and tantalizing, wrapping a few silky wisps around her face. An unusual heat coursed through her, even though she was dressed only in a T-shirt, jeans tucked into riding boots. She raised her head against the breeze, letting the briny air course over her body, willing it to drive away this unfamiliar disquiet from her mind.

Gradually her sense of foreboding subsided and the awesome setting regained its hold. She felt an exhilaration and breadth of freedom in the vast solitude of the deserted beach and the wide horizons of the sea. The intense blue of the bay lay before her in the late afternoon sun. The lines of the land were so recognizable to her: no trees, no shrubs, no delicate tinting nor soft beauty, but a pure, distinct outline of form, almost terrifying in its austerity. Then, from time to time, there were the shadows of great clouds moving overhead, staining this infinite expanse of dunes that stretched before her like a vast tapestry in shades of cream, greys and silver. Galloping in the wind on the back of her beautiful white mare, Luz felt in harmony with the Andalucían landscape and with herself. She had left her flat in Chelsea, finished her job in Scotland and now she was back in Spain, a newly born post-Franco Spain, ruled by an energetic young king and teetering on the edge of new possibilities. She was back at last in her beloved country, this time to stay.

Luz María Cervantes de Rueda was the only child to Count Salvador Cervantes de Rueda and his beautiful half-English, half-Spanish wife, Alexandra. At the time, their love story had made newspaper headlines and had been a favoured subject for wagging tongues in the drawing rooms of Spanish society. There had been a scandal involving Count Salvador, a young gypsy girl and her ne'er-do-well brothers. To add to the gossip, Alexandra de Falla was not from a pure Spanish background. Her foreign ways had caused suspicion and disapproval among the cloistered circles, their traditions still so deeply rooted in conservative Spanish society. The fact that she was a romantic novelist, too, had caused many raised eyebrows. Some predicted doom when the couple's fairy-tale marriage was announced but, as in all fairy tales, the pair had surprised everyone and were still living happily ever after.

For the first eleven years of her life Luz had lived in Spain, spending July and August in Kent with her Great-Aunt Geraldine. Later, when she was sent to boarding school in Gloucestershire, she would return three times a year to El Pavón, the ancestral home of her father outside the city of Jerez: at Christmas, Easter and for part of the summer holidays.

Luz had just arrived in Cádiz that morning, straight from England. She intended to spend at least a week at L'Estrella, the family's summer house, before going on to see her parents at El Pavón. She was excited, pulsing with life, feeling as though she was on the verge of embarking on a great adventure.

It had been a long haul that had started with Cheltenham Ladies' College when she was eleven, through a master's degree in history and modern languages at Cambridge and, finally, two years spent in the Highlands of Scotland penning the biography of an ancestor for one of the great families of Britain. Now that book was delivered, she could feel that Spain was where she was meant to be, where she was *always* meant to be. Here, she could breathe, feel her body come alive under the Spanish sun, and let all the pent-up, reckless instincts she had tried so hard to tame all through boarding school in England run wild and free. Luz had never thought that those compulsive feelings she had were the secret machinations of 'destiny'; there was a sceptical, no-nonsense side to her inherited from her mother, along with a talent for writing, but she knew that the fiery Spanish nature that was her father's – and always got the better of her – had finally pulled her back to Andalucía.

Only that morning, when Luz had arrived at L'Estrella laden with suitcases, Carmela had handed her a letter that had come the day before. Ever since she had replied to an advertisement in the local paper for a biographer, she'd been praying for an interview. And here it was: a letter inviting her for a first meeting that week. Luz had barely been able to contain her relief and joy as she pulled the housekeeper into a delighted hug. She had really set her heart on this job, not only because she would be writing about Count Eduardo Raphael Ruiz de Salazar, one of the great painters of modern Spain, but also because the artist was from this part of the world and a large portion of the research would be done locally in Cádiz and its neighbouring towns. It seemed that now Luz had been given her reason to stay.

She brought Zeyna to a halt at the edge of the shore. The wild salty air seemed to be sweeping up from the beach as it brushed her cheek. She closed her eyes to savour its breath, delicious odours laden with iodine and fruits of the deep. The sun was setting in the late afternoon and the sky, gloriously mottled with apricot-pink and lilac, was broken here and there by shafts of light reflecting on the surface of the water, turning the calm ocean into a spectrum of peacock colours.

Now she could make out the fishing boats in the distance returning after a day's work: black toy insects, the antennae of their masts bristling against the flamingo-tinted sky. Gulls and terns mingled overhead, screeching, impatient for the laden fleet's arrival. Luz did not care much for birds. She found them – even the beautiful ones – eerie and menacing. It was time to be starting back.

The beach was no longer deserted. As she cantered along the shore she passed a few joggers and a couple of lovers strolling hand in hand. A child and his mother were flying a bright-red kite; a bunch of gypsies loitered on one of the dunes by an upturned wreck of a rowing boat. She was used to seeing these vagabonds around; they did not bother her – on the contrary, she found them colourful and mysterious, stirring her imagination. Today the gentle agitation in her moved a step further and, for a second, Luz's thoughts flashed back to the young gypsy who had so unnerved her. Her parents were wary of *gitanos* and Luz suspected that the reason she had been swept off to the protective cocoon of an English boarding school was to shield her from something. She had heard whispered snatches of gossip concerning the *gitanos'* involvement with her family. She had often attempted to prise some answers from her parents but they had always dismissed her questions, brushing off the stories as servants' tittle-tattle and malicious rumour. Not everyone approved of their marriage, they explained, and there were always narrow-minded and prejudiced people in the world. Every time Luz pushed, she found herself no further forward than before and although her inquisitive nature was dissatisfied by their explanations, she had given up asking questions and, for the time being, dismissed the whole thing from her mind.

As Luz approached the group, she noticed that the young gypsy was among them. She was nearly level with the *gitanos* when he turned, his eyes rising slowly to meet her gaze. For all their lazy manner they were sharp, green and sparkling, shadowed by thick, long dark lashes. Transfixed, Luz felt herself blushing under the watchful lion's gaze. Her stomach gave a little flutter; her concentration wavered. Then it all happened very quickly.

From the corner of her eye she was aware of the red kite falling. Spooked, Zeyna shied suddenly. The young woman tried to control her, but it was too late: the mare swerved to the right. Luz put her weight on the stirrup to steady herself but the girth was not tight enough and the saddle slipped sideways. Slowly and inexorably, she came off her mount with a cry. As she hit the hard sandy ground with a sickening thud to her head, the landscape swirled around her and she felt herself sinking into a deep black well. She fought to regain consciousness, hearing rushing footsteps, noises and voices all around her. Then two powerful arms lifted her; she felt her head fall back against a strong shoulder, then the shutters came down and she was plunged into oblivion. The blackout was complete.

*   *   *

'I'm taking her back to the camp,' Leandro announced to his companions as he scooped the unconscious young woman carefully into his arms.

His words were greeted with roars of laughter.

'I'm sure this will improve your relationship with Rosa no end,' scoffed a lanky youth with tattoos on both arms.

Leandro shrugged and took the lead, heading back up the beach. 'Her horse has bolted and we must make sure she's all right. That was a bad fall.'

'Yeah, yeah, talk about taking advantage of a chaotic situation. Do you think we've all been struck blind, *amigo*? We all saw the look you gave each other. And now you're her rescuing hero.' The lanky youth grinned, ruffling Leandro's hair, and playfully dodged the responding sideways kick of his friend's foot. '*A rio revuelto, ganancia de pescadores*, it is good fishing in troubled waters!'

'And you are paddling in the wrong river, Juan. You're lucky I have my hands full or I'd clip your ear.'

'Yeah, yeah. But your hands are full, *amigo*.' Juan winked at him.

'You're too cynical.' Leandro gently adjusted the svelte form higher in his arms and shook his head nonchalantly. 'I just want to make sure she's not hurt.'

'Do you know her?' Juan and the others fell into step alongside him.

'I've seen her around a few times,' Leandro said lightly. He deliberately kept his gaze level. Yes, he had seen her around often, going to and from the port at Cádiz every few months, or when his wanderings had taken him along the cliff, close to the house in the clouds. Usually she went riding along the beach and sometimes he saw her jogging; she always seemed to be on the move. He couldn't fail to notice that her body was supple and strong, yet so graceful. The first time he'd seen her, elegantly stepping out of her boat on to the quay, it was like a goddess had leapt into his vision and his heart had given a corresponding somersault. It was a feeling that had disturbed him. He had always observed her from afar after that, always without being noticed.

Today it had been different. By pure chance he had been at the port to see her motorboat drive in. She was back. He had known she would come down to the beach that afternoon – she always did on the day of her arrival in Cádiz – and he had deliberately waited for her at the side of the track. This time he was fixed on drawing her attention to him. It was his swift glance that had made her look at him; he had *willed* her to look at him. Then, as he had guessed, she headed slowly for the beach and it hadn't taken long for him to rejoin the others, knowing she would pass by. It was his fault that she had been distracted and fallen off her mount. She was normally a brilliant rider: he had watched her many times as she cantered up and down the beach on her white mare, a beautiful Amazon with her long raven-black mane flying behind her as though she was racing the wind. But he had needed those startling eyes to lock on to his once more.

Guilt washed over him. Protectively, his arms tightened a fraction around her and he clenched the slim, inert body a little closer to his muscular chest. The white V-neck T-shirt she was wearing was close-fitting, making him conscious of the curves beneath his hands. His chin brushed accidentally against her hair. Delicate whiffs of wild rose, jasmine and sandalwood, the essence of the bath oils she had bathed in before going down to the beach, came to him. The disturbance he felt was deep and strong. He moistened his dry lips and walked up the steep slope of rock, his gaze still fixed straight ahead, not daring to look down at her in case he lost control and gave himself away. The situation was awkward enough as it was. He was breathing hard. Some may have thought it was because his burden was too heavy, but Luz was light as a feather. No, it was not her weight that was making his chest rise and fall laboriously but the warmth of her soft curves pressing against him.

The sun was setting. A little distance from the sea in a glade as dry as brown wrapping paper, wild and barren lay the encampment. Yawning with caves and split by rocky gorges, it was a smaller than usual site and somewhat modern compared with most gypsy camps. It was close enough to Cádiz to be hooked up with electricity and running water. The caves had been excavated from the soft rock hundreds of years before, during the Moorish conquest of Spain, and after the Arabs' expulsion the *gitanos* quickly appropriated them as their own. Formed in a rough crescent along the hillside skirting the glade, many of these homes had crude rectangular doorways in front of which were assembled rickety chairs, tables and lines of washing.

Several tents and wooden caravans were grouped here and there, painted in bright reds, pinks, yellows and greens, and embellished with a wealth of carving. They were set up in an uneven semicircle facing the caves and completed the wide enclosure of haphazard dwellings. Right at the front of the camp, near the track leading down to the beach, was a solid bank of sacks and boxes of rubbish that marked the entrance.

Great wood fires were burning, above which large copper containers filled with stew – the powerful smelling *pirriá* for the evening meal – hung from iron hooks. Two gypsies were singing while beating metal horseshoes on an anvil over a fire, their strong, hoarse voices resounding loudly in the camp. Men sat in groups of three or four in front of their tents, chatting or playing cards; decrepit-looking mongrels sniffed around the cooking pots, hoping for a bone; olive-faced urchins of various ages played hopscotch or ball in front of their doorways.

They ran towards Leandro, clamouring, and clustered around him as he walked into the camp, carrying the girl. Children liked Leandro. He would usually take time to play and joke with them or hand out the sweets and chewing gum that were always kept in his pockets. Today, however, he walked right past them, his face grave, towards the largest and most elaborate-looking cave.

A *gitana* was standing at the entrance. She must have been in her late forties or early fifties, still handsome and well preserved for a gypsy, not a wrinkle on her olive skin, which nonetheless had a somewhat pallid look. A mass of tousled black hair undulated wildly around a fiercely sensual but hard face, and down to her shoulders. The gold and silver chains and bracelets she wore spoke of her status within the camp: a striking gypsy queen. A big black cat idled beside her as she stooped to stir the steaming contents of a large pot on the fire. Upon Leandro's approach, her blazing dark eyes broke into a smile, softening her features and making her look almost gentle.

'Where have you been, my boy, and what have you there?' Her voice was low-pitched and slightly husky.

Leandro gestured with his head towards the dunes. 'Her horse bolted so I brought her back here to make sure she wasn't hurt. She hit her head and lost consciousness.'

The *gitana* flicked a glance over Luz. 'Huh, this one's a *gajo*! We don't let their sort in the camp, you know that.' She pushed the ladle roughly through the stew, a heavily ringed hand resting on her hip.

'*Mamacita*, what would you have me do with her? I couldn't just leave her on the beach, she needed help.'

She met his expectant gaze and stopped stirring. 'So now I'm to let a *gajo* into my house because you decide to play rescuer, eh?' She sighed, her expression losing its hardness. 'You have a kind heart, my son, maybe too kind … very much like your father, may God rest his soul.' For a moment, her eyes filled with dreaming, and then the look was gone. She nodded curtly towards the cave. 'Take the stranger to my room. Lay her on my bed and I'll make her a brew for when she wakes up.'

Leandro pulled Luz closer, feeling her steady breathing against his chest, but made sure not to look down. His mother was keen-eyed, the last person he wanted to guess at any attachment he might have formed to a *gajo*.

'No one in the whole of Andalucía has your healing touch,' Leandro offered quickly. He grinned. 'If anyone can put her right, it's you.'

'We'll see,' she murmured begrudgingly and watched her son as he went inside.

Many of the caves were one room, though some of the larger ones had two or three, fashioned out of the knobbly rock with low-domed ceilings and rough terracotta tiles on the floor. This cave was vast, its thick whitewashed walls hung with a scattering of religious pictures. In the bedroom an old iron lantern had been fixed into the rock of the eight-feet-high arched ceiling above the brass double bed. The floor was tastefully tiled and the space richly furnished, somewhat in conflict with the outside surroundings. There was a heavily carved wooden cupboard, an ancient armchair draped with brightly coloured brocade and a delicate chair that stood in front of a good-quality *coiffeuse* dating from the nineteenth century.

Leandro lay Luz gently on his mother's bed and arranged the pillows behind her head. He gazed down at her, aching to run his fingers through the long raven-black hair that splayed out in lustrous strands on the pillow like spun silk. The alabaster colour of her skin and the purity of her bone structure seemed to him the most exquisite and serene beauty he had ever beheld in a woman. Her thick dark lashes spread fanwise on her cheeks, like those of a Madonna in repose. Luz shifted slightly and her soft full lips parted a little, as though offering a subconscious invitation in her sleep.

The gypsy's blood stirred. Never before had he felt desire so strong – not even Rosa had awakened his senses with such vibrancy – coupled with immense tenderness. For a moment he thought ruefully of the gypsy girl whose savage and primitive beauty had once driven him wild, but that was before. He knew now that he could no longer continue his dalliance with Rosa and that he would have to extricate himself from it: everything had changed.

Leandro's eyes travelled over Luz. The urge to reach out and touch her, to feel the smoothness of her skin beneath his hands, was overwhelming. For a few moments he fought to keep a check on his movements and then abruptly left the room.

He went out into the night to get some air and made his way to the wooden hut that served as a stable for some of the gypsies' horses. It made sense to saddle up Ventarrón, his black stallion, so he could take Luz back to her house once she had woken. Much as he would have liked to keep her close by him for just a little longer, he knew that this would be opening a Pandora's box of trouble if he were to encourage any sort of intimacy with a *gajo* inside the camp.

In the meantime Leandro's mother had returned to her bedroom carrying a cup of herbal brew, which she laid on the dressing table. She went over to the bed and leaned over Luz, sucking in her breath as she noted the girl's fine and unmistakable features and her undeniable beauty. A shadow passed over the gypsy's face and, just then, the gold locket that hung around Luz's neck caught her eye. With the nimble fingers that had served her well all her life, she flicked it open. There was a fierce gleam in the jet-black eyes and they narrowed a little, blazing now with a strange expression. With just as much dexterity, she detached the clasp, took the locket and slipped it in her pocket. As she did so, her big black cat uncurled himself from the bed, jumped to the floor and padded towards the *gitana*, mewing and waving his tail. He brushed against her legs, purring loudly, winding himself around her ankles.

'Yes, *mi caballo negro*, my black knight, we're in luck,' she whispered, a look of triumph on her face. 'We are most certainly in luck.'

The *gitana* went to a shelf and pulled down a pot, from which she retrieved some dark purple pods. She crushed the seeds they contained into the cup of liquid on the dressing table and returned to the bed. There, she placed a thumb over one of Luz's eyes, opened the lid and peered at the pupil.

'Mmm, nothing wrong. She'll be awake soon,' she muttered.

She scooped up the cat, stroking it slowly as she stared down at Luz, who groaned a little and then was still again.

'Better she doesn't wake here.'

Leandro returned, carrying a blanket. 'How is she?' he asked. 'Has she woken up?'

His mother's face set itself into an impenetrable mask. 'She has stirred a few times. I've examined her. She's unharmed, but she must have had a nasty shock.'

'She looks pale.'

'Yes, she needs time to recover.'

The gypsy let the cat jump from her arms and motioned to the cup on the dressing table. 'There, feed her that brew. It will calm her, but most of all it will make her sleep deeply till morning. I must attend to our dinner. Lucas and some other dealers are coming over to discuss the next horse fair with Juanillo and your brothers.'

But he wasn't in the mood to put up with them at the moment; besides, he had a trip to make up the cliffs. 'I won't be around for that tonight.'

'Suit yourself.' She coughed roughly.

Leandro sensed the change in his mother's mood but he was used to her erratic behaviour. She was a creature of impulse: sometimes mischievous and diabolical; a vociferous spitfire in anger, vengeful and unyielding; and at other times so loving, so caring … at least to him, her eldest son.

'You should look after that cough and give up the pipe. You know you're not well.'

His mother threw him a dark look. 'You worry too much, my boy. We gypsies are tough,' she said gruffly, waving him away with her hand.

He picked up the cup as she swept out of the room and sniffed at the pungent brew. *Valerian root*, he thought. Indeed he, too, was once given some of this concoction by his mother, he recalled, while suffering with insomnia and it had sent him off to sleep for many hours. He sat on the edge of the bed. Luz stirred and opened her eyes briefly; they were sapphire-blue with the depth and mystery of the ocean he loved so much. He smiled at her, but the long black lashes shuttered down again. Placing an arm around her shoulder he lifted her slightly to give her the tea his mother had concocted.

'Here, drink this,' he whispered, leaning over her as he held the cup to her lips. 'You'll feel better.'

Luz seemed to revive slightly at the sound of his voice and the feel of the liquid at her lips. She forced open her heavy eyelids and sipped a few mouthfuls of the brew but then looked faint and a pained expression crossed her face. Despite her wrenching effort to sit up and talk, she fell back on the pillows with a little groan and closed her eyes, once more overcome by sleep.

Leandro glanced at his watch: it was getting late. They must be looking for her by now if the mare had returned to its stable. Maybe it would be better if she were examined by a doctor, but the colour had returned to her cheeks and she looked perfectly serene in her slumber. She had just been shaken by the fall. His mother's potions were renowned for their powerful healing properties. Hopefully, the herbal brew would have a beneficial effect and she would rest till the morning.

He found his mother sitting on a stool at the entrance to the cave, smoking a hubble-bubble.

'I'll take her home to her family, they must be looking for her. If the horse found its way back, they're sure to be concerned.'

The *gitana* stopped smoking and tossed her head back arrogantly. 'What is it to us? Anyhow, do you know where she lives?'

'I have a pretty good idea.'

'Do you know her name and who she is?'

He paused. 'No, but I can find her house.'

The *gitana* turned to look at her son, pipe in her mouth, her bright, hawkish eyes considering him pensively. She shrugged and returned to her hubble-bubble. 'Well, my son, do as you please, but when you get back, come and see me. It's a full moon tonight, a night of good omens, the night I've been waiting for so long.' She flicked an inscrutable glance at him. 'I will not rest until you have said goodnight.'

Leandro smiled and kissed his mother. 'Always mysterious, always speaking in riddles, *Mamacita*! Tell me, do I ever go to bed without first saying goodnight?'

Her gaze softened. 'No, my boy, you never do. You're a good son, and your father would have been proud. I'm a lucky woman.'

Her expression changed as the sound of boisterous cheering rose up from a group of young men opposite. Wineskins were being passed around while a couple of youths sent pebbles flying through the air from large catapults, knocking over tins lined up on barrels.

'But your brother is another matter,' she murmured, watching one of the youths detach himself from the group and saunter towards them.

'*Mamacita*, did you see that? Twenty-three in a row! Brought them all down, even after a skinful. Hey, Leandro, want to try your hand?' The youth was swerving slightly and came to an unsteady halt in front of them.

'No, thanks, Toñito. I've got better things to do tonight.'

'Better things, eh?' Toñito, who wore faded jeans and a petrol-stained T-shirt, curved his overly full lips into a sneer. 'Yes, always better things, brother.' The young *gitano* pulled at the catapult in his hand, stretching the sinuous elastic. His eyes were like his mother's, jet-black and fiery, and now they were fixed on Leandro, who stood calmly watching him, arms folded.

'Isn't that right, *Mamacita*?' Toñito gesticulated dismissively with his catapult. 'Angel Boy here, your pride and joy, has better things to do than share a bottle of brandy with his brother and play a little target practice. Anyone would think you only had one son. Well, I need a little respect too.'

He punched his chest with his fist, swaying a little.

Leandro narrowed his eyes. 'Take a look in the mirror sometime. Respect is earned, little brother.'

'*Earned*? And what have you earned in your life, eh? You think you're so much better than me, isn't that right, Angel Boy?'

Leandro took a step forward, looking his brother straight in the eye. 'Call me that one more time and we'll see who's an angel.'

Toñito was too drunk to catch the dangerous expression on Leandro's face and jeered at him, '*Espetiede bastardo*!'

'Toñito, watch your tongue, or one day someone will tire of it and have it out.' The *gitana* glared at her younger son, who scowled back at her.

Toñito started to say something, then, obviously thinking better of a confrontation, raised his arms in mock defeat and grinned crookedly.

'Okay, okay, I'm off.' He shoved the catapult in his back pocket.

Just then another gale of laughter erupted from the group of men opposite. An older man had joined them and was playing with a knife while a couple of the *gitanos* rushed to pour him a cup of brandy.

'Hey, Toñito,' one of young men shouted, 'our Uncle Juanillo here reckons he can beat your record with his *navaja* and there's a bottle in it for the winner!'

Toñito turned his bleary gaze to Leandro. 'Enjoy your better things, brother.' He spat on the ground and took a step backwards. 'Diego, you can tell him I accept his challenge,' he called back. As he turned, he almost unbalanced, then staggered off to rejoin his group.

The *gitana* sucked on her pipe. 'Foolish boy! He may come from my loins but he'll never amount to anything.'

'He's young and foolish, true, but he'll grow up soon.' Leandro stared after his brother for a moment, then sighed. He picked up a stick and threw it on to the fire. 'He's just trying to please you, that's all.'

'Please me, eh? Before you came along, my little brother Pablo was the only one I could rely on. Since he left us, it's just you. Anyway, be off with you now. Do what you need to do with this girl and hurry back.'

'I'll take her back on Ventarrón,' the young man told his mother but she was not listening any more. She smoked placidly, her eyes staring vacantly, the shadow of a smile hovering across her face.

In the still of the night, under a velvet sky studded with stars like diamonds and a bright golden moon hanging in the heavens like a big porcelain saucer, Leandro rode to L'Estrella, holding Luz to him on his jet-black stallion. The sea was quiet, the air soft with an all-pervasive smell of iodine and seaweed. They made their way, corkscrewing along the empty cobbled backstreets of Cádiz that snaked uphill to the top of the cliffs. There, L'Estrella lay; the focal point of an enchanting setting, a tiny jewel-like circular house in calm seclusion, halfway between fascinating reality and a mirage. Its whitewashed walls gleamed almost luminous under the full moon and a faint breeze whispered through the cluster of almond trees fringing the entrance.

The house was dark. Luz was still asleep – the concoction must have been strong, his mother perhaps a little heavy-handed with the herbs. Leandro was perplexed: no one seemed to be waiting up for her. The lights were off but the front gate was wide open. He quietly steered Ventarrón to a holm oak in the courtyard. Carefully leaning Luz forward against the stallion's mane and holding on to her with one hand, he slid to the ground. With the other, Leandro tied the horse to the trunk of the tree and then carried the young woman into the hacienda.

The grounds of the villa were all steps and corners, arches and angles, linked by patios and punctuated by sweet-smelling shrubs and orchard trees. Leandro walked up to the house and circled round it: the place seemed deserted. Gently hitching Luz closer to him, he searched her pockets for a key but there was none – it must have been lost when she fell. He was toying with the idea of taking her back to camp when he noticed, in the light of the moon, Zeyna grazing on one of the expanses of grass at the edge of the garden. The creature lifted its head and regarded Leandro for a few moments before bending back down to the ground. 'Well, at least the mare is back,' he muttered to himself.

As he turned with Luz in his arms, a veranda draped in wisteria caught his eye, flanked by a handsome flight of stone steps. He climbed to the top of them and was relieved to find a French window slightly ajar. Nudging it open with his foot, he gazed into the moonlit room. It was a bedroom – Luz's bedroom by the look of it. He walked in.

She was still fast asleep against his shoulder. He laid her carefully on the bed and slowly removed her riding boots. He spotted a blanket neatly folded on a chest next to the window and gently tucked it around her. For a moment he stood there, feasting his eyes on the ripe perfection of his Sleeping Beauty. Her eyes were closed, her mouth pink, and thick dark lashes feathered against her pale face. She was lovely, but unconscious and remote. What would she, a rich *gajo*, say if she woke to find that he had brought her home and was standing in her bedroom alone with her? What had she thought of him when she had looked his way? She fascinated him. He stretched out a cautious hand and touched her silky black hair. A slight frown creased his brow and he hesitated, then stooped and gently, ever so gently, brushed her soft, parted lips with a kiss. There was a hint of worship in his caress.

*   *   *

Later that night Leandro rode back slowly from L'Estrella. He hadn't returned immediately, wishing to avoid Lucas, the visiting horse dealer, and the rest of his family. Instead, he had sat on the beach near Luz's cliff house for a long time, staring at the inky, glistening ocean.

Now, as he made his way through the gypsy camp, he watched the dark clouds drift towards the large shining moon as if intent on devouring it whole. So vibrant by day, the camp was now bleached of colour in the pale light. The fires were almost out, copper pots lay discarded and some caravans and makeshift improvised tents glowed from the lamps inside. The place smelt of burnt wood and petrol. A few figures were huddled round the dying embers, murmuring to one another, and some were passed out next to the dogs on the ground. The sound of a donkey braying somewhere was replaced with the harsh miaow of squabbling cats. Leandro nudged Ventarrón on, the bells on the horse's reins jingling softly. He sighed. Tonight, for the first time, the encampment was the last place he wanted to be.

His mother was waiting for him, sitting at the cave entrance with a tall *gitano* with long, greying, wiry hair and a worn face, who had a deep scar down one of his cheeks. He put the wineskin he was holding down at his feet and dragged on his long cigar.

'Juanillo.' Leandro brought his horse to a stop and nodded a greeting. He had never liked his uncle and was irritated that he was still there.

'Leandro,' Juanillo responded in a gravelly voice, nodding back. 'We missed you earlier.' He regarded his nephew with a squint as the smoke curled out of his nostrils. His hawkish eyes were black as coal, with a hard edge that made many give him a wide berth when passing him on the street.

Leandro met his gaze unflinchingly. 'I was busy. I trust you and Lucas struck a good deal for your two horses and those mules you wanted rid of?'

'I did – Lucas is a thieving rascal but I've always managed to make him see sense.'

'I'm sure, *Tío*.' Leandro dismounted and began unfastening the saddle.

'Your business tonight must have been important to take you away for so long, *sobrino*, nephew.'

'Important enough.'

'Well, take care you don't leave your mother alone for too long. There's no more important business than family and Marujita's already suffered plenty for hers.' Juanillo took out a small whetstone from his pocket and played with it while smiling sardonically.

'That she has, *Tío*.' Leandro pulled the saddle off Ventarrón without looking up.

'Be off with you, Juanillo!' Marujita patted her brother's back. 'You've had enough brandy to kill the Devil in you today and I need to talk to my son.' Her features were glowing, her midnight eyes shining with an intensity Leandro had never noticed in them before – he could see she was agitated.

Juanillo allowed his gaze to linger a little on Leandro before he rose to his feet with his wineskin. 'Yes, you talk to your son. And if the Devil wants to come and get me any time soon, he knows where I am,' he grunted and lurched off into the darkness.

When Leandro had put Ventarrón away for the night, the *gitana* emptied her pipe on the ground and stood up. 'Come,' she commanded in a tone that bore no contradiction, 'we must talk.'

Once they were in the privacy of her bedroom she poured a couple of glasses of manzanilla and sat in one of the wooden chairs flanking a low round table at the foot of the bed. She swigged at her glass and dangled a gold locket hanging at the end of a chain in front of him as he took up the chair opposite her.

'Look what I've found,' she chuckled.

Leandro recognized it immediately. 'Oh, *Mamacita*! Why did you have to take that?' he said reproachfully. 'I'll get you a hundred gold lockets, if you want. You know you don't need to do that any more.'

'This is different, my son, you don't understand. Saint Cyprian, the King of Sorcerers and patron of all fortune tellers, has finally answered my prayers.'

Leandro's mouth twitched with amusement as he gulped a mouthful of the sherry. '*Mamacita*, Saint Cyprian might be the patron of diviners but if I remember right, he gave up being the King of Sorcerers when he renounced Satan. He converted to Christianity and died a martyr. Trust me, he would not condone theft. I will take that back to its owner tomorrow.'

His mother lifted her eyes to the ceiling. 'You will do no such thing,' she retorted, clutching the locket tighter. 'Sometimes I wonder if you really are my son,' she declared in an exasperated tone. 'Listen to me carefully.' There was urgency in her voice. 'This illness claws at me like the Devil himself. I don't have long to live.'

'But if you let me take you back to the doctors, things could be different for you,' Leandro stood up and started pacing. 'If you would just try—'

'I don't need any more doctors,' she cut in. 'Doctors cannot give me more life than God intends. I have seen it in the fire … in my dreams … cast in the runes. I know my fate.' Her grim expression turned to something fiercer as she studied Leandro's face. 'But my wish has been granted and only you, my beloved son, can carry it out to its final closure so I may die in peace.'

A curious, blank feeling came over him, a kind of foreboding that froze him to the bone. 'What are we talking about here?'

Marujita opened the locket. Inside were miniatures of a man and a woman.

'Don Salvador and the high and mighty Doña Alexandra de Rueda,' the *gitana* enunciated triumphantly. 'Can't you see? They are that chit's parents,' she snorted. 'My lifelong enemies: the whore who stole Don Salvador from me, and the man himself, who not only rejected my love but threw me in prison and was the cause of my eldest brother's death.'

Leandro paused as the meaning of her words sunk in. An icy heaviness took hold. '*Mamacita*, all this happened such a long time ago. Can't you forgive and forget?'

A sudden flush burned her cheeks. She rose to her feet, her finger stabbing at the air, sending her bracelets ringing again like a warning. 'Don't you dare speak like a *gajo* and forget you're a gypsy. You are Marujita's son!' Her mien had altered with the speed of a chameleon changing its colour. The *gitana's* eyes shone wildly and her features contracted in an ugly spasm, a look that had caused her to be branded *Il Diabólica*, the evil one, by some. 'Gypsies never forget a bad deed, you know that. The evil actions of our enemies must be returned upon them or their children, it's our law,' she rasped, holding the locket up to him again as if the two faces contained within it were already her grisly war trophies. '*La venganza de Calés* is not something to be bargained with. Fate has put that girl in your way for a reason.'

'Perhaps.' Leandro stared at Marujita. Even though he had often seen the darker side of her, she was scarcely recognizable to him at this moment. He had never anticipated that he would be placing Luz in danger by bringing her there. The story of Don Salvador and his wife from England was well known to him; his mother had bitterly reminded him often enough how it had affected their lives. And now he had unwittingly brought the daughter of Marujita's sworn enemies straight to the *gitana*. The look in his mother's eyes was clear and chilled his blood. So he was to be the instrument of her revenge.

Leandro paused, watching her. 'Why me?'

Her laugh was bitter, more like a sneer. 'Why *me*, he asks! Remember that because of them, you saw your first light of day in prison and, for that reason only, you were torn away from me. My baby son, wrenched from my arms. Even though you were only days' old, you clung to me. I can still hear you crying as I watched you through the bars of my cell, disappearing down the long dark corridor of that prison.'

There was pain as well as anger now in her dark irises and it caught at the strings of Leandro's heart.

'What do you want me to do?' he asked quietly. He knew her well enough to dread the answer.

The *gitana* moved over to him, her eyes shining coldly as she smiled up at her son. 'You are a handsome young man,' she whispered, brushing his cheek with her tapering fingers. 'It is a known fact that *gajo* women go mad for *Caló* men. It would not be difficult to seduce her and if you get her with child, even better. Let's see how her stuck-up family likes that!' She paused to take a breath, which set off a fit of coughing. Leandro was in the process of turning away but she held up a hand. 'Then ... then, you will toss her aside as her father did me.'

Marujita stepped back and flicked up her fingers, sending her bracelets jangling roughly. 'She will be used goods. No honourable Spanish man will marry her after that. *La honra* in those aristocratic circles obeys rules just as fierce as ours. It will ruin her life and her parents will shed tears of blood, as I have. And trust me, their punishment will be nothing compared with the pain they caused me, your mother!'

Leandro stepped back from her. 'What you're demanding of me is an evil thing. Do you really want your son to be a part of this?'

Glaring at him, she lifted her chin with a haughty movement of her head. 'Why not? Anyway, what they did to me and your uncle was not evil?' She ran a hand through her untidy hair and turned away from him as if to hide the effect those painful memories had on her. 'May God and all the Saints preserve you from ever being in prison. In the summer we were scorched with heat, eaten up with vermin. In the winter we slept, without either bed or rug, on the cold stone floor, with one wretched meal a day of coarse *rancho* or foul-tasting soup to fill our starving bellies. The place had hardly any windows, no drains worth speaking of – the stench was unbelievable. But we are gypsies and we're not supposed to be able to feel or smell.' She turned sharply back round. 'Do you want me to continue my list? My brother died young, in a filthy hovel, away from his people as a direct result of that and those wretched *gajos*.'

Leandro returned the look steadily. 'Your brother knifed Don Salvador, who would probably have let you go if not for that. Don Salvador was taken to hospital. There was no choice, the police had to get involved.'

'Why?' she retorted resentfully. 'They could have called the family doctor and let us go. After all, it was thanks to me that Don Salvador became a whole man again in the first place. If it hadn't been for my gifted hands, he would still be lying in his bed, a shadow of himself and no use to anybody.'

She walked over to the table to drain the last of the manzanilla in her glass and shook her head, her fiery eyes fixed on some invisible point. 'There is an old Moorish saying: "He eats the dates and then attacks with the stones." Those people think of us as dirt. Our caste is ostracized by them and they spit on us at every opportunity.' Her voice began to rise. 'Do not speak to me about evil. He who sows the thorn does not reap the grape. And in this case they would be reaping only half the thorns they sowed.' She spoke vehemently, her whole body trembling with the force of her hatred.

Leandro guessed any other woman would be letting her tears fall but not Marujita, the gypsy queen. Instead she wore her pain like a battle shield. Suddenly, he pitied her and took her, still quivering with anger, in his arms. He smoothed her hair, trying to soothe the hurt away, and kissed her forehead tenderly. 'Please, *Mamacita*,' he whispered hoarsely in her ear, 'don't make me do this, I …'

But she pushed him away with the strength of a virago, eyeing him with contempt. 'Huh, you're soft like your father! I have brought a coward into this world.' She laughed then, though it was more like a bitter cackle. '*Un ombre de versa*, a real man would be proud to take his revenge but you whimper like a woman. I will die of a broken heart before this illness kills me. What's more, I will leave this earth ashamed to be your mother and curse you forever from my grave.'

Leandro took another step back as though she had struck him. The force of her vitriol shook him deeply. Until then he had never realized how much his mother had been consumed by the hostility she felt towards Luz's parents. She was as pathetic in her wrath as she was frightening yet what was more disturbing to him was the idea that some of her darkness might have infiltrated his blood, imprinting itself upon his own nature. That he was the son of this vengeful, dying gypsy queen with a duty to carry out her *venganza* now lay on him heavily like an iron cloak.

He turned without a word and left his mother standing in the cave, the chain of the locket still wound tightly between her fingers, her eyes a blaze of black fire.

*   *   *

It was early morning when Luz woke up. At first, she seemed to have lost her bearings. Then, still in a dreamy state, she realized she was in her own room. A vague memory kept returning of the previous day's incident on the beach and the time spent in the gypsy encampment. Initially in a haze, then clearer, as though her mind had taken in details that at the time she had scarcely noticed, she remembered the powerful smell of smoky log fires and cooking food, the shrill banging of a hammer on iron that echoed noisily in her head and seemed to increase the pain across her eyes, the clamouring of children's voices and the sense of a glittering-eyed woman leaning over her. But, first and foremost, it was the face of the young gypsy that kept floating into her mind's eye. She saw his features in detail now: the prominent cheekbones in a narrow, burnished face, the short nose and the generous mouth with full, curved lips. Most of all she remembered his eyes, those elongated green eyes set under perfect brows that had ensnared hers and burned with such fire she had been conscious of little else.

For a while she remained still, aware of a rare sense of wellbeing. She felt strangely rested – odd after the previous day's events. Then, in some alarm, she realized she was still fully dressed and that she was wrapped up in a blanket. How had she got here? Who had brought her back? It must have been him. Who had let him in? Carmela and Pedro were away for the night; they were due to return today so it couldn't have been them. Then she remembered she had left both the gate and her window open, not expecting her outing to be a long one. How did he know her house? It was not as though she was well known down in the town – up until now she had only spent time at L'Estrella during the holidays. And Zeyna ... she remembered her horse had bolted. Had the mare found its own way back to L'Estrella?

She tumbled out of bed. Beyond the French windows opposite, the sea glistened in the distance. The sky was a clear and endless blue, paling at the horizon; the air was soft and the whiteness of the light filled it, dazzling her eyes, still full of sleep. Lost in thought, she went to the bathroom and ran herself a bath. She washed quickly then pulled on her jeans and a loose white shirt tied at the waist with a white leather belt. Images, voices, scraps of conversation kept rising then receding to the back of her mind like the ebb and flow of tidewater. The only thing that remained clear was the disconcerting impact of the *gitano's* eyes and the way it had shot through her like a bolt of lightning. It still startled her when she thought of it.

As she surveyed herself in the mirror, she noticed that her locket was missing. She cherished that pendant more than any of her other jewels for it contained the miniature portraits of her mother and father. It never left her neck. It had belonged to her great-grandmother, Doña Maria Dolores, who had given it to Luz on her tenth birthday, a year before the old lady died. Luz was definitely wearing it when riding on the beach.

For a moment her parents' warnings echoed dimly in her head and the disturbing thought that the young gypsy might have taken it crossed her mind. She dismissed it immediately. Even if she couldn't vouch for any of the other gypsies, something told her this one was different. He would never do such a thing.

No, the chain must have broken when she fell off her horse, she thought gloomily. It would probably be hopeless to attempt to find it on the beach, though she would certainly try; and the idea of reporting it lost to the police, as she would have done in England, was pointless here in Spain, she conceded. The morning would have to be spent doing some important chores she had put off, including making arrangements for the rest of her things to be shipped from England, but as soon as that was done she would go down to the beach to look for it. Perhaps she might bump into her rescuer and she could thank him personally for his kindness, she told herself. But before any of that, she had to make sure Zeyna had come back and was unharmed.

The house was quiet. Pedro and Carmela had obviously not returned yet. She went straight down to the stable block. Zeyna was there in her box, happily munching on a handful of hay. As Luz reached out and patted her mare's nose, the animal snorted and started to paw the ground.

'There, there, my beautiful girl, calm down. We're not going anywhere together today. I just wonder how you got here and who put you in your box.' *It must be the gypsy*, she thought. This afternoon, after searching for her locket, she would go looking for him. She felt her pulse race and her stomach churn at the idea of seeing him again. There was something about the gypsy that sparked an unknown thrill deep inside her.

Luz went to the kitchen and made herself a cup of coffee, taking it back up to her bedroom with some fruit. She loved the fruit in Spain – the peaches and oranges had such a delicious scent and they tasted of sunshine. So much more succulent than the pale imitations endured back in England, she thought with a sigh, biting into the sweet flesh of an apricot.

The sun was benevolent today so she seated herself comfortably on the veranda. A particularly fecund crop of orange and lemon trees hung like illuminated lanterns on one side of the terrace, backed by the whitewashed walls of the villa.

A veranda encircled the house on two floors and the entire outside walls were festooned with green creepers, purple wisteria, morning glory and pink-stained bougainvillea, which spilled over the awning roofs. In the cool interior of the villa, the elegant and rustic look of exposed beams, white walls, high wood-inlaid arches and warm flagstone floors were typically Andalucían.

Count Salvador Cervantes de Rueda had bought the summer house in Cádiz to celebrate his wedding anniversary and his only daughter's twenty-first birthday. On the edge of the Atlantic Ocean, the house looked across to Puerto de Santa María and the church where he had first caught sight of Alexandra. Their daughter had been conceived in Cádiz, the 'city of light', on the last euphoric night of their honeymoon and when she came screaming lustily into the world, nine months later, both Salvador and Alexandra instantly agreed that Luz, meaning 'light' in Spanish, was the only fitting name for their adored little girl. She had now grown into a charismatically beautiful and spirited young woman.

Luz loved the house on the cliff – *La Casa Sobre las Nubes*, the house in the clouds. The villagers had given it this name because on some moonless nights, when the far-off lights shone from its windows, it seemed to be the only bright spot twinkling in the darkness, suspended above the clouds. Salvador and Alexandra named it L'Estrella, the star.

After L'Estrella was purchased, Luz spent most of her time there. She loved the sense of freedom it gave her to be perched high above the sea, as if in a magical tower, removed from the cluster of other village houses dotting the cliff further down. It didn't matter whether her parents accompanied her there or not – it was only forty-five minutes away by ferry from Puerto de Santa María and transport into the mainland. Anyhow, she used her father's small motorboat or the family launch to take her to and fro across the water, which was much quicker. Sometimes she would remain at L'Estrella for a few days; the housekeeper, Carmela, and her husband, Pedro, made sure she wanted for nothing. They lived in a separate annexe in the grounds; Carmela took care of the cleaning, laundry and cooking while Pedro looked after the horses and the garden.

The bright and airy summer house was so different from the imposing hacienda of El Pavón and for those who knew her well, it was little wonder that Luz found as many excuses as possible to escape here, where she could be near the wild and windswept cliffs and let the invigorating smell of the sea fill her lungs.

The views from her vantage point on the terrace at the back of the villa were wondrous; there was so much incident to the ever-changing skyscape and to the land itself. It was as if nature was behaving like a magician with a wand, revealing or concealing vistas of the most beguiling beauty. Under a huge arc of sky, where racing cotton-wool clouds folded and unfolded, appeared and disappeared, an enamelled sea the colour of pure cobalt spread itself in front of her. Dancing waves unwound over stretches of glistening white sand, extending infinitely in a straight line. On the opposite shore Puerto de Santa María, the shimmering salt plains and marshy wetlands of Las Salinas behind it, was edged by a far-off screen of pine trees and the masts of ships. In front of the town, boats and yachts painted in bright Van Gogh colours bobbed up and down in the port.

Luz's thoughts meandered back to the previous day and the gypsy youth. Events only vaguely recollected when she woke up that morning gradually clarified in her mind. She realized most of the time she had not been deeply asleep, more like visited by a strange faintness, a sort of doziness where her eyelids felt as though weights were forcing them shut and her hearing was fuzzy. How her blood had thundered when the gypsy lifted her up after the fall and later, when he put his arm around her to help her drink, a tingling feeling ran through the whole of her body as she sensed the warmth of his lean strength against her. Though he was rugged – his jaw firm and with a hard, piercing stare in those green eyes – there had been something infinitely soothing in his deep voice when she tried to raise herself up from bleary-headed stupor to be civil.

Despite her twenty-four years and having spent most of them in a modern and liberal society, particularly compared with that of Spain, Luz was surprisingly conservative in her ideals. Her disposition was a complex mixture of passion and principle; her acute physical drives and boundless energy did not translate into a liberal attitude towards sex. Most of her English friends had done with their virginity by the time they were her age. She was by no means narrow minded but to her it represented a precious one-time gift, whether in marriage or outside it, that she would preserve until the right time and the right person came along – and for Luz that had simply never happened. She considered the act of love to be just that, provoked by deeply felt emotion, and for love itself to be a passionate adventure. Her English friends teased her, claiming her Spanish genes were to blame for such a regressive philosophy, labelling her an old-fashioned romantic and sentimental fool, but she simply shrugged and laughed and kept to her principles.

Luz was pulled in two directions: it was the troublesome Latin fire in her blood that tempted her to follow her passions in exactly the way her friends encouraged but, ironically, it was the traditional notions of *la honra* in her Andalucían upbringing that also held her back. Luz's Spanish nature was both the agent of her passions and her protection from them.

She had many admirers and her family, both in England and Spain, were pressing her to get married. Her doting parents, having just one child, fervently hoped that Luz would find the same blissful happiness and companionship as they themselves had in marriage. What few friends she'd had the time to make in Spain, notably her best friend Alba, never ceased to point out eligible young Spanish men. Luz herself did not think she had ever really fallen in love. Sure, her heart had beaten a little faster sometimes and she'd had a few boyfriends, but the feeling had always been skin-deep and short-lived. Even Cameron Hunt, England's tennis heartthrob with whom she'd had a very short-lived romance after she left Cambridge and whose biography she had begun to write, had not set her heart racing at this sort of speed. His superficiality and fickleness had finally become apparent; she should have known better than to mix work with pleasure. In the end he had driven away any respect she had for him, regardless of his chiselled good looks. And so this morning she puzzled at the overpowering reaction her whole being had clearly had to the gypsy. This emotion was unlike anything she had experienced in the past and it was deeply confusing.

'*Buenos días,* I hope you slept well on your first night home?' Carmela's cheerful greeting invaded Luz's daydreaming as she breezed on to the veranda, tying an apron around her ample waist.

Carmela, the housekeeper, was a plump young woman with twinkling dark eyes and lush curly black hair. In her early thirties, she came from peasant stock and was a force of nature. She looked happily built for children, though she and her devoted husband Pedro had yet to be blessed with young ones of their own. Carmela more than made up for this by mothering half the children in the village. Her family were simple folk who had lived all their lives in Cádiz; her father was a labourer, her mother a waitress at one of the many ice-cream parlours in the Old Town.

Everything about Carmela was endearing, from her sunny, uncomplicated and bumptious personality to her total lack of self-discipline where punctuality was concerned – and whenever a string of chorizos or a box of chocolates appeared on the horizon. She was a mixture of shrewdness, calculation, devotion and benevolence, with a happy-go-lucky attitude that carried her through everyday difficulties and problems and would no doubt ensure a long life. Her rippling laughter was infectious and it pealed through the house at any time of day with no consideration for its residents. Carmela put up with long hours and hard work but did not hesitate to give her opinion or deliver a reproof, should she deem it necessary. She would never have survived in the silent, dark corridors of El Pavón, but here at L'Estrella, irritating as they might sometimes find her, Luz and her parents adored her. Carmela was more like an older sister to Luz, who secretly delighted in being fussed over by the Spanish woman and regarded her as a breath of fresh air.

'I slept very deeply, thank you, Carmela.'

This was the truth and Luz had no intention of talking about last night's adventure. Carmela knew everybody and everybody knew Carmela; she was a born gossip, too. You just had to walk into Cádiz with her to witness the joyous greetings that assailed her from all sides. Besides, the housekeeper was no different from most people – to her, the *gitanos* were pariahs and she would probably make the incident into a major drama. In no time the fishmonger, the butcher and the vegetable man would be told about it, with added embellishments that Carmela would feel free to supply. No, Luz reasoned, she would keep this to herself.

Luz and Carmela chatted happily for the good part of an hour, catching up on the town's tittle-tattle. Time was of no essence, at least for Carmela, when there were such colourful stories to relay. Finally, Luz noticed the clock.

'Goodness, Carmela, what happened to the time?' She sprang up from the table. 'I've got a lot to do this morning.'

Carmela stood up and smoothed her apron, tutting, '*No te dés prisa*, rush, rush! I can't see that you've even eaten a proper breakfast yet. Doña Luz, you must eat. Every time I see you, I want to feed you, to put the Spanish colour back into those cheeks, eh?' Carmela nipped Luz's chin. 'What do they feed you in England, nuts and lettuce? Come, what shall I make you? Maybe some *tortillas de patatas* or paella or some chorizo? You always love my paella. I try to build you up,' she chuckled, winking at Luz.

'You're trying to make me fat, Carmela. I'll have a light lunch of salad and smoked sausage, *gracias*,' Luz informed her with a wry smile, 'and then I'll go down to the beach. I need to … I could do with some exercise,' she added quickly, her cheeks colouring slightly. A confession that she had lost her locket had almost tumbled from her lips. An explanation of how that had happened would have led to all sorts of trouble.

Carmela seemed not to have noticed Luz's awkwardness and rolled her eyes playfully. 'Always racing around. *Si eso es lo que quieres*, if that's what you want. Would you like Pedro to saddle up Zeyna?'

'No, no thank you. I think I prefer to walk.' She eyed Carmela with exaggerated obedience. 'I promise I'll see you for lunch before I go.'

Carmela chuckled and shooed her out of the kitchen.

For the rest of the morning Luz busied herself making phone calls, writing letters and completing paperwork. She took time to have lunch with Carmela, humouring her by eating one of her special warm, crispy *leche frita* for dessert, but then had to spend longer afterwards finishing off her tasks. So it was late afternoon, at around four o'clock, when Luz finally walked down to the beach. A pleasurable anticipation warmed her heart and her body at the thought of once more encountering the gypsy.

On arrival she found that the shore was bustling with activity. The boats had come in earlier and the fishermen were busy with their brown nets and fishing boats as crowds gathered round for the fish auction. Peering down, Luz slowly retraced her steps to the upturned boat where the gypsies had been the day before. The sand was soft and dry here, high up on the beach, studded with razor clam shells and tufts of dune grass. No sign of the sparkle of a golden chain to give away its presence. This was like looking for a needle in a haystack, she decided with sad resignation. Perhaps her beloved locket was lost to her the moment it fell from her neck.

Luz stood still, shading her eyes with her hand, and scanned the beach. A jolly group of picnickers under a garish-looking umbrella were finishing off their meal. Little brown children gambolled in and out of the waves, laughing and splashing. The boy with the red kite that had frightened Zeyna the day before was there again with his mother.

And then suddenly she saw them: young men, bare-armed and bare-legged in shorts, scarlet scarves around their throats, cantering bareback at the edge of the ocean. They seemed to be competing, pressing their horses' flanks and goading them on to greater speeds; awe-inspiring on their wild-looking horses with long, flying tails. Racing past Luz at flash-speed, they raised a whirlwind of sand in their wake, taking her breath away. Her *gitano* was not among them. Still, she remained there, staring after them as they disappeared into the distance. They did not return, and there was no sign of her gypsy, but she was here now and determined to find him. Their camp could not be that far off, surely. At a loss, she looked around her, not knowing quite where to start. Then, bracing herself, she set out haphazardly, instinct her only guide.

Luz scrambled up and down the sandy dunes and descended into a greener and gentler land, past a little house with fruit trees in bloom that were fenced off from the road, through a timbered yard, then up again into wilder countryside. A strangely seductive combination of the voluptuous and the austere pervaded the scenery all the way. She had walked for almost a mile in the golden early evening when, around a narrow turning, she emerged on to a plateau. Nearby, the ground fell away sharply. She drew in her breath and her heart began to race: beneath her lay the rugged expanse of the gypsy camp.

Within that enchanted circle of caves, tents and wagons, bright fires glowed fiercely, flickering upon the gypsies seated outside their dwellings. In the dusk there was something unearthly about the scene. She had come across the camp from the back, where the steep slope led down to the caves. There was no way she could make her way down there without breaking her neck. Still, she was not discouraged, far from it; waves of excitement rippled through her. She had discovered the gypsies' den. Tomorrow she would look for a different route to reach it and no doubt find the entrance.

A curious elation swept over her as she headed back the way she had come.

*   *   *

That night Luz had a dream. It was not altogether a nightmare, but it was strange and it made her uneasy. She was not accustomed to dreaming or, if she did, she never remembered her dreams. But that morning, when she woke up, the dream was still with her, the details disturbingly vivid, and images of fire all around still flickering inside her head. She had always regarded dreams as meaningless nonsense but, in this part of the world, where superstitions abounded, they were regarded as omens of good or bad luck.

Her country was steeped in ancient myths and gypsy legends and had a complex heritage of religious shibboleths left by the Christians and Moors; this had produced beliefs that Luz found less easy to identify with, though she always harboured a curiosity about this shadowy wisdom and its potency was undeniable. Luz's dream had been intense – so real. Could there be some underlying meaning to it? But she felt faintly ridiculous entertaining such notions. Carmela was always talking about her dreams and it was clear that they had a great influence on her behaviour. Perhaps she would have an interesting interpretation to offer.

Luz showered and dressed quickly. The night before she had been so charged up by her discovery of the gypsy encampment that she scarcely touched her food at dinner. Now she was famished. Carmela was singing in the kitchen and beamed as the young woman came in, her greeting as effusive as usual.

'*Buenos días*, Doña Luz, *has dormido bien*? Did you sleep well? I have made you some fresh *churros*; they are still warm. Would you prefer to have *café con leche* or hot chocolate for breakfast?'

'Hot chocolate would be lovely, thank you, Carmela,' said Luz enthusiastically. 'I'm really hungry this morning.'

Carmela laughed, showing two rows of brilliant white teeth in her copper-tanned face. '*A mucha hambre, no hay pan duro*, hunger is the best sauce.'

Luz seated herself at the kitchen table and started to tuck into the appetizing doughnuts that Carmela had prepared, while the latter hovered attentively round her, chattering merrily, dashing in and out of the room as she went about her chores.

'Mmm ... delicious,' said Luz, biting gingerly into the little golden cakes and taking a mouthful of the thick chocolate.

Rays of sunshine poured into the room. The open window afforded a magical view of the garden. Olive trees coexisted cheerfully with orange, lemon and fig trees, as well as oleander, hibiscus, grapevines and a sprinkling of cactus and palms. Beyond this eclectic world fashioned by man and nature she could see gulls in the distance, in a huge arc of sky, their white wings flashing in the sunlight as they swooped over the phosphorescent ocean. Their far-off cries filled the air, punctuated by the chirruping sound of nearby cicadas. She let out a small sigh of pleasure. This was bliss.

'Carmela,' she called out suddenly to the housekeeper, who was sweeping the patio outside.

'Would you like some more coffee? Another cup of chocolate?' the other asked, coming back into the kitchen.

Luz helped herself to a bunch of grapes from a pristine bowl of fruit in the middle of the table. She popped one into her mouth and smiled. 'No, no, thank you, I've already eaten too much. You're a superb cook, Carmela.'

The maid grinned in radiant gratification. 'You have so much energy, Doña Luz, and that needs food!' She paused as Luz glanced at her sheepishly. 'I know that look, you have something on your mind. What is it?'

'I want to ask you something. I had a dream last night. I suppose I must have dreams like most people, but I never remember them. This time I've remembered it, though. You believe in dreams, don't you? I wondered if you could tell me what mine means.'

'*Cuéntame, cuéntame*, tell me.' Carmela's eyes grew wide as she set aside her broom, entering wholeheartedly into the spirit of this new subject of conversation. She leaned against one of the kitchen cabinets, hands in her apron, her black eyes steadily watching Luz who, with some amusement, could almost see the housekeeper's ears twitching in eager anticipation.

'I dreamt I was on a vast dark plain, in the middle of which a bright fire was burning. I went up to it with a mixture of fear and awe. It became brighter and brighter as I approached and then, even though I was scared, without the least hesitation I walked right into it. The flames were all around me. They licked me but didn't burn, and I wasn't afraid any more. I walked through the fire and as I emerged from it I saw a shadow, the silhouette of a person. I couldn't distinguish whether it was a man or a woman. The figure was a shape without features. It took my two hands and together we rose into the sky towards another fire which, when we reached it, suddenly turned into a sun.'

Carmela went into raptures. '*Esto es un sueño maravilloso*, a wonderful dream,' she burst out enthusiastically. 'Fire in a dream is a very lucky omen!'

'Does the dream have a particular meaning, do you think?'

'*Fuera de curso*, of course,' she declared with unshakeable conviction as she flung up her arms, her black eyes glittering with barely contained excitement. 'All dreams have a meaning. This one says that soon your heart will be burning with a very powerful fire. You will have a *novio*, a boyfriend, *un gran amor y pasión*.'

Luz gave her an uncertain look then broke into peals of laughter. 'Dear Carmela, you're such a romantic!' She leapt to her feet and hugged the Spanish woman affectionately.

That Carmela was hurt by the young woman's obvious scepticism was written all over her face. Her penetrating eyes regarded Luz with undisguised reproach. 'You don't believe me? You think I say this to please you, but I am very good at deciphering dreams. *Podrás ver*, you'll see – Carmela is always right. Soon, very soon, this will happen. Maybe it's someone you already know, maybe not. Perhaps you feel the flames already, but you are not yet burning. Believe me, it will happen, Doña Luz, *muy pronto*, very soon.'

'For all I know you could be right,' Luz said, still laughing. 'I don't think I've ever been in love, let alone felt any sort of *gran pasión*. It'll be a novel experience.'

'You should not joke about this, Doña Luz. *Es mala suerte*, it's unlucky to make fun of these things.' She considered the young woman with a grave face.

Luz had never seen Carmela looking so serious and self-important. Perhaps she'd been a little hasty in telling her about the dream. She had to admit she found the maid's words exhilarating because they were so uncanny given yesterday's events, but the last thing she needed was for the subject of a *novio* to become one of those topics of conversation that Carmela would obsess about, turning it into part of the trifling daily rumours that she and her friends found so absorbing. Luz picked up another grape, kissed Carmela affectionately on the cheek and gave her a reassuring smile before she went off to sort out some of the books she had still to unpack.

The morning was gone before she knew it. So in the afternoon, armed with a map of Cádiz, Luz set off yet again on foot in search of the gypsy encampment, hoping that this time she would find a decent entrance to it.

Luck was on her side. She went down the sun-gold path she usually took to the beach. As she neared the carob tree, where the gypsy had appeared on her first day back in Cádiz, she noticed a narrow lane. Instinctively, she turned into it. Gradually it wound uphill. She threaded her way between sand dunes, wild fig and carob trees and banks overgrown with brambles. As she drew closer to the top of one of the banks, she could see spirals of black smoke in the distance, coiling up into the darkening sky.

All of a sudden a cluster of half-naked, brown-faced children erupted out of a dirt track, the entrance to which was scarcely visible, being concealed by mounds of rubble and rubbish. They raced past her towards the beach, scrambling down the dunes like mountain goats, kicking up the sand behind them.

She decided to turn into the narrow track. Underfoot, the soil was red and rough, more of a bridle path than a proper track. She doubted the heavy-looking caravans she'd seen the other day would be able to tackle it. Now the path dipped down towards what she hoped would be the gypsy encampment, though still she could not see it. The silence was awesome, the landscape barren and even rockier; a countryside petrified in desolation. She could not even hear the sea. There must be another way in. Suddenly she felt incredibly weary. The eeriness of the place was getting to her but she soldiered on; she had come so far, she was not going to turn back now, and the entrance had to be closer than where she'd ended up the day before after her much longer ramble. Up another hill, down again almost perpendicularly and she was there – at the same solid portal of debris she had spotted the previous day.

The gypsy tents were pitched near a jumble of a few cave homes amid the rubble and rocks, cacti, prickly pears and refuse bags that littered the camp. They were interspersed here and there with the high-wheeled caravans she had already seen, but now she noticed motorcycles, strange-looking wagons loaded with wood and a couple of heavily dented cars.

The place was heaving with gypsies, many more than had been there the day before when she'd first come across the camp. Fires from copper *braseros* roared into a sky rapidly turning from azure to purple and now a paler shade of blue. Men, women and children all sat round them in small circles. There were murmurs and laughs, but mostly they were silent and there seemed to be an air of expectancy about the place.

Luz stood hidden behind a large clump of bristling cactus, peering over the spiky plants in search of the gypsy youth, carefully scanning the faces lit up by the flickering glow of the fires. Soon, a couple of *gitanas* came out of a cave carrying large trays of glasses filled with manzanilla. They passed the drinks around and so the Romani revelry began.

A tall, wild-faced man with black hair standing out in tousled tufts around a face with thick black side whiskers and moustache walked to the middle of the clearing with his guitar, followed by three other musicians carrying a tambourine, cymbals and a fiddle. As they started their instrumental prelude, the audience acted as a chorus, stimulating the musicians by clapping and stamping in time with the rhythm. Some gypsies banged stones on rocks as the noise grew to a crescendo and a few women came forward, hitching their colourful skirts up to cock their hips and swirl to the chaotic music. It was a most vibrant spectacle, the sounds echoing and reverberating through the atmosphere.

While the performance was taking place, the sun had sunk and twilight turned into evening. The moon beamed in a starless sky but it was still light and visibility was good. Fascinated, Luz had lost count of time. The musicians had ended their show and she was about to turn back when one man moved out from the crowded circle and came forward, a guitar hanging across his chest. Trays of manzanilla went round again. Luz's heart skipped a beat. She had to smother a gasp as the flickering firelight fell on the face of the man she was looking for.

The young gypsy took his place in the middle of the circle, which the previous performers had vacated. His long, copper-tanned fingers began thrumming his guitar. The prelude continued for some time and the shouts, clapping of hands and stamping of feet worked his audience up to a state of rhythmic excitement. Suddenly, in a convulsive movement, his features contracted into a mask of agony. He closed his eyes and lifted one hand to his forehead as he broke into a long, tragic high-pitched cry: 'Aye ... Aye ... Aye ... Ayeeeeee!' He repeated this lament a few times against the frenzied accompaniment of his guitar, the open strings of which he played with the other hand. Then he began singing in a deep masculine voice as if telling the world of his sorrows and misfortune. He sang in *Caló*, the language of the gypsies, which Luz did not understand. Despite the tension of feeling in the full, vigorous notes, he sang with an air of dignity that the young woman had never witnessed before and she had listened to many Flamenco singers in the clubs of Cádiz.

Like the rest of the audience Luz stood breathless, spellbound, stirred to her innermost fibres. Tears in her eyes; the music awakened a fierce impulse that sent her heart hammering. He sang one song after the other, seemingly oblivious to his audience and of anything save the notes, which formed themselves in the air before him as if independent of his body. Some of the songs were passionate, heart-wrenching ballads about faithless or separated lovers, unending longing, death, prison and revenge, which he appeared to be improvising. Those few songs in *Caló* remained frustratingly mysterious to Luz but the words of his closing song she understood, though she found them strange. He sang in a kind of trance, as if reaching deep down into his soul to uproot the pain, drawing out the final notes in a prolonged, descending strain, with seemingly never-ending turns and tremolos. It was a haunting sound, so poignant Luz had great difficulty in controlling her urge to reach out to him. Did those *coplas* recall some experience in his life, she wondered.

From birth I was rejected
From birth I was evicted
Where was my mother?
Where was my father?
They left me without a kiss
And threw me out of Paradise's bliss
My life was barren, I was alone
How could my heart not turn to stone?
My heart is crying out to melt
Will love reverse the cruelty fate dealt?

As he opened his eyes, the gypsy turned towards where Luz was standing. Like deep opals his green irises shone in the

CHAPTER 2

The next few days were spent preparing for her first interview. Luz's mornings were wholly taken up by visits to the Eduardo Raphael Ruiz de Salazar museum, which housed most of the artist's works, and the small library attached to it.

The Salazar museum nestled in one of the many plazas in the Old Town that were connected by narrow cobbled streets. This anachronistic building had been built specially to house the artist's surreal and mysterious work. Tall narrow windows sat beneath macabre fairy-tale spires and an external wrought-iron staircase marched up the outside of each floor, one storey completely comprised of glass-fronted pods that jutted from the building like bulbous eyes. It was a perfect setting and Luz was pleased that she had made the trip here before her interview. Already, she would have more to talk about with de Salazar's nephew – if she got that far.

The interview letter had explained that the initial examination and discussion was to be carried out by the directors of the artist's estate. A shortlist would eventually be drawn up and presented to the nephew and only heir, who would see the candidates and make the final choice. While she was at the museum Luz thought she would do some research on Count Eduardo de Salazar, his work and his life in Cádiz, just to get a little more background. She could start putting together a file; that way, she would go to the meeting fully prepared.

She had always been blessed with great powers of concentration but on this occasion it had been difficult to blank Leandro from her mind. *Leandro*, that's what they had called him … the gypsy's face had a name now. His handsome features kept springing up in her mind unbidden, obscuring the text she was reading. They had such vivid clarity that each time her heart thudded uncontrollably and she had to call on every ounce of willpower as she struggled to drive his image away.

After mornings spent poring over books and paintings at the museum library, Luz went down to the beach, partly to try to find her locket but always in the secret hope of seeing Leandro. Added to that, the beach was where she felt most free. There she could ride Zeyna, go for a run, take a swim or simply walk for miles and feel the sun and sea air on her face. She liked to look back at the mesmerizing view of the city rising up behind her, so bright it was blinding to those approaching it by sea. Luz loved Cádiz, with its mellow-stone churches and whitewashed houses shining under a bright blue sky like a spray of water lilies on the dancing, glittering waters of the Atlantic. She had read the nineteenth-century French writer and traveller Théophile Gautier at university and his description of it as a city that was 'lively and luminous' had always stayed with her. It was named *Cádiz Joyosa* as though it was laughing in the sun.

During her long solitary walks on the beach, and at night while she waited for sleep to come, thoughts of her unusual, powerful dream and of Carmela's prediction of a *novio* preyed on Luz. She had never really given much consideration to love and marriage. Her parents were the natural embodiment of true love, and perhaps because they made it seem entirely fated, Luz had always assumed that it would just happen to her one day and her future would fall neatly into place.

She was perfectly open to romance but always regarded herself as someone with her feet firmly planted on the ground. It had never occurred to her that she could fall in love with someone her parents would find unacceptable. And now she was behaving like one of the love-struck heroines in her mother's romantic novels. Wasn't she more down-to-earth than that? Hadn't she been trying so hard all her life to be the cool English rose? But the gypsy Leandro, so mysterious and exciting to her in every way, had infiltrated her system like a fever.

You're a fool to allow yourself to fantasize about Leandro, she told herself fiercely again and again. *What do you know about him? Nothing can come of such a union. Anyhow, how can you fall in love with someone you've never even spoken to? This is all schoolgirl infatuation.* Yet no matter how often she recited this litany to herself, she was not convinced. Something had been awoken in her that she had never felt before. Their eyes had met only twice and she'd had no real physical contact with the gypsy apart from the few moments when he had lifted her up on the beach and later when he had given her the tea to sip. Apparently, that had been enough. No man had set a fire in her belly the way he had. She was shocked at some of the sensations and images her fantasies conjured up when she let them run wild.

Though the idea seemed mad, some sort of sixth sense told her this must be love at first sight. After all, wasn't this what had happened to her parents? And if that were the case, it was useless trying to fight Leandro's haunting power over her; the hungering need she felt for him was likely to intensify with time unless she did something about it, whatever that might be. Still, for now she must concentrate on the task at hand, which was to secure the book assignment with the directors of the Eduardo Raphael Ruiz de Salazar estate.

It was on one of those solitary afternoon walks along the beach that Luz encountered Paquita the gypsy for the first time.

Luz was sitting on a boulder gazing down through the crystal-clear waters at the subaqueous jungle of swaying seaweed that was crinkling, twisting, curling and uncurling as the waves washed against the reef. Silver fish and velvety brown baby crabs darted in and out of rocks; a gaggle of colourful sailboats bobbed up and down on the little white crests of the waves as they slowly floated past her; not too far away a small group of winkle pickers were was hard at work with their spades and nets.

Luz closed her eyes and lifted her face to the sky; she wanted to savour the delicious warmth of the sun on her skin. When she opened them again the old witch was there, peering at her with hooded eyes beneath bushy eyebrows, a mask-like expression on her swarthy, wrinkled face. She had come out of nowhere, making no noise as she approached. Short and bent as she stood there in the sand, she wore a red scarf over her white scraggly hair. Her nose was strong and hooked.

Luz gave a start and instinctively recoiled in fear. The old gypsy's eyes flashed with cunning and her mouth curved into a smile, albeit one like a grimace that uncovered toothless gums.

'*Hermosa jovencita*, beautiful young lady, don't be afraid, Paquita means you no harm,' she rasped.

Luz suddenly realized how isolated she was. People rarely strolled so far along the beach and the gypsies had a reputation for being quick with knives, even old women like this one. If she screamed, no one would hear her.

'Please go away,' she said politely. 'I have no money on me and nothing else to give you.'

'Paquita isn't looking for money or anything else from you. Give me your palm, I know who you are.' Insistent and slyly menacing in her manner, the old woman moved surprisingly swiftly towards her and claimed her wrist with thin, gnarled fingers.

'What do you mean, you know who I am?' Luz demanded. She tried to pull away from the gypsy's iron grip. Her eyes fell on the old woman's long nails – they reminded her of a bird of prey's talons. She shivered.

'Gypsies never forget.' The sharp black irises glowed with a strange fire. 'You have your father's bewitching eyes and your mother's clear complexion, a happy combination. Paquita is an old friend of the family … a *very* old friend. Ask your parents about me, they will tell you.'

'I doubt they will remember you,' said Luz sceptically, jerking her wrist out of the witch's claws. Even supposing they did, she very much doubted that it would be a welcome topic of conversation.

The old hag gave a hoarse chuckle. Her wizened old face lit up with a wicked grin. 'They'll remember me all right. I was there – I saw it all. If they had listened, they would have heard, but they ignored Paquita.' She scoffed and shrugged her bony shoulders, a look of contempt on her sharp features. 'And now, *hermosa jovencita*, you must listen to me,' she said, peering at Luz again through narrowed eyes.

Luz's brows lifted. 'And why is that?' she asked, trying to seem detached.

The tone of the witch's voice changed a little. 'Because I see into the future, I know the unknown!' she replied. 'So tell me, child, what are you looking for, or should I say, *who* are you looking for?'

'You tell me, since you can see into the past and the future.' Luz fixed Paquita with fierce, steely blue eyes.

The old crone winked and, once again exposing her ungainly jaws, broke into hideous crackles of laughter that resonated eerily in the silence. 'A tongue and personality to equal your beauty, eh?' she said in her hoarse voice. 'Quite a rare jewel!'

She paused and seemed to be pondering for a moment. Suddenly, under her untidy bushy eyebrows, her eyes lit up with a wild fire. She grabbed hold of Luz's arm, clutching it tightly in her horny hand. 'You want to know your *bahi*, your fortune? I will tell you. I have seen the *simachi*, the sign in the full moon,' she whispered, pulling closer, her breath warm and garlicky on Luz's cheek. 'Gemini! You're looking for Gemini! He is your *sustiri*, your fate. Many men covet you, but your *bahi* lies with him of the *moreno*, dark skin and the lion's eyes, eyes as green and deep as African forests. A gypsy *hidalgo de la mas pura rati*, of the purest descent. Do not try to avoid your destiny or the curse will come upon you. I tell you, I have seen the sign in the full moon this month. Every word I speak is true.'

Luz's heart filled with a dark unease as the crone's flow of words screeched to a halt. The image of Leandro's face danced in front of her and while the old harpy's description fitted him like a glove, nothing else made sense. It was one thing fantasizing about the handsome gypsy, quite another for a sinister old *gitana* to tell her that she was fated to be with him and would be cursed should she choose to ignore her destiny. Again she tried to rid herself of the ensnaring fingers.

'What are you talking about? What do you mean, "curse"? I don't know any "Gemini" and I don't understand a word you're saying,' she cried out.

Rolling her eyes, Paquita loosened her hold and released her prisoner. She did not reply immediately. A faraway look came into her jet-black irises and beads of perspiration rolled down her forehead. She began to chant a strange incantation in a cavernous voice while moving slowly away over the dunes as if in a daze. A sea wind started up gently. As it blew, the old witch's haunting sing-song voice was carried back on its breath across the sands:

Gemini, Gemini ... Deceptive Gemini.
You think you know them, blinded by their wit and charm,

Today they love you, tomorrow they may harm.
Chameleons of the Zodiac, they'll lead your mind astray,
Into their murky waters, they'll drag you as their prey.
One body, two people, one heart, one mind, one soul;
One total complete entity; two sides to the same coin,
Evil lurks in every shadow for mile and mile and mile,
Behind a friendly mask, behind the friendly smile.
Deceit is all around, the curse you cannot break.
And it will last forever because of the mistake.
Unless love and its power can repair and erase
The scalding pain of hatred, and good it will embrace.
Forever rid of malice, at last you will be free.
Dear child, the truth reflects in this duality.

A group of black crows shrieked as they took off from a nearby rock, adding their own final cadence. Luz stood for a moment, her wide eyes following the old woman, her hands trembling a little as she rubbed her wrist where the gypsy had gripped it so tightly. A despairing sense of unreality swept over her and she let out a long, shuddering sigh. Suddenly, she felt vulnerable and afraid. What did it all mean? She could make neither head nor tail of those odd, chilling words.

Gradually, logic took over. This was just gypsy nonsense with the sole intention of intimidating her, she told herself. These people were renowned for their quick, dramatic language. As for Paquita's predictions, the old woman must have seen Leandro bring her back to the camp the day she fell off her horse and had deduced that his good looks must have captured her heart – which was not far from the truth. Luz herself had witnessed female reactions to the young man's charms; she remembered how the young *gitanas* had crowded round him after his bewitching song at the camp. Presumably the old hag had not been able to resist the temptation of spinning a yarn that she could later use as a weapon to extort money and any other favour from Luz, maybe even from her family.

With a sense of final conviction, Luz determinedly pushed away these sombre thoughts. Slowly she started back to L'Estrella, head down against the wind, her hands thrust deeply into her jeans pockets.

She got home to find her parents had arrived from El Pavón. They greeted her effusively as they always did. Whether they had been apart for a few months or a couple of days, it mattered not – Salvador and Alexandra de Rueda doted on their daughter and were always delighted to see her.

Luz was never adept at hiding anything from her mother. 'You're a little pale,' Alexandra remarked, taking her daughter's hand in both of hers and leading the way into the airy living room. 'Is anything the matter?' Luz had inherited her mother's glorious complexion, which today seemed a little sallow. Like Alexandra, she was tall for a woman. She had what the French call *allure*, with a neat perfection about her dainty figure. There the physical resemblance between mother and daughter ended. Luz had inherited Salvador's sleek raven hair and his fine aristocratic features; she was also possessed of the most amazing cobalt-blue eyes, which could turn a contemptuous steel-grey, just as her father's did, when riled.

Luz went over to the window so her mother could not read her eyes, which did not know how to lie. 'No, I'm fine, really, *Mamá*. I just need a good night's sleep,' she replied, giving her slow smile.

'She's been working too hard,' Salvador declared as he came over to his daughter and hugged her. She lifted her head up to receive his kiss. Her father was a tall, handsome man with a fierce love for his one and only daughter that meant that he could be quickly moved to worry over any matter concerning her. He regarded Luz fondly, keeping an arm around her. 'It's this job you want so badly. I've told you that with one call to

Santiago de Calderón, the father of the young man who'll be interviewing you, I could get you hired. We haven't seen each other for a while but he's an old friend. It would make everything so much easier for you.'

'That's not the point, *Papá*,' Luz protested. 'I know you're just trying to help, but you can't protect me the whole time from what's difficult. I need to do this myself. You know how I hate nepotism,' she told him firmly.

'Nepotism! Nepotism! You're always going on about nepotism. What are parents for, *niña*, if it's not to help their children?' he countered, giving her a final squeeze and shaking his head. 'You are one stubborn woman, just like your mother.' At this Salvador glanced towards Alexandra, his eyes sparking with the same fire that had burned in them when the pair had first met.

His wife laughed as she fussed with some cushions on the sofa before sitting down. 'Don't look at me, I have nothing to do with this,' she said.

Luz gently pulled away from her father and wandered over to the dining table. She plucked a ruby-coloured grape from the fruit bowl and bit into it. 'By the way, talking of old friends, I met one of yours today,' she ventured, only the slightest hesitation in her voice.

'Yes?' Salvador's eyebrows shot up quizzically. 'Who?'

'Paquita, she said she was called. The gypsy fortune teller.'

At the name Alexandra paled, while Salvador looked towards Luz, then burst out laughing. 'Paquita, eh? I'm surprised the old hag is still alive. She must be at least ninety. What has the witch been up to now?'

'I met her on the beach, she recognized me. She said I had your eyes and my mother's complexion,' Luz told him. Now that she had this opportunity, perhaps she could unravel the mystery of her parents' connection with the gypsies.

'That's very shrewd of her,' Salvador said evenly.

'What else did she say?' Alexandra whispered. There was a light in her irises and a tremor in her voice that did not escape Luz.

Uneasily conscious of her mother's eyes searching her face, Luz shrugged. 'Nothing really, nothing of great interest.' She tried to take on a bored expression as she pulled a small bunch of grapes from its stem. 'Did she ever tell your fortune?' she went on, keeping her tone light.

Salvador did not reply immediately. Absently, he drew a cigarette from the packet in his pocket and lit it. After inhaling a few puffs he went to sit next to his wife on the sofa.

'*Niña*, you must understand that these people get good money to tell the future,' he explained at length. 'It's a very ancient game and their old grandmothers taught them the words to say – it's always the same thing. They don't see any harm in feigning clairvoyance, they regard it as a respectable job. If *gajos*, as they call us, are naïve enough to believe their stories, more fool them.

'Anyhow, I'd prefer it if you didn't have any more to do with these nomads,' he added, a sudden gravity in his voice. 'They're always up to tricks and can become unpleasant. Better to keep away.'

Luz laughed: 'Don't worry about me, *Papá*, I can look after myself. I'm very sensible, you know that. Besides I always manage to fall on my feet.'

She was about to ask whether he'd experienced this unpleasantness himself but then glanced sideways at her mother. Luz was struck by how tense she looked, her cheeks flushed pink. She had never seen her look quite so agitated at the mention of gypsies. Even though Luz felt she was edging closer to something with her mention of Paquita, she sensed this was the wrong moment. Anyhow, if it also came out that the old woman had predicted Luz's fate as one aligned with that of the gypsy, Leandro … Well, that was not a conversation she was ready to have. Reluctantly, she decided to change the subject, at least for now.

She smiled brightly and went to sit on the opposite sofa, tucking her bare feet under her. 'In two days' time I will have had my first interview for the Salazar job. Apparently, at this stage I'll have to face a written examination followed, if I'm successful, by a panel of examiners at a later date before the final meeting with Andrés de Calderón, Eduardo de Salazar's heir. I can't wait! Have you met him, *Papá*?'

'No, I haven't, but I've heard much about him. His father, Santiago, spoke of him often. He's energetic, travels a good deal and is certainly highly respected in society circles. He chairs Caldezar Corporación, SA, a family-owned business that started out producing olive oil. I've known people who've had dealings with the firm. Their holdings consist of olive groves and factories extending all over the Province of Cádiz. I've heard they've lately broken into the international market.'

'Mmm ... what a great success story Señor de Calderón is,' Luz grinned playfully at her father. 'He sounds like the sort of man even you would approve of, *Papá*.'

Salvador ignored his daughter's ribbing. 'What's impressive is that under his own name he has also acquired some sort of testing laboratory that tries out new products and technologies before they are allowed to be released to the public, a kind of agent for new manufacturers around Europe. Just the sort of innovator the economy needs at the moment. Yes, a very enterprising young man, by all accounts.'

By now Alexandra looked a little more composed as she reached over for the jug of water on the coffee table and poured herself a glass. 'I've heard that he's quite eccentric in his testing of each product.'

'Eccentric?' Luz asked, popping another grape into her mouth. Suddenly this sounded more interesting.

'Well, I'm not entirely sure,' her mother conceded, 'but apparently he likes to try out all the products himself, which is a little unusual for a man in his position, wouldn't you say? His office is full of the latest things. Everyone had calculators in their drawers as soon as they were available, I'm told. And I'm sure he was one of the first people in Spain to try out Polaroid cameras. Now, of course, they're all the rage.'

'For someone who's involved in the arts, I can see why photographic technology would interest him,' said Luz. 'Have you heard anything else about him, *Mamá*? The more I know before the interview, the better.'

'He's very handsome in a sultry sort of way,' Alexandra continued. 'I've seen him around. His heart's in the right place, too – he's on the board of a few charities. But from what I hear he leads a fast life, burning the candle at both ends, and has the reputation of being a bit of a womanizer.' She raised a slightly disapproving eyebrow. Alexandra's English roots were still discernible despite many years spent in Spain.

Salvador chuckled. 'Like his uncle! Eduardo de Salazar never married – too dedicated to his career – but he was well known for his romantic adventures. We Spanish men are driven by our passions until we are tamed by the right woman.' He winked at Luz as he leaned over to his wife, kissing her hand. Alexandra's expression softened and she rolled her eyes.

Luz chuckled. 'In which case a Spanish man had better beware of the tamer's whip. Womanizers aren't so very difficult to deal with.'

'My little Luz, you are far too wise for your own good.' Salvador laughed and took another puff of his cigarette. 'By the way, I have tickets for the opening night of *Carmen* at the Gran Teatro Falla tomorrow, a new touring production,' he announced. 'The reviews have been excellent.'

Luz's face lit up. 'What a wonderful idea! We haven't been for a while. I love that theatre, even though it's a little tatty. I read there are plans to refurbish it by 1980.'

'It's high time they did something about it,' her father replied. 'I believe it's one of the notable monuments of Andalucía, a lovely example of the neo-Mudéjar style. It's important to keep our Moorish heritage alive.' He stubbed out his cigarette and sighed. 'Perhaps now we have a new king and the beginnings of a new government they will actually put their energies in the right places.'

'Nothing's certain at the moment, that's true.' Alexandra placed her hand on her husband's. 'You never know, perhaps it's men like Andrés de Calderón, with his entrepreneurial spirit and international perspective, who are the future of Spain. The sort we need to give our beautiful cities a new lease of life.'

But Luz had ceased to listen by now and instead gazed dreamily out of the window at the sea. A trip to the theatre might be just what she needed as a distraction – though the irony that the opera would involve the tale of a beguiling gypsy was not lost on her.

*　　*　　*

A first night at the Gran Teatro Falla had a charm of its own. Standing in the Plaza Fragela in the north-west quarter of the Old Town, the grand and atmospheric theatre welcomed its visitors with beckoning mystery, like a magician inviting one to step back in time. The century-old coral brick building, with its distinctive red- and white-banded arches wrapped around three vast keyhole-shaped doorways, was filling up when they arrived. There was a festive atmosphere about the place and the lobby was buzzing with different languages. The audience was a mixed assortment of Spaniards and foreigners, an attractive, cheerful crowd made up of distinguished-looking men and women, all of them united by their love of opera.

As they walked in through the large arches of the main entrance, Luz was unaware of the effect her singular beauty was having on people. Men turned their heads as she passed and women threw her envious glances. She wore a blue, silk, full-length dress, which skimmed her body and moulded her form to perfection. Its deep colour reflected in her large eyes, giving her irises a violet tint and setting off the radiant nature of her skin, which glowed even more warmly under her newly caught tan from the beach. The dress had a plunging neckline and a knotted bodice from which the skirt fell into a profusion of soft folds. A fabulous necklace cascading with different-sized gold beads hung down to her cleavage, ending in a cluster of small gems fashioned as grapes. She had teamed it with a matching pair of earrings and stiletto sandals. Her long raven-black hair was tonight worn loose to the hips and acted as a cloak around her naked shoulders. The whole effect was striking.

The theatre was horseshoe shaped; the de Ruedas stood in the large ground-floor foyer facing a handsome marble staircase that led to the stalls, the gallery, the mezzanine boxes and the upper floors of the widely curving auditorium. The decor was a sumptuous mixture of antiquated gold and claret, soft drapes and mouldings, though everything had faded somewhat with the passage of time.

Salvador and Alexandra knew almost everyone in Cádiz and they were soon joined by quite a few of their wide circle of friends. Luz had met many of them; the names and faces were familiar, but mostly they were family acquaintances she'd had little to do with, being so often away. As she was greeted by kisses and handshakes, Luz smiled politely and tried to take part in the small talk.

Suddenly, across the room, she caught sight of a figure standing with a group of young, smartly dressed men and women. The men wore black tie and the women were all in evening gowns and richly bejewelled. Though he stood with his back to her, something about his stance was vaguely familiar. His dark hair was tied back in a ponytail and, as he turned a little, the light from the chandelier fell obliquely on his profile, throwing into relief its chiselled lines. Luz paled and inwardly flinched. *Leandro?* Was it possible? What was he doing here?

Her mother's hand on her arm jerked her back to reality. 'We'd better take our seats. The theatre is crowded tonight and the performance will soon be starting. I hate queues.' Alexandra frowned. 'You looked strained, is everything all right, darling?'

'Yes, *Mamá*, everything's fine … I'm just a little worried about tomorrow's test.' Luz forced her features weakly into a smile. 'I really do want this job very badly.'

Alexandra gave her daughter's arm an affectionate squeeze. 'You'll do very well, as you've always done. Don't worry, just try to relax and enjoy the show,' she said.

'Yes, of course, *Mamá*.' She took a calming breath, then, when she looked up again, the little group of jetsetters had moved away.

The de Rueda family were ushered down the corridor to their box. The auditorium, like the rest of the theatre, was decorated in Moorish revival style, with ornate arches stretching along cream-coloured balconies, its boxes hung with red velvet curtains. Luz took her seat at the front of their box with her mother, while Salvador took his place at the back.

She tried to relax and enjoy the scene, tilting her head to gaze at the nineteenth-century ceiling fresco, Felipe Abárzuza's vast allegory of Paradise, but she was fidgety. She felt like wandering around, but the thick velvet curtain had been pulled behind them and the padded doors were now closed; she would have to wait for the interval. Luz could not get the young man in the lobby out of her mind. She was not sure it was Leandro, he had been too far away, and though she'd had a brief glimpse of his profile she really couldn't be certain. Besides, logic told her it didn't make sense: what would a gypsy be doing among such a smart crowd? He looked so much at ease, too. She must have been mistaken.

The orchestra was tuning up in the pit. Luz rather liked the slightly cacophonic sound it made. After a while she picked up the small opera glasses on the side of her armrest and started to scan the crowd. The lights were dimming, and she was on the verge of putting them down when she breathed in sharply. She found herself looking directly into another person's pair of binoculars, those of a man seated in the box opposite. Luz just had time to notice the slow smile that curled at the side of the stranger's mouth before the place fell into darkness. The curtain lifted and the first notes of *Carmen*'s overture resonated in the vast auditorium.

Throughout the performance she could barely concentrate, despite the intensely passionate drama unfolding on stage. Once or twice her eyes dared to flit across the auditorium to where he sat, her pulse quickening every time she thought he was watching her. Then the next time she looked up, he was gone. Only now did she notice that the opposite box was also occupied by an elderly couple and a very smart and beautiful blonde-haired young woman.

Luz looked for him during the intermission but he was nowhere to be found. Returning to her seat, she sat through the rest of the performance waiting for the stranger to reappear, but he had vanished. She wondered if it had not all been a figment of her imagination.

*　　*　　*

The sun woke Luz early the next morning. She was surprised to find that she had gone off into a deep, dreamless sleep as soon as her head hit the pillow. A quick glance at her alarm clock showed that it was only seven-thirty. She had plenty of time to soak in a hot bath to calm the butterflies in her stomach that besieged her every time she thought of the impending examination. Despite all her careful preparation, this morning she did not feel too brave.

As she turned on the taps and dropped some scented oils under the running water, her thoughts ventured back to the previous evening and the stranger she had seen at the theatre. Why had he left before the end of the performance? Had he really looked so much like Leandro or was it all just a trick of the light? Admittedly, she had never really got a good look at him – it had all happened so fast and then the auditorium had been plunged into darkness. Luz slipped into the steamy bubbles and dripped her sponge over her face, trying to wash away her uneasy thoughts. Time to get a grip and focus on the interview. It was only a few hours away. *I can do this*, she told herself. The priority now was to master her wayward thoughts, to focus and look the part. After her hot soak Luz took extra care with her clothes and her make-up. She had learned from her experience with interviews in London that appearance was half the battle.

Both Carmela and Alexandra were in the kitchen with steaming coffee and pastries when she came downstairs for breakfast. Luz looked sophisticated and businesslike in a slick, dark, figure-hugging Givenchy suit she had bought in London, teamed with a pair of Gucci high-heeled shoes and a matching Gucci bag. Her beautiful raven hair was not worn loose as usual; this morning she had it in a braided chignon at the base of her neck. Her eyes, though bright, were tinged with the steely grey that denoted her frame of mind: she was going out there today with the firm resolution of winning.

Alexandra smiled. 'Darling, you look perfect.'

Luz kissed her mother, gulped down her coffee and squinted at her watch as she bit into one of Carmela's warm *churros*. *Best get moving*, she thought, determined not to be late for her appointment.

It was a pleasant walk from L'Estrella down the hill into the walled city. She arrived outside the office building twenty minutes early and decided to go for a brisk walk along the port's promenade to clear her head. The image of Leandro and the stranger tried to intrude into her thoughts a few times, but she made a conscious effort to obliterate them from her mind and to go over what she wanted to say instead. This was her big break if she wanted to establish herself as a serious biographer in Spain. She must give her best and not get distracted. Anyhow, despite the eerie encounter with Paquita the day before, she was not inclined to be forced into something of someone else's design, particularly that of a deranged old witch. She should forget about Leandro and the gypsies. No good could come of entertaining unrealistic dreams so it would be best to put all that behind her.

Caldezar Corporación, SA was an imposing faded-yellow brick building, which stood four storeys tall in the tree-shaded Plaza de España, very close to the port. Outside, punctuating its walls were elegant wrought-iron balconies, above which tall, green-shuttered windows were topped with ornate mouldings. Luz took a deep breath and walked into the building, heart beating but head held high. Inside, the enormous grand lobby was all marble and stone with a large staircase and cool flagstone floors.

Luz gave her name to the uniformed porter. After he had made a brief phone call, a smartly dressed young woman, who could not yet have been in her twenties, came down to greet her and together they went up in the lift to the third floor. The reception area was vast and light, with huge ceiling-to-floor windows that looked out over the square, with its palm trees and fountain, and beyond that to the port. Despite the air-conditioning, the honey-coloured wooden parquet, combined with the sunshine that poured into the room, gave warmth to the place.

She was asked to wait, so Luz perched on the edge of an armchair and looked around her. The furnishings were expensive: an oak desk, oak tables and black leather armchairs. Beautiful oils by renowned artists adorned the walls. She recognized most of them but, strangely, none of the paintings was by Eduardo de Salazar. Though the taste was impeccable, the room remained impersonal. There was nothing there to indicate what kind of person Andrés de Calderón was.

One of the communicating doors opened and a hatchet-faced middle-aged woman entered.

'Doña Luz de Rueda?' She seemed to size up Luz as she came towards her. '*Buenos días.* I understand you're here for the biographer's job.'

Luz stood up, held out her hand and smiled. '*Buenos días, Señora.* Yes, I have an appointment to take a preliminary test, I believe.'

The assistant shook her hand curtly. 'Follow me,' she said, and she made her way down a corridor, guiding Luz to a room at the far end. 'You're the last of a long string of candidates. We've had a parade of all sorts, but I doubt any of them fit the bill.' Luz raised an eyebrow but was nonetheless heartened by the woman's forthright observation.

The room was small with a single desk and a typewriter. The assistant handed Luz a typewritten sheet. 'First of all,' she said, 'you must read through this questionnaire and answer it to the best of your knowledge. Secondly, you should write a thousand-word essay on why you think you are right for this job, and what you know about Eduardo Raphael Ruiz de Salazar and his work.' She paused, went to a cabinet and took out some sheets of paper and some pens. 'Here, or you're quite welcome to use the typewriter if you prefer.' She smiled faintly. 'Good luck,' she added, and left the room.

It was a strange list. Most of the questions about her education, her experience, her knowledge of languages, expected salary, etc had already been answered on her CV, but there were other questions, a little more probing and less discreet, about her family, her life, the state of her health and her friends; even whether or not she was engaged to be married. These seemed slightly untoward, but they did not disturb her. After all, she had nothing to hide. Luz sat down at the typewriter and began to tap out her answers.

She came away an hour and a half later feeling quite pleased with herself. The ordeal had been much easier than she had anticipated. Her hours in the de Salazar museum had paid off and for the essay she had confidently poured on to the page all the fascinating material she'd researched on the artist. Now she would have to wait patiently for an answer.

Back in reception, the hatchet-faced woman was now sitting behind the smart oak desk that Luz had noticed before. 'There's been a slight change of plan,' she announced. 'Don Andrés would like to see you later on today if that's all right. He would like to conduct his interview over lunch and has asked me to convey to you his apologies for inviting you at such short notice. Is it convenient to meet him at that time? If you have other engagements, he said he would quite understand. The thing is, he's away for the rest of the week and the meeting would otherwise have to be postponed to a later date.'

Luz swallowed hard and stiffened as a wave of panic washed through her. *Andrés de Calderón wanted to see her today?* She was unprepared for this. Wasn't there supposed to be an interview panel to get through before being shortlisted to meet de Salazar's nephew? Her instinctive reaction was to put it off till the coming week when she would have had the time to collect her wits and think about what she would say. Still, she wanted this job badly. *Stop being a coward and just go for it,* a voice at the back of her head told her. Good to get it over with, anyway. This would be her chance.

Mustering every ounce of composure she possessed, she smiled graciously. 'How very kind of Don Andrés. Please tell him that I have no other engagements today and that I would be honoured to join him for lunch.'

The woman looked her up and down again and nodded brusquely. 'Very well, it is now eleven-thirty. Don Andrés will be waiting for you in our dining room on the top floor at two o'clock. You should present yourself at the reception downstairs as you did earlier and someone will escort you there.'

*   *   *

Andrés de Calderón sat at his desk in his vast office on the fourth floor overlooking the harbour. He closed the file he had been reading for the last hour and passed his lean brown hand over his eyes, pondering on the contents. It was a detailed history to date of the candidate he had chosen to write Eduardo's biography. Her CV had been impressive: head and shoulders above that of any other candidate. So good, in fact, that he'd had her checked out to ensure there was nothing in her history that might jeopardize the project, should he select her for the job.

He read through the answers to the questionnaire that his assistant had brought in half an hour ago. As with the CV, they left out one important item: Luz María Cervantes de Rueda had conveniently omitted to mention that she had walked out of her first job without completing it.

It was only because he'd already had her checked out that this issue had come to light. He had been handed a copy of an

English newspaper article: '*Miffed biographer walks off job!*' The gossip was that it had happened after a lovers' tiff. Now he once again scrutinized Luz's snapshot, which was clipped to her CV. Indeed, she was a beautiful young woman. Still, the photograph did not do her justice. He smiled as he recalled seeing her at the theatre last night; even at a distance, through opera glasses, she was certainly the loveliest creature he had ever set eyes upon. Now she was here, at his offices, applying for the biographer's post. He frowned as his eyes scanned the article again. Luz de Rueda did not seem the type to walk out of anything, let alone a breakthrough in her career. He must clarify this at the interview today, he told himself. Not that it would make the slightest difference: his mind was already made up.

A knock at the door interrupted his thoughts. He put the file down on his desk and looked up. 'Enter.'

His assistant popped her head around the door. 'Señor de Calderón, *la Señorita* de Rueda has accepted your invitation for lunch.'

'Excellent. *Gracias*, Señora Herminia. Please cancel all my afternoon appointments.'

The woman nodded and closed the door behind her.

Andrés de Calderón turned back to the window and watched the seagulls as they squawked their way across the plaza towards the harbour. His mouth curled into a smile. In a few hours he would have the pleasure of finding out more about the complicated and captivating Luz de Rueda.

*   *   *

When Luz arrived at Caldezar Corporación, SA at five minutes to two she was escorted to the top floor by the same young woman who had met her that morning. 'Señor de Calderón is waiting for you on the terrace,' the woman informed her as they went up in the lift. Luz had always enjoyed the challenge of one-to-one interviews but today nerves were warring with her usual confidence. She wished she had taken the time to find out more about Eduardo de Salazar's nephew for herself, rather than rely on the snippets of information her parents had supplied. Was he truly a womanizer? Normally, she was so thorough and would certainly have done her homework on the man she was about to meet. Lately, however, she had become distracted and now she could kick herself.

The gated lift seemed to take an interminable time before it came smoothly to a halt. Luz was ushered through a large, empty dining room where French doors led out on to a patio. The young assistant smiled, held the door open and nodded politely.

Luz stepped out into the strong Spanish sunlight that drenched the veranda. Handsome tiles were inserted into the stuccoed walls in a random pattern and, together with the simple terracotta flooring and the two sets of graceful double arches dividing the patio, they gave a pleasing and coherent first impression. Breathtaking vistas unfolded on all sides over the terraced roofs of the luminous white city cut deep with blue shadows.

Andrés de Calderón was waiting for her, seated at a table half shaded by a vine-trellised loggia, looking suitably cool in a beige linen suit, crisp white shirt and Hermès tie with a gold-printed pattern of Andalucían horses. He rose indolently to greet her, a broad grin revealing a set of perfect white teeth in a copper-bronzed face. Luz's heart somersaulted twice. She stared at him as if struck by lightning. *It can't be*, she thought. Her eyes, her mind were playing havoc with her imagination. The man who stood before her with wraparound dark glasses that completely screened his eyes was a startling echo of Leandro the gypsy, although the latter was swarthy and wild-looking whereas this man was elegant and chiselled as cut glass. Could this be the man she'd glimpsed at the theatre last night?

'Ah, Doña Luz, you're on time, congratulations,' he said as he held out a tanned hand with perfectly manicured fingers. His voice was deep and warm, like brandy and caramel. 'It must be your English blood. Spaniards, I'm sad to say, are notoriously unpunctual.'

As Luz shook his hand, the touch of his fingers sent an odd frisson of excitement through her and she pulled her hand away quickly, hoping her astonishment was not as evident as it was felt. She caught a glimpse of humour quivering around his mouth as if he was appreciating some private joke. Although his eyes were not visible, she had a fair idea that Andrés de Calderón was mightily amused and she did not like it one bit.

Her eyes lightened from dark blue to grey. '*La puntualidad es la cortesia de los reyes*, punctuality is the politeness of kings,' she said coolly, noting that his own courtesy had not extended to removing his sunglasses, at least to greet her.

'Quite.' He signalled her to take a seat and sank back into his own. 'Can I offer you a drink before lunch, maybe some crisp white wine from our vineyards?' he suggested. 'It's very refreshing on a hot day like this.'

The way the day was turning out she had better stay away from alcohol; despite this suave invitation she did not need anything else to add to her confusion. Luz shook her head. 'No, thank you, I won't have anything for the moment.' She took her place opposite him with the sun on her back.

'A glass of fino or a stiff whisky, maybe? That is what the English drink, *no es asi*, is that not so?' he asked, his face completely straight, although she knew he was making fun of her.

'Not at lunchtime they don't, *señor*.' She coloured slightly at her own directness and tried to smile. Would he think her rude? 'Thank you, I'm fine, really.'

'There is no pleasing you, *señorita*,' he continued, apparently ignoring her comment. He was obviously enjoying this little game of testing his will against hers. 'A glass of iced water then,' he ended, with the most disarming smile.

The curve of his mouth was very distracting and she could not help but smile back at him. 'Yes, all right, I'd love a glass of water, thank you.'

'Ah, third time lucky! You drive a hard bargain, *señorita*,' he laughed and signalled to a waiter discreetly hovering in the background. '*Un vaso de agua para la joven por favour.*' The ice was broken.

A moment passed while Luz surveyed the man sitting opposite, still not quite over her shock. Tall, lean and dark, glossy brown hair neatly pulled back into a ponytail and a perfect profile that would make Rudolph Valentino jealous. It disturbed her that she could not stop staring at his sensual lips, which were the only clue to his expression. This man was dangerously attractive. She wished he would take off those dark glasses so that she could see his eyes; besides, they unnerved her. Logic told her that Andrés and Leandro could not be one and the same person. Anyhow, there was something much more sophisticated about Andrés de Calderón, a quiet confidence as opposed to the pent-up energy that emanated from the gypsy.

'I saw you at the theatre yesterday,' he volunteered, breaking into her thoughts. 'I recognized you from your photograph, even though it's a poor reflection of the reality. You are a very beautiful young lady.'

So he *was* the stranger she had glimpsed observing her through his opera glasses. Her eyes flicked down again and watched him run a finger pensively across his bottom lip. To her great annoyance Luz felt a pink blush rise to her cheeks. *And it's true, you really are a most shocking womanizer.*

'Thank you, you are very kind, *señor*.' She wondered when this pantomime of small talk would end. He was dragging on the suspense and she was increasingly more edgy by the second. It was clear he was flirting with her and she was at loss to know how to react. In different circumstances she would have had no problem in dealing with him – she had never found it difficult to respond to male attention or give men short shrift if she felt like it, but given the present situation and her need to be courteous ...

A waiter brought in the first course: medallions of steaming lobster served with an olive oil, garlic, caper and parsley sauce. They waited as he poured a glass of chilled white wine for Andrés and filled Luz's glass with icy water.

'I'm very impressed by your credentials,' Andrés said, again the first to talk. Appearing not to look at her, he breathed in the aroma of the wine before sipping it. 'You obviously know your job. The work you presented this morning was outstanding and far superior to that of the other candidates. We've been inundated with applications, as you can guess, but luckily for you, none of them suitable.' His tone was mild and businesslike. It was a good opening and Luz felt cheered. Realizing suddenly how hungry she was, she started to tuck into the delicious appetizer.

'I've always been interested in art,' she ventured, 'especially Spanish contemporary art and Surrealism. I've read extensively about your uncle and I'm fascinated by his work, always have been.' She paused to take a sip of her water. 'We own a house outside Puerto de Santa María and one in Cádiz,' – but he probably knew that already – 'so this is an ideal opportunity for me, given most of de Salazar's work is around the Costa de Luz. It would be very easy and practical for me to carry out the work.'

Andrés speared some lobster with his fork. 'I see you spent most of your childhood in England. Are you planning to stay in Spain for good?' His face was impassive.

'I have lots of friends from boarding school and my great-aunt is in England, but my parents are here and this is where my heart lies,' she explained.

He nodded as if satisfied with her answer. 'Did you find it difficult growing up away from home?'

Luz glanced up at him in surprise at this sudden intimate question. 'I would have preferred to stay in Spain, I think, but I learned to be independent there and think for myself.'

'You think that an English boarding school education is the reason for that?'

'Yes, in a way.' She took a sip of water and looked at him, suddenly a little bolder. 'Forgive me for saying so, but you yourself said that my written work today was far superior to that of the other applicants and I can't take all the credit for that.'

Andrés cocked his head to one side, studying her. 'You can't?'

'I might not be sitting here if I hadn't lived and studied abroad. Boarding school taught me to be self-sufficient and rely on myself and not others. That gave me the drive to be as good as I could be at everything I do.'

Now one side of his mouth lifted with amusement. 'I'm sure you are good at everything you do, Doña Luz.' His gaze stayed on her as he sipped his wine, making her flush once more. 'Perhaps there is a connection, as you say. You were the only candidate educated abroad, I believe.'

'As I said, though, Spain is where I belong,' Luz went on, keen to reassure him that she was committed. 'That's why I wanted to find challenging work in this part of the country. I love it so much.'

'This biography will certainly be a challenge. No one has ever written anything of much quality about Eduardo's work.'

'Then I shall be the first,' she answered, without thinking, taking another mouthful of the delicious, creamy shellfish.

'Are you always this straightforward, Doña Luz? I like that.' His broad smile flashed at her and Luz coloured again slightly, though relieved that she seemed to be making a good impression.

'What I meant, I suppose, is that I've always had high expectations of myself.'

He was still smiling as he took a sip of his wine. 'And in all things?'

Her brow furrowed. 'Of course. How can one live without expectations and standards in life?'

He raised his eyebrows at her artless response and then chuckled. 'That sounds like your English boarding school speaking.'

Realizing how earnest she must have sounded, Luz smiled sheepishly at his obvious amusement. 'Yes, maybe it is.' He was perceptive as well as ridiculously handsome.

They talked and ate, and Luz found herself laughing in spite of her nerves. She was starting to feel more confident now, even beginning to enjoy Andrés' playful banter.

A waiter cleared the first course as another brought in the second: poussin filled with a Provençal stuffing, made distinctive by the addition of spicy local sausage, he told her. Andrés de Calderón was obviously a gourmet.

Now that she was at ease, she sensed the more rigorous part of the interview was about to start.

Andrés refilled Luz's glass with water. 'Eduardo's Surrealist influences are well known but how would you say they informed his architecture?' His polite, professional tone had returned.

'Yes, people often cite Magritte, Dalí, Ernst and Miró as influences for his paintings, but his extraordinary, strident colours are often reminiscent of Fauvism. And there's no doubt that he admired the old masters too, especially Velázquez and Caravaggio for their dramatic realism. You can see how it shaped the more representational aspects of his style.' Luz felt him watching her intently as she spoke and realized that she was gazing at his mouth again. Already she was moving off the point.

'And his architecture?' he asked, a faint smile playing around his lips as if he knew what she was thinking.

Annoyed with herself, she pulled her distracted attention back to the question. 'Some say, and I agree, that his architecture as well as his paintings owe the greatest debt to Escher and his use of impossible constructions, all those odd perspectives and the exploration of infinity in his black-and-white woodcuts.'

'For example?'

'For example, the interlocking stairs in many of the elaborate castles and towers that Eduardo painted and his doorways placed in bizarre, illogical places. For Eduardo, Escher was a genius.' Luz began to relax into her subject. 'And just look at his museum in Cádiz. It's an obvious homage to both Escher and the Surrealists. There's no doubt that the Surrealist painters he was exposed to in Paris when he was an art student also inspired him to create buildings like that, as well as his landscaped gardens – they're fantastical, too.'

Andrés broke in here, fully locked now into the debate. 'André Breton, who, as you know, was the father of Surrealism, said: "The imaginary is what tends to become real."' He gave a wry smile. 'The boundary between illusion and reality is a fictitious one.'

Luz stared at Andrés' unfeasibly handsome face. Now that he was fired with enthusiasm, it was almost as if Leandro was sitting opposite her. 'Does that apply to your own life?' The words had left Luz's lips before she had a chance to think.

'I have my uncle's blood running through my veins so I have a certain way of looking at the world, yes. Life is a masquerade, as Eduardo knew. What is truth from one angle is a lie from another.' He ate a mouthful of food and seemed to regard her appraisingly. 'People suppress their inner truths and desires all the time and present an illusion to the world and even to themselves, wouldn't you say, Doña Luz?'

She glanced down at her plate, feeling like the conversation was suddenly moving in a direction with which she did not feel comfortable. Though it had been tempting to fish for information about Andrés, he was clearly adept at turning the tables. Luz shifted in her chair. Not being able to see the expression in his eyes was intimidating. The thought crossed her mind that he had worn them for just that reason. She sat a little more upright in her chair, determined to return to the subject of Eduardo.

'Yes, illusion and reality is at the heart of Surrealism and what you say fits with Eduardo, and even more so with Dalí. But then Dalí was such a strong influence in all those years Eduardo lived in France after he finished art school.'

Andrés gave a slight wave of his fork. 'True, but Eduardo was not fond of Dalí's grandiose behaviour and the publicity stunts that so often eclipsed his actual work.'

Relieved they were firmly back on track, Luz continued the thread: 'And, of course, he didn't share Dalí's politics either. Having said that, he may have frowned upon Dalí's support of Franco, but he didn't return to Spain to fight for the Republican cause.'

'His war protest was in his art, like Picasso and Miró. Like many of the Surrealists.' Andrés broke off some bread and continued to look at her. 'But I see you're not about to let Eduardo off lightly.'

'I don't think you can write an insightful account of an artist's life unless you look squarely at those things for which they can be criticized …' She paused. Would he take exception to that?

'Indeed,' Andrés nodded his head, conceding the point. 'But life is not just black and white, right and wrong. Circumstances often weave a complicated pattern that can obscure the way forward,' he said softly.

A furrow appeared between his brows and as he said no more, Luz carried on.

'I've always found the darker side of Eduardo's paintings interesting. His use of magic and fairy tale can either feel uplifting or menacing and despairing.'

'Yes, some of the images are unsettling, even when beautifully painted. His obsession with death is as potent as his celebration of life. Which works do you prefer, Doña Luz?'

Luz thought for a moment. She knew exactly which painting was her favourite. It was *The Immortality of the Crab*, in which a naked woman sat on a chair on the beach, her face covered with a giant butterfly, the sea calm behind her. Out of her head protruded two long feelers and from her lower belly a huge lotus flower with giant petals bloomed, on which a whole new fantastic, vibrant landscape was rendered in miniature. The flower's long stem plunged straight into the ground, where thick roots tendrilled outwards to take hold of the earth. The image always spoke to her own desire for something suppressed within her, fighting to get out, and was strangely erotic. This particular painting was not one she wanted to discuss with Andrés.

'The ones dealing with freedom, release and rebirth – *The Mannequin and the Princess*, *Song to the Mountain*, *Gypsy Carnival*, *Dominion of the Phoenix*. I love the jewel-like colours and sense of magic and movement. The element of surprise and wild imagination is breathtaking.'

'The element of surprise and mystery was what Eduardo excelled at,' he observed.

Eduardo wasn't the only one, Luz mused. She sensed his nephew was an unpredictable puzzle and it made her uncharacteristically wary. She watched the long, perfectly formed fingers of his hand reach for his glass and for some unknown reason it made her cheeks warm.

'The symbols of sex, death, hope and love are equally fascinating …' Luz hesitated, not knowing how to finish her train of thought.

'Go on, Doña Luz,' Andrés said smoothly.

'Well … it's a combination of traditions. The mythological and pagan, but also harking back to medieval and renaissance

Christian symbolism, which was used so that the illiterate masses could readily understand its meaning ... the pomegranate as a symbol of eternal life and resurrection, the fig as the loss of innocence, and so on. In those days people were constantly reminded that Satan would be ready with his pitchfork in the fires of Hell for anyone indulging in carnal pleasures or even indecent thoughts.' She blushed again as her eyes inadvertently took in the smooth line of his jaw and she took a sip of water.

Andrés put his fork down and leaned back in his chair. His amused smile had reappeared. 'And you think that Eduardo was warning against the dangers of carnal pleasure?'

Luz cleared her throat. 'No, not at all! His paintings are far too erotic for that.' *Why was she finding this so difficult to talk about?* She needed to steer towards safer ground. 'I mean that he depicted human experience and also saw the repercussions that our actions have. His symbolism was deeply personal, too. There are so many references to the fact that he witnessed his mother fall from a horse that trampled her to death. Horses figure repeatedly in his paintings – *The Lady of the Forest* with the woman on horseback riding through the trees, her head facing the wrong way on her shoulders.'

'Ah, yes, that's one of his best. Beautiful and disturbing at the same time.' Andrés cupped his chin in his hand and his brow furrowed. 'Her neck was broken when they found her.'

Luz nodded and pushed her plate away. 'It must have been hideous, completely devastating. Psychoanalysts would say that the loss of his mother was Eduardo's reason for shifting back and forth between reality and illusion in his paintings, refusing to accept what had happened.'

'Yes, he never got over it. He understood loss and loneliness very well.' Andrés frowned again and then seemed to be on the point of saying more when the waiter appeared to clear their plates. Luz watched Andrés for a moment and although his sunglasses rendered him inscrutable, for the first time he seemed genuinely awkward. Aware of her gaze, he broke the moment by changing the subject: 'We could talk for hours about Eduardo's symbolism and I'm sure we will again, but there are other matters we should move on to.'

All through the remainder of the meal, Andrés put her through a searching and thorough examination, asking intricate, ambiguous questions pertaining to Spain and its place in the international art world. She was aware that he arranged them purposely to trip her, but she was well trained and gave swift, instinctive answers.

He seemed satisfied and just when she thought that he was going to offer her the post, once the table had been cleared he leaned over and took a file that was sitting on one of the chairs, fingering it absentmindedly for a moment before opening it.

His face looked suddenly grave and the mouth that had often been so animated during their meal was set in an impassive line. He leaned on the chair arm, chin resting on his thumb and index finger. For a few disquieting seconds Luz knew he was surveying her closely from behind those dark glasses. 'Is there anything you feel might be of issue if I were to employ you? Anything at all?' He paused a few moments. Luz cast about in her mind for anything she thought he needed to know. She remained silent.

'Well then, Doña Luz, can you please tell me why you walked away from your first job and why you mentioned it neither in your CV nor in this morning's questionnaire?'

The words slipped coolly off his tongue but she could see that he was not enjoying this part of the interview. His question was unexpected, of course, but it was the first that really felt like an intrusion into her private life. How did he know? Then again, he was an experienced businessman. He wouldn't take any chances; he'd research a person's background first and be a master at extracting more information from them in the interview than they wanted to relay. Then Luz's eye caught sight of a tabloid clipping in his open file. He followed her gaze. A couple of uncomfortable seconds passed.

'Did you think it was of no importance to a future employer? Such an attitude deserves a little condemnation, does it not?'

It was as if a bucket of icy water had just been hurled in her face. Earlier, he had been nothing but complimentary; where was he coming from with this? He had made a good job of unnerving her, if that was his intention.

The words stuck in her throat. She drew a breath. 'It was my first job, I was inexperienced … I mishandled a difficult situation …' Her heart was hammering now as if she had run a marathon.

'Why did you not mention it? Do you not find that dishonest? I'm paying a generous fee for this biography, assigning the writer copyright and putting their name on the cover. Don't you think I had the right to know?' The dark tone of his voice was dry and inflexible.

Something tightened inside her at his hostility. *For God's sake, did he not understand that it wasn't dishonesty that had prevented her from disclosing the facts but embarrassment?* Her only crime in that first job had been that she was too innocent, too trusting. Lifting her chin defiantly, she gave Andrés a look of thunder, her stormy eyes threatening to fill with the tears that she willed away. 'I honestly did not think you would be interested,' she replied finally.

'On the contrary, I'm *very* interested. I'd like to know what would make a dedicated, passionate and talented young woman walk out of her first assignment.'

'There was a difference of opinion between myself and my employer.'

'This man, Cameron Hunt, he was your lover.' It was not a question but a statement.

Before Andrés could go any further with his accusations, she put up a peremptory hand. 'Just wait a second, *señor*. What gives you the right to presume that he was my lover?'

'Wasn't he?' he asked quietly.

'I don't think it's any of your business who I do or do not sleep with.' Luz forced herself to remain calm. 'Still, I will enlighten you out of courtesy and because I admit that it was possibly wrong of me not to mention the fact. Mr Hunt and myself were never lovers. He commissioned me to write the biography of his ancestor. We went on a few dates, yes. All the rest is newspaper hype.'

'But you walked off the job ...' He was still toying with her and his relentless confrontation was throwing her off balance.

How she wished he would take off those dreadful glasses so she could speak to him eye-to-eye. This was like talking to a blank wall and it unsettled her. Luz was starting to think that he had worn them as a deliberate ploy. She clenched her fists slightly.

'Yes, as I have told you already, I was young and I didn't know how to handle a difficult situation. I had no option but to resign from the job and return the advance paid. Still, I don't see what my personal life has to do with you, or with whether or not I'm fit to write your uncle's biography. Maybe if you had a better look at my CV instead of reading trashy tabloids like the *Daily Messenger* you would have a fuller picture of my capabilities.' She was staring at him with fiery eyes.

The smile that flitted across his lips was darker now. 'Come now, Doña Luz, you are a very beautiful woman. You were, as you said, very young, just out of university. Were you so naïve as to think that a man of Cameron Hunt's status would have given you that important assignment without an ulterior motive?'

'Do I take it then, *señor*, that if you decide to give me this job – and I'm aware it would only be my second significant assignment – you too would have an ulterior motive?' She blurted out the answer and regretted her words as soon as she had said them but it was too late to take them back.

One of his black eyebrows flicked up a fraction and she had the horrible feeling that he was trying to assess the reason for her question. The suggestion behind it made Luz suddenly very self-conscious. For a fleeting moment she caught some kind of smouldering emotion burning silently beneath his elegant and composed exterior. Then suddenly Andrés threw his head back and, for the first time, burst out laughing, his handsome, masculine face vibrating with life.

'*Touché, señorita*!' He closed the file and slapped it down on the table. 'You've got the job if you still want it. It's been a pleasure fencing with you,' he ended with a good-humoured nod of his head.

Luz was flabbergasted by this condescending admission and by his mercurial mood. Fascination and indignation caught her in a tug of war. She could walk away – it would be enormously satisfying but so short-sighted. He was watching her now with that disarming smile of his. Andrés de Calderón was most definitely a charmer and whether she cared to admit it or not, Luz was suitably charmed. Anger died as relief settled in. She looked at him steadily, her deep-blue eyes trying to penetrate the mask of his dark glasses.

'Thank you, *señor*, I'll do my best to live up to *your* expectations.'

The warmth in his smile would have melted all the glaciers in Alaska. 'Splendid, you've just made me a happy man.' Though she could not see his eyes, she sensed they were caressing her. He pushed back his chair and stood up. 'I'll get my office to draw up the contract. Unfortunately I've been called away this week on business. If you don't mind, the signing will have to wait a few days, so I'll understand if you want to delay starting work until then. My assistant will make an appointment with you. I hope this will be the beginning of a very fruitful and enjoyable partnership.'

By the time he had finished, any belligerent thoughts she had been nurturing had evaporated. He led the way to the lift and held the gated door open for her. She took his outstretched hand and again a tiny shock of awareness ran through her nerve-endings at his touch. That slow, secret smile of his reappeared and once more she wished she could see the expression in his eyes. How like the gypsy he was, but how very different, too.

Her curiosity had been piqued and even though she remained wary, as she left Caldezar Corporación, SA Luz was already under the notorious Andrés de Calderón's spell.

CHAPTER 3

A couple of days had passed since her interview at Caldezar Corporación, SA. Alexandra and Salvador had returned to Jerez for the preparations of the El Pavón annual masked ball, but Luz had elected to stay in Cádiz. The fancy dress ball had been a tradition at El Pavón since the time of Count Rodriguez Cervantes de Rueda, Salvador's grandfather, almost a century before. It had started off as a celebration of late spring and the last harvest of oranges. In the old days it was a much grander event, which lasted a week, and to which a great number of the European nobility were invited. Today, it was done on a smaller scale and only the great Spanish families were asked, along with famous names in the art and literary worlds.

Luz had loved the romantic glamour of it all ever since she was a teenager, when she'd been allowed to stay up late to see the guests arrive: the music, the dancing and the fascination of watching a host of characters in costume, guessing who was beneath their velvety and bejewelled masks. It had always been a magical event for her.

But now she had other things on her mind, her new job as biographer being uppermost. On her first morning alone, without her parents, Luz was just finishing her breakfast and reading her notebook when Carmela breezed on to the veranda.

'*Por favor, señorita,* please make sure you lock your windows properly if you leave the house today.' Carmela stood next to the table with her hands on her hips. 'The gypsy horse fair's in Cádiz and the town is apparently flooded with these people. I don't need to tell you what *ladrones,* thieves, they are! They have more than one trick in their bags to rob from you. Pickpocketing, house breaking ... nothing is beyond them. Every year they bring chaos to the area.'

'I don't think I'll be going out today, I've some work to do.' Luz told her. 'Thank you for warning me, though. It's true, I do have the habit of leaving the house without locking my windows, but it's so isolated and calm here. It saves me taking my keys.' She glanced up at Carmela. Of course she wasn't going to admit that only a few days ago a young *gitano* had walked straight into the villa and through her bedroom door, not to mention the fact that he had carried her, unconscious, from his gypsy camp. She almost giggled at the thought and took a sip of coffee. 'Anyhow, today if I decide to take a walk, I'll make an exception.' She smiled at Carmela.

As the housekeeper turned to go, Luz asked nonchalantly, 'Where does this fair take place?'

'Oh, I think they usually set up camp on a plain the other side of the hills, always the same site. You know, that big space of derelict land just beyond the old forge,' Carmela told Luz, waving a dismissive hand. 'But that doesn't stop them from coming over and invading the town.'

Yes, Luz knew exactly where that was; she had seen the large area of scrubland on one of her long walks and wondered why it had remained undeveloped. She wouldn't need a map to find it.

Carmela paused and untied her apron, not noticing that Luz had put down her notebook and was deep in thought. 'The *gitanos* overrun the taverns with their wild music and brawls. The women – *iay!* – the women are often the worst when they come to blows … more like claws than hands … and it's usually over a man or money, or both. You should see them, carrying on with the sailors down at the port,' she tutted and prattled on, folding her apron and tying her long dark curls back with a brightly coloured scarf.

Luz's attention returned to the housekeeper. 'But Carmela, surely you've seen the Flamenco dancing and heard their music?' She picked up a peach from her plate and moved to the marbled balcony wall of the veranda, leaning back against it. Her sapphire-blue eyes fixed on Carmela brightly. 'Aren't you the tiniest bit impressed by the spectacle – the passion, the skill, the grace of the dancers? It's like watching colourful birds swirling, about to take flight.'

She gazed out to sea and the sound of Leandro pouring his heart out over the strings of his guitar echoed through her mind. 'And the music is exciting and sad, all at once, as if your heart will stop just from listening to it.'

She looked up to see Carmela regarding her curiously. 'Doña Luz, mark my words, these *gitanos* can hypnotize you with their music and sultry looks, but no good ever came of us *gajos* mixing with them. They have their world, we have ours. *Así tiene que ser*, that's the way it's meant to be.' She sighed. 'Now I must be off and back to my kitchen or Pedro will be wondering where his favourite baked cinnamon *ensaimada* are!' She chuckled and gave the young woman a wave as she disappeared around the side of the villa.

The sun baked fiercely over the great expanse of the Atlantic. Luz thought of Leandro and of Andrés, the two men who had made such a strong impression on her in the past week. Both were so similar physically but so completely different. How could they look so alike? Were they related? The idea sounded preposterous.

Luz bit into the ripe peach, exposing the dark core. She had never come across the kind of man who tested her feelings and excited her in a way she'd always thought a woman should be excited, but who also made her nervous and unsure of herself. Generally, the opposite sex did not affect Luz to this extent. She was astonished at herself.

She had never spoken to Leandro; still, the gypsy stirred emotions to the depth of her soul. Andrés, the cool, sophisticated businessman, had captivated her in quite a different manner. She had the vague impression of being the prisoner of an invisible net, cast by some strange twist of fate; and though it mystified her – disturbed her even – she found it enormously exhilarating. Now, whether she knew it or not, Luz was giving herself up to the current of destiny.

Somewhere, an unfathomable need to see Leandro again swept through her. Her eyes skimmed over the distant view of dazzling water; it shimmered like a spangled sheet of silk, dotted here and there with little beads of gold. She could hear the seagulls squalling and the horns of big ships booming in the harbour. Luz glanced down at the manuscript she had been reading and then at her book of notes. Such a beautiful afternoon and there she was, cooped up at home working. Her decision to start before the contract was signed, to get ahead with the job – and perhaps impress Andrés de Calderón in the process, she conceded – now seemed an onerous task.

Her mind automatically wandered back to his green-eyed gypsy doppelgänger. *Becoming involved with gypsies is a bad idea*, a small voice at the back of her mind nagged. She thought of her parents and their strange reticence about the *gitanos*, and about Carmela, who had made no bones about her opinion. Certainly, such behaviour wasn't in keeping with the sense of decorum she'd tried to adopt while growing up in England either. *But I'm not going to get involved, I'm just curious about these people*, another part of her argued. The dialogue went on in her head: curiosity killed the cat, went the proverb. Ah, but curiosity alone inspires every step, according to Goethe. Anyway, it was all part of her research, she told herself. One or two of Eduardo's best pieces portrayed aspects of their lives.

She searched her wardrobe for a scruffy-looking sleeveless top and a pair of faded denims and pulled her hair back into a loose ponytail with wispy strands coming away from the band. A last glance in the mirror assured her that she was inconspicuous enough; it would not do to be noticed. Luz was unaware that her kind of beauty was never unobtrusive and, however much she tried to blend into the crowd, she would always be noticed.

She found the fairground without any difficulty. The hilly route she took was hot and dusty with no merciful shade. At last, though, the road fell away and the old forge appeared in the near distance on the edge of a scrubby plain; a matter of minutes and she would be there. As she approached the site she could hear the low, continuous, rumbling murmur of the gypsy gathering, like the raging winds that thundered over the coast on stormy nights. The commotion held numerous sounds. There was the resonating clamour of speech and laughter; the whinnying of excited horses stamping their hooves and the clanking of the brass ornaments on their harnesses as they shook their beautiful manes. There was the barking of dogs and the rattling of their chains as they pulled on them. And now, as the camp came into view, there was the distinctive, heavy pounding of her heartbeat filling her ears.

The scene was humming with life. Under the fire of the sun a rainbow tapestry of people, beasts and inanimate objects came together in happy, organised chaos. Mules and donkeys mingled with goats and pigs, braying, bleating and squealing as children ran around whooping and chasing each other with catapults. Men led horses round on ropes while others gesticulated on the merits of a particular beast as they huddled in groups, smoking cigarettes and grunting their approval or rejection. The *chaláns*, the gypsy horse dealers, with their bronzed faces and broad-brimmed felt hats, presided over the buying and selling of every beast under the shade of a huge wooden shed roof. They stood in front of a bigger crowd who shouted things back at them in *Caló*. Men and women chatted and laughed behind stalls of food, copper pans, bright clothes and baskets. There was even a barrel-organ player, grinning toothlessly and nodding along to his music as some gypsies clapped and danced, or swigged from glasses of manzanilla. The air was a heady mix of smells: earth, sweat, dung, tobacco and strong coffee.

At first Luz was overwhelmed by it all; but as she slipped through the crowd and roamed around the stalls, feasting her eyes on this colourful and mysterious world, she began to enjoy herself.

She had almost forgotten what she had come for when she spotted him in a group of men gathered under the shed roof. Leandro was accompanied by the lanky, tattooed youth she had seen with him on the beach. His back was to Luz and he was busy arguing with the owner of a beautiful horse, explaining himself with animated gestures. He was dressed in a faded olive-green vest and washed-out black Bermuda shorts, a dark scarf around his throat. Despite his slim build, Leandro's whole body was the picture of vitality and strength. When looking at him, the words 'tall', 'lean' and 'energetic' came to mind. Luz's gaze lingered on his bare arms and thighs, which were evenly tanned and knotted with muscles. He had held her in those arms against his powerful chest and she had been unconscious: how infuriating! She wondered what it would be like to live the life of a wild gypsy. Luz felt herself blush as sensual, unfamiliar images invaded her mind and delicious warm sensations flooded her body. What was wrong with her? Never in her whole life had she been subjected to such unbelievable inner mayhem. *It must be the heat*, she thought. She had read somewhere that the sun sometimes did strange things to a person.

His friend was the first to notice her. He nudged Leandro and whispered something in his ear. Leandro turned to look over his shoulder and she felt the strength of his magnetic stare. He nodded in acknowledgement of her and smiled, then returned to his business, shaking his head at the owner of the horse: no deal. The seller said something. Leandro yawned, shrugged his shoulders and scratched his head, then his chin. Finally he laughed, shook hands with the trader and came towards Luz, pulling the beautiful animal behind him. The deal was done after all.

'*Buenas tardes, señorita,*' he greeted her courteously as he drew nearer. '*Que me han traído suerte,* you've brought me luck,' he declared, his glittering eyes arresting hers with an enigmatic stare. He raked long, slender fingers through his unruly shock of shiny dark hair. For the first time she had a clear view of him. He was around her own age, she guessed, though something about him seemed older somehow. Under the two-day stubble his narrow face had a golden darkness, different to the usual rougher gypsy tan, with a pronounced bone structure and regular features. It was highlighted by the deep green of his irises that watched her now between thick black eyelashes with a strange remoteness.

He glanced casually behind him before returning his gaze to her. 'You have to be doubly careful at these fairs. Some dealers can make you believe that oranges grow on cactus trees.' His voice had a gypsy cadence to it that she did not find unattractive. This was certainly not the measured, sophisticated drawl of Andrés de Calderón.

Luz laughed, mustering up enough courage not to run away and hide. 'I've been meaning to thank you for taking care of me after my fall and returning me safely home. It was very kind of you.'

'You were hurt, what else could I do?'

She thought she glimpsed a spark of something in his eyes: frustration, anger, impatience, but then it was gone and his expression became unreadable again.

'Still, not everyone would have been so ... gallant,' she stammered, trying to find the right word. As she said it, she thought of him delivering her directly to her bedroom and felt her face warm at the suggestion of just how gallant he had been.

As if reading her mind he looked down at her and gave a slow, mischievous smile. 'This is true. But we gypsies can be honourable, too.' Green eyes glittered at her with amusement as he lowered his face closer to hers and added: 'Or did you think we were all rogues and bandits, perhaps?'

'Of course not, I didn't mean to ...'

'But I see you're fully recovered,' he interrupted, straightening up. His gaze travelled over her in a way that made her insides blaze and melt at the same time.

'Yes, I slept well and felt fine the next morning, thank you.'

'Your bed is very comfortable, that always helps.' His voice was low and provocative.

Luz's eyes widened. 'You were ...' was all she could manage as the heat deepened in her cheeks.

He laughed. 'Don't look so shocked, *señorita*. I laid you down on your bed, that's all. As I told you, we gypsies are honourable, though you would sorely test any man's control, I think.'

She blinked rapidly, telling herself to concentrate. He was standing close enough for her to reach out and touch him and although she yearned to, she would never have dared. Men did not normally have this effect on her and her heart was thundering in her chest as though she had just finished a run on the beach.

'And are all gypsies so forward?'

'No, just me ... and only with you.' He flashed a grin and began stroking the side of his horse absentmindedly. 'Do you often ride on the beach?'

Luz noticed the way the smooth muscles in his arm flexed as his hand moved up and down the creature. She swallowed before saying, 'Yes, most days. I love the sea air and the exercise.'

He nodded, wicked humour still alight in his bright green eyes, which remained fixed on Luz's. 'Exercise is good. What other exercise do you enjoy, *señorita*?' His gaze darkened and flicked down to her mouth before settling back on her eyes.

Luz felt an involuntary quiver in a strange and uncharted place deep in her belly. He was flirting outrageously and she found it intoxicating. 'I often swim, too. Do you swim?' she found herself saying, huskily.

An eyebrow arched. 'Yes, of course – we are sea gypsies. I should take you swimming one day, I think we would both like it. You can race me. Though I warn you, you wouldn't win.'

'You think not? I was on our school swim team,' she answered, still trying to control her breathy voice. Suddenly she realized that she hadn't even introduced herself. 'By the way, my name is Luz. Doña Luz de Rueda.'

'Yes, I know.' He lifted an eyebrow and gave a lazy, enigmatic smile. 'So why is a girl like you alone at the horse fair, Doña Luz de Rueda?' He pulled gently on the reins of his stallion as it snorted and tossed its head.

Luz was distracted from the fact that he already knew her name and was more concerned about how to explain her appearance there. She could not possibly admit that she had gone there solely to find him, and yet the fairground was too out of the way to pretend she had just been out for a walk.

'I heard the fair was on at the moment and I've always wanted to see it for myself. Your horse is beautiful, I'm quite envious.'

He was about to answer when two young *gitanas* came out of nowhere, joining their little group.

'Oh, Leandro, what have you got there?' said one as she trailed her hand over the horse's chestnut coat. 'He's a beauty!'

'Indeed, he's quite a find,' Leandro agreed, his well-defined mouth breaking into a satisfied smile. He patted the creature's flank and stared at Luz for a brief moment before looking away.

'You're so clever, you have a real business talent,' the other gypsy girl told him in a sugary tone, sliding an arm around his waist possessively and cuddling up to him. Her flame-coloured hair framed a striking face and there was a boldness about her that Luz found slightly vulgar.

'Rosa, you flatter me, as always. But yes, it's true,' he shrugged, grinning impishly.

Leandro obviously had a large fan club, Luz noted. Feeling distinctly *de trop*, she started to turn but he caught her eye. The gypsy gave her a fleeting glance as if he was pretending not to notice her but something flickered in his expression that she couldn't interpret. Did he recognize her discomfort? Was that a glance of understanding or sudden dismissal now that he had a new female audience? Whatever he was thinking, Luz sensed that the circle now excluded her. She felt like she'd been cast aside but was determined no one would see such emotion betrayed by her face.

A rigid smile touched her lips as she moved away, leaving the three gypsies engrossed in a lively conversation about the newly bought horse. Luz held her chin up, but knives cruelly pierced her heart. All her unrealistic dreams were crumbling into a pile of cinders. Her imagination, not normally quite so febrile, had spun a web of romantic fantasies in which she was now caught. The wretchedness that consumed her now was not the gypsy's fault but all of her own making, she told herself. From the very first moment she had laid eyes on Leandro, she had been wrong; in her head she had fabricated his interest and misjudged the situation all along. Now, she had only herself to blame.

The air had grown cooler. In different circumstances Luz would have enjoyed the walk back but, as it was, her thoughts weighed heavily on her, making her head hang down. She was weary and humiliated. What had possessed her to act in such a foolhardy way? she pondered miserably. Perhaps Leandro had always been out to make fun of her. Dimly, she could hear her parents' warnings to keep away from gypsies. Only the other day her father had told her that the *gitanos* were fond of tricks. Why had she not taken heed of those wise words?

'My beautiful red roses, my lovely scented roses, who will buy? Fair lady, gracious *señorita*, why are you so sad?'

Luz jumped, jerked out of her sombre thoughts. A *gitana* dressed all in black was accosting her at the side of the road with a bunch of blood-red roses, which she clutched tightly in her long brown fingers, despite the spiky thorns. She had come right up to Luz, her dark hawkish eyes peering inquisitively into the young woman's face. Luz shook her head politely and tried to move on, doing her best to ignore the flower seller.

'Let me help you, let me make things better,' the gypsy persisted, close on Luz's heels. 'Believe me, I have the remedy. Today he doesn't love you, tomorrow with this talisman he will be unable to live without you.'

'Leave me alone, thank you. I've no money on me, so just go away,' Luz told her, accelerating her step. Perhaps fate was laughing at her, too.

'I do not want any money, fair lady,' the gypsy said sharply as she caught the young woman's arm, forcing her to halt, the gold and silver bracelets clinking on her arms as she did so. She then coughed slightly and ran the back of her hand over her mouth. For the first time Luz looked into the *gitana*'s face. She was a fine-looking woman, with large, blazing, charcoal pupils fixed keenly on the young woman's eyes. Brass hoop earrings pushed through her blue-black curly hair, which was obviously dyed and fell well below her shoulders in thick unruly locks. Her face was heavily made-up and Luz found it difficult to guess her age, but it was clear that, while she must have been a great beauty in her youth, life had not been kind. There was an ashen pallor to her complexion underneath the make-up.

Exasperated, Luz sighed. 'So if it's not money you're looking for, what is it you want?'

'I have taken a shine to you, *hermosa jovencita*. You remind me of the daughter I lost through sickness when she was still a blooming flower,' she said, switching to a whimpering tone. 'I want to help you, you seem so sad. Here, take this talisman and wear it underneath your clothes,' she went on with urgency, as she tried to press a tiny package into the young woman's hand.

'What are you up to this time, Jezebel?' croaked an old woman loudly, moving out of the shadow of a gnarled olive tree. It was Paquita.

The younger *gitana* turned sharply round as Paquita crossed the narrow road to join them, saying: 'Show me what you've got there.' She snatched the tiny package from the other gypsy's hand, throwing her a contemptuous look. 'Shame on you!'

Then turning to Luz, she gazed at her with shrewd, hooded eyes that were unusually alert and penetrating for an old woman. 'Go on your way, beautiful lady, go on your way and beware of red roses! The rose is a dangerous flower … it does not just hold the blossom, it also has thorns.'

After both gypsies had disappeared back up hill towards the camp, Luz hurried home in a kind of haze. To Carmela's dismay she evaded dinner and went straight to her room. She sat for a long time on the veranda, looking out over the beautiful vista before her without seeing it, ruminating on this painful confusion that was so unfamiliar to her. The waves crashed on to the rocks in the soft light of the fading day. Something had been unleashed in her that she dearly wished she could return whence it came. Nothing made sense and nothing gave her comfort.

That night Luz's dreams of fire returned, all-consuming this time, and she could not walk out of the flames.

*   *   *

Luz threw herself fully into her work. Contract or no contract, she must keep her mind occupied and pull herself together. Thank goodness she had swallowed her pride at the interview and secured the job with Caldezar Corporación, SA. She spent her days scanning libraries, museums and art galleries for information about Eduardo de Salazar. In the evenings she would return, exhausted, to L'Estrella and after a quick snack in brooding silence, retreat to her bedroom. So long as she was working, she was safe, but at night, in the deep quiet of darkness, that was when the torment began. Assailed by nightmares and humiliating thoughts she would toss and turn, but also, and that was the worst of it, by a powerful, aching need that was unfamiliar to her. Those brief moments when she'd been aware of Leandro's strong masculine physique at the horse fair haunted her. No matter how much she fought it, he was always there, his green opal eyes boring into hers, caressing her, calling her.

A new day dawned. She was scheduled to meet Andrés de Calderón that morning to sign her contract. A fresh surge of energy seized her. The sun was shining, the sky was blue without a cloud – a perfect travel-brochure day. There was also the El Pavón annual masked ball to look forward to in a few days' time. Thinking she should extend the courtesy of inviting Andrés, Luz sealed an envelope containing his invitation and put it in her briefcase. As she quickly pulled on her blue silk robe, she wondered with what costume the charming, urbane businessman might choose to disguise himself. Today she assumed she would be seeing him without sunglasses; if not, it would be a strange reversal to see his eyes for the first time behind a mask if he came to the ball. The thought gave her a curious feeling in the pit of her stomach but she chose to ignore it and ran downstairs to breakfast.

The smell of coffee greeted her as she burst into the kitchen. 'Good morning, Carmela, what have you made me this morning?' she said cheerfully, picking up the cup the housekeeper had already poured for her and seating herself at the table on the patio.

Carmela followed, and her features broke into a warm smile. 'Ah, that's better, *señorita*. You are your happy self again, I was beginning to get worried.' She put down a tray of milk, cinnamon *ensaimada* and fruit.

'I've been working too hard these past few days and I suppose I was just tired,' Luz murmured, pouring some steaming hot milk over her coffee. She bit into a peach from the fruit bowl.

The housekeeper eyed her quizzically. 'I wondered if you had a *novio. No hay nada como el amor para que el corazón sufra*, there's nothing like love to make the heart suffer. Tell me about it – I had a lot of experience with my dear Pedro before we married.'

She breathed a deep, knowing sigh as she placed the basket of fresh warm pastries in front of the young woman.

'You may rest assured, there is no *novio* in sight and it's unlikely that there will be for a long time,' said Luz with a hollow laugh, helping herself to an *ensaimada*. The image of Leandro's face flickered in her mind but she resolutely pushed it away.

'You never know, these things happen when you least expect them. It's fate.'

Luz shrugged and grabbed another *ensaimada*. She was suddenly very hungry. Since the horse fair she had picked at her food and nothing seemed to have much taste, but this idyllic morning heralded a brand new day in her life and she intended to make the most of it.

She loved her work. Eduardo de Salazar's paintings excited her and it had been phenomenal to view the originals in the museum.

Some were vivid and flirtatious: behind the picture you could perceive the humour of a mischievous mind; others were darker, showing creatures that were half-human, half-horse, many of them disturbingly sexual. She was sure she would thoroughly enjoy writing the biography of such an artist, not only to get to know his artworks but also to gain a deeper insight into the life and psychology of the man. Her thoughts drifted to Eduardo's nephew and she wondered what else she might discover about him, too.

An hour later Luz was sailing through the doors of Calderón Corporación, SA, in a businesslike but feminine cream Yves Saint Laurent suit, the knee-length skirt flaring out above her shapely legs. Her notes were tidily collated in her briefcase; her mood was curious, if cautious. She was immediately taken to the top floor and this time not shown to the veranda but directly to Andrés de Calderón's office.

It was a huge room, with tall windows that generously let in the light, made even brighter by the white painted walls. A row of six Eduardo de Salazar paintings adorned them, a wild splash of colour against the stark background. It was as if this room, unlike the reception area in which Luz previously waited, was the only place where Eduardo's presence was allowed to be felt, though no clue to its occupant's personality was immediately apparent. A cabinet held two televisions side by side, one of which showed a computer-style screen with 'TVE Teletext' across the top in colourful letters and beneath it a list of the latest international news stories. No doubt this was one of the eccentric 'latest things' her mother had spoken about. A large modern oak desk sat in front of the windows, behind which Andrés de Calderón watched the screen with concentration.

He looked up as she entered the room and greeted her with a beaming smile. '*Buenos días*, Doña Luz. How lovely to meet you again. I hope you've had a good week,' he said, rising from an imposing leather chair behind his desk and extending his hand as he came towards her. As their hands touched there it was again, that fascinating shiver.

'*Buenos días*, Don Andrés,' she said, turning her discerning sapphire eyes on him.

This time the sunglasses were gone. Finally, Luz had the opportunity to scrutinize him more closely. Jet-black eyes met hers and, despite being strikingly different in colour to those of Leandro, she was reminded of the uncanny resemblance between the smooth businessman and the dishevelled gypsy.

She nodded towards the TV screen. 'How fascinating. I've heard of teletext but I've never seen it before.'

'I pride myself on being up to date with technology. Knowledge is success.' His voice sounded amused but the smile was merely polite. 'Please have a seat.' He indicated the chair opposite and resumed his own.

Funnily enough, she thought as she sat down facing him, even though Andrés de Calderón had a good deal of presence in his impeccably cut city suit, immaculately starched white shirt and designer tie, somehow he lacked the energetic and bewitching sortilege which Leandro oozed from every pore.

She must have been staring because Andrés was watching her with slight humour in his sooty irises. 'Well, do I meet with your approval?' he asked, his lips twitching. Luz felt her cheeks deepen in colour. Telling him that he resembled a gypsy she had met was hardly an appropriate response.

He looked down. 'Perhaps the suit needs cleaning ...' She was at a loss for words but he put up a hand, coming to her rescue. 'Don't take any notice, *señorita*, I say strange things sometimes. I'm told it's all part of my mercurial character.'

He had taken the words right out of her mouth.

'And do you agree?'

'It's a fair assessment.' His expression was still one of amusement. She searched for something witty to say, but found herself tongue-tied and only managed a sunny smile.

Andrés opened a folder and scanned it briefly. His eyes came back to hers as he handed it over.

'Our lawyers have drawn up the contract. I hope you will find the terms satisfactory. Please read through it carefully and if there's anything you don't agree with, don't hesitate to let me know. I'm always open to discussion, nothing is cast in stone.' He had reverted to a businesslike tone, his dark eyes not giving anything away, but he was watching her closely.

'Before I forget,' she said, relieved to have an excuse to look down as she opened her briefcase and handed him the invitation to the ball, 'we have a traditional annual masked ball at El Pavón. I hope that you'll be able to come.'

His glance held soft mockery, glittering with mischief. 'A masked ball, hey? What an ingenious idea. Everybody has something to hide and it's so much easier to have fun when under a false identity, don't you agree? Though Oscar Wilde, I think it was, said: "Give a man a mask and he will tell you the truth."' Again, Andrés' mouth seemed to be suppressing a laugh. 'Thank you, *señorita*. If I'm not away on business I will certainly do my utmost to attend your ball.'

Luz smiled uncertainly. *I really don't get his humour, or is there something wrong with me this morning?* she pondered, a little discouraged. *Best read the contract and get it over with.*

'Good, in that case I'll just take a minute to look at this,' said Luz, picking up the folder.

Andrés waved a hand. 'Please, take all the time you need.'

Luz pored over the document for the next five minutes, aware that Andrés had risen from his chair and moved over to the window, his back to her, hands in pockets. She resisted the urge to look up at him. The contract was pretty straightforward except for one clause, she realized with a disquieting stab. It stipulated that he had the right to decide at a later date whether he would keep the copyright entirely or allow her to share it with him.

Stiffening, she shut the folder and prepared to do battle. She must keep her cool. Considering he had already mentioned assigning the copyright to the author, albeit before he had given her the job, the clause felt insulting, as if she was undeserving of respectful treatment.

'Well?' he said, flashing her one of his devastating smiles and returning to his chair. 'Do we sign?'

She had to restrain herself from giving a straightforward, *no, we don't*. Instead, she cleared her throat and drew in a steadying breath.

'I'm sorry, Don Andrés ...'

'Call me Andrés, please,' he interrupted, unsettling her and causing her to drop the thread of her thoughts.

In a flash she recovered her cool. 'Please, let me finish, *señor*,' she said softly. Her tone held a dangerous undercurrent that she was sure did not go unnoticed. 'I'm a little disappointed to find that your terms imply that you are going to own the copyright of this biography, one which *I* will be writing.'

'That's normal, *señorita*. We are the employer, so naturally all rights rest with us.'

For a few moments their eyes locked. Luz was stung into a new belligerence. *The arrogance and cheek of the man!*

'Permit me to contradict you, *señor*. There is a slight misunderstanding here ...' She tried to keep an even tone despite her seething anger. 'You seem to be under the impression that I am working for your company, when actually I'm a freelance writer to whom Caldezar Corporación, SA is assigning the job of writing this biography. Therefore the copyright, by law, is entirely mine. You have already stated the rights were to be assigned to the author. Are you now going back on that?'

His lips quirked. 'Did I? I think that would be subject to your probationary period. If you read the contract carefully you will find that this is our arrangement,' he said coolly.

'I have read the contract very carefully and that is why I am objecting to its contents,' she snapped, outraged.

Andrés sighed wearily. 'You're making a mountain out of a molehill, *señorita*,' he went on as he opened an ornate silver cigarette case resting on his desk and offered her one. She declined, gritting her teeth, enraged still more at this new interruption.

'Do you mind if I smoke?' he asked.

'Go ahead, please,' she said tersely, repressing an irritated gesture.

His jaw tightened. He helped himself to a cigarette and flicked a flame from his lighter, then inhaled deeply before leaning back in his seat to contemplate the glowing tip for a few seconds. His dark eyes rested intently on her.

'As I was saying, *señorita*, you're making a big drama over a very small issue. We could go back and forth like this, but of what importance is it who keeps the copyright?' *Why did she get the impression he was trying to make her feel small and petty?*

'The main objective here is to combine our efforts to make this work an *obra maestra*, a masterpiece, one worthy of Eduardo de Salazar's genius, is it not?' he ended in a low voice, his eyes studying her flushed, angry face.

'You don't understand, *señor*.' Luz shifted edgily in the large leather chair, trying to keep the cool that her flashing, stormy eyes belied.

'Oh, but I do, *señorita*, I do. This is a very important issue for your pride.'

'No, it has nothing to do with pride,' she cut in. Once more, he was doing a pretty good job of riling her. She had to concede he was better at this game than she was. 'It has nothing to do with pride,' she repeated angrily, 'and everything to do with what is lawful and right. The copyright of this book – if I write it – would be my due.'

'*If?*' His lips twisted sardonically.

He was goading her. A voice at the back of her head urged caution. She was on slippery ground; this job was perfect in every way. What if he gave it to someone else? She must swallow her pride and try to put the conversation back on a friendlier footing, make concessions, even if they were to her disadvantage. A lump formed in her throat as anger, hurt and frustration all bubbled up tightly, but she forced herself to ignore his mocking tone.

'I mean, if we do not come to some sort of agreement that would satisfy both parties,' she said, looking abruptly away so he could not see the intense emotion in her eyes.

'You disappoint me. You're giving up too easily, Luz. Can I call you Luz?' His tone was now caressingly reprimanding.

The man was hideous. At that moment she loathed him with a passion for all his contemptible mind games, but for Luz this was new territory and her responses were in chaos. First Leandro, now Andrés: her sense of humiliation was increasing layer upon layer, dangerously swaying her equilibrium. She swallowed hard, shrugged and turned back to face him. He had filled a glass with water and was handing it to her, his charcoal eyes staring at her gravely.

Ignoring the offer, Luz smoothed back a stray tendril of hair.

'You haven't answered. May I call you Luz? It's such a beautiful name and it suits your luminous beauty to perfection.'

She blinked, her large blue eyes confounded. So now he was resorting to compliments. What next? There was an intense look about him that made her heart beat a little faster. Was it excitement or fear? She was so close to getting the job and yet so far. Never had a man challenged her in this way and she was torn between fascination and abhorrence.

'I don't understand you,' she said. 'What is it that you want?'

'According to Nietzsche, "The true man wants two things: danger and play. For that reason he wants woman, as the most dangerous plaything ..."' He was staring at her, his finger on his mouth, and she had to look away. This was more than she could handle.

'Maybe if you got off your high horse you would understand me better,' he continued softly, his voice deep and melodious. She glanced back at him sharply. His eyes were stroking her with a dark, sensuous touch. He was becoming more personal by the minute and she found it deeply disturbing. She shook her head.

Her lips parted to say something, but he was in there before her. 'Has it not occurred to you that this discussion may be part of the examination?'

She frowned. 'What examination? I thought I'd finished with examinations!' Her voice was tight, her sapphire eyes reverting to steel grey as tension mounted inside her.

He nodded and met her frozen expression. 'Don't I have a right to make sure that you're serious about this assignment? That, no matter what disagreement we might have in the future, under no circumstance whatsoever will you walk away from this job?' He gestured with his hand and continued to look at her steadily. 'I need unconditional commitment, nothing less. You're intelligent and, I'm sure, very skilled in your field, but also quite impulsive, as you proved with your first job.'

Now that was the last straw. His condescending tone incensed her. Luz glared at him, her stormy eyes colliding with his cool arrogant look.

'How dare you patronize me! I have a good mind to ...'

'Yes?' His dark eyebrows lifted quizzically.

He's decided what you're like. Don't give him the satisfaction of proving him right, the voice of reason advised, but she wasn't listening.

'Are you threatening me? Do you want me to resign before even starting?'

'Not at all, on the contrary. You are deliberately misunderstanding me, Luz. I needed to see just how impetuous you could be. Your passion is your strength, but also your weakness. You are so busy lashing out that you're entirely missing the point. Actually, my greatest wish is that we join forces to honour and immortalize the works and the name of a great artist.' He put his hand on his heart, his dark gaze glued to her face. 'Luz, I really feel deep in here that we would make a formidable partnership.'

'You have a funny way of showing it,' she said sceptically.

He smiled ruefully. 'If you had more trust in your worth, and your instincts, you would have seen through this little ruse.' A strange expression flashed in those dark chocolate eyes or was it her imagination? He opened a drawer and took out a folder similar to the one she still held. 'Just to prove I'm not lying to you, have a look at this.'

She eyed him mutinously and took the file from his hand. Still trembling inside, she quickly flipped through the contents and then looked up. The copyright in this contract was clearly assigned to her.

'I resent being toyed with,' she told him icily.

'Who doesn't? I apologize. Unfortunately, it's sometimes necessary to use disagreeable means to get to the bottom of things. Did you really think we are so unprofessional that we would deliberately change the terms of an agreement?' There was a shadow of reproach in his tone.

This man was the limit – he really had the knack of antagonizing her.

'And do you find it professional to expressly mislead a person, especially when you're in a position of power?' she replied contemptuously. 'Are those honourable tactics as far as you're concerned? Personally, I think it is rather unsavoury and I don't care for it one bit,' she ended, lightning flashing dangerously from her eyes.

To her surprise, he was silent. His face had become very serious, impassive, like a statue of a Roman god that she had once seen in the Prado, fierce in its dangerous, masculine beauty. The intensity of his gaze made her heart thunder mercilessly. *I've blown it*, she thought, sudden panic rushing through her. *He's going to throw me out.* Suddenly she wished she had swallowed that last retort. She looked at him blankly.

Andrés wrenched a sigh deep from his chest and something in his expression flickered. He looked genuinely troubled, anxious even.

'Luz …' Her name had never been so tenderly uttered. 'Luz, I'm sorry. You're right, it was not an honourable way to approach things. Perhaps … I went a little too far,' he murmured, rubbing his finger across his chin as he gazed at her. 'Could we start again, do you think?'

His tone was deep and soft; his eyes caught hers in a dark, compelling search for a response. Once more this man was wielding his power over her, whether he knew it or not, and the spell was working. She sat like a statue, staring into those midnight eyes.

Then, very subtly, Andrés recovered himself. 'Well?' he said at last. 'Friend or foe?'

Without a word she opened the second folder, signed her name at the bottom of the document and gave the contract back to him. She was defeated.

He walked around the desk and passed her a duplicate, one he had already signed. As she stood up to take it from him, he swiftly caught her hand and lifted it to his lips. 'Thank you,' he murmured, gazing down at her. 'I promise you won't regret it.'

His lips were warm and soft with the smoothness of velvet; their heat ran through her like a current of electricity, causing every nerve in her body to shudder imperceptibly. Luz met his brooding gaze and pulled her hand away, painfully aware of his proximity and the dynamic sexuality that he exuded. Stepping back, she rapidly shoved the folder into her briefcase and was about to take her leave when there was a knock at the door.

A couple walked in.

'Ah, Lorenzo and Adalia, you've arrived just in time to meet Doña Luz de Rueda, who will be writing Eduardo's biography.' He turned his gaze on Luz, making her cheeks colour. 'She has outstanding credentials and I've already been impressed by her in every way.'

Andrés went over to greet his guests. 'Don Lorenzo and Doña Adalia Herrera are my partners in our new venture, Los Laboratorios Calderra, SA,' he told Luz. 'Don Lorenzo is also an accomplished *torero* – he has perpetuated the Herrera myth.'

As Andrés spoke, Don Lorenzo nodded towards Luz, his eyes raking over her as his friend continued: 'His father was one of the great toreadors of our time. Lorenzo takes part in some of the most important *corridas* in Spain.'

As she smiled a greeting, Luz surreptitiously studied the handsome pair. They could almost have been Scandinavian. Tall, slim and fair, with large pale-blue eyes and almost regal features, their mien was elegant and striking. Luz recognized the sister as the beautiful woman she had seen that night at the opera, sitting in the box opposite.

'Andrés, *cariño*, you really are incorrigible!' Adalia reprimanded silkily, her hand moving to touch his arm lightly. Her pale eyes flicked between Andrés and Luz. 'You never told me you had already found someone for the post.' She fixed Luz with a look of curiosity.

'But how wonderful that you are just what dear Andrés is looking for!' she gushed, smiling briefly at Luz before immediately turning back to Andrés, regarding him closely. 'I've never heard Andrés speak about anyone with quite such enthusiasm.'

Luz felt herself flush again, then tense inwardly. The whole meeting with Andrés, not to mention the thrilling current that had run through her at his touch, had made her feel thoroughly exposed. Now she wanted nothing more than to exit his office without further scrutiny.

'I am sure that Señor de Calderón is just being kind.' The explanation was delivered in an even, calm voice; no one could have guessed the turmoil that bubbled away inside Luz, though Andrés cast her a wry glance.

Without waiting for Andrés to say anything, she picked up her briefcase and held out her hand to him. She made the handshake as brief as possible, trying to ignore the feeling of his strong fingers on her skin. 'I'm afraid I'm already late for another appointment,' she said, evading his eyes, though she could sense them on her. 'Thank you, Don Andrés, for your confidence. I will make sure my work lives up to your expectations.'

She nodded to his visitors and walked swiftly to the door, opening it before either man could do so for her. Without a backward glance she left the room, head high, managing to conceal, she hoped, her confused and fractious feelings.

*　　*　　*

When Luz got home she was surprised to find that her parents had arrived for the weekend. Her father was on the sofa in the living room reading the paper, her mother curled up in a chair with a book.

'Darling,' exclaimed Alexandra as she got up to hug her daughter. 'I hope you don't mind us descending on you like this.'

Salvador rested his paper on his lap. 'El Pavón is unbearable at the moment with all the preparations for the ball so we thought we'd run away for a couple of days and take a break from it all.' He winked at Luz and patted the cushion beside him.

Alexandra sighed. 'Poor Agustina does her best, but she's not so young any more. The trouble is, she won't give up the reins to anyone else and we have to tiptoe around her so as not to upset her. But tell us, didn't you have an appointment today with your new boss? How …'

'Don't you start all that, *Mamá*, I've had a morning of it already!' Luz interrupted, claws out. 'I am not working *for* Andrés de Calderón, I have been assigned to write this biography about his uncle. That doesn't make de Salazar's nephew my boss.' She ran her fingers through her long black hair in an irritated gesture.

'Don't get so angry, Luz, it's only a slip of the tongue,' Alexandra said, giving her daughter a kiss and smoothing her hand across the back of Luz's head.

'*Iay, iay,* who's had a bad day?' Her father looked at her teasingly. 'Come and sit down beside me, *querida*, and tell *Papá* all about it,' he said affectionately.

'It's been a challenging, if exhausting, morning. That man is the most arrogant, manipulative, high-handed scoundrel I have ever met.' Luz flopped down on the sofa next to her father.

'And charming with it, I suppose,' Alexandra interjected.

'And you've fallen under his spell. Yes? No?' Salvador added playfully.

'Will you stop second-guessing me, both of you, this isn't helpful!' Luz cried out, her eyes flashing. 'I would have happily told him to go to the Devil if it hadn't been for the fact that I'm passionate about Eduardo de Salazar's work and I'd give my right arm to write his biography. Plus, I've done so much research already.'

Never before had she felt this out of control and it made her so agitated.

'Most importantly, did you sign the contract?' her mother asked.

'Yes.'

'And in your favour?'

'Yes. I've got the copyright, there's no time limit on the work and I'm being handsomely paid,' she conceded.

'So what's the problem, *querida*?' Her father flung up his hands. 'What more do you want? Ah, you women! You are never so happy as when there's a drama.'

What she wasn't telling them was that Andrés de Calderón had humiliated her and made her feel vulnerable as never before. It felt like this was all part of some master plan to undermine her. In the end she'd got what she wanted, not because she'd won it, but because he had wanted to give it to her, and Andrés had made quite sure she understood that. He had proved great gamesmanship and had scored a point in what seemed like a battle for authority … *for this round*, she thought disdainfully. Given Leandro's indifference at the horse fair, it was the second indignity her pride had suffered in the last twenty-four hours and she was not about to invite the experience again.

They moved into the dining room, where Carmela had laid out a light lunch. But in her father's playful company, Luz could never stay angry for long and when she next spoke she was more relaxed. 'Andrés certainly seems to have glamorous friends, although I wasn't sure I liked the look of them,' she remarked.

'You met his friends? How so? I wonder if we know them. What are their names, *querida*?' Salvador asked lightly. It wasn't in Luz's nature to be derogatory about people, though today she seemed to be making a feast of it.

'They're a brother and sister, Lorenzo and Adalia Herrera. Clearly from an important family, but I don't recall you ever mentioning them. You may know their parents. They're not on the ball's invitation list, though.'

Salvador exchanged a look of understanding with Alexandra, who was about to say something, but he spoke first. 'Yes, the Herreras are a well-known family that extend all over Spain. I think we may have met their parents at some point,' he said quickly. 'What did you think of them?'

Luz couldn't bring herself to admit that she'd sensed Adalia's condescension and hadn't liked the way her brother had looked her over and shrugged. 'Oh, I didn't speak to them really … they were coming in as I was going out. I found them somewhat superior but perhaps I was just feeling out of sorts.'

She cringed internally as she recalled how Adalia had greeted her 'partner'. What was she to Andrés? From the way she had spoken to him, almost as if her words were an intimate caress, they were obviously very close, more than just business partners. And, of course, she had been his guest at the opera. Anyhow, what did she care? In the two meetings she'd had with Andrés, it was already clear he was a charmer who had a golden touch when it came to women. Hundreds of them must be throwing themselves at him. Well, so long as he kept his tentacles away from her, it was none of her business what he got up to.

Salvador scoffed. 'Superior? You are Count Salvador de Rueda's daughter, you have no reason to inferior to anyone! Anyway, since when do such people worry you? You're becoming too sensitive, *niña*.' He changed the subject and they proceeded to discuss the main topic of conversation of the moment: the masked ball at El Pavón.

They had just risen from the table and were enjoying coffee on the veranda when Carmela came bursting on to the terrace, wheezing and chuckling, carrying an enormous bunch of red roses. Eyes flashing with excitement, she laid the glorious bouquet on the table in front of Luz to everybody's surprise, not least Luz's.

'Your *novio*, Doña Luz.' She gave a huge wink. 'Your *novio* has finally taken pity on you and appeared. He has sent you these beautiful flowers as a token of his love,' she announced.

Salvador and Alexandra turned to their daughter with questioning expressions.

'Don't look at me,' Luz cried out laughingly. 'I promise I haven't the faintest idea what Carmela's talking about.'

'There's a card, Doña Luz,' said Carmela, barely able to restrain her impatience. She detached the envelope from the magnificent bouquet and handed it to the young woman, her features quivering with anticipation, dark eyes intent on Luz's face.

Salvador regarded the housekeeper with contained amusement. '*Gracias, Carmela, usted puede ir ahora*, thank you, Carmela, you can go now.' He and his daughter exchanged knowing glances. They both understood that by the evening the whole of Cádiz would know that she had received red roses, and who knows what else Carmela's vivid imagination might conjure up as gossip?

Determined not to be banished just yet, Carmela had more to say. 'A driver delivered them,' she said, her eyes glittering. 'Is there not to be an answer then? He's waiting.'

'Don't worry about an answer,' Salvador told her dismissively. 'Thank the driver and tell him she'll reply in due course.'

Carmela's face fell. 'As you wish, Don Salvador.'

Obviously fathers were unaware of their daughter's aches of the heart. Disappointment was written all over her as she walked slowly round the side of the hacienda.

Luz had already recognized the coat of arms on the envelope. She opened it. The card read: 'Have dinner with me and let me make amends. I remain your faithful servant, Andrés.' The writing was generous and energetic. Luz's heart beat a little faster and a pale rose coloured her cheeks. *Damn him for being so charming!* She handed the note to her mother and tried to look cool.

'There's nothing like a romantic note to entangle a sensitive woman's heart,' Alexandra declared as she gazed lovingly at her husband, clearly remembering the days of their courtship.

Salvador laughed. 'We Spaniards are masters in the language of love, is that not so, *mi amor*?' He picked up Alexandra's hand and kissed it before turning to his daughter. 'So he's not arrogant and insufferable now!' Irony twisted his lips and Luz blushed and looked away.

Yes, but he is *manipulative*, she thought.

Handsome, successful and manipulative – that was her verdict. No doubt leagues of pining women queued outside the door to his heart. Yes, she would have dinner with him, but not immediately. Andrés de Calderón was used to his wishes being granted at the snap of his fingers. She was not one of his enslaved admirers. She would not rush to his command – let him stew for a while.

CHAPTER 4

The architecture of El Pavón, the de Fallas' ancestral home, was defined by function and tradition. It had a local style with a touch of neoclassical inspiration that gave the hacienda a look of prosperity, permanence and grandeur. The sun-drenched old house stood on copper-tinted soil, surrounded by hibiscus, begonias and oleanders, and was approached by an avenue of stooping willows. Solid and sedate it lay in its eclectic landscape of manicured lawns, exuberant foliage, fruit orchards and noble trees. The whitewashed walls wore shawls of bougainvillea, wisteria and mimosa, their vivid colours softening its severe lines during most months of the year. On arrival, the first impression was of green and red and white, punctuated here and there with yellow. Through the years nature and man had joined forces to create a strangely seductive combination of voluptuous beauty and austerity. It had atmosphere and, generation after generation, the edifice continued to live up to its name: El Pavón, the peacock.

After his great-aunt Doña María Dolores had passed away, Salvador and Alexandra had taken over the hacienda. The couple decided to leave the core of the house intact. It was a palace in miniature, with marble floors and rich but worn silk hangings, dark brown furniture and heavy Persian rugs. Though Alexandra loved the aura of past history that permeated

El Pavón, its brooding spirit depressed her. She preferred contemporary furniture and light airy spaces. So Salvador built a new wing and gave his wife carte blanche to decorate it in her own style, so she could give it her personal touch and furnish it to her own taste.

Luz had always preferred to stay in this new part of the house as well, finding the rest of the hacienda strangely claustrophobic, despite its great size. The sprawling, colourful grounds of El Pavón were her favourite part and her parents had succeeded in enhancing their secret allure and making them their own. At the request of Alexandra, Salvador even had a small lake dug out beyond the back gardens in a beautiful spot surrounded by lilac trees. To escape the hacienda, Luz often walked down to the lake on warm afternoons and lazed on the bench there with a book.

Leaning against her bedroom balcony, Luz looked out on to the garden, which seemed to dream in the declining day. She had arrived from Cádiz with her parents the day before to help them oversee the finishing touches to the masked ball. There were only a few hours before the guests arrived, but for now she wanted to savour this magical hour when El Pavón looked its best. Her bedroom was at the back of the house, the view from there dominated by the more private and shaded areas of the hacienda: Alexandra and Salvador's creation. Here, cool rose-scented walks mingled with wrought-iron gateways framed by honeysuckle and old fountains with gently murmuring water splashing or flowing lazily into stone-edged ponds. In the distance, over the high walls of the property, the lights of Jerez were beginning to twinkle. Luz's eyes moved from one beautiful aspect to another. Roses, begonias and evergreen shrubs were everywhere. A soft, warm evening breeze touched her, stirring her long, silky black hair. After the heat of the day, the cool air was refreshing. The heady aroma of flowers released by dusk aroused a sort of excitement within her.

Year after year since her eighteenth birthday, she had attended the El Pavón traditional masked ball but never before had she experienced such a feeling of anticipation. Tonight would be the stuff of fairy tales as her ancestral home was transformed into an enchanted world of swirling colours, twinkling lights and sweeping music, where anything could happen.

Luz had welcomed the comforting presence of her parents at L'Estrella over the past week and her mind was easier than it had been for a while. Yet as the hour of the ball approached and the power of its spell started to gather, she was aware of a sensation of longing still budding within her.

She thought of Leandro and Andrés, two men who only a few weeks earlier had been strangers to her and, since then, had filled her mind. Would Andrés show up tonight and would she recognize him? she wondered. For some reason he had been particularly enthused by the idea of a masked ball, though his infuriating habit of playing games perhaps made that hardly surprising, she concluded. Yes, Andrés de Calderón would play his part in a masquerade with relish. In her mind's eye, she could still see the soft mockery that had flashed in those dark velvety irises and deep down she knew that if he did honour them with his presence, he would do his utmost to mystify her at every turn.

Though she had sent him a brief note to thank him for the roses, she had refused his invitation to dinner. She wondered how he would have reacted to that. Luz could usually read people, but she had no clue as to this man's thoughts. He was dangerously attractive, she realized that, but did she *like* him? Something in her rebelled against his arrogant treatment of her. One moment she was being rigorously interviewed, the next, almost wooed; by turns she had been charmed, enraged and perplexed. Flirtation was a duel of wits for Andrés, a sport for his amusement. The man was egotistical, complicated and maddening. Still, she could not deny feeling a certain piquancy in his presence, which, though disquieting at times, was also oddly thrilling.

She frowned at the thought. Her reaction to him had been an aberration, she decided, and one that she had no intention of repeating. In fact after tonight, she concluded, it would be extreme folly to see Andrés de Calderón more than was absolutely necessary in the course of researching Eduardo's biography.

Luz watched as an eagle circled high in the sky before diving for some invisible prey in the dusky air. Her thoughts turned to Leandro, the gypsy with the deep, soft voice and the mesmerizing eyes. Emotion welled up in her. A stab of pain shot through her heart as she thought back to the horse fair and to the redheaded *gitana* with her arm around him, obviously claiming him as her man. He had not disengaged from her and Luz had taken the hint. But what was she to think? That afternoon on the beach she was sure she hadn't misread the turbulent undercurrents of passion in his fiery gaze and then, when they had talked at the fair, the desire in his eyes as he flirted with her was obvious. The memory of it stirred her with a sudden acuteness that made something flutter and blaze bright near her heart.

A knot formed in her throat. Surely she wasn't going to let the gypsy's magnetism weave its spell over her? Wasn't this just the way of the *gitanos*? She swallowed hard. It was only a sexual attraction, mere hormones at play. Anyway, as she'd already told herself, nothing could ever come of such a relationship. The gypsies' world was not hers; she must put Leandro and his people out of her mind.

Luz looked up at the darkening, violet sky as an opalescent moon floated into view from behind a cloud. Still, she thought wistfully, had he been free and truly wanted her, she would not have denied herself the chance of love simply because he was a gypsy; she would have fought anyone and anything for her happiness.

There was a knock at the door. Luz sighed quietly and moved away from the balcony. 'Come in,' she called, walking back into her bedroom.

The door opened and Agustina, the old housekeeper at El Pavón, came in, carrying a shimmering costume which she ceremoniously laid out on the bed as if it were a sacred robe. '*Buenas tardes*, Doña Luz, I have brought your outfit for tonight's ball.'

'How very kind of you, Agustina, but that's Valentina's job. You shouldn't be climbing all those stairs, you're disobeying doctor's orders,' she remonstrated sweetly as she gave the old servant a hug.

'*Iay!* Doctors!' Agustina gave a dismissive wave. 'And Valentina does what I tell her,' she added with a twinkle in her eye.

Agustina had been with the family for two generations and, in her elevated role in the house, had come to know and love both Alexandra and Salvador with a fierce loyalty. Though in her early seventies, she still had the same matronly figure of her middle age years and a round, serene face with barely a wrinkle. Her eyes were still vivacious and held a sharpness belying her age. Luz had always admired her hair, which in her youth, she guessed, must have been raven black and was now a lustrous white, held in the nape of her neck by a net and a wide tortoiseshell comb.

Agustina smiled kindly and took Luz's arm, her dark pupils gazing up earnestly at the young woman. 'This costume is very special, as your mother must have told you. It was the dress of a genuine Moorish sultana. Doña Alexandra wore it the night she met your father. I helped her dress for the ball on that evening and I would like to do the same today for you. This is a family heirloom, which is very dear to your parents. Now you're back in Spain for good and making your home here, it's time you had it.'

Though Luz was not accustomed to being pampered in such a way – in fact, she actively disliked anyone hovering around her while she was dressing – she didn't have the heart to turn the *duenna* away.

'That's a lovely idea,' she said, trying to sound enthusiastic as she moved to the bathroom. 'Let me have a shower, and I'll be right with you.'

'*Si, si, tómese su tiempo*, take your time, I will sit for a minute. It's true, my old legs aren't as strong as they were,' replied Agustina, lowering herself slowly into a chair.

Ten minutes later Luz reappeared clad in a white bath towel. Agustina smiled as the young woman came into the room.

'You have the best features from each of your parents,' she declared, surveying her with affection.

She invited Luz to sit at the dressing table in front of the mirror. 'I will first dry your hair and then give it Agustina's special treatment,' she declared as she removed the towelling turban wrapped around the young woman's head.

'Yours is a different beauty to your mother's … it is more exotic and mysterious,' she said, 'so for tonight I may let your hair fall loosely down your back. It is lush and heavy like your great-grandmother's and should be seen in all its glory. Will you trust me to bring out the best so that when I have finished every woman at the ball will be envious?' She patted Luz's shoulder and her smile uncovered two rows of perfect teeth.

Luz nodded enthusiastically as the old housekeeper's still dextrous fingers threaded expertly through strands of silken black hair. Suddenly she felt light-hearted, getting into the spirit of the whole event.

'Do as you please, Agustina,' she replied, 'I'm entirely in your hands.'

At this she relaxed and let her imagination run free. She was a princess in this beautiful castle and perhaps tonight fate would steer her away from its recent thorny path and she would meet her Prince Charming. Wasn't that what had happened to her mother almost thirty years ago?

Without delay, the *duenna* began massaging Luz's scalp, applying strange creams and oils, drying, brushing, combing. Before becoming the housekeeper at El Pavón, Agustina had been personal maid to Doña María Dolores, Alexandra's grandmother. In her youth the *Duquesa* had possessed the lushest and most beautiful head of hair and Agustina was accustomed to dressing and handling long hair. She worked swiftly and expertly.

Suddenly, as the buzzing of the hairdryer ceased, Luz thought she could hear the thud of distant drumbeats. At first she assumed the musicians had arrived early and were practising for the ball but, as it went on and she listened carefully, she realized these were not the melodious tones of a fully fledged orchestra, but a more monotonous, repetitive thumping that seemed to flow continuously like an endless river of sound.

'What's that sound?' she asked. 'It's an odd sort of dull, throbbing beat. Can you hear it?'

Luz felt Agustina's hands jerk slightly. Without lifting her head or pausing, the housekeeper shrugged. 'Oh, don't take any notice,' she said a little too dismissively.

That sort of evasiveness irritated Luz and was enough to alert her curiosity. 'Come on, Agustina.' she coaxed. 'I've not heard drums like that at El Pavón before. It sounds more like some African or South American jungle ritual …'

'I don't know anything about jungle rituals. The only thing clear to me at this moment is that you should not be moving your head,' came the stern answer.

Suddenly Luz burst out laughing, the crystal-clear notes filling the room. 'Of course! Why hadn't I thought of it before? Gypsies! The gypsies are having their own party at the bottom of the garden. Isn't that so, Agustina? And you didn't want me to get on to the subject. What's wrong with you all? As soon as the word "gypsy" is in the air, everybody gets into a tizzy.'

'And quite rightly so,' Agustina said grimly, as though to herself.

Luz raised her eyes to the ceiling. 'Why? I've met a couple of gypsies who have been really kind to me.'

'Nothing good can come from these people if you aren't one of them.'

'Agustina, why be so pessimistic?' Luz sighed. 'It's probably that sort of prejudice that makes them unfriendly.'

'As the saying goes: "The believer is happy, the doubter is wise." To be a pessimist is to be clear headed, my child, and often that comes with experience.'

'Please, what does that mean, exactly? Have the gypsies ever harmed you or any of your loved ones?' There was a note of impatience in Luz's tone.

Agustina shook her head regretfully. 'I prefer not to talk about this. In life, one must know when to let sleeping dogs lie. There is no good in stirring up old grievances and in this case it is most important that you should leave well alone. And you should certainly not consort with them. These are hot-blooded people, they are ruled by customs and traditions that we will never understand. God knows what they will start if you rub them up the wrong way.'

Luz listened in silence. She had heard those words so many times before she found them tedious. True, it was probably sensible advice; still, for Luz, this made the subject only more interesting.

'I met an old gypsy the other day who told me that she knew my parents. Her name is Paquita. Do you know her?' She tried to sound casual. Whether Agustina wanted to or not, she was now talking and Luz spotted her chance to probe further.

Agustina's hands paused. 'What else did the old hag say?' the housekeeper muttered under her breath, echoing Alexandra's words of a few weeks earlier.

'She said that a great love awaits me.'

'Did she now? Don't you know that's the yarn they all spin to get your attention? Sometimes I wonder at how gullible you can be.'

Luz ignored her and persisted stubbornly. 'Did she have a hand in my parents meeting?'

'Nonsense, child!' Agustina broke out with swift irritation.

The old servant was not prone to outbursts of discourtesy to her employers and, unlike Carmela, was very conscious of her place – even though she had always been considered to be a confidante and a friend by the family – but she regarded it as her duty to counsel and protect its members. A look of something akin to worry crossed her face before she spoke, but then she fixed Luz with a steady gaze before her hands resumed their work on the young woman's hair.

'Your parents, Doña Luz, met in this house – they are, as you well know, distant cousins. They were fated to meet and fall in love. Both young and handsome, it was bound to happen. Their love affair and marriage had nothing to do with the *gitanos*. If anything, it occurred despite those people and trust me when I tell you that was not for lack of trying on the part of the gypsies. Now, are you satisfied? I've said too much already, and you will not get a word more out of me on the subject.'

Luz smiled and wrinkled her nose in appeasement. 'Dear Agustina, don't be cross. Isn't it normal that I should be interested in my parents' romance?'

Agustina regarded her indulgently, but replied without mincing her words. 'Don't try and hoodwink me, child,' she said shortly. 'Like most people who are ignorant of those tribes and their ways, you are attracted to them. And I know you, Doña Luz ... You find them mysterious and romantic, yes? They have the beguiling scent of the unknown with a spicy undercurrent that spells danger. You are young and the young are often foolish ... I trust you are not so. And now, I must stop lecturing – we should get on with dressing you.'

Luz could see that she would not get anything more out of the stubborn housekeeper on this occasion and chuckled. 'All right, you win, Agustina. I'll say no more, I promise.'

Luz's abundant hair was now a shining mass of tumbling jet-black waves. Agustina had artistically threaded a handful of tiny iridescent pearls through it, which caught the light with every movement. It formed the most luscious, bejewelled mantle around the young woman's bare shoulders and fell all the way to her hips. The effect was stunning.

'Oh, Agustina, you have such magic fingers,' Luz cried out with delight as she leapt from her stool and surveyed herself in the cheval mirror that had once stood in her mother's dressing room. 'I love the effect of those seed-like beads you've woven into my hair.' She ran her palms over them. 'Shall I put on my make-up now or after I've dressed?'

'It would be wiser if you did that now – you don't want to get any on the garment, it's very delicate,' the housekeeper warned.

Luz applied some blush to her cheekbones and a little gloss to her lips. She had clear, luminous skin, which the sea air and sun had turned a golden honey, and her features were fine. Nature had been generous and Luz needed little embellishment from make-up. She concentrated on her eyes, intensifying their natural sapphire blue and giving them a sensuous, smoky oriental look with kohl. In an effort to enhance the enigmatic and mysterious effect, she paid special attention to her eyelashes, which were already thick and naturally long.

'There,' she said, finally putting down her colours and brushes, 'I think that's enough. I'm not used to all this greasepaint – any more and I'll feel a bit of a clown.'

'You could never look like a clown, my child,' Agustina said warmly, her eyes glittering approvingly.

Together they moved to the bed, where the magnificent sultana's costume lay. Looking down at it, Luz marvelled at its beauty: there were six distinct parts to it, each one a work of art in its own right. She slipped on the close-fitting jerkin of fine and sheer cotton. It felt soft and snug against her body. Over it hung a tunic, called a *gömlek*, of the purest, sheer ivory-coloured silk, with a round neck slit vertically to the bust and closed by four miniature pearl buttons. This smock had long, full sleeves that bunched at the wrists and fastened tightly with the same iridescent buttons. Then, over the top of this, was the *antery*, a magnificent fitted waistcoat in heavy off-white damask silk, which boasted the most intricate embroidery of silver thread, seed pearls and precious stones. Luz fastened the buttons and passed her hand over the rich workmanship.

'I wonder how much time and effort was invested in creating this garment?' she said, taking the next item of clothing from Agustina's hands.

'A great many hours, I'm sure. I suppose it was a way for women to support themselves.' Agustina helped the young woman into a pair of loose-fitting trousers, the *shalwar*. 'Careful now, these are extremely delicate and could easily tear.' They fell in graceful folds of fine ivory silk and tapered to the ankles, where they were gathered by narrow cuffs of bias-cut fabric, which contrasted subtly with the rest of the ensemble. Luz's tiny waist was clad in a wide belt, also richly embroidered in silver, gold and small jewels.

'And now for the final touch,' Agustina said, holding up the veil of fine voile, to which was attached a black comb. She fixed it gently to the hair on Luz's crown. 'I plaited your mother's hair into a braided chignon when she wore this costume,' she told her, 'but, as I said to you before, I will leave your hair loose and hold the veil in place simply with the tiara. The pear-shaped pearl, which is the centre of the jewel, will hang over your forehead like this,' she went on as she affixed the coronet on the young woman's head. 'There! Now, put on the matching earrings and those dainty-looking sandals.' Luz obeyed without argument.

'*Es decir que ce*, that's it! *Parece como si ha salido de una cuento de hadas moro*, you look as if you've just walked out of a Moorish fairy tale.'

Luz rushed to the mirror and was amazed at the transformation – she hardly recognized herself. The figure who looked back at her was a stranger, from a faraway country and a different era. Alexandra had given her daughter the matching set of jewellery, referred to as 'Princess Gulinar's jewels', on her twenty-first birthday. Originally they had been given as a gift to Alexandra by Doña María Dolores when she first came to El Pavón. They consisted of a tiara, a bracelet, a pair of earrings and a necklace, all minutely worked in gold and encrusted with tiny pearls. Luz fingered the necklace, debating whether or not to wear it. She decided against it. The earrings that hung gracefully from her lobes were long enough. Her neck was left bare; and though she was unaware of it, to admiring eyes it made her look more vulnerable and artless. She turned to Agustina.

'How do I look?' she asked, eyes dancing with excitement.

'*Perfecto*! You look very enigmatic, completely transformed, a real sultana from the East. With that mask across your face, if it were not for your beautiful hair even I would not be able to recognize you.' The Spanish woman's face filled with pride as she contemplated Luz and her mouth broke into a wide smile. At the same time, though, a shadow passed over her aged features. 'Many men will lose their hearts to you tonight, my child. Be careful who you lose yours to,' she said softly. 'I have read the cards and witnessed this before many years ago and, though I can't see any immediate danger, I can sense deception and evil lurking in the shadows.'

'Oh, dear Agustina,' the young woman cried out, half laughing, her heart too full of dreams and brimming with hope to take in such enigmatic and dramatic words. 'Don't dampen my fun. Fancy saying something like that to me just as I'm off to a ball!'

'It is exactly for that reason that I urge caution. Remember, snakes prefer to hide under flowers. I have found that the world outside El Pavón has always been greatly populated with snakes and today *mi paloma*, my dove, it's no different. And now you have just enough time to show yourself off to your parents before your guests start to arrive.'

*   *   *

In the glow of a warm late-spring evening, with crisp linens, flickering candles, the house's special sangria, champagne and glorious tapas generous enough to make a meal, El Pavón was the most romantic place on earth. The great ballroom, the terrace and the garden gradually filled up with a host of glamorous people in more or less elaborate disguises. It resembled a scene from Verdi's opera, *Un Ballo in Maschera*. In this world of fantasy, of illusion and surprise, despite the formal mood, dress and setting, men and women were offered a chance to reveal everything that was normally left unexpressed for the rest of the year. As she stood alongside her parents, welcoming the first guests, Luz was struck by the liberating power of this glittering camouflage. *It's so much easier to have fun under a false identity ...* Suddenly Andrés' words made sense to her and, strangely enough, they filled her with an added excitement she had not felt at the previous balls.

Under a sky blinking with stars, the roof of the great hacienda was ablaze with light from multicoloured lanterns, like fireballs, strewn in trees or hanging by slender chains from tall, curved iron poles. An oversize moon beamed enigmatically in the dark sapphire canopy of sky. The atmosphere was warm and scented. It was a night made for lovers.

The ballroom at El Pavón took up most of the width of the ground floor on the east side of the hacienda. It was regarded as an architectural masterpiece, with its vaulted ceiling and French windows looking over the gardens. A gallery, supported by marble columns and with an intricate wrought-iron surround, was where the orchestra was playing tonight.

Guests were still arriving and meandering into the vast ballroom, laughing and admiring each other's costumes. Luz's mood was elevated, as though she was waiting for something wonderful to happen. She stood in the wide doorway, her glittering dark-blue eyes peering through the narrow slits of her delicate black-velvet mask at the brightly lit ballroom scene. The atmosphere was charged with myth and fantasy.

Masked couples, living out fantastic identities, swirled, swung, twirled, twisted and glided across the highly polished parquet floor to the haunting melodies of Tchaikovsky and Delibes waltzes that filled every corner of the room. A black and yellow honeybee in black stockings and dainty golden wings was dancing with Peter Pan. Pocahontas in her brown suede outfit and feathered headband looked somewhat swamped by her partner, Minotaur, in his oversized bull mask with snout and horns. Two clowns, one jolly, the other grumpy, were fooling about on the dancefloor in their colourful three-toned jumpsuits with blue pom-pom buttons and matching hats. El Cid and Chimène were making their way to the terrace and nearly bumped into Don Quixote and Sancho Panza, who were coming back into the room. In a corner, gossiping and giggling as they watched the dancers, stood three lady buccaneers sporting ruffles, headscarves and eye-patches.

Some moments passed before Luz spotted him. There was no mistaking the dark figure that turned around on the dancefloor. He wore a close-fitting black jumpsuit that was moulded to his body to perfection. Across the chest was a gold symbol representing the sign of Gemini, the twins. It was his baroque-style papier-mâché mask, cut vertically into half profile, that was the biggest giveaway: it represented his own face with uncanny realism. Secured above the brow with a fine black-and-gold ribbon, it was decorated with a gold frieze on the half forehead and chin. There was something eerie and fascinating about it.

He was dancing with a beautiful blonde fairy in a purple tutu of thin voile and a set of large wings made of the daintiest pink and silver gossamer studded with diamonds. She was leaning back into his arms, looking up into his face, and he was laughing. Luz guessed from their stance that they were equally charmed and was immediately struck by an almost insane jealousy that took her by surprise.

Before she had time to wonder at the violence of her reaction, a pair of gorilla hands suddenly grabbed her waist and King Kong carried her away on to the dancefloor. As they waltzed past Gemini and his graceful partner, she met Andrés' eyes through his mask. But he made no sign of recognition – he was talking animatedly and the fairy lady was hanging on to his words, spellbound. Although he had taken no notice when they passed, Luz had the feeling that he had seen her, but was deliberately holding back. During this 'cutting-in' dance, King Kong had ceded his place to a handsome Cossack, who now chattered away non-stop, distracting Luz's attention. She lost sight of Gemini but then, out of the corner of her eye, she she noticed he was no longer dancing but standing at the side of the floor, sipping a glass of champagne in the company of Cleopatra and a Roman soldier.

Dinner would soon be announced. If she could get nearer to the door of the dining room there might be a better chance of waylaying him without it looking too conspicuous. With some satisfaction Luz had deliberately left him dangling with her refusal of his dinner invitation and now she had the feeling that tonight he was turning the tables, playing her at her own game. She was quite sure that he was unaccustomed to being turned down; more likely he was in the habit of always having his own way. Well, he was in for a nasty surprise …

'If you'll excuse me,' she said sweetly to her partner, 'I think I must see to dinner.' The Cossack, who had become somewhat proprietorial, let go of her reluctantly. Luz moved swiftly towards the dining-room door. She looked towards the spot where Gemini had been standing; he was still there. He then became hidden by taller couples and when she looked again he was gone. She scanned the crowded dancefloor but couldn't see him among the dancers. It was difficult to spot anyone in the throng of moving disguises, even though his was so very obvious. No doubt he was sitting on the terrace, murmuring sweet nothings to some gullible belle.

But then he was back, standing on the opposite side of the room, the familiar amused smile hovering around his lips while he chatted with the beautiful blonde fairy. Standing there, he could have been Leandro, she thought with a sudden pang of confusion; but he was so different, so poised and sophisticated, with nothing of the untamed spirit of the young *gitano*. The first trumpeted notes of the popular song 'Granada' rang out and Andrés' partner dragged him on to the dancefloor. Then they were off, jostling other couples as they went. He was moving deliberately and steadily towards Luz, who held her breath, rooted to the spot, unable to tear her eyes away from him. They passed her and there was no mistaking the expression of curiosity in his velvet-black eyes as they locked with hers, or the whimsical smile he slanted at her as everything else, in the flash of a second, spun away into the background.

He was introducing a new game of cat and mouse, provoking her with his evasions, and once again she was playing straight into his hands.

Luz took a deep breath and decided to ignore him for the rest of the evening; she would concentrate on having a good time. After all, she told herself, why was she getting so annoyed? If that was what he wanted, so be it: that was what he would get! There were enough handsome and interesting men here tonight to keep her amused, she concluded, as she flipped from the arms of one eager dancing partner to another.

The music played on and occasionally their paths crossed on the dancefloor, neither making the slightest attempt at eye contact. The masks of shepherds and shepherdesses, Romans and Vikings, cats and witches all floated round the enormous ballroom beneath the gilded ceiling. Time went by …

The setting for dinner had been designed to make the guests feel as if they were living in a beautiful dream. After all, this was El Pavón's traditional annual ball, one of the biggest events in the social calendar, a time for partying, a time to let go and reach for the stars. In the big, airy dining room, with its floor-to-ceiling French windows that opened on to lawns and beds of sweet-smelling shrubs, tables were laid for a banquet. The effect was an impressive spectacle of ornate gilt, with mounds of colourful luscious fruits and bright displays of exotic flowers. The flickering candles in tall candelabra, which stood on the tables, threw long shadows on to the pale walls and softened the contours of faces under a clement semi-darkness that made everybody look their best. In this subtle romantic light, delicate off-white lace tablecloths laden with glittering crystal, silver and fine china gave the setting a magical fairy-tale appearance and every guest seemed to wear the same bemused air on contemplating this Shangri-La. Once again, the ball at El Pavón would be the talk of the town for weeks to come.

This year, Alexandra and Salvador had decided to have a sit-down dinner instead of the usual buffet. It meant that more thought had to be given to the menu, but also to the seating of guests. In the past everyone had chosen where they wanted to sit and more often than not, the seat coveted would be already taken, if you were not quick enough. Besides, every now and again newcomers would find themselves left out on a limb, which to Alexandra seemed unfriendly and inhospitable. So on this occasion the hosts had allotted places to their guests, who mingled in front of the seating plan at the entrance to the dining room, excited and curious to see where they had been placed.

As Luz located her seat, she noted that Andrés was settled a couple of tables along from hers with his back to her. She had not been involved in the seating plan, so was not surprised that he had not been allocated a place at her table. Was she relieved or frustrated? He had got under her skin once again that evening and a momentary irritation prickled away at her. She watched him lean forward and clink glasses with a woman dressed as the Roman goddess Ceres in a revealing off-the-shoulder white toga. Luz bit her lip and sat down, smiling graciously at the guests who came to sit beside her.

As she unfolded her napkin, a note fell out. She picked it up, glanced at it and put it aside, her heart hammering against her ribcage: 'Meet me at the lake at midnight.' It was left unsigned, but she had no doubt as to the identity of the author. Her cheeks felt warm and it was nothing to do with the wine she had been sipping. She was thankful that Andrés was unable to witness her reaction – she had no intention of giving him the satisfaction of seeing her loss of composure. In a different situation she might have found it romantic, but given the present infuriating circumstances … Anyhow, she was not yet sure whether she would run to his cavalier summons, but would she be able to resist such an intriguing invitation? Perhaps it would be just the excuse she needed to put Andrés de Calderón in his place for his general rudeness and childish behaviour.

Luz barely ate or spoke at dinner, too preoccupied with the message to engage in the revelry around her table; she merely smiled and nodded in all the right places in the conversation, her eyes every now and then flicking to the table opposite. She did not need to turn to see Andrés; his back was in full view. By the look of it, he was being entertained by Ceres and a maharani in a rather garish sari, each seated on either side of him, openly vying for his attention. There was no evidence that he knew he was being watched furtively by Luz; not once did he cast a glance behind him to acknowledge her presence.

There were many courses and the meal was a slow process. A bewildering number of waiting staff came and went, fluttering around the tables like moths, lavishing their attentions on guests. Luz had longed with scarcely concealed impatience for the meal to end and now, at last, it was over. After dinner, coffee and sherry were brought round. She glanced surreptitiously at her watch. Soon it would be midnight and everybody would line up in the ballroom for the moment of truth, when masks and headdresses would be removed and identities revealed. She was waiting to see how Andrés would extricate himself to go down to the lake. It seemed his dining partners had no intention of letting him out of their sight.

Eleven forty-five; guests were getting up. Some were shown to cloakrooms while others were ushered into the brightly lit ballroom. Luz saw Andrés making his way through the throng towards the ballroom. She lost him for a moment but he soon emerged again in the company of his blonde fairy companion. If he wanted to get down to the lake before midnight, he'd better get going, she thought. She felt someone brush against her back and turned: it was the Cossack.

'Beautiful Sultana, I'm curious to know your real identity,' he whispered, catching hold of her arm and grinning down at her, hot breath against her ear. 'Will you do me the honour of standing with me when the masks are lowered?'

Desperation tinted her smile as she tried to disengage herself from his predatory grip. She knew that he was perfectly aware of her identity and did not care much for this sort of lame duplicity. These society beaus with their small talk bored her to tears and, besides, she had other business to attend to.

'Let me relieve you from the suspense, *señor*,' she said, lifting her mask a little and turning innocent blue eyes on him. 'As you can see, I am your hostess, Doña Luz. And now, if you will excuse me, I must take care of the allocation of prizes for the winners.' Before the Cossack could protest, she swept off into the crowd.

A rapid look around the room assured her that Andrés was no longer there. He was almost certainly already down at the lake. It was no use pretending now. All evening she had been on tenterhooks; she might as well admit to herself that she was going to meet him, though she was at a loss to know why her reactions to him were so volatile. She had made her point by turning him down once; it was no use persisting down that road. Besides, there was not much to gain from rubbing him up the wrong way. She had agreed to work with him on his uncle's biography so she might as well clear the air between them and start afresh. Was that not what he was trying to do in raising the white flag and asking her to meet him at midnight, even if his message read more like a summons than an invitation?

It was five minutes to midnight. Luz moved swiftly to the veranda and, from there, down the steps into the garden. She was aware of exotic scents emanating from the sleeping flowers and of the unruly beating of her heart that thumped so hard that she thought it might break like glass. It was cooler now and the breeze caused the leaves to rustle in the trees, making her think of smothered footfalls.

Luz didn't notice the pair of eyes watching her from behind dark branches as she wandered silently along the path like a spirit of this enchanting night. Her observer glanced furtively over his shoulder to make sure no one was following her or watching him. But all was still in romantic silence. His lips curled in a satisfied smile. He moved quietly and just as rapidly, keeping up with her on a parallel footway screened by a tall hedge of oleanders.

The lake lay dark, except for a wide golden path reflecting an expansive arc of moon hanging among myriad blinking stars in the inky sky. A stone plinth bench was tucked behind a lilac tree further up from the water, conspicuously empty. Luz looked around her. With a sickening lurch of her heart, she noted Gemini was not there. Indeed the place was deserted. An owl hooted, making her jump, and a branch cracked behind her. She turned sharply.

'Is someone there? Andrés, is that you?' she called out uncertainly, slightly unnerved by the silence and darkness.

There was a rustling in the coppice. Her eyes widened in alarm as a man wearing a Tuareg costume suddenly materialized in the shadows from behind a bush. He was clad in a long, loose-fitting dark robe, a turban and a veil that covered his entire face except for his eyes. He took a few steps forward. Luz froze and felt the colour drain from her face.

'Stop right there,' she ordered, battling to control the tremor in her voice. 'Who are you and what do you want?' Her heart was pounding wildly against her ribcage. At all costs she must retain a semblance of calm. The man did not stop, nor did he answer, but continued to move purposefully towards her.

In the distance the church clock boomed the first slow, sonorous strokes of midnight. As the vibrations died away upon the air and once more silence reigned, the scarf covering the stranger's face fell.

Luz breathed in sharply and now her pulse had a new reason to hammer violently as she met Leandro's green eyes and recognized the glitter of raw desire that mirrored her own.

The next moment the gypsy drew her strongly into the circle of his arms. His head came down and, like a bird of prey, he claimed her mouth with a passion that took her breath away. She did not struggle; it would have been useless for he was stronger than her. Besides it was what she wanted.

All evening Luz had ridden a wave of exhilaration, tension and frustration, and now her warring emotions blazed in her blood. Her lips parted under the skilful persuasion of his kisses and the expert wandering of his hands over her young curves as their softness brushed up against his hard thighs. His tongue coaxed hers more urgently as one of his hands came up to tangle in her hair. She pressed closer and closer against him, her nipples hardening, her body responding and promising as the floodgates opened still further and all the suppressed need that had haunted her for weeks surfaced in a rush.

Through the open French windows, spasmodic clapping broke out into the night as masks fell and prizes were announced, bringing Luz reluctantly back to earth. She drew away, her heart pounding, though her body was yearning for more. As she stared at the man standing before her, confusion and doubt shadowed her eyes. The breath caught once more in her throat as she looked at him. Faced with his sexual magnetism, her head was swimming … she felt weak … but characteristically, something stronger and proud stepped up in her defence.

'How dare you! What are you doing here? How did you get in?' she demanded, staring at him in disbelief, still incredulous at his presence at El Pavón and at the situation she found herself in.

He did not answer, but simply gave her one of his slow, lazy smiles. A shaft of moonlight touched his face. Once again Luz was reminded of how devastatingly attractive she found him. He was a restless creature with eyes as secretive and deep as the ocean, reflecting the fire that burned silently within him. It was definitely those eyes that revealed Leandro's gypsy blood: wild, flashing, magnificent. Still, as she looked deeper into them for the first time, Luz was aware of a trace of dreamy softness concealed behind his devil-may-care attitude.

'What do you want?' she went on.

He stared into her dark-blue eyes without comment and was silent for so long that she began to wonder if he intended to say anything at all.

He moved away a little and, taking out a packet of thin paper and a small box of tobacco, proceeded to roll a cigarette. Once he had lit it, he inhaled deeply, leaned against a nearby tree and surveyed her idly. 'I want to make love to you,' he said coolly.

Luz blinked and looked away from him so he couldn't see the effect of aching tension his boldness had produced in her. Hopefully, the semi-darkness would hide the flame sweeping her cheeks. She could still feel his passionate embrace, his feverish kisses burning her lips, and the tautness of his arousal that had made her innermost parts pulsate with a desire of which she had never thought herself capable. Still, she remembered how easily he had dismissed her at the fair when the redheaded gypsy girl, Rosa, had appeared on the scene and she searched for a cutting response.

'Don't you think you're being a little brazen?' was the only phrase she could come up with, making her inwardly wince.

Leandro favoured her with a long, speculative look through the smoke of his cigarette. He laughed deep in his throat. 'No, I do not. There's no shield from the forces of destiny. I think you want it as much as I do – it was there from the first moment we laid eyes on each other. When two consenting adults are in agreement, where is the problem?' His gypsy intonation had a questioning lift as he voiced his forthright challenge, but his eyes were watching her steadily.

Luz frowned. For a few moments she was lost for words.

'I see,' she said evenly, still evading his gaze. 'But I don't believe I've given my consent to anything of the sort so I think your presumption is a little misplaced.'

She looked directly at him and saw that his sparkling green eyes held mischief.

'We're going to have to do something about your old-fashioned ways, Luz.'

'I'm not old-fashioned, I simply don't …'

'Don't what, Luz?' As before, his eyes travelled up and down her in a way that made her legs go weak and her stomach fill with butterflies. 'I think you are a little tense, then.'

'I'm not tense,' she lied, instinctively taking two paces back and crossing her arms against her chest. She needed some distance between them; to put their relationship – such as it was – back on a more formal footing. 'What you're so casually suggesting is not something a decent woman does lightly, that's all. And no decent man should demand it either.'

'It's not *gallant*, you mean?' His green gaze was twinkling again.

She couldn't help but smile at that quaint description she'd once used with regard to him. 'It's a question of *la honra* as even rogues and bandits know.' She arched a brow, batting his own words back to him.

He tilted his head to one side. 'Are you now playing with me, Doña Luz?' He grinned with a flash of white teeth, making her marvel again at how stunningly handsome he was. As he leant his forearm against the tree trunk, she imagined how his muscled shoulder might look beneath his dark Tuareg robe. She blinked rapidly.

'Decency is irrelevant to passion and even *la honra* bows to the laws of love and destiny,' he continued.

'Is that the convenient mantra of all gypsies?'

'We gypsies have many mantras, but that one is my own.' His comment was accompanied by a twisted smile. She couldn't make out whether or not he was amused. Still, she wanted more of that smile, she craved it, and in that craving, she knew, was a danger more extreme than any other.

'I've been warned about gypsies …' Perturbed, she blurted it out before she could stop herself.

He arched a brow. 'And what warnings would those be? That we are wild and untrustworthy? That rich, fine girls like you will be corrupted by our wicked ways?'

'Well, you certainly seem free with your affections.' Her voice was low and husky and she regarded him warily. That was exactly the impression she had been given.

'I am not free with anything, believe me, Luz,' he murmured, tossing his cigarette to the ground and stubbing it out with the heel of his boot. He was still watching her.

Luz took a breath, her heart in her throat almost choking her. 'Not even Rosa, I suppose?' She stood staring at him defiantly, a pang of jealousy mixing uncomfortably with the butterflies that had returned to her stomach. Why did he have this effect on her?

Leandro finally pushed away from the tree, his lips quirking in a half smile as he took a step towards her. 'Does she bother you, Luz?'

'Why should she bother me? What you do with women is none of my concern.' She shrugged, trying to feign indifference as she met his gaze. 'You and I do not own each other.'

'Don't we, *querida*?' he said softly. He stood observing her with a scrutiny she found unnerving. 'You want me as much as I want you but you're too afraid to admit it. Afraid to give in to your passion, afraid of your own nature.' He paused, his eyes still searching her face, dropping suddenly and settling on her mouth. 'Rosa is nothing to me.' He took another step nearer and her legs felt disinclined to hold her up. 'You have yet to understand that submitting to your passion is your destiny. Not only that, it is what you really want.'

'You do have some nerve, you know,' Luz breathed, turning away to break the hold he had on her. She wanted to run back to the terrace but somehow she couldn't move, her heart was pounding so hard. She was so aware of him behind her.

Muffled voices and strains of violin music from the orchestra trickled into the garden as a tango started up, eventually sweeping towards them into the deepening night.

He must have covered the space between them silently and with agile swiftness because Luz was stunned when she felt his hands slide over her shoulders as he came to stand behind her. She longed to lean against his lithe, vigorous body, but instead she turned sharply to face the young gypsy with all her efforts concentrated on resisting him. As she drew new breath to argue, she collided with the blaze of those hypnotic, devouring eyes.

'Please don't look at me like that,' she whispered in earnest, her courage deflated. 'When you do, I find it hard to behave as I know I should. It's not fair.'

She drew away with a little shake of her head. Luz's deep sapphire eyes reflected the uncontrollable desire churning inside her but the struggle to suppress it was also written on her face, as was her resolution to reject him.

A deep groove appeared between Leandro's brows as he took in her refusal. He straightened, and his chin lifted a little with resigned determination. The devil-may-care look that earlier glittered in his eyes and the faint smile that tugged at the corners of his mouth had now disappeared. They were replaced by a stark expression she couldn't understand, as if his pride was battling with some far more complicated melancholic emotion. His voice dropped to a husky note.

'I will not pressure you,' he said ruefully, tracing a finger across the beautiful curve of her cheekbone. 'I'll go now and not bother you again.'

His reaction took Luz by surprise. She had no intention of surrendering to him at the drop of a hat, and yet nor was she expecting him to give up so easily, or for it to be so final. While her mind grappled with the right thing to do, Luz's body had already betrayed her and the words he clearly wanted to hear were there, quivering on the tip of her tongue: a longing to tell him how she felt, how this yearning for him consumed her. She only needed a little more time; he was being absurd.

He started to turn away. Her heart sank and panic struck her as a thousand conflicting thoughts fought for sovereignty. Her upbringing, her parents' hints and Agustina's plainer words surfaced and nagged away at her but her restless heart and chaotic hormones chanted a different tune. *He'll disappear like gypsies do, never to be seen or heard of again. He'll never hold you like he did tonight … His burning kisses will be just a memory, never to return.* The terrible finality of it suddenly struck her. No, she couldn't bear that.

'Leandro …'

It was the first time she had uttered his name out loud and her cry resonated in the night. Drawn from within her, it was an anguished reflex, not heeding of consequences, and it stopped him in his tracks. He turned. For a brief moment in the moonlight the consuming, raw passion they felt erupted between them as they held each other's gaze and then there was no stopping them. Swept away by the current of their aching desire, they sailed tumultuous waves of eroticism into a world of their own.

Luz had been held and kissed before, but never like this. In fact, she had often wondered what all the fuss was about. Now she understood. In Leandro's arms she felt feminine, wanted, alive. The strength of his arousal sent sensations spinning through her like liquid fire and scorched every intimate part of her. His mouth was voracious on hers, probing and enticing her with his tongue, and when she shyly pursued with hers, hot and moist, he gave a low groan in his throat. As he teased, kissed and caressed, she shivered and burned, gasping with need and pleasure. Luz was equally fierce, freeing the shackles of repressed longing, holding nothing back. They knew nothing of each other yet still their bodies were perfectly attuned: he led and she followed. There was no tenderness either in his kisses or his caresses. They were wild, like everything about him, and Luz revelled in his touch with an ever-growing hunger as she responded blindly, giving as much as she took.

So it came as a bolt from the blue when fireworks began to explode, loud enough to shock them out of their ecstasy and bright enough to transform the natural wonder of El Pavón's garden into a surreal world bathed in bright kaleidoscopic colours.

They gazed at each other with their hearts in their eyes, still trembling with the passion that had rocked them so. Leandro lifted Luz up urgently and carried her to the stone bench at the edge of the lake. Though the flowers were asleep for the night their heady scent filled the air. A soft breeze had started up its occasional whisper, rushing eerily through the waterside plants. They were quiet for a while, a little subdued by the quick passion that had shaken them both and dazed by the last of the lights bursting and falling to nothing in the night sky. There was no need to talk. Together, in silence, they watched the golden shafts of moonlight blazing on the rippling black expanse of water that lay at their feet.

Luz was the first to speak. 'How were you able to get your message to me?' She lifted her dark-blue eyes to him.

Leandro fixed his gaze on her face, and then down the long and graceful line of her throat, beautiful as a swan's neck, without decoration of any kind. His laugh was deep and hoarse;

the yearning for her still burning like flames in his eyes while he seemed to ponder his answer.

'We gypsies rise from the mist like an illusion, a dream. We ride the wind and, like the wind, we breeze in and out of places at our leisure, anywhere and at any time,' he said with that slow smile that was becoming familiar to her.

True enough, she thought. In Cádiz, after her fall, not only had he been able to bring her back to L'Estrella but he'd also managed to find his way to her bedroom. And then today he had somehow managed to get a note to her table.

She gave him a bright, direct smile. 'Very resourceful, very enterprising.'

'I believe that if someone wants something enough, he must reach out and take it, don't you think?' he said calmly, the arrogant gleam returning to his eyes.

'Erm … Yes, I suppose so,' she muttered awkwardly.

'Don't be afraid, relax, let yourself go,' he whispered as his head came down and he claimed her lips once more. It was a different sort of kiss now, Luz thought dreamily, her body flooded with warmth as his mouth moved slowly and lovingly from her lips to her cheeks and down to the hollow in her throat where a tiny nerve pulsed almost imperceptibly, a manifest giveaway of what he was doing to her senses. His hands swept over the curve of her breasts, lingeringly. She felt them swell beneath her costume and knew he could feel it too, which sent another rush of heat down between her thighs. Luz shuddered and her arms moved up to his neck as fire raced through her. She pulled him down towards her on the bench and he covered her with his body. Arching her back wantonly to mould herself to him, she could feel the strength of his virility. Her obvious arousal made Leandro lose control. His fingers moved urgently, impatiently seeking an entrance to her bodice. He buried his face in the warmth of her neck, enveloped in the sweet scent of her silken hair.

'*Yo te quiero, yo te quiero*, I want you, *querida*,' he groaned as he found and began to undo the three buttons that protected the intimate upper part of her from his scorching touch.

The loud noise of shrill klaxons and roaring motors brought them down to earth again with a bang, their breathing fast and uneven as they drew back from each other in alarm. Leandro looked at Luz enquiringly, still exhaling heavily.

'Oh, no,' she protested, her hand to her mouth, 'it must be one o'clock. The guests will be leaving. You must go, Leandro! I have to get back to the hacienda before I'm missed.'

A faint smile crossed his handsome face as his eyes stroked her mouth but it was edged with frustration. 'Pity, *querida*. We were getting on so well.'

'Will I see you again?' A shadow darkened her eyes. Why was he suddenly looking so desolate? 'Where can I find you? Where can we meet?' she asked desperately. Luz surprised herself, realizing only too well how forward she must sound and how far she had wanted – and still wanted – to go with this man who had so bewitched her.

Leandro's eyes slid away as he stood up, a strange figure, sombre as his own shadow. Then he looked back at her with an intense, absorbing stare that held her in its spell.

'I am forgetting myself, *querida*.' He pulled the scarf back over his face so only the glimmer of his green eyes was visible once more. 'Flowers in the darkness of night have an intoxicating scent,' he murmured. 'Are you sure that in the cold light of day you won't turn away from it?' But he didn't wait for a reply. He looked her over with hooded eyes, bowed and then was gone, sucked up by the black hole of the night.

As his shadow disappeared behind the trees, Luz blinked, disorientated. She sat for a moment, looking after him uneasily, biting her lower lip. Then she turned her attention back to the lake. The evening had ended a little too abruptly and she had the vague impression that Leandro's mood had darkened. Had he been hurt by the fact that she had asked him to go? His parting words had undertones of bitterness, somehow intimating that Luz might be one of those society belles who got a kick out of flirting with gypsies. How wrong he was; she had lost her heart to him, she knew that now. Whenever he was there, everything else was eclipsed. She was twenty-four and had never fallen in love. If he wanted, she would follow him anywhere.

She shivered. The air had turned cold and a gentle wind sighed through the trees, penetrating her flimsy garments. She started back to the hacienda, a little heavy hearted.

Guests were still queuing to take leave of their hosts. As she made her way through the hall to the staircase leading up to her room, she glimpsed Andrés talking to her father at the front door. He had taken off his mask and his long chestnut hair, usually drawn back into a neat ponytail, was a little ruffled. She had forgotten all about him. A feeling she couldn't identify made Luz linger on the stairs, watching him. The shadow of a smile crossed her face. So he had stayed until the bitter end; he must have been having a good time. *That, I hope, should win me some brownie points*, she told herself as she climbed the stairs to bed.

An hour later Luz still lay awake, replaying everything that had happened that evening and, with the recollection, came a flash of realization that she was leaping blindfolded into a marsh of quicksand that could totally engulf her. Her feelings for Leandro were overwhelming. What would happen, she wondered dreamily, if she just went with the flow, guided only by intuition and her newfound love? Or should she walk away now, before it was too late, turning her back and shutting the door firmly on all that might be? Should she try to fight for her gypsy or would it be more sensible to fight against her love for him?

Suddenly the events of the past few hours seemed to crowd in upon her. Unbidden, the face of Andrés swam into her vision and she remembered the sting of his evasiveness. Why was she thinking of him at the very moment of contemplating her love for Leandro? She turned and pulled a pillow to her chest in frustration. Why did everything with the young gypsy have to be fraught with such complications?

Luz couldn't cope with the dizzying spin of her emotions, but still she clung to her pride and the tears that threatened her eyes burned like acid. She would not cry, even though she was on her own and could let her body have the release it needed.

Sleep did not come easily that night.

*   *   *

Not too far away in the darkness, Leandro sat beneath the stars, strumming a melancholy tune on his guitar, deep in thought. The young gypsy was in one of his dark moods. He leaned his head back against the stump of an ancient olive tree. The moon that a couple of hours ago had witnessed his passion now smiled benignly on him.

What was he doing? Where would all this lead? Well-bred *gajo* ladies didn't bring home gypsies. Luz, in turn, could never live in his world. He remembered how she had looked at him as if she was fighting with all her might not to give in to her own desire. The thought sliced through him. He was a gypsy, what did he expect from a *gajo*? But he was proud; he would not beg. He had never had to beg. So he had almost walked away from her then. Still, it would be she who would one day turn her back on him. 'The day obliterates the promises of the night,' went the ancient Moorish saying. Luz would soon realize her mistake and flee. Heartbreaking as it was, he had to concede he was on a road to nowhere. Their short-lived idyll could only end in disaster. Hadn't he already had warning of that?

The night he'd argued with his mother after taking Luz back to L'Estrella was still vivid in his mind, as well as what had happened subsequently.

When he'd walked briskly away from Marujita's cave, dread and horror burning within him, his uncle Juanillo had been hunched over on a bench. The older gypsy was leaning one arm, gnarled with muscle, on his knee while slowly dragging his whetstone across a short *navaja*. The butt of a cigar was clenched between his teeth.

Juanillo was still as strong as an ox despite his greying hair and side-whiskers. In fact Leandro had once seen him throw a man, who had drunkenly challenged him, across a table as if he were a bag of old rags. Leandro had never gone out of his way to befriend his uncle and, in turn, Juanillo usually kept his distance. Perhaps he sensed and respected his nephew's own fearless flashes of temper. As a result the two men managed to preserve a wary tolerance of each other.

Juanillo glanced up when he saw his nephew and narrowed his eyes. 'You've a face like boiled milk, *sobrino*,' he rasped, his voice like a heel over broken glass. 'I'm thinking that you didn't like what your mother had to say.'

'That's between me and her,' answered Leandro in a flat voice as he came level with his uncle. He wasn't about to get into a discussion with Juanillo about Marujita's plans for revenge against the man and woman she regarded as her sworn enemies – or that she wanted an innocent young woman to pay the price.

He would have walked on but Juanillo stuck a booted foot across Leandro's path, halting his progress.

'Nephew, the dishonour of my sister concerns me, too.'

Leandro looked down at the boot before his gaze settled coolly on Juanillo's coal-black eyes. His uncle clearly knew what Marujita planned to do.

'We gypsies must stick to our *lachirí*, justice, or where would we be? No better than the filthy *gajos*.' He spat out the butt of his cigar on the ground.

'What is your point, *Tío*?'

Juanillo let out a dramatic sigh, drawing in his outstretched leg. 'You run too fast in the opposite direction, *sobrino*. You've always been that way. Anyone would think that you're shunning your own kind. You should know who you are.'

'I know who I am.'

'That's good.' The older gypsy nodded slowly, raising his eyebrows. 'Then you also know that as the eldest son of Marujita, our queen, your duty is clear.'

'I have always done my duty by my mother,' Leandro said quietly. 'She knows that, and so do you.' What he didn't say was that never before had he felt the need to challenge her, or their way of life. Yet what she was asking of him now was tearing at his insides.

Juanillo stuck his knife into the bench beside him and leaned forward. 'What I know is that your mother is owed her *lachirí* now,' he growled.

Leandro didn't react but continued to gaze steadily at the older man.

'My sister has the power of the *olajai*, curse,' Juanillo continued, 'and *Il Diabolica* is feared by any man with sense in his head. Me, I'm different. I don't need the power of curses, I have this.' He held up his knife. 'This is my power ... I'm not afraid to draw my *navaja* against another man who wrongs me, or a *gitano* who breaks gypsy law either.'

Juanillo stood, drawing himself up to his full height. 'Do not make your mother go to her grave unavenged and cursing you for it.' He wrenched his dagger out of the seat and shoved it under his belt. 'You may be my sister's son but if you fail her, you will suffer a fate worse than death for a gypsy. We will cast you out forever. And then I will hunt you down and kill you, make no mistake. Remember, the Devil always sleeps with one eye open and that eye can still burn a man to nothing.' He began to saunter away. 'You can't escape who you are.'

Leandro opened his eyes and shook his head, as if banishing the memory. He returned his gaze to the dark outline of olive trees, lit by the ghostly moonlight. Juanillo had simply stated the truth: if he ignored his mother's demands there would be repercussions. He couldn't imagine turning his back on his own people, but the pull of familial loyalties fought against the pull of his heart. As he plucked a few notes from his guitar, he tried to push Luz from his mind but it was no good. How could he ever do that? She ran through his blood like his very life force.

He stared into space, visualizing Luz, an exquisite, slim-hipped creature in a moon-flooded garden. How beautiful and graceful she had looked running down to the lake as he followed her. He recalled the soft bloom on her face, the slender curved line of her brows, the look in her deep-blue eyes when he had threatened to go and the shiny silken waves of her raven-black hair.

But mostly, he remembered the way her body, soft and pliable as a liana, had pulsated and quivered under his touch, willing and responsive, with a generosity and abandonment the like of which he had never imagined a woman capable. Ever since Leandro had turned fifteen, women from all walks of life, young and old, solicited and unsolicited, had fallen for him and come to his bed. The years had long gone when a woman had surprised him, but tonight, even though in his book their embraces had been relatively innocent – after all, they were fully dressed – Luz had thrilled him like no other.

He had pulled back from her in amazed wonderment, never having felt so much unbridled desire, never so alive, but then reality swept back over him like an ominous thundercloud in the angry heavens. He knew it now: he loved Luz with all his heart, but he found himself in a terrible situation and had no idea how to deal with it.

CHAPTER 5

Luz woke with a start. The first pale rays of dawn gleamed through the windows. She sat up in a daze, still breathless, her body throbbing and on fire. She had just been dreaming of Leandro naked in the Garden of Eden – or was it Andrés? – as he moved swiftly through the magical paradise, trying to elude her. All through her dream she could glimpse his glistening bronzed figure appearing then disappearing behind trees and shrubberies, only to resurface next to a marble colonnade and vanish again suddenly without warning, always inaccessible.

Sliding out of bed she made her way shakily to the bathroom: she needed a shower. She discarded her damp, flimsy nightdress that clung to her uncomfortably, stepped into the cubicle and turned on the tap. Yes, that felt good. She lingered for a long time under the jet of cool water, her eyes closed, recalling her passionate rendezvous the night before at the lake. Carrying the image of Leandro and the feel of him powerfully in her mind, she let the stream drizzle slowly down the length of her body, caressing her hair, her face, her neck, refreshing her overheated breasts, her stomach, her hips and her thighs.

Whether this overpowering emotion assailing her was motivated by love or purely lust for the young gypsy, she couldn't tell. The only thing she knew was that she must see him again. Every time Luz remembered the way his hands had touched her body, she lost the ability to analyze it; and every time his bleak parting words drifted back to her mind, she grew more determined to find him. She hated the way he had raced off so abruptly and the uncertainty in which he had left her.

She was wide awake now. The idea that Leandro might be down at the orange grove with the gypsies crossed her mind, starting up a sudden flutter in her stomach. The El Pavón annual ball was held to celebrate the harvesting of Valencia late oranges, but the gathering would still be going on for another couple of days. Each year gypsies would come from all parts of Andalucía to help, rolling up on wagons and pitching their tents among the fruit trees. They were paid well for a long day's work, filling the baskets and giant boxes. At night, the sound of guitars, pipes and raucous laughter, encouraged no doubt by the generous sharing of manzanilla, floated up through the orchards and gardens of the hacienda. Even as a child, Luz often lay awake listening to the distant sounds, imagining what it would be like to run down to the orchard in her nightdress and join in with the gypsies' wild dancing.

As a rule they started the picking in the early morning, long before the sun reached its zenith. Luz glanced at the clock on her bedside table: just gone seven o'clock. She quickly pulled on a pair of jeans and a short, blue-and-white gingham top, eager to escape before her parents woke up. They would surely have noticed her absence at the prize giving at midnight and later as the guests were leaving the ball. No doubt they would question her. She had already dreamt up an excuse but she loathed the idea of lying to them, so was postponing the time of reckoning for as long as possible.

She walked down to the orange grove where she knew the harvesting would be well under way. It was a cool and tranquil morning. Everything at that hour glistened with moisture and sunshine and the ground was saturated with dew. Later in the day it would have evaporated and the bare earth would become scorching hot. The singing of birds was enchanting. There was buzzing in the branches overhead: humming bees, chirruping crickets and the soft murmur of leaves. The sunny path that led down to the grove was streaked with broad patches of shadow, which flitted to and fro, uniting and breaking asunder again.

As Luz drew closer she could hear the harvesters chanting. Dense rows of orange, lemon and tangerine trees appeared in the distance, stretching out where the land sloped down. The air around her was filled with the sweet smell of orange blossom brought out by the first heat of the day. She quickened her pace, the tempo of her heart rising as it moved into racing mode at the thought of Leandro.

Men, women and children gathered in the harvest. The men were dressed all in brown with black broad-brimmed hats; the women wore bright-coloured handkerchiefs tied round their heads. They had bare arms and feet, either skirts hitched up and tucked into waistbands or trousers rolled to the knee, toiling under the huge blue dome of the sky. Some of them used ladders to reach fruit in the top branches; others simply shook the trees, allowing the oranges to fall to the ground before placing them in their picking sacks. The heavy jute receptacles were then emptied into bin boxes, which were carried and stacked on the side of the grove, ready to be loaded on to trailers for transportation to the packing house.

The harvesters were very merry, cheering and singing as they picked. On one side of the grove, a group would sing a monotone refrain while another on the opposite side would answer, echoing the preceding verse. There was a close and intimate feeling among them, an atmosphere of mirth and comradeship.

Luz scanned the grove looking for him. Though the sight was a magnificent one, it was hard to distinguish anything at this distance. The trees were planted very close to each other; there were ladders, tall baskets and a sea of people milling under the dappled branches. This year's crop was especially large and the oranges and lemons hung like illuminated lanterns in the foliage. For a while she stood at the edge of the orchard, staring at the beauty of lines and colours. The scene reminded her of a vivid turn-of-the-century Fauvist painting.

She hesitated before walking further into the orchard. The change of ambiance was instant. Before she knew it, the rows of men and women widened to let her pass. The singing stopped. There was complete silence, save for the trickling murmur of a nearby stream as it rippled gently over stones, the rustle of leaves in the branches as fruit was broken off, and the continuous buzzing of insects. As she walked past, men removed their caps, dark eyes flashed upon her their slow fire; lips parted in courteous, aloof smiles. Luz wanted to stop and be with them but she felt cut off. It was plain they could not really relate to her. *Gajos*, cocooned in their alien shells, with their fancy ways, were too far removed from them. She was sorely aware that her presence was more of an intimidation and it made her feel awkward and uneasy. Still, she wanted to find Leandro and so she walked on, ignoring the new, stilted atmosphere.

As she came to the end of one of the rows, she saw the rose seller, who had accosted her on the way back from the horse fair. The *gitana* was standing halfway up a ladder, a sardonic grin on her sunburnt face, watching Luz. As the young woman approached, she came down from her perch, a basket of oranges under her arm, propped against her hip. She paused for a moment, gave in to a fit of coughing and then plucked an orange from her basket.

'Juicy and warm from the first rays of the sun,' she said, offering it to Luz.

Close up, Luz could see that there was a sickly hue beneath the bronzed complexion of the gypsy. Immediately she felt a pang as she realized that her family was employing someone so obviously unwell, but then she met the powerful gaze of the older woman's jet-black eyes, gleaming with an unconcealed malevolence that belied the smile of welcome on her face.

'Thank you,' Luz managed to say, taking the lustrous fruit from her before turning away to move on.

The *gitana* coughed roughly and laid a hand on her arm as if to steady herself as much as to grab Luz's attention. She quickly straightened, putting her hands on her hips. 'The one you are looking for is not here today,' she said with an arrogantly triumphant air.

Luz's cheeks flamed hotly. 'I don't know what you're talking about …' The invisible wall around her was vibrating with defensive caution.

The gypsy's mouth drew back from her teeth in a wide smile teetering on the edge of a sneer. 'You have refused me your palm once before but you can't deceive my gypsy eye. I don't need to look at the lines on your hand to read you, my girl!'

Luz felt her gut tighten. This woman had a menacing power over her. She wanted to run but moving away now was an admission of fear. She looked the gypsy straight in the eye and shook her head. 'How can you be so sure it was me you spoke to? I don't remember ever having laid eyes on you before. I would have remembered, you are a very handsome woman.'

The *gitana*'s sardonic smile died away, her eyes glittering dangerously as her gaze fixed hard on Luz. 'Ah, beautiful lady, but I never forget a face. Remember, gypsies have long memories.' With those words she turned and, without a backward glance, climbed on to the ladder.

Luz stood for a moment, not knowing where to look, then squared her shoulders. She thought of all the clever, dignified responses she could have made but the moment was gone. Leandro was clearly gone, too. The harvesters parted once more as she walked back through the grove, hearing the soft murmur of their chant start up again behind her as she left.

*   *   *

Luz had been back at L'Estrella since the beginning of the week. After her eerie conversation with the gypsy on the day of the harvest at El Pavón, she made a conscious effort to push Leandro out of her mind. No matter that she had feelings for him that were new to her, he had disappeared into thin air and had scarcely beaten a path to her door. She wanted to forget him and the crazy fantasy that had taken hold on the night of the ball. What would be the point of continuing with it all?

Confusion and the nag of common sense clouded Luz's mind but now they seemed to go hand in hand with some other feeling, darker and more threatening. Every time she had encountered one of the gypsies, be it Paquita, the dusky flower seller or even Leandro himself, she sensed something obscure lurking in the shadows. The way they appeared out of nowhere, with their convoluted words and eerie gift of divination, was making her feel increasingly uncomfortable. She was beginning to understand what Agustina meant. Perhaps she was right and no good could ever come to those who became mixed up with the *gitanos*. They were an uncanny lot who seemed to project a sinister aura around them or, at the very least, a dangerous and beguiling lure to the unwary, as the housekeeper had warned. Given the choice, it was better to have nothing to do with them. Still, forgetting did not come easily to her.

Luz knew the gypsies were still camped in the grounds of the El Pavón estate and there was still the chance that Leandro might be somewhere among them. Secretly, so very secretly, she hoped that he would somehow materialize in front of her, his astonishing eyes mesmerizing her as they always did, so that she would be made to submit to him. However, Leandro carried on being elusive and Luz therefore remained safe.

Since the masked ball the phone had not stopped ringing at the hacienda; she was the flavour of the month. Word was out that Luz, after years of working abroad, was now back in Spain for good. Invitations were showered upon her as covetous mothers saw in her an enviable catch, and endless queues of young men pursued her. But she was not one for wild parties, particularly those frequented by the Andalucían aristocracy. She found the people in that particular circle shallow and two-faced. To her parents' exasperation, she much preferred quiet evenings spent with the same handful of friends, long walks in the countryside around Jerez and riding her mare.

So, as soon as she could, she returned to L'Estrella.

She spent her mornings working on Eduardo de Salazar's biography and her afternoons swimming. On one of her outings of exploration, as she climbed through the opaque forest of thick vegetation that wound up and down the coast, she had burst into a clearing. From there, as if out of nowhere, she had come upon an expanse of shimmering blue ocean enclosed within a small cove. It lay at the bottom of the escarpment, surrounded by little creeks and rocky caves, with lonely golden beaches sandwiched between haciendas. Since it was impossible to reach by foot, the next day she hired a small boat and, using her sense of direction, found one of the approaches to this magical place through the rocks. It looked lonely, with only a few seagulls strutting about on the wet sand at the water's edge. And there, in complete seclusion, she bathed until sunset. After that, she came every day.

She was scheduled to meet Andrés at the end of the week for a first review of the book's plan and to discuss the way to proceed. Pleased with the progress of her outline, she hoped that Andrés would be, too. It would be a working dinner at his hacienda, Puesta de Sol, his secretary had told her when she rang to make the appointment. Don Andrés had a very busy diary during the days ahead and hoped that this invitation would not inconvenience her. *Very cunning*, Luz thought, *he was going to have his intimate tête-à-tête dinner after all. Nothing like determination!*

Now that her previously tangled emotions over the urbane businessman had been cloaked by an overwhelming desire for the young gypsy, Luz's antagonism towards Andrés had faded into a more convenient indulgence, or at least that's how she chose to view it. Whereas she had been infuriated that night of the masked ball and even piqued by his attentions towards other women, now, every time she recalled the way he had tried to elude her, it made her smile. It had been his way of capturing her attention: matching her rejection of him. She told herself that this playful brand of mischievousness had a childish charm, safe enough now she would not fall for it again. Nonetheless, it kept her amused.

Luz's reflection stared back at her as she surveyed herself in the mirror before setting off for her dinner engagement. In England, a working dinner suggested smart-casual attire. Spain had a completely different etiquette. If you were invited to dinner, be it for leisure or work, you dressed up and never down – anything less would be insulting to your hosts.

Luz had complied, wanting to make the right impression and at least feel armed with the confidence to handle this unpredictable man who was, she admitted, to all intents and purposes her new boss. Whether she liked it or not, Andrés de Calderón would have a good deal of input into her work. Besides, if he decided to engage her in another battle of wills, she would be armoured appropriately.

She had slipped on a black silk-chiffon dress with ruched shoulder straps and a figure-hugging bodice flaring into a delicately draped skirt, and wore towering heels. A ridged cuff in 22-carat gold adorned her wrist, while oversized but dainty gold hoops hung from her earlobes. She debated whether or not to put her hair up and finally opted for a straightforward ponytail. Her make-up was minimal: a hint of eye shadow, a stroke of mascara and a tinge of tinted gloss applied to her cheekbones and lips. The copper tan she had acquired on the beach deepened the blue of her eyes, making them look wider and more vivid. She satisfied herself that she had achieved a glamorous look, without being overdone, but wished it was Leandro she was meeting instead of Andrés.

Luz drove her Volkswagen cabriolet up through the hills of Cádiz, following the directions she'd been given, and passed a final screen of cypress trees artfully concealing the house and the sea behind, like curtains on a stage. The first sight she had of Puesta de Sol was breathtaking. She arrived at the hacienda just as the sun was sinking behind the horizon. Its last flamboyant pink-and-orange flush still lingered overhead, making the Atlantic Ocean that unfolded before her seem on fire. It was such a sight that she stopped the car abruptly and watched as a flying boat taxied across the water, flurrying the golden path of the sun. In the twilight the luxurious villa appeared as a mosaic of smoky green and toasted bronze, white and terracotta, scalloped by low mellow stone walls and delineated by a mass of turrets, columns and sloping roofs.

Puesta de Sol – Sunset – was a most appropriate name for the place, she thought as she drove up to the house.

She leaned forward and switched off the ignition. Before she had time to move, he was at her side, gallantly helping her out of the car. A half smile touched the corner of his mouth.

'Welcome to Puesta de Sol, Doña Luz,' he said softly. 'You look dazzling.'

'Señor de Calderón.' She nodded politely at Andrés as she stepped from the car. His gaze was warm and, as his eyes met hers, Luz looked swiftly away. She was still not accustomed to his uncanny resemblance to Leandro but more than that: she had forgotten how potent his presence was.

She scanned the view. The driveway was flanked by elaborate gardens whose fantastic colours complemented the bizarre fairy-tale nature of the hacienda itself. 'A magnificent setting you've got here,' she said, wishing she had found more original words to describe the awe-inspiring surroundings.

Andrés gave an easy smile, deepening the faint lines that fanned out at the side of his eyes. 'Unfortunately, I can take no credit for it. Puesta de Sol is the creation of my Uncle Eduardo, a very spirited and whimsical man, as you know. This is the translation of his empathy with the dramatic into visual terms – I'm just the very lucky man to whom he chose to give it.'

'Yes, I can see, it's a marvellous present,' she agreed, letting her gaze wander across the rippling waters to the now darkening horizon so that she didn't have to look at him. Handsome as the Devil in his white dinner jacket and dark trousers, his ensemble brought out the bronze shade of his skin, which glowed with health and vitality. His glossy chestnut hair was swept back from a high forehead. Though his gleaming dark eyes didn't sparkle with the same life as the gypsy's, they were just as compelling in a calm, enigmatic way and she felt their power already threatening her control over the evening.

He took her elbow briefly, making her nerve endings quiver, and proceeded to guide her through the poetic garden. They passed graceful playing fountains and patios of mild stone, hedges sculpted into tall, moving figures and green leaves wrapped around exotic flowers, which bloomed elaborately inside.

'I'm pleased that you could come here for dinner tonight. I thought it would help you properly understand the breadth of spirit in my uncle's work.'

'Of course,' Luz agreed quickly.

He paused and she caught his glittering dark stare before he carried on, his tone cool and his manner easy. 'Eduardo began training his eye when he was very young. My grandparents were keen art collectors and they took him and his sister, my mother, around with them to exhibitions and museums. Of course, after he left the School of Fine Arts in Barcelona he went on to study architecture. As you know, he built and landscaped many important haciendas and gardens in Andalucía.' He gestured towards the garden. 'He sketched the idea for this landscaped garden while in Paris.'

She nodded and smiled. 'Yes, the more I discover about him, the more I realize how great he was.'

Luz was annoyed with herself that she felt a small pang of disappointment on finding that Andrés' invitation to dinner seemed prompted by business after all and not because he actually wanted her company. In fact, why should she have thought otherwise? His first request for dinner had been refused and now he had clearly chosen to put the two of them on a different footing. As a rebuke this was a kind one and probably sensible, too. She had hated his game-playing after all.

His deep, warm voice startled her from her internal battle of self-reproach.

'Did you know that Eduardo often used napkins to sketch his visions on?'

She nodded as they made their way along a path, momentarily distracted by a statue of a Minotaur roaring silently to the heavens. 'Yes, I've read about that. He spent so much time frequenting the Café de Flore, the famous haunt of Surrealists of the day, he often resorted to grabbing napkins to draw on. Unfortunately, hardly any of those sketches survive.'

'Absolutely right – except for the one of this garden, which is preserved in the house.'

Luz looked up at him and nearly gasped. 'Really?' This was an intriguing revelation. She touched a fragrant cluster of yellow jasmine overhanging the path, wondering how these extraordinary surroundings looked originally when they were nothing more than a set of scribbles. 'Can I see it?'

'Yes, you must,' Andrés answered mildly, glancing sideways at her, 'but you need to see everything in its full glory first. I'm afraid you won't be able to see much tonight, it's already getting dark. The place comes to life in the sunshine,' he continued, as his shapely lips curved into a wide smile, showing perfect white teeth. 'We will have to make a lunch appointment next time, or maybe a breakfast one? The garden at dawn is at its most spectacular.' He was beaming down at her with the sort of contrived innocence she was sure he had certainly never known. That mouth of his was so familiar, so dangerous.

Luz managed a stilted smile. 'Of course, whatever it takes,' she said, realizing too late how he would interpret those words and wanting to eat them as soon as they were out of her mouth.

Predictably, his eyebrows shot up; soft irony twisted his mouth as wicked midnight eyes fixed on hers. Luz looked away, feeling his continued amusement as if he were scanning her thoughts.

'I saw you at the ball,' he said, changing the subject. 'You looked ravishing, a real, mysterious Princess of the East.'

Now it was her turn to lift a quizzical brow. 'So you recognized me?'

'Immediately.'

Luz felt her cheeks burn. She had missed neither the challenge in his voice nor the sardonic glint in the look he gave her. This was tantamount to admitting he had consciously avoided her company.

'Is that why you spent most of the evening running away from me? After all, I was your hostess ...' she parried, deliberately insinuating his conduct had been rude. She knew she sounded nettled but she had ceased to worry what the high-and-mighty Andrés de Calderón thought of her, she told herself.

'So you thought I was running away?'

'You never made yourself known to me.'

'And that upset you, did it?' His face was deadpan, though his mouth held the ghost of a smile.

He was laughing at her, she decided, and her face began to heat. His arrogant and patronizing manner was intolerable. In his suave way he seemed to want to humiliate her again. It was incomprehensible. If he was still annoyed at her omitting to mention her first job on her CV, why had he gone ahead and offered her the assignment? How he expected them to work together in this sort of atmosphere defied logic. She had tried to ignore it before, but she had never been a doormat and he was not about to turn her into one. She was very tempted to tell him to take his biography to the Devil, but the words 'act in haste, repent at leisure' rang in her head so she bit her tongue. Still, she would find a way of showing him she was a match for him any day.

'It's not the way one's guests normally behave on such occasions ...' Gritting her teeth, she kept walking.

He looked at her and came to a sudden standstill, his hand resting on her arm. A half-moon had risen in the smooth, cerulean sky. Luz was conscious of his nearness and masculinity as they stood facing each other in silence. Very gently he lifted her chin and met her stormy gaze.

'I had no idea you would be offended by my behaviour,' he murmured, his velvet-black eyes gently stroking. 'I simply didn't want to bother you. As you had turned down my dinner invitation without giving a reason, I thought it would be thick-skinned of me to force myself on you.' He dropped his hand. 'I was your guest, as you say, which would have made it difficult for you to refuse me a dance. I made sure my own costume left no doubt as to my identity, giving you the choice to speak to me or not.' His stare was unwavering, his tone almost humble. 'And that, Luz, is the honest truth.'

No words came to her in reply. At that point she was struck by the sheer force of Andrés' personality and lamented her inexperience of men and their games. This man had a way of making her lose her usual self-assurance and feel disorientated and emotional. She knew that he had enjoyed toying with her at the ball, as if he couldn't help himself, but there was something else in his eyes now: a warring of pride, caution and something so intense that it made her stare back at him. Luz could see he was fighting to control the emotions that she seemed to inspire and she abruptly lost her breath.

His gaze bored into her. In that moment his features blurred and fused in her mind with those of Leandro so, when his head bent down towards her and his mouth brushed hers with infinite tenderness, soft, warm and eloquent, her eyes closed and her lips parted to receive the kiss. He smelled clean, fresh, with a hint of tantalizing aftershave. Her heart pounded and she didn't know what to do with her hands, still lying limply by her side. The world began to tilt and left her sliding away into the whisper of that kiss. Yet beneath the silky intensity of it she sensed a sort of thorniness to him, something she could not put her arms around but at the same time was begging her to try. She found herself wanting to, but then it was too late.

'And now, shall we have dinner?' he murmured softly against her lips, lifting his head away. For a second he stared at her again before recovering himself and gracing her with his devilish smile.

Slightly taken aback by this abrupt change in mood, but nonetheless relieved that he had not taken the interlude further, Luz acquiesced, a little shaken. The taste of his mouth was still on hers and she realized that some shocking, unknown part of her had urged not to break away.

They dined in secluded privacy on a small terrace at the bottom of the garden that jutted out, suspended like a ship's prow above the ocean. Below, where miles of white sand skirted the bay, a series of rocks and creeks with deep pools of blue water shielded a private beach. Shallow flights of steps led down to it from the terrace and the rhythmic drum and sigh of the sea sounded through the night air.

The moon and the stars, pendant in a sapphire sky, watched over them as they worked their way through a three-course dinner of caviar, *filets mignons* with mustard-and-port sauce and a sumptuous cold chocolate soufflé. They talked in detail about the plan for Eduardo's biography, fleshing out subjects for every chapter, each of them getting caught up in different ideas but agreeing on most things, which surprised Luz. All the while, she felt his ebony eyes on her, attentive, appraising, often inscrutable. On occasion, she found herself ensnared in their dark mystery, so much so that she found it hard to concentrate on the thread of the conversation.

Around the terrace were long stone troughs filled with water, the sides of which held reliefs of winged water creatures – nymphs, perhaps. Exquisite white lotus flowers floated on the surface and Luz immediately thought back to her favourite Eduardo painting, *The Immortality of the Crab*, with its giant lotus petals holding other worlds within them. She had noticed the flowers as soon as they had taken their seats and being surrounded by them as they discussed Eduardo's work gave her a curious feeling, as if her secret longings were being whispered to her in this magical place.

'You like lotus flowers?' Andrés cocked his head to one side, watching her.

'Lotus flowers? Oh, yes. Yes, I do.'

'I couldn't help but notice you've been looking at them all evening. They're beautiful, aren't they?'

'Stunning, and so captivating displayed like this. Eduardo certainly seemed to have a penchant for them.'

'Birth and rebirth, fertility and creation, all themes that fascinated my uncle. The long stems symbolize our connection to our origins.'

Luz stared at them again. 'Of course, I hadn't thought of that. How funny.'

'Funny?' He raised an eyebrow.

'Oh … just that I had forgotten that.' Luz glanced at him, noticing his finger was touching his perfectly sculpted lips again. It was a habit he had when something bemused him, she noticed, and she found it as distracting as ever.

Andrés pulled a bowl of fruit across the table between them. It was piled with figs, grapes and pears. 'Eduardo often worked these into his images, too. It's that Renaissance symbolism you so rightly pointed out. May I?' He offered her a plate.

'Yes, please do. I love fruit,' she answered graciously, though her antennae were already switched on. She knew full well their symbolism.

'Figs for loss of innocence.' He placed one on his plate and reached for the grapes. 'Lustful thoughts.' His gaze settled on her face as he pulled off a bunch. 'And pears for faithfulness.'

Luz felt the inevitable blush steal up her cheeks and inwardly cursed herself. 'An interesting combination.'

He waved a hand. 'Oh, all of these grow in the grounds. The choice was already made for me.' He smiled his secret, amused smile and began to peel a fig. She had noticed his hands before and couldn't help but glance at them again as he deftly removed the tender skin. Tanned and perfectly groomed, with lean, long fingers, they were the hands of an artist, the hands of a gentleman.

'Eduardo was fascinated by loss of innocence and the repression of sexual desire,' he continued, his eyes not leaving her face.

She met his gaze, needing to prove that she could discuss this topic with him and remain clear-headed and focused. 'Repressed sexual desire was the obsession of all the Surrealists in some form or other,' she replied, sipping the chilled white wine he had poured her. 'Dalí most of all, of course. His controversial love life is testimony to that.'

Andrés took a bite of fig. 'True. Dalí's most disturbing sexual images are the most powerful and, of course, the most shocking to society – Spanish society in particular. Some say he's a showman who prostitutes his art, others that he simply lives his brand of Surrealism. Do you find such imagery morally unacceptable?' He regarded her intently.

Luz raised an eyebrow. 'Well, no … I don't know, really.' She wondered if he thought her conservative, even unworldly, and took a breath. 'I think sexual desire is complicated.' She paused and looked down into her glass, fiddling with the stem. 'What's socially unacceptable isn't necessarily morally wrong.'

'Would you condone doing something socially unacceptable, Luz?'

'Perhaps, in the right circumstances.' She glanced up at him quickly. 'Wouldn't you?'

His long finger was stroking his bottom lip once more in contemplation. Suddenly his mouth broke into a broad grin. 'I think I would find it all too easy.'

Luz looked at him for a moment and then burst out laughing. 'I believe you would!'

He nodded an acknowledgement, his eyes flashing with twinkling humour. 'I see you are getting to know me, Doña Luz.'

'Perhaps I am,' she answered over the rim of her glass as she took a sip of wine.

The soft, steady rush of waves against rock filled the silence that hung for a moment in the air.

'This really is a fabulous setting,' Luz continued, breathing in deeply and looking up at the twinkling stars overhead.

'One day, I'll take you to explore the labyrinth of sea caves that lie at the bottom of this cliff,' Andrés said, leaning back in his chair and cloaking Luz in his smoky gaze. 'It's a warren of grottos, formed by the wave action of the sea, that lies all along this part of the coastline. The caves emerge on little coves and beaches and are mostly interlinked. Nearly all of them are dry now. Some are very beautiful, real relics. Salt crystals form on the walls and when the chamber is open to the sky, the sun and the play of shadow and light make those formations look like little jewels,' he told her.

She smiled inwardly and helped herself to some fruit. 'Actually, I've already discovered the little coves and secluded beaches.' She hadn't explored the caves yet, but that was a pleasure in store.

'You like to swim?' he asked.

'Yes.' Instantly, she was reminded of similar words in her flirtatious conversation with Leandro at the gypsy fair, not so very long ago. She quickly cut into a ripe pear and glanced up at him. 'I try to swim every day. It helps clear my head, particularly when I've been writing all morning,' she added, popping a piece of fruit into her mouth, hoping her discomfort didn't show.

'What else do you like to do, besides your work, that is, and swimming?' His eyes were alight with curiosity.

'Oh, well, I sometimes run, and I ride whenever I can along the beach. There are often gypsies with their horses down there and I enjoy watching them race each other.' *Where had that come from?* Why could she not have thought of something else? Was she deliberately trying to provoke him and expose herself to his ridicule?

To her surprise he looked almost amused at this. 'You're curious about the gypsies, I can see,' he answered. 'Well, I would steer clear of them if I were you.'

Patronizing hound, she thought. To Luz this was beginning to sound like a familiar refrain and despite previous misgivings about falling into this subject, she felt like challenging him.

'You don't approve of gypsies?'

He paused and fixed her with a stare. 'I think they're a wild and unpredictable people.'

'And that's a bad thing?'

'I think they lack control.'

'Perhaps a lack of control is sometimes necessary to feel alive.' She frowned, feeling the irony of her own words.

'Indeed.' He gazed into the night and then back at her. 'It's easy to become bewitched by their free and untamed natures, Luz. Somehow they speak to the primitive soul in all of us, something Eduardo was also intrigued by, of course ... But there's a darkness to their passion, born of suffering and death, that has walked with them for centuries. It is not a life that we *gajos* can easily understand.'

'No, I'm sure you certainly wouldn't,' she agreed, trying not to sound pointed. She noticed that his eyes had become darker than she had ever seen them. 'Perhaps if there were less prejudice towards them, we would understand them better,' she murmured.

'Perhaps, Luz.' He nodded gravely, searching her face. 'That world is a long way off. Their way of life cannot be changed overnight and neither can ours.' His expression softened. 'I think your time abroad has given you an unusual perspective.'

It was her turn to change the subject. 'It feels like you know more about me than I do about you. You've not told me much about yourself.'

He settled back further in his seat and crossed his long legs under the table. She was aware of how easily he moved his body, with masculine confidence.

'What do you want to know?'

'Did you grow up in Cádiz?'

'Yes, I grew up near Eduardo's house. I was an only child and we spent a lot of time together when I was young. We were very close.'

'What about your parents, were you close to them, too?' But something about him made her guess the answer.

He shrugged lightly. 'Not really, my father was away most of the time, the result being that I was left to my own devices, which suited me well enough, I suppose.'

'But wasn't your mother around?' She felt like she was prying now, but her curiosity was aroused.

'My mother wasn't really present in reality, shall we say? She lived in a world of make-believe.' His tone was a little terse.

'I see.' Luz instantly regretted her probing. She smiled weakly, not knowing the right thing to say. 'Perhaps a world of make-believe is a necessary refuge for some.'

Rubbing his chin, he pondered for a moment. '"*We are so accustomed to disguise ourselves to others that in the end we become disguised to ourselves.*" One of La Rochefoucauld's maxims. He was a shrewd man for his time.' He cocked his head and met her gaze. 'Tell me, what's your disguise, Luz?'

She blinked. 'I have no disguise, what you see is what you get,' she blurted out, still unnerved by her attraction to him. The recollection of their fleeting kiss chose to flash into her mind at that moment and she had to force her gaze away from his perfect mouth.

'I don't doubt it. You are very open and I like that. But I sense something else beneath your pride and your sense of propriety, Luz, that you wrestle so very hard with.'

Luz looked up at him, startled. He seemed to be stealing into her soul with those sooty eyes that now watched her with a mixture of playfulness and intensity. His continual piquing of her was exasperating but she found it strangely thrilling to have him look at her that way.

'So you think me too proud,' was all she could think of saying. 'And I suppose you are without faults?'

He laced his fingers together and paused. "*If we had no faults of our own, we should not take so much pleasure in noticing those in others.*"

At that, she couldn't help but laugh. 'Mmm, don't tell me … La Rochefoucauld?'

He raised his eyebrows and smiled broadly at her.

Now they sipped their wine, listening to the steady rumble of the waves trapped below in the ankle-deep coves. Its resonance reminded Luz of the slow-rolling thud of a storm-tossed vessel slamming into choppy waters. An all-pervasive smell of iodine and seaweed filled the air.

They were silent, both lost in thought. She took the opportunity of this quiet moment to study Andrés. Looking at him now, he was nothing like Leandro. The shape of their features might be a carbon copy of each other, but there the similarity ended. For a start, their eyes were different, not only in colour but in intensity. Leandro's vibrated with the fire of his wild dreams whereas Andrés' had the calmness of unwavering self-confidence and the caress of a practised womanizer. His whole demeanour was unlike that of the gypsy's: he looked older, rather preoccupied, and had the studied veneer of the sophisticate. She had noticed that he smiled but seldom laughed whole-heartedly; Leandro was full of laughter and cheek, his entire being redolent of merriment, joy and pent-up energy. These two could be brothers, even twins perhaps, but she could not see how …

It would be so simple just to confront Andrés now and ask him outright. Wouldn't it clear up this mystery once and for all? Though how could she ask such a question? 'Andrés, tell me, do you happen to have a gypsy twin who lives in a totally different world to your own, whom you've neglected to mention?' It sounded so ridiculous! Anyhow, the problem of her convoluted emotions at this point meant she was afraid to admit to either of them the existence of the other. It would lead to uncomfortable questions from both men, questions she would rather not face. Luz could imagine Andrés' potential distaste at her confession that she'd had contact with a gypsy, even if she managed to put it casually. No, it was too complicated a situation.

'A penny for your thoughts.' Andrés' voice brought her back to earth with a bump.

'It's a foolish sheep that makes the wolf his confessor,' came her quick answer as she looked him straight in the face, smiling.

He raised one eyebrow and smiled back at her. 'Luz, it saddens me to hear that you see our new partnership in those terms. You, a sheep? You certainly don't strike me as weak, quite the reverse. I think you're an intelligent, strong and high-spirited young woman, very capable of taking care of herself.' He sighed. 'As for me: *un perro que ladra no muerde*, a dog that barks seldom bites.'

She flung back her head and laughed, the crystal-clear peal resounding in the empty night around them. 'You may not bite, *señor*, but you certainly sting.'

Beneath the humour there was undisguised hurt in her voice. His face clouded slightly. He took out a packet of cigarettes and offered her one, which she declined.

'May I?' he enquired. When she nodded, he lit one, inhaled and leant back against the frame of his chair. He appeared to be pondering what to say. 'Luz, we seem to have started out on the wrong footing …' His voice was husky and strained. Something stirred inside her as slowly his eyes met hers. What was it with eyes? she wondered, it was clear they did curious things to her these days.

He smiled a wry, apologetic smile. 'This, I admit, is probably my fault. I was harsh and insensitive over my handling of our contract meeting. I realized it at the time and regret it profoundly.' He sighed heavily. 'That's why I sent you the roses. It was not only to ask your forgiveness for my boorish ways, but also to herald a fresh start to this partnership – and to our friendship. Obviously I also misjudged your feelings at the ball ...' His gaze still held hers. 'I hope we can wipe the slate clean. It's not too late, is it?'

What was she supposed to answer? The caressing promise in his velvet gaze was drawing Luz under. Once again the Andrés de Calderón charm had worked its magic and disarmed her. It was her turn to lean back in her chair, inhaling the heady smells of the sea.

'No, no, of course not, Andrés,' she said softly. 'I've probably been oversensitive ... perhaps over-reacted a little.' In fact Luz wasn't sure any more whether or not she had. She no longer knew what she thought about anything, but the way he was scrutinizing her so intently made strange muscles tighten deep in her belly.

'Friends then?' he asked, the question reflecting in the depths of his eyes as he extended his hand to her.

Luz took a steadying breath. Where had she heard that one before, and not so long ago, too? Leopards never change their spots and she wondered whether there would be more games to come.

'Yes, yes, of course,' she said, conflicting emotions mirrored on her face as she offered her hand to him.

Andrés held it and was about to lift it to his lips but changed his mind midway. Instead, he encircled her wrist with his long fingers.

'Shall we go for a walk on the beach?' he suggested, standing up and coming round to her.

'What, now?' She looked at him in confusion.

'Yes, now,' he said in a low, gentle tone. 'Look at the sky above you. It's such a magical night, why waste it?' His voice was charged with some new, subtle emotion, a softened quality.

Luz turned her face upwards. It was true, the stars shone like floodlights.

'You may want to take those off.'

'Sorry?' Her eyes widened.

'Your shoes,' Andrés murmured. His sensual mouth curved in secret amusement. 'It's a little precarious down there for high heels.'

'Yes, of course, you're right.' For some reason Luz felt her cheeks warm as she slipped off her shoes to stand in bare feet.

He took her hand. The subtle surprise of it made her breathe in suddenly as his warm skin made contact with hers, but she didn't pull her hand away. In his strong, wide palm it felt small to her. The current that raced through Luz made her heartbeat quicken as he guided her down the zigzag steps that led to the breeze-cooled beach. Rather than let go when they reached the bottom of the steps, Andrés kept her hand clasped in his, which took her by surprise.

They walked along the beach in tranquil silence, moving gently beneath a navy-blue canopy patterned with merry stars that winked in the night as though they shared a private joke. The night here was tender. Most of the fishing boats, which had dotted the blue ocean so picturesquely with pinprick lights, had gone. Luz glanced up at him as she carried her shoes, enjoying the sensation of the cool sand between her toes. She was aware of the aggressively male muscled body an inch away from hers. It gave her a sense of security that she had never experienced before.

He looked like Apollyon, his head tilted back a little in haughty disdain and his swarthy profile limned clear-cut against the vaulted backcloth of brilliant darkness: proud and arrogant, belonging to the distinguished physique of a man born to dominate and rule. She was aware of a fluttering stir in her gut, shooting pulses at her nerve-endings that were becoming all too familiar.

The hold on her hand tightened and she was astonished to find that instead of a calming effect, it made her tremble inside. She stiffened slightly and only now did she try to pull away from him. He resisted for an instant before suddenly letting go. After the warmth of his touch, the biting chill of the night on her skin was almost painful. They had come to the end of one section of beach; high rocks separated it from the next.

Andrés turned. His eyes, once dark caverns of mystery, now blazed with a strange light as he looked down at Luz's, which were enormous and anxious. For a split second they were like two people caught up in a tidal wave and lifted out of their depth. They were standing so close, she could sense him catch his breath. She heard her shoes drop on the sand with a soft thud. *He's going to kiss me,* she realized, sudden panic hitting her like a hammer. Luz didn't know why, but she wanted to run away, to have nothing more to do with this man ever again.

She was afraid to hold that burning gaze any longer in case she was lost to herself, but then he smiled, his eyes clouding over again as they became inscrutable. 'Shall we go back?' he said tightly. 'It's late and I don't want to tire you.' He stepped away from her and thrust his hands deep in his pockets.

Luz remained looking up at him for a moment, adrenaline coursing through her blood, leaving her heart stuck in her throat. There was nothing she could find to say as she fought for composure. Something was shifting in her and she didn't know how to stop it. She bent down to retrieve her shoes from the sand and felt his gaze following her darkly as she moved in front of him. Together they started back up the beach towards the house.

*   *   *

Andrés watched Luz drive out of the hacienda. A heavy ache tore at his heart. He had seen the rejection on her upturned face as he had almost kissed her – and the fear. Unwilling to trust himself, almost unable any longer to control the wild emotion that had clamoured for some physical expression, he had forced himself to stop. His mouth had been so close to hers, so soft and full, so sweet … He sighed, a deep harrowing sigh. Sleep would evade him tonight.

Slowly he retraced his steps to the terrace they had just left. He sat under the stars, looking out to sea, listening to the boom and thunder of the waves dashing against the rocks below, a lonely figure in the drowsy cloak of night. Behind pensive eyes, his thoughts ran chaotically as he tried to catch up with them. He felt at a disadvantage, as if the situation he was trying to cope with was already beyond him. His plan was flawed; he had not given it enough thought. It was all clear now, so clear that he could only curse his blindness in not seeing it all before; he must find a way of tipping the scales back.

For years his heart had been closed. Up until now he had led a free and easy life. Of course he'd had liaisons, forgetting them almost as quickly as they began. He had wanted nothing more from life than a good time … until the day he had laid eyes on Luz. Her lively intelligence and spirit were as captivating as her beauty. And now he had the feeling that he had come to a turning point in his life, one from which there would be no return. For the first time his heart had decided its destiny and all he had managed to do was hurt her. The yearning that had swept over him as she walked beside him in her floating black dress, a black-and-gold butterfly, beautiful and fragile, was still with him. To add to the burning in his blood he had noticed the melting look that for a mere second had surged like the rushing blue sea in her glorious eyes. And he knew himself well enough to realize that like a parched man's need for water in the desert, his thirst would not recede until it had been quenched.

*   *   *

As if she were running away from Lucifer himself, Luz drove home in a frenzy of shock and confusion. She could not believe or accept what she had actually felt for a split second down there on the beach. Still, no matter how much she hated to admit it, she had been intensely aroused by Andrés; the physical stir she had experienced at his touch, at his mere proximity, had been no figment of her imagination. She could find no excuse or reason for this, except of course his undeniable resemblance to Leandro. That had to be it, didn't it?

The gypsy still filled her heart despite her determination to fight the emotions she believed were doomed. She had not forgotten Leandro's lively and passionate nature that so intrigued her, or that colourful, mysterious edge he had; and yet he was so direct in his desire for her that it made her senses run rampant. No, her love for the young gypsy could not be dislodged so easily and perhaps that was why she had felt so disturbed by her reaction to the sophisticated hidalgo.

Andrés always seemed to make her play a dark and dangerous game, a struggle for power that both appalled and excited her. She knew he wanted her and his quietly self-assured demeanour should have made her feel safe but she was also aware of something else between them: a psychological undercurrent more potent and reckless. It spoke to something deep inside her and triggered the panic that had struck her on the beach. Now she had no idea how to deal with this new sense of guilt. The situation as it was could not go on.

She was relieved to find the lights off in the annexe when she arrived back home and slipped quietly into her room. Luz lay propped up in bed for a long time, staring ahead of her. Through the open window she could see the dark, colourless water glimmering in the distance under the glow of the moon, streaked with trembling golden lights reflected from the town and the ships in the harbour. Finally she got up and went on to the veranda. The velvet canopy of an ink-like sky hung above; the stars seemed so near to earth that Luz felt if she stretched out her hand she could touch them. She wondered about both Leandro and Andrés. Were they sleeping soundly, oblivious to the chaos they had created?

Lately, there had been times when Luz studied herself in the mirror to see if she was the same young woman who had left England not so long ago. As she had earlier tonight, before she had gone out to meet Andrés. Though she looked no different, maybe a little healthier and tanned, she had changed inwardly. Back in England it had suited her to tether her wilder instincts. Since her arrival in Andalucía, life had now revealed much to her: unsuspected things, feelings, which had probably always lain dormant within her. She was not sure she much liked the confused, wanton new her, but there was nothing she could do about it for she felt helpless against the tide of emotion that rose repeatedly inside her like a flood-surge.

She had three alternatives, she told herself wearily. Firstly, she could leave Spain and go back to England for six months, but that was running away, which was not in her nature. Secondly, she could decide that Leandro was the man for her and fight the world to accept their love; but how could she be sure he even wanted this? After all, he was a gypsy, a nomad, free as the wind, to use his own words. Finally, she could simply leave matters as they stood and try and get a grip, somehow curb her feelings for Leandro and face the situation with Andrés. The latter was surely the most difficult but eminently sensible choice. She would sleep on it; in the morning things might seem clearer.

That night she dreamed again of the Garden of Eden. This time Leandro and Andrés, joined at the shoulder, were playing hide and seek with her through the trees. They were the twins and each wore the Gemini half-mask. Suddenly they seemed to be moving towards her. As they neared, their image gradually merged into one, with the mask covering the whole face until the irises behind it were so close to her, glancing through the leaves, that a green eye and a black one stared with saturnine mockery into the horror of her own.

Luz woke with a hoarse cry, her heart beating hard against her ribs. She sat up, trembling, in haunting semi-darkness. The room was hot and airless; she needed to breathe. She ran out on to the veranda and inhaled deeply.

The air was light and salty. She focused sleepy eyes on the familiar view. Though the moon had not yet quite beaten its retreat, a blood-red dawn streaked across the horizon. The chorus of birds had begun their cheerful calling. A young wind ruffled the surface of the clean-swept ocean and the lighthouse over in Puerto de Santa María still winked steadfastly, its lonely message breaking the monotony at the end of the night.

Luz leant against the balcony, aware of the images from her dream flickering on through her mind, and the turmoil and confusion they reflected. Running away was not the answer. As for her passionate romance with Leandro ... she smiled sadly to herself. Where *was* Leandro? She felt a little like Don Quixote with his naïve and unrealistic quests. What was real and what was illusion? She raised her hands and pressed both knuckles into her eyes, which were now welling up with tears. Nothing and no one had ever had this effect on her; she must not let events overwhelm her so. Her mother would say it was all part of the rich pattern of life. She must get a grip and rise above these problems. They were trivial when compared with some of the dreadful things that happened in the world.

Luz stayed like this for a long time and, as she stood there witnessing the glorious flamboyant colours of the sun rising out of the mist, a certain peace came to her after the rush and emotion of the previous evening. She watched some fishing vessels sail smoothly and slowly through a sapphire sea towards the horizon.

It was still early by the time she shook herself out of her reverie so she went back to bed. Perhaps because she had almost reached the end of thought, Luz fell into a deep, dreamless sleep and a couple of hours later woke feeling heavy-headed.

She had a light breakfast in silence under the steady, scrutinizing dark gaze of Carmela.

'Doña Luz, *la cara es el espejo del alma*, the face is the mirror of the soul and yours is not happy. Come now, you can tell Carmela. Is it a man that makes those pretty eyes so gloomy, eh?'

Luz sighed. 'Am I gloomy? Sorry, Carmela,' she answered. 'I didn't sleep well, but I'm fine otherwise.' Nevertheless, she had caught sight of her reflection in the mirror on the way to breakfast and knew that Carmela would not be fooled. The telltale signs of sleepless nights were there on her face, her eyes shadowed by dark circles left from the tears of frustration that she had given into in the early hours.

'Looks to me as though you're not sleeping for a good reason,' observed Carmela, arching an eyebrow.

'Carmela, there's no *novio* for you to get excited about, I assure you.' Luz managed a wan smile and sipped her coffee. 'Now, I need to get dressed and down to the motorboat as I'm off for the day. A swim will wake me up, I'm sure,' she told the housekeeper, giving her a quick peck on the cheek.

Carmela tried to probe a little further, clearly surmising Luz was up to mischief, and though Luz assured her that all was well and there was no important man in her life, Carmela looked highly sceptical as she packed a basket of food and then waved her out of the door.

Luz sailed to her favourite beach early, long before most bathers were up. The little secret cove, with its fine sand strewn with a multitude of chromatic shells, lay dreaming under a clear and moist blue sky. It was a lovely, isolated spot. She peeled off her outer clothes, under which was her bikini. The sea temperature was fresh as she floated alongside the rocks and there was a certain purity and cleanliness in the air like balm to the spirit. She spent an easy morning turning burnished gold on the white sand, swimming, snorkelling and idly watching the boats as they came and went from Cádiz's harbour. At midday she unrolled her towel next to a large rock and lunched on the melon and delicious *jamón* Ibérico Carmela had provided. She fell asleep in the shade of the rock, her thoughts hazy and her senses suddenly dulled by tiredness, the ceaseless sound of the sea and the drowsy heat of the afternoon.

The sun was still blazing when she woke up, hot and clammy. Her bikini was sticking to her like a second skin and her hair was damp, unpleasant against her nape. She padded across the sun-warmed sand and stood digging her toes deep in the fine ivory-coloured strip, feasting her eyes on the crystal-clear waters lapping at her feet. Golden sunbeams danced on the glasslike surface; it was seductively inviting. Luz looked around her; she was tempted to strip and bathe naked. She had never done so before, but had heard it was the most sensuous experience. Ocean-battered rocks towered a hundred feet above her. This was such a private place that no one would know. Without a second thought, she stripped off her bikini and ran boldly into the sea.

She shuddered with pleasure as her hot skin hit the cold water. The rippling cool envelope that caressed her nakedness felt delicious. With a curious ecstasy that was all new to her, she swam out a little way into the open. She could feel the long hot sunbeams on her back as she went, then, diving down, eyes wide open, she scanned the deep, exploring the spectacular kaleidoscopic undersea world. There were beds of coloured coral and fields of strange grasses, pink and green and lavender, waving in the underwater currents. Baby octopus, tiny crabs and a startling array of variegated fish darted in and out of the rocks, busily going about their business on the highways of sparkling white sand stirred up from the seabed. Life below the surface might be joyously lively, but above the air was sweet and fresh, she thought, slowly bringing her face up again.

Luz turned on to her back and floated like an exotic mermaid playing in the sunshine, her lustrous black hair trailing behind her. In the broad afternoon glare the outline of hills, olive groves and vineyards rising behind the town were visible in the distance and immediately above her, perched high, was the quaint little brown church with its green bench where she had often sat to gaze at the sea, the ships and the port. It seemed so remote, standing sentinel up there on the cliffs.

That is when Luz saw him. He was standing at the top of the cliffs, not far from the church, on a huge grey rock that stretched like a tongue over the sea. Dressed only in Bermuda shorts, his muscled torso bronzed from the sun, he was very still, a hand shielding his eyes, gazing down at her. The empathy between them was such that, in the first moment of seeing the man silhouetted up there against the sky, Luz knew without a shadow of a doubt it was Leandro.

But she did not anticipate what happened next. She watched wide-eyed, holding her breath, her heart beating furiously as the faraway figure sprang into the air and plunged over the cliff. His lean limbs uncoiled slowly in the air, like the wings of a magnificent bird. Arms stretched out in front of him, he dived headfirst, his body a lean, sinewy line, darting like a missile into the depths of the sea.

There was another breathless moment while he disappeared into the blue abyss when Luz waited for him to resurface. And then his head came up in the sunlit spray as he swam towards her with a powerful over-arm stroke. She hurried to meet him, her heart leaping tumultuously in her breast. Both reached the bobbing red buoy a little out of breath. The droplets on Leandro's head glistened like diamonds; his green eyes the limpid colour of peridot. He leant his strongly muscled arms on the anchored float and passed a hand over his face and hair to sweep off the surplus water.

'I was walking along the cliff, hoping you would turn up somewhere. Then I saw you in the water. Even though I couldn't see you clearly, I knew it was you.' He laughed, his gaze travelling over her face.

Luz smiled, flushed with pleasure. 'I knew it was you, too, but I never expected you to launch yourself into the air the way you did. You nearly gave me a heart attack.' Her voice was low and unsteady, due in part to the light glinting off his broad, wet shoulders submerged in the water.

He shrugged, green eyes sparkling. 'I've told you, we're sea gypsies. Besides, we *gitanos* are pretty good acrobats. I've never worked in a circus but I'm sure many of my forbears did. It's in our blood.'

They were treading water, their eyes locked, as if the other was something precious they had lost and found again at a most unexpected moment, in a most unexpected place. All alone, completely closed to the world around them.

'You always appear out of nowhere when I least expect it and then you disappear just as suddenly, like a dream. Sometimes I wonder if you're even real,' she pondered. 'I find it a little unnerving.' Her voice was hesitant, trying to suppress the slight reproach in it.

'You can't hold a gypsy, Doña Luz ... we roam the world freely as the seas and the wind,' he whispered, confounding her with a grin of utter boyish mischievousness.

The current suddenly pulled them together. Their bodies collided. Only then did Luz remember she was bare from head to toe. Leandro shuddered and his eyes flared as he clearly felt her nakedness against him. He let go of the buoy and took her in his arms.

'Do you still doubt that I'm real?' he murmured.

'No, I don't,' she whispered and, despite the cool of the water, heat rushed through her body, pulsating between her thighs. His mouth found hers; his lips were firm, cool and mobile, his kiss deep, passionate and familiar. Luz wrapped her thighs around his hips, feeling the length of his firm arousal. She clung to him; all thought and reason and past resolve evaporating, her skin fluttering beneath his touch, intoxicated by love, by desire and by the sun.

Leandro was now ploughing into the surf with one arm as he held her against him with the other, keeping them both afloat. He swam powerfully towards the shore, striking out with strong strokes, and with vigorous thrusts of his leg muscles.

He carried her, naked and dripping, out of the sea and laid her on the towel she had rolled out on the sand earlier. Though the sun was still warm, she was shivering uncontrollably. Torrents of words rushed to her tongue but were not uttered. He covered her with his hard body, still wet from the sea, and held her tightly in his warmth for a while without moving. At last Luz was where she had longed to be. She was aware of his smooth, tanned skin and beneath it the solid outline of his back and shoulders. His broad chest, with its tantalizing dark hair, was pressed against her naked breasts and his breath grew more ragged. Her heart was pounding loudly, or was it his she could hear? But it was of no importance: nothing mattered but the storm of emotion and the ache inside her crying out for the song of his lovemaking. So he sang.

His mouth was sizzling hot when it came down on hers and she was lost. It seemed to explode into her as he sucked at her lips and her tongue with a primitive, starved ferocity, drinking up her soul. She welcomed his assaulting overture with a wanton fervour that fuelled the already raging flame Luz could sense within him. As though wild for the taste of her, his lips moved from her mouth to her cheek, down to her neck. A sob of raw desire caught in her throat, every part of her pulsating and alive as he continued to seek out her soft vulnerable places, branding them with the fire of his kisses.

The sea appeared to be dancing in the afternoon sunshine.

The tempo of Leandro's lovemaking deepened as his hands joined his lips, a new instrument in the orchestration of foreplay and sensuality. As he explored, Luz's eyes closed, shutting out the world around them, while his palms trailed over her slim curves, bathing her with the heat that radiated from him. Her body opened up to him like a flower in the sunlight, inviting, yielding, relishing this intimate contact as she spiralled smoothly down into a whirlpool of shameless, voluptuous pleasure.

She moaned beneath him as the heat of his body flooded back into her skin and she felt his throbbing hardness press against her, powerful and insistent. The intolerable need to touch him made her dizzy. Luz knew she was inexperienced in this field in which he was master, but let her intuition guide her: a little hesitantly, her fingers trailed feverishly over the muscles of his arms, his shoulders and down the arch of his ribs and his back.

Leandro's athletic frame shook with tension as she found and unfastened the button of his shorts. She helped him slide them off, desperate to feel the strength of his virility against her softness. He groaned as they touched, the contact of skin on skin scorching them both. Flames of passion burst between them as she arched and he pressed, brushing, rubbing, and they moved against each other in perfect unison.

A gust of wind rippled the ocean as the sun's rays played on its surface, making rainbows through the spray that broke on the rocks.

Luz slid her palms across his quivering flesh, feeling his need spiral with every stroke and caress. With her lips she explored the contours of his beautiful body, tasting the salt on his skin. His breathing became laboured, the sounds rasping in his throat. Gaining in confidence, her hands moved lower and her fingers touched him tentatively, softly, marvelling at his sizeable manhood. Staring down into her face, Leandro let out a rough gasp and she watched as a more intense quiver of excitement shot through him; and so the pressure of her fingers became bolder and more intimate, guided by the gratifying feeling of his encouraging response. She had not expected him to react to her touch in this way; the thundering heart against her breast and the fierce arousal that pushed against her were living proof of what she was doing to him and she rejoiced in the pleasure she was giving.

Luz met his penetrating gaze and watched as the colour in his eyes deepened to dark green; they were almost black now. She read a quiet question in them and was suddenly aware he was holding back as he fought to control a need oscillating dangerously on a knife-edge.

Did she want to jump off this wild rollercoaster before it led them into an abyss from which there was no return? Was she prepared to leap into the unknown? Did she want him to be the first? There was probably no future for them together, and it was a gift Luz could only make once. If she had any misgivings, then she must stop him now; he was letting her decide.

But he did not need her to answer: Luz wanted to be his. There was no hesitation and there would be no inhibition either. The response was there, vibrating irrefutably between them. Her body was crying out for his; it was clear in her wildly dilated blue eyes, in the flame that stained her face, in the burgeoning, rosy twin peaks of her small breasts that were taunt and throbbing, and in the tiny bud at the centre of her, all swollen and moist.

Every part of her was waiting, pleading to be stroked and soothed, to be relieved from the ache and the longing deep within her, which only he, Leandro, had the power to fulfil.

The sea, less tranquil now, foamed, splashed and dashed with almost frolicsome delight over the numerous small islets, some of which were no more than big rocks in the sea.

Leandro responded to the potent, erotic invitation of her arousal. '*Mi amor, mi querida amor,*' he murmured, his voice caressing and vibrant with desire, his eyes blazing with his own need. His lips searched hers hungrily, hard and possessive. One hand found the sweet curve of her breasts, while the other found its way to the moist bud between her thighs.

Luz's eyes closed; her mind, her limbs, her soul, her entire being drenched in sensual pleasure ... She had never dreamed of such delicious agony. The more she moaned with ecstasy, the more he explored and caressed until every inch of her flesh was on fire, every nerve in her body was quivering, and every cell in her brain crying out for him to fill the waiting void within her.

The wind had strengthened a little. Now the sea rushed into the deep holes in the rocks with an echoing roar. The trapped water, trying to escape the way it had come in, was met with a slamming, booming impact as the next wave banged and battered its way in.

Leandro paused once more but Luz opened her eyes, feeling his hesitation, and touched his face. Her eyes met his in a silent cry for him as her fingers moved to the back of his head and wound themselves tightly in his hair. It was enough. Leandro slid his hands under Luz and lifted her gently as he parted her thighs, supporting her with his arms. Instinctively she arched towards him, hips pressed against his, craving the feel of him inside her.

Then as she felt his hardness push against the wall of her femininity for a split second her delirious moan was edged with alarm. His driving thrust was like a burning spear as he conquered her and she cried out his name. It was a cry of pain and of passion, of aching need and release. As though in triumph, the gulls perched on the rocks nearby rose in flight and seemed to echo the thin sound.

He froze and raised his head, looking down at her, breathing heavily; his eyes wide with shocked surprise. 'Luz, *mi querida amor*, you're still … I didn't …' he gasped before she stilled his mouth with her fingers.

'It's all right, it's what I want, Leandro. It's you that I want. Now.' She smiled up at him and their eyes locked, enraptured, both still hungry with desire and primal longing. She drew his head back down to her, kissing him deeply. Gradually, the pain subsided and she felt the delicious warmth of him in her centre. She wrapped her thighs around him, hugging his body closer to her, an explicit demand for his force to thrust deeper into her again.

And then they were moving together, rocking to the same rhythm, their enthralled bodies in tune with each other, rising and falling in an erotic feast. It was like trying to hold on to a dream so it would never end. Their whole beings were centred on the waves of exquisite pleasure that raced through them, savouring each precious moment. They were free and wild, a man and a woman joined as one, writhing on the edge of ecstasy in total abandonment.

Release when it came was an explosive thunderclap of liquid fire as they soared together to the pinnacle of ecstasy. Their bodies convulsed feverishly, their minds empty to everything but the heavenly space in which they were floating. After those dizzy heights, they lay clasped together, still panting and trembling, weak, languid and sated with the warm honey of fulfilment; the finale to their beautiful song.

CHAPTER 6

A ship's siren blasted rudely, blotting out all other sounds and bringing them back down to earth. The smudge of smoke from her funnel trailed in soft grey plumage against the sky. Now that the wind had dropped, the air was soft and warm, and filled with the golden, limpid light that always came before dusk.

Leandro's arms still encircled Luz, locking her in his embrace. The heat and the scent of his masculine body wrapped around her. He caressed her with a soothing hand, submerging her with his warmth. As he lifted his head, strands of bleached chestnut hair fell across his face. She pushed them away and he stared down at her, a bleak expression darkening his features.

Luz sat up, covering herself with her towel as he rolled over. 'Are you all right?' she asked, alarmed at his sudden change of mood.

And though he smiled up at her, she thought there was an odd look on his face, as though it was an effort for him to smile. He was so near, yet he seemed so far away. Her mind frantically searched for a reason why shock was now churning in his gaze. She wanted to probe, to find out what he was thinking, and still she remained simply watchful.

Leandro sat up but looked away from her, a muscle in his cheek contracting. He let out a strained breath.

'Do you have any idea what you do to me?' he whispered.

Then, without waiting for Luz's answer, he pulled her against him once more. His arms tightened around her as though he never wanted to let her go and he buried his face in her neck, trembling violently.

Luz didn't know what to think. The only thing clear to her was that he was in distress. Her fingers ran slowly through the strands of his hair, caressing him soothingly as they sat in the sand holding each other.

'I love you,' she murmured, her lips close to his ear.

Leandro lifted his head, his face etched with pain, and his eyes shone as they met her steady gaze. He drew a ragged breath. 'I know,' he said. 'And all I've done to repay you is behave in a blind, selfish way.'

He had not spoken of his love for her but only of his blindness, his selfishness. Luz's romantic haze shifted and pulled apart. As realization started to dawn, an uneasy feeling crept in with it. She forced a smile to her lips. 'Nothing happened today that I didn't want,' she said quietly.

'Maybe, but I had no right to accept such a precious gift,' he whispered as though to himself. 'It was your first time and you chose me. Did I hurt you?' He frowned and touched her cheek lightly with his thumb.

'Everything I felt was wonderful …'

'I didn't realize … If only I'd known, I would never have allowed myself to touch you.'

She looked at him intently. 'Someone once told me there is no shield from the forces of destiny,' she murmured, repeating the words he had said to her at the masked ball. Whatever he was trying to say to her now, she didn't care to hear. 'We both wanted this. It was boiling inside us from the first moment we laid eyes on each other. Isn't that what you told me not so long ago?'

'Still, I shouldn't have ... It shouldn't have happened, not now ... not like this,' he repeated dully and pulled away, sitting with his forearms resting on his knees.

Luz drew a long, shaky breath. 'In what other way would you have had it? Leandro, this was an incredible, spontaneous explosion of love. Nothing could have stopped it.' She knelt back on her heels. Her body was still burning from his lovemaking but now her mind was filling with cool, quiet dread. Surely she had not been the only one to feel how perfect it had been?

He stared at her for a moment. 'I've defiled your innocence. Can't you see, Luz? I took advantage of you.' His tone had become brisk as he passed a weary hand over his brow.

'How can you have taken advantage of me if I was willing?' she asked softly.

Leandro let out a mocking, self-deprecating laugh that sounded more like a cry of despair. '*Madre de Dios!* Because I'm a gypsy bastard!'

Under the red glow of the setting sun, the whiplash of his words echoed eerily on the lonely beach. His eyes moved over her, wild and intense; the fire in them scorched her skin. For a split second she thought he was going to say something more, but he turned his face away again and the moment was gone.

Luz felt the struggle in him, just as it was in her. All she'd ever wanted was here beside her, his coppery skin glowing under the softening light of the day, but his eyes were too angry and remote for her to reach him. His bitterness stunned her and she wanted to understand what was beneath it. Gypsy or hidalgo, she would have taken him, but a mist of confusion rolled in with his reaction and strangled her throat. She raised an unsteady hand towards his arm, wanting to silently convey the love she felt for him, and then let it fall back on to the sand. His body language indicated all he wanted now was distance from her.

A golden light from the dying sun spread like a paling sheet on the washed sky. Without touching, each one lost in thought, they watched a liner move forward slowly, doggedly, into the great expanse of the sea.

When he spoke again, his voice was slightly raw. 'For what it's worth, Luz, I've never felt this way about a woman … but we must both forget what has happened today. I will disappear from your life.'

'For what it's worth …' she repeated. What was all this worth to him, she wondered? Could he not see how much it meant to *her*? And how could either of them forget what had happened? Wild-eyed, Luz raised a hand to her forehead, trying to stop the dizzying thoughts that left her reeling from such a blow.

Had she weaved romantic notions around herself and him without even realizing it? What a sentimental fool she'd been. All along he had known that she was in love with him and still he chose to push her away.

'So, you're disappearing again.'

'Luz …' Leandro's green irises gleamed fiercely as he gazed into hers, and his palm reached out to touch her cheek. She flinched, evading it, and swallowed a lump of hysteria.

'Don't pull back from me, Luz,' he whispered.

She cursed herself as her heart went out to him, even though her body seemed to freeze.

'I've just given you the most precious thing that a woman can give to a man and you announce that we mustn't see each other again. And you expect me not to pull back from you?'

Leandro stared at her, compelling her to look at him. She tried to remain rigidly composed but she was melting inside, knowing there was nowhere for her to hide for he could read in her deep-blue eyes the passion, desire and need that reflected his own. She was swimming against the current; once more he was in control. The hand that had been gently cupping her face now closed possessively around it. Leandro focused intently on her features as if to etch them on his mind. Then he drew back, his breathing unsteady.

Dusk spread slowly across the sky. Luz stared silently at him. The inevitable truth cut through her like a knife to the stomach and left her bleeding: Leandro was leaving her and she had to let him go. Her eyes turned to skim the surface of the ocean but she found no refuge in the beauty of the dark, sparkling depths that usually moved her at this hour. So this was how things were done in his world. Love was cast like a spell, potent and fierce, and then longing and love thrown aside, broken.

It was not yet night. The evening was startlingly clear; an early single star gazed down at them, twinkling brightly in the darkening sky. The briny tang of seaweed was carried on the fresh breeze now whipping up. In the silence the only sounds were of the lapping of water against the motorboat, which Luz had moored close by, and the gentle swish of the sea breaking over the low rocks.

It was turning cold. They rose as though by common consent and put on their clothes. There was nothing more to be said. Slowly they paced side by side to the boat in bemused silence, without a backward glance. Luz stared straight ahead of her, close to tears. She was making a determined effort to forget that for a few precious moments they had nestled in each other's arms and had loved one another in a rapturous communion of body and soul.

When they climbed into the boat, she turned and caught in the gathering darkness an urgent questioning in Leandro's look that matched the confusion in her heart. But what point was there in raking over what had already been said? Throughout the twenty-minute journey back she could feel his eyes on her but, even if she had looked up at him, she would not have seen him through the mist clouding her vision.

Leandro was the first to get out of the boat. He held out his hand to help her but Luz chose not to see it, convinced now that if she valued her own peace of mind, she must never have anything to do with the gypsy again.

'Will you not let me help you, Luz?'

'I don't need help. I can manage on my own, thank you.'

The air between them, usually crackling with a powerful charge, was now thick with unexpressed emotion but neither could manage any more words. Luz caught something unfathomable in Leandro's gaze before he turned away from her and her heart gave one final lurch before she ordered it to be still.

She must walk away without a backward look, but she did look back and watched him go with an unbearable sense of loss, her eyes following him as he disappeared over the dunes. Part of her mind taunted her: he'd had her, enjoyed her and now he was moving on. The shock and disbelief were such that it gave way to nothing but a strange emptiness deep inside her. The real hurt would come afterwards.

*   *   *

A short time later, as evening faded into night, Leandro lay back on the soft dunes among cactuses and wild shrubs watching the old lighthouse come alive. In Cádiz, the cobalt-blue sky always darkened and thickened in the couple of hours before nightfall. Shadows devoured him, bruising his soul, while he marvelled at how the evening's slow descent matched his own. Under the ever-changing skyscape, high above the sea, a sweep of glorious coastline dimmed as it unfolded.

He looked on as the last ferry of the day plied its way into Cádiz Harbour. A small crowd of travellers had gathered at the port's terminal gate, waiting to embark. Here was the leisure of enforced patience, for nothing would hasten the arrival of the multi-storey boat. It docked and discharged its passengers before reloading. As darkness settled, the ramp was raised and the ferry gradually vanished into the night. It was more satisfying to watch it go, he decided. He was not a patient man.

As the balmy breeze caressed him, he contemplated the obvious: the texture of the sand, the bands of iridescence where waves ran up the beach, the sea sparkling like diamonds under a silver half-moon. Memories of Luz floated through his mind to keep him company. It was not the burn of passion that stirred him now but an emotion that was tender and cherishing.

As they had walked in silence back to the boat, he had wanted to ask her again if she was all right, but he sensed with that rare intuition so unique to lovers that she had withdrawn from him. Though it had cost him dearly, he had forced himself to lie to her and now he must keep his distance. That he had claimed her virginity still resounded like a shockwave through him; he'd taken it for granted that, like most liberal Englishwomen of her age, she'd already had physical experience of men. What a fool, he should have known better – there was a purity to Luz's beauty that shone like the evening star on a clear Andalucían night. He'd read the challenging question in her eyes, the confusion and hurt as they'd climbed into the boat. There were so many ways in which he'd been a fool, but there was also so much he had to unravel before he could answer her with the truth.

The craving to touch her had been overwhelming and yet he had not done so, afraid he would be unable to quench the strong flames of desire still blazing through him like an uncontrollable fire. Covertly, his eyes had dwelt on her soft, satiny skin and the purity of her profile: how fresh she had looked, and so utterly defenceless. His heart aching, he thought wildly, *ti adoro querida, perdóname, forgive me, Luz.* He had stared at her continuously until they arrived at the shore and it was all he could do to stop himself from taking her in his arms, clasping her close to him, never to let her go. But the reality was not that simple. When he came to think of it, life for a long time had been anything but simple. '*You can't escape who you are.*' Isn't that what his uncle had told him?

Leandro settled back in the dunes. In the distance the old lighthouse threw its steady beam out into the night. Gradually a deep understanding came to him, so overpowering in its strength that he sensed it almost physically – a kind of ecstatic pain, so much easier to bear than the pangs of guilt that had gnawed away at him for weeks. He could see light at the end of the tunnel.

The secret fires slumbering in Leandro's heart burst into flames and he knew that things could not continue as they were any longer. It would take decisiveness, determination and courage to deal with the situation – a certain amount of tact, too – but he couldn't see any alternative. He must take the bull by the horns and act. What he was about to do would threaten his very existence as a *gitano*, dishonour the ways of his people perhaps, and offend their sense of justice. Yet he had his own sense of *lachirí* and he could no longer bear this battle within himself, even if it pitted him against his own kind and made an enemy of them, even if he had to die to do it. He would carry his war right into that enemy's camp and meet whatever challenge awaited him, whatever fate would now be his. But his adversary was like a wild animal when crossed. He had to do this without awakening the creature's wrath, which would be fierce and unforgiving.

He thought again of his life: of the world of the *gitanos*, these people who lived by implacable, harsh rules but who were part of him; of his mother, consumed by a slow illness that would eventually kill her. She could be a passionate, vindictive woman to others – *Il Diabólica* – terrible and ruthless in her fury, but also the most loving and caring person when it came to him, her beloved eldest son.

He thought of Luz, and her eyes, which, as they met his for a fleeting second on the boat, had held that odd look of both defiance and despair in their dark-blue depths. He had hurt her, of this he was in no doubt, but still he hoped that he had not lost her.

His whole life's happiness was at stake and that was the only truth of which he was sure. Oh, he knew all about the gypsies' deep-rooted horror of marriages between *gitano* and *gajo*, and this case was so much more complicated. Sacrifices would have to be made. No, it would not be easy. Still, he was a great believer in the saying: 'Nothing in life worth having is easy.' But at all costs, for now, he must distance himself from the one thing he wanted most dearly; he could see no other way.

*   *   *

Luz was still in stunned shock when she got back to L'Estrella. Drained of all emotion and completely worn out, her heart felt like a lump of lead in her chest. In no mood to eat anything, she undressed by moonlight, not bothering even to turn on her bedside lamp. She padded barefoot across the rattan matting to the open window and spent the next few hours on the veranda staring bleakly into the night. Odd nebulous thoughts drifted across her mind, going round in convoluted circles until she felt her brain would explode.

She had forced herself not to weep on that miserable trip back to the harbour with Leandro. But tears of hurt and frustration flowed now, streaming down her face as she looked up at the ivory curve of the moon. Maybe he was looking at it too, wherever he was. How could so much change in the space of one afternoon? It had been a wonderful dream, which then turned into a nightmare.

She closed her eyes and hugged herself, aching for the feel of him. Her body felt cold and lifeless after the radiating warmth of his skin and his touch. She longed for him and tried desperately not to think about her heart breaking.

Luz's feelings switched from one extreme to the other as her mind impulsively picked over everything that had happened since she first laid eyes on the gypsy. Stray images flitted before her vision like a film reel. She remembered the day she had seen him on the path down to the beach and how, despite her initial wariness, she was helplessly stirred by his audacious, compelling gaze; how much incitement she had seen in those wild green eyes. And then at the horse fair, how provocatively he had looked at her, even from a distance, stoking the flames already lit within her. No man had ever affected her in this way. Her spirit soared when she recalled his burning kisses at the masked ball, the electric skin-to-skin contact, and then the ecstasy they had shared just a few hours earlier, only to plummet in the same breath as she relived the agony of his subsequent rejection and accepted the reality of her short-lived idyll.

The truth of the matter was that gypsies and *gajos* did not mix well; and the sooner she accepted this cruel fact, the quicker she would be able to get on with her life. Luz buried her face in her hands and sobbed. An owl hooted as if to second her grief and commiserate, but it had no answers. However much life without Leandro seemed inconceivable, it was inevitable: as a couple they would be outcasts. The gypsies' contempt for *gajos* was no secret, nor did she doubt her parents' reaction if she were to come home with a Romany *chalán* in tow. Still, something inside her rebelled. Luz hated the world she lived in and refused to be defeated by its bias and bigotry. She swept her tears away with the back of her hand. Even if this special dream of her life was doomed to go the way of all dreams, she would not let that happen, she vowed: true love would prevail.

True love, was that what it was? Leandro had never really told her he loved her. At the end of the day he was a *gitano*, a free spirit. If she were truly honest, what might be real love to her could be construed as real lust as far as he was concerned. Yes, what she had taken for love at first sight had actually been a more primitive need for sex. He had simply been displaying his knowledge of the female body and his art in her arousal. Both times he had taken her by surprise, first at the ball and now on the beach, overwhelming her with his passion and blatant virility. She had not just welcomed his lovemaking, she had offered herself to each thrust of his demand, revelling in each stage of his wild possession, yearning to belong to him, body and soul forever. Her heart was full of him, bursting with an emotion she was *sure* was love ... or was it just hormones spinning out of control?

At that thought, she felt belittled and ashamed of herself. It was no good, she had to get him out of her mind, to quash this physical attraction not only burning her body but also threatening her sanity. She must snap out of it and smother the romantic core in her heart that wept for him. It was just a schoolgirl infatuation, she remonstrated.

Luz stared up at the moon again. Her imagination told her it was hinting at something; suddenly, the half-sphere in profile reminded her a little of Andrés' cryptic mask at the ball. Come to think of it now, there had been something a little unnerving about his disguise. She shivered. It disturbed her that Andrés had come unbidden into her mind when her heart was in turmoil over Leandro.

Finally, she went to bed, physically and mentally exhausted. She was met with unrest, tossing and turning as the recurrent nightmare of Leandro and Andrés in the Garden of Eden assailed her each time she closed her eyes. This time it was so much more erotic and explicit than any dream she'd ever had and she was shocked at the wantonness of her fantasies.

*   *   *

When Luz woke the next day, thoughts of Leandro were still spinning around in her head. Pushing back the covers, she sat up. She made a concerted effort to get out of bed and then shower and dress, refusing to give in to the depression and lethargy that were weighing her down like a heavy mist.

Work was the answer, she decided. She would find solace there. Research for the Eduardo de Salazar biography was taxing and she knew it would take up most of her time and all of her energy. It would stop her from indulging in daydreaming and self-pity. So she threw herself wholeheartedly into gathering notes, pictures, articles and any other material she could get her hands on, all the while under the watchful and concerned gaze of Carmela. The days slipped quietly from one week into the next, except when unwelcome thoughts intruded on her peace, which was more often than she liked.

Leandro, as expected, remained elusive as the proverbial pimpernel. As much as it pained her deep down, true to his word he had not pursued her, but Luz did not go looking for him either.

Andrés had rung l'Estrella just as she had come in from the beach after a particularly vigorous ride on Zeyna to clear her mind. It was the first time they had spoken since she had walked hand-in-hand with him on the sand that night at Puesta de Sol, when they had parted with that strange charge between them that she so wanted to ignore.

'Luz, I have to go away on business tomorrow.' Hearing his strong, caramel voice again had given her that uncomfortable familiar reaction deep in her stomach. He sounded almost apologetic and she wondered what expression was in those mysterious dark eyes at that moment. Perhaps he regretted the intimacy they had shared and was deliberately going away to avoid her. *Well, that made two of them.*

'Really? Are you going far?' Why had she asked that? Not that she cared where he went and, in any case, she was relieved she wouldn't see him for a while.

'No, not far. I'll be gone for a few weeks, though,' He paused as if not knowing what to say, which Luz found surprising. 'I just wanted to know how you're getting on with the book.'

'Things are progressing very well, thank you.'

'And you don't need anything else from me? You'll be all right while I'm gone?' His tone was soft, concerned even.

'Yes, of course. In any case, I need to build up my notes more before we speak again.'

'Luz ... I ...' Andrés paused again and something in his voice made her fervently hope he would not ask to meet up before his departure.

'Yes, Andrés?' She almost snapped the words, irritated he was saying nothing and inexplicably annoyed that he would be gone for so long. Suddenly she wanted the conversation to be over so that she wouldn't have to think about him, or the way he might have looked at her right then had they been face to face.

'Nothing. I look forward to seeing you when I'm back, I'm sure we'll have much to talk about by then.' She had waited for his customary note of amused arrogance to surface, when she would visualize the devilish gleam in his eyes, but he seemed strangely subdued. This false-footed her, somehow, and she swiftly closed the conversation.

'I'm sure we will. Goodbye, Andrés.' She hung up the phone with some relief but couldn't understand why the conversation had left her restless and thrown off balance.

A good part of a month had elapsed by now. Luz had gone back to El Pavón a couple of times. Both her parents had sensed that there was something untoward going on in their daughter's life. They had tried to quiz her discreetly but were met with a brick wall. Since her return from England Luz had lost touch with the few Spanish friends she had, fully absorbed as she had been in her personal life and work on the biography. Salvador and Alexandra encouraged her to reacquaint herself with her local social circle and get out of the rut she was in. Luz began to accompany her parents to parties at the haciendas of their friends near El Pavón and, when she took trips into Jerez, she would meet the people she knew there for tapas, even shopping jaunts – something she did not ordinarily enjoy much but now welcomed as a distraction.

Slowly the wound that had been painfully raw was beginning to heal, but fate had other plans for Luz. It came in the form of an invitation from Carlos Alvarez, the brother of her friend Alba, who had a house in Pamplona in the Navarre region, to watch the town's Festival of San Fermin and the *Encierro*, the Running of the Bulls.

It had been on her mind to take a break and visit parts of Spain still unknown to her, and she hadn't seen Alba, her closest friend in Spain, since she had returned. So when Alba rang to suggest they attended the *Sanfermines*, Luz welcomed this offer wholeheartedly, although it meant she would have to interrupt her work for a week as Navarre was a long distance from Andalucía in the north of Spain and the fiesta would go on for a whole seven days.

In all Luz's visits back to her country, she had never been to the Pamplona bull-running festival and although bullfighting was not to her taste, the renowned *Encierro* was the centre of an exciting celebration where the whole town took to the streets in a colourful riot of music, dancing, eating and drinking that enveloped the place in a joyous party atmosphere. It would do her soul good to be among such high spirits, she decided.

'Luz, I'm so glad you're coming to stay!' Alba squeaked excitedly to her friend down the phone. Still living at home with her parents, Alba found every chance to stay with her brother in Pamplona and having Luz to herself for a week to swap news and hear about life in England while enjoying the fiesta was clearly a delightful arrangement in every way. 'It's been such a long time. We have so much to catch up on. But are you sure it won't get in the way of your work?'

'I'm sure, Alba, don't worry. Besides, I could really do with a break.'

Luz thought of Andrés and their conversation earlier. He would be away for a few weeks, enough time for her to catch up with her notes.

'Excellent! Carlos and I will pick you up from the station the day after tomorrow at lunchtime. We'll have a wonderful week.'

*   *   *

The sound of bands playing everywhere was the first thing Luz woke up to on the day of the *Encierro* in Pamplona. She rushed to the window. Dawn, pale, warm and sweet, was lighting the white streets. She could see it would be a brilliant gold and blue morning of sunshine and cloudless sky. It had rained a little during the night and the air was fresh and cool. Any strange, troubled thoughts still lingering in her mind evaporated as her eyes took in the scene on the street. Despite the early hour, the town was heaving with enthusiasts heading towards the bullring to await the arrival of the young men racing ahead of the bulls from their corrals.

Luz had been on edge for so long and now felt calmer than she had in weeks. It was good to be away from Cádiz and El Pavón, which were full of memories she longed to forget. As soon as Alba and Carlos had met her at the station in Pamplona, and hugs and animated greetings had been exchanged between the three of them, she could feel herself relax.

Carlos had given her such a bear-hug that her feet had left the ground and Luz thought her bones might crunch, so she couldn't help but giggle as he eventually put her down. He had a round, rather boyish face, framed by unruly curly brown hair that made him look even more appealingly cherubic. She didn't know him that well, certainly not as well as his sister, Alba, but she liked him and his easy, friendly manner always made her feel welcome whenever they met. Alba had lighter, almost blonde hair and a pretty, heart-shaped face that although not beautiful, was made more attractive by her lively and expressive brown eyes, which had been wide with excitement at Luz's arrival at the station.

Carlos, a banker who lived on his own, had a large, comfortable bachelor flat in the heart of the city. Luz had been given a lovely room that was light and airy, next door to Alba's. She washed and dressed swiftly, eager to be part of the buzz and excitement that were growing by the minute outside. Pulling on jeans and a close-fitting sleeveless black T-shirt, she fastened a silky red scarf around her slim neck, all of which accentuated her golden tan and shapely figure. She quickly tied her hair back in a ponytail and went to see if her friends were up and about.

When she hit the street half an hour later with Carlos and Alba, there was already a great atmosphere of anticipation about the place, even though it was still only six o'clock in the morning. Balconies, the tops of buildings and every bit of spare ground were solid with clusters of people. The romantic sound of oboes coupled with the dull pounding of drums gave a haunting effect to the notes that echoed through the town. Wooden and iron barricades had been erected along the pavements and through the heart of the city to block off side streets so the bulls could not stray during the length of the run. There were gaps in some parts of the fences, narrow enough to block an animal but sufficiently wide for a person to slip through.

The three of them walked down to Plaza Santo Domingo, following the throng who had donned the traditional costume of the festival, consisting of white trousers, red sashes and neckerchiefs. A stone's throw away, the runners waited for the rockets to go off. On the way to the square, Luz bought a couple of postcards to send to her parents and Carmela.

'*Siñorinas*, I think it's time for something to eat, don't you? I know just the place,' suggested Carlos, his face breaking into an enthusiastic grin. Alba's brother loved his food and already Luz had enjoyed a delicious plate of tapas the night before that he had cooked himself. They stopped at a café, well known to him, and ordered a quick breakfast of warm golden *churros* and thick hot chocolate flavoured with cinnamon and topped with whipped cream. The place was full of smoke, some customers already singing and downing beers. A carefree festive atmosphere was king. Outside, the course was being swept and carefully looked over by the authorities. The whole town was now awake and humming.

They had managed to get a table at the front of the café, where the friendly owner had reserved some spaces at the edge of the pavement with a good view of the runners and the start of the *encierro*. At eight o'clock the whole spectacle would explode into life when the first rocket was let off to alert the town that the gates had been opened and the bulls released.

Suddenly, at five to eight, the runners started their chant, raising their rolled newspapers, which would be used to draw the bulls' attention from them should the need arise. The words were a prayer to the statue of San Fermin, taken from an engraving in a niche in a wall of the Cuesta de Santo Domingo asking for the saint's protection during the run.

By this time the sun had come out and the early-morning mists had dissipated. At three minutes to eight, the runners repeated their chant. The street was now lined on both sides with spectators closely pressed against each other and most shops were shuttered. The three friends joined the crowds on the pavement, jostling their way through the throng to find a place next to each other at the front of one of the barricades. Luz could feel the air about her vibrating with tense, mounting expectation amid the hubbub of the multitude. With one minute to go, the chant went up again, louder this time; and then a few seconds of hush fell over the crowd …

The clock of the Church of San Fermin struck eight and the first rocket was set off. It flew into the air and the explosion was met with a great roar from the masses. Suddenly a red-and-white mob, the *mansos*, came swarming down the street, whizzing by at tremendous speed.

Just as the next batch of runners appeared and the second rocket exploded, an over-enthusiastic photographer pushed his way between Carlos and Luz, propelling her against the barricade as he shoved his way to the front. She grasped the barrier to prevent herself falling and was almost pitched forward over it, pushed by the crowds. Luz struggled to straighten, raising her eyes as she did so.

Her heart lurched uncontrollably as she glimpsed Leandro. He was running at the edge of the route, a little apart from the others, looking down, completely engrossed in the race. Without seeing her, he brushed past. Behind him came the bulls and the sweep-up bullocks, slower and smaller, pounding at full speed, formidable thundering beasts tossing their heads up and down, the echo of their heavy hoofs resounding on the cobbled street as they pressed on. Close on their heels came the *pastores*, the bull herders, armed with long sticks to keep the herd in check.

Luz jumped back, breathing raggedly, her eyes dazed and incredulous, legs trembling. It was as if a volt of electricity had been injected right into her veins. How could it be? What was Leandro doing here, miles away from Cádiz?

'Are you all right?' enquired Alba, her face intent with concern. 'You look as if you've seen a ghost.' But Luz was not listening.

Another wave of *mansos* passed, their red sashes flying. Before her friends could stop her, Luz pushed through one of the gaps in the barricades and was off. Her heart was hammering in her ribcage as she tore down the street with the rest of the crowd who were headed for the arena, their final destination half a mile away. Buzzing with adrenaline, she ran at a steady pace, oblivious to the pushing and shoving and the extreme danger she was putting herself in, ignoring the din of the crowd urging them on, yelling: '*Ahí va! Ahí va!*' She had only one thought in her mind: Leandro. If someone had asked her what she hoped to achieve once she had caught up with him, she would have been incapable of answering. The shock of seeing him had made her act on sheer impulse.

At the Plaza del Ayuntamiento, following the mob, Luz turned left into Calles Mercaderes. The third rocket went off as she reached the crossing, signalling the bulls had entered the arena. She squeezed through to the strait, pushing slightly uphill and along La Calle Estafeta alongside hordes of others, then right again in front of the telephone exchange. Now, at last, she dived into the narrow passageway leading to their final destination. Just as she erupted into the sunshine-bathed bullring, the fourth firecracker exploded, indicating the bulls were in the pens. The run had ended.

Here, the colourful human sea, the deafening music and the handful of loose calves capering around for the amusement of the crowd created total mayhem. Luz stood for a moment, looking around in a daze, not quite grasping what she was doing there.

Suddenly, strong arms pushed her behind the safety barriers lining the ring and Leandro swept her off her feet, carrying her up to the stand and out of danger. He was received with hurrahs of approval and great slaps on the back, and a drink was shoved into his hand. But he was distracted: his attention claimed by Luz.

'What in God's name did you think you were doing, you stupid girl?' he growled in his strong *Caló* accent, glittering green eyes boring into hers with a terrifying air of menace. 'Do I need this to torture my conscience and add to my remorse?' His hands were clasping the side of her arms now, pulling her slightly towards him. She thought he was going to shake her, but instead he tossed his head and swore under his breath.

Shock finally took over and Luz swallowed painfully. 'I saw you … in the crowd of runners … so I …'

A flame flickered in his translucent green eyes as they narrowed dangerously. 'And so you what?' he snapped. 'Do you realize what could have happened to you out there?' He glared at her, his hands still gripping her arms. 'The *Encierro* is not a *game*, people get gored by the bulls every year.' he rasped before releasing her and turning away in disgust.

Luz was trembling now, partly because Leandro was standing there in front of her, so obviously caring violently for her safety, but also because she realized what a fool she had been. He was right: she could have been badly hurt.

'I'm sorry,' she whispered shakily, longing to throw herself into his arms, every nerve in her body in a reckless burst of wanting. She could see his gypsy blood was still boiling, though; his whole demeanour reminded her of a wild animal in fury. No, she would not be kissed by him today, or any other day, she thought with a heavy heart.

'I need to get back,' she said suddenly. 'My friends must be worried.'

He scowled. 'Where are your friends? And what were they doing, letting you behave like a halfwit?'

'They're outside a small café on Calle Santo Domingo. I can't recall its name now,' she admitted sheepishly.

He pondered a moment. 'I will accompany you half way,' he declared finally. 'Will you know how to get back to your friends? What if they've moved on?'

'Don't worry, I know where the café is. They won't have gone anywhere. Some of Carlos's friends are supposed to be joining us after the run.' She let out a breath. 'Thank you, Leandro, you mustn't worry about me. I am an adult, you know.' At this point she had the sense to look contrite as she met his fiercely unwavering gaze. 'I admit I acted stupidly, I realize that now. I'm really sorry.' Her deep-blue eyes looked up at him dejectedly.

'You scared me half to death … when I saw you standing there … looking so lost.' His voice was husky and a little shaky. She sensed the undertones of tenderness, registered the emotion in his eyes, and a wild hope surged in her. As she opened her mouth to say something he stiffened and pressed two fingers against her lips.

'Shush,' he murmured, 'it's no use. It would never work. The mountain between us is unscalable. Trust me, this way is the best. Come on, let's go. Your friends will be looking for you.'

His fingers were warm and she thought she would melt under their touch. She looked up at him again, silently pleading, and met with his impassive features. Then she turned away so he could not see the tears stinging her eyes.

Pushing through the crowds, they made their way out of the bullring. Once or twice, Luz was painfully aware of his strong hand in the small of her back, steering her, and the thrill of it flooded her whole body. Caught up in the crowds again, they reached the Plaza del Ayuntamiento once more and she felt his hand brush against hers. She turned around but before she could say anything, Leandro's figure disappeared into the sea of people. Once again, desperation and frustration coursed through her. Would she ever see him again?

Carlos and Alba were still at the café when Luz got there. They were sitting at a large table with a number of young men and women who had joined them. The room buzzed with sound. They greeted her with enthusiastic shouts.

'Luz, *de aquí!*, over here! We've been worried about you. What happened? Come and have a drink, you look like you need it.'

Alba poured a glass of wine while Carlos stood to let Luz through, pulling out a chair for her as he did so.

A wave of self-consciousness swept over Luz as she took her place at the table. Introductions were made and Carlos called a waiter to bring more drinks. To her relief, no one seemed very interested as to why she had gone off. Her friends had obviously been drinking solidly since the end of the run and although she herself had never been very fond of alcohol, she was feeling so dispirited that it seemed a very good idea. She swiftly drank a chilled glass of sangria and Carlos refilled it from the jug. Now, at last, she was beginning to relax and get into the spirit of the fiesta.

The moment didn't last long, though, before she was aware of a great noise and commotion behind her. She turned in her chair to watch a crowd of people invading the café, singing loudly and dancing a conga, pushing their way through the throng to the table next to theirs. Luz recognized Lorenzo Herrera and his sister Adalia among the revellers and she gave an inward sigh, immediately on her mettle.

The short-haired brunette sitting next to Luz, who had introduced herself as Doña Lilliana Cortés, nudged her.

'Do you know who that is?' Her eyes were glittering as she trained her sights on the handsome blond young man. 'Lorenzo Herrera, the great *matador*. He's going to be bullfighting this week. Have you ever seen him in the arena? He's a god!'

'I've met him briefly,' Luz told her with a fixed smile. At this the young woman was beside herself with excitement. 'Oh, you're so lucky! Will you take me to meet him?' She pushed her chair back and stood up, not waiting for Luz to answer.

'Hey, wait a minute,' Luz said, alarmed. 'We were introduced *en passant* some time ago. I doubt he remembers me. Besides, I'm not used to barging uninvited into a party.'

'Oh, come on, don't be a wet blanket. He has millions of fans, I'm sure he wouldn't mind,' said the other woman with a pout.

Luz was spared the unpleasantness of an argument when Doña Lilliana suddenly sat down again: Lorenzo Herrera was coming towards their table. He stopped a few paces from Luz as Carlos rose from his chair to greet him. 'Carlos, *amigo*, how are you?' she heard him say. She half looked the other way and pretended to be engrossed in the conversation at the other end of the table. 'It's been a long time!' Carlos's face was beaming and the two men embraced.

'Yes, much too long,' Carlos agreed, slapping the *torero* affectionately on the back. 'I'm told that you've practically retired from bullfighting. Is it true that you've become a respected businessman?'

'To a certain extent, but I still take part in quite a few *corridas*. With me, as you know, it's a passion inherited from my dear *Papá*, may God rest his soul.'

'Yes, yes, of course. He was the best,' Carlos nodded solemnly. 'So where is Adalia? I thought I saw you come in with her.'

'Oh, doing what Adalia does best, flitting about and being charming with someone, no doubt. I think she spotted some other friends as we arrived.'

'That sister of yours can charm the birds from the trees.' Carlos grinned and took a gulp of his sangria. 'So what brings you to our part of the world?'

'You forget, my dear friend, that my mother is half from Castile and half from Navarre. We have a house here.'

Carlos laughed. 'Ah, yes, that is where you get your wonderful pale complexion and those large blue eyes that make all the ladies swoon when you enter the arena.' He nudged him playfully. 'Not like the rest of us mortal Spanish men.'

'You exaggerate, *amigo*.' Lorenzo laughed, obviously delighted by his friend's little crack. 'Anyhow, I have never taken part in a *corrida* in Pamplona, so I thought I'd give it a go this year.'

'An excellent idea. When is it happening?'

'It's scheduled for the last day of the fiesta. I'll take part in the running in the morning and the *corrida* in the afternoon.'

'Well, I for one wouldn't miss it for the world, and nor would Alba. We also have her friend staying, Doña Luz de Rueda. If she's still here, she'd love to come, too, I'm sure.'

Luz took a sip of her sangria, slanting a look at the two men. *I will be gone by then*, she thought. She had never enjoyed *corridas*. In that regard she was definitely not Spanish.

Lorenzo's pale brows knitted together. 'Doña Luz de Rueda, you said?' He shook his head, perplexed. 'I seem to recall that name.'

'She's sitting right opposite Alba at the table,' Carlos told him.

Lorenzo turned and glanced over. Luz looked the other way. The last thing she wanted was for him to realize that she had been eavesdropping. She hoped he wouldn't come over to introduce himself. Although Lorenzo had said nothing at their first meeting, she remembered the way his eyes had looked her up and down; she didn't feel he was someone whose attentions she wanted to encourage.

'Yes, yes, I remember now,' she heard him reply warmly. 'I met her very briefly a couple of months ago at my business partner's offices in Cádiz. Yes, of course. Doña Luz de Rueda, a most arresting young lady. A real beauty.' He seemed to be hesitating, a question hovering on the tip of his tongue.

Carlos, too, paused and then the smile was audible in his voice. 'She is a good friend of my sister's and an acquaintance of mine. Does that give you the answer you were looking for?'

'May I pay my respects?'

'Even if I had any designs on her myself, with you as a rival what chance would I have?' Carlos laughed teasingly and gave his friend another slap on the back. 'Go ahead, *amigo*. I'm sure she'll be flattered.'

Luz stiffened as she saw the young *torero* turn again to look at her. Carlos might be an old friend of the bullfighter but did he really think she'd be interested in such an obviously pompous and self-regarding young man?

'You are very kind, *amigo*. I'm having a few friends over to dinner at La Fortaleza on the thirteenth, the night before my *corrida*, to mark the end of the festival. I hope you'll all be able to come,' said Lorenzo.

Carlos beamed. 'I've been to your parties before, my friend, and I wouldn't miss one for the world.'

'*Espléndido!* Nine o'clock. I'll send you three invitations.'

Before Lorenzo could make his way over to Luz, a group of adoring fans gathered around the young *torero*, asking for autographs.

Luz quickly turned towards Doña Lilliana and started up a conversation. By the time Lorenzo had come over to her, they were deep in discussion about the cruelty of *corridas*. He placed a hand on her shoulder and because her nerves were still on edge from the stressful morning, she jumped and abruptly swung round in her seat.

'Doña Luz, I'm sorry to interrupt. How wonderful to see you again. It's been a long time, too long actually,' he drawled, leaning over her, his pale-blue eyes searching her face intently, as though to say, *I know how attracted you are to me.*

She suppressed the sarcastic comment itching on her tongue. Clearly the type of man who went around with a bevy of beauties tagging at his heels, he was not the sort to impress Luz.

'Ah, Don Lorenzo. I've just been hearing all about your prowess in the bullring. Doña Lilliana Cortés here is an ardent fan of yours,' she told him with a polite smile.

'I have attended all of the *corridas* you've taken part in,' Doña Lilliana gushed as she gazed adoringly at her hero. 'Your fans are very sad that you have … retired, so to speak.'

'I am deeply flattered, Doña Lilliana,' Lorenzo said in a suave voice, the conceited smile he flashed belying the humility of his answer. 'You must come and watch me. I'll be performing here in Pamplona on the last day of the fiesta. I can promise you a good *corrida*. The bulls from that ranch are well known for their boldness and courage.' Then, addressing Luz again, he assumed a solemn air. 'I hope to see you there, too, Doña Luz,' he said softly, gently squeezing her shoulder. Luz pasted a gracious smile on her face, fighting the desire to shrug off his hand, once again thinking, *I dislike this man intensely.*

At that moment Doña Lilliana was pulled to her feet by the boisterous young man on her left as another burst of singing erupted in the bar and a few revellers began dancing in a snaking line between the tables.

'Lorenzo, are you flirting again? Really, I can't leave you alone for one minute!'

Luz looked up at the sound of the velvety female tones to see Lorenzo's sister appear beside him from the crowd. She looked stylishly cool in a navy polka-dot dress with a ruffled halterneck, her blonde hair neatly swept up into a sophisticated chignon. Luz felt decidedly underdressed in her black T-shirt and jeans.

'Doña Adalia, how lovely to see you again,' Luz said, not entirely welcoming the arrival of the blonde socialite but relieved, at least, that she wouldn't be left alone with the preening matador.

Adalia tilted her head to one side. 'Why, it's Doña Luz, isn't it?' After the tiniest of pauses, she gave a dazzling smile. 'How are you? Working hard on the book? Andrés tells me how committed you are. But of course you need a break from all that, so what better place to be? I'm sure Andrés can be a hard taskmaster when he wants to be.'

Before Luz could answer, Don Lorenzo said: 'Doña Luz is staying with Carlos and Alba. You remember them ...'

'Oh, Carlos, yes, I've just seen him. He really is one of your nicest friends, Lorenzo. So entertaining!' She turned to Luz again. 'Lucky you to be staying with him.' Her pale blue eyes fixed on Luz intently. What confused Luz was how she so suddenly seemed perfectly charming and attentive compared with the relative coolness she had displayed in Andrés' office. She didn't quite know what to make of Lorenzo's sister and she felt a little guarded as a result.

Adalia glanced at her brother and then back at Luz, smiling sweetly. 'Is my brother trying to dazzle you with his charms, Doña Luz? He can't resist a pretty face, you know.' She then surprised Luz by giving her a conspiratorial glance. 'Lorenzo, be a good boy and get us some more drinks, will you?'

'Doña Luz and I were just …'

'Oh, Doña Luz can spare you for a few minutes.' She tapped his arm impatiently. 'Besides, how are we ever to have any girl talk and get to know each other properly with you hanging around?'

Lorenzo arched an eyebrow at his sister and turned to Luz. 'I'll be back soon,' he said, gazing at her apologetically as if he must be breaking her heart by leaving her side. Luz resisted the temptation to roll her eyes as he disappeared towards the bar. She hoped the smile she gave Adalia didn't look too grateful; the brother and sister seemed very close and she wouldn't want to give the merest hint how irritating she found Lorenzo.

Adalia took the seat that Doña Lilliana had vacated and sipped the last of her sangria. 'I think my brother is quite taken with you, Doña Luz.' She looked at her over the rim of her glass. 'But then you must be used to having that effect on men …'

Luz shifted uncomfortably in her chair. Her experience with men so far was a little too painful to contemplate. 'Well, I don't know about that.'

Adalia waved a perfectly manicured hand. 'Oh, come on, you must have noticed how men look at you! You're so gorgeous, it's hard not to. Any man would be *madly* attracted to you.' She gave a high laugh. 'Lorenzo is clearly smitten. As for our dear Andrés, he can't stop singing your praises. It really is getting rather silly. I told him that he needed to be a little more professional or it wouldn't be fair on you. After all, you're trying to get a job done, which I'm sure you'll do admirably. The last thing you want is your boss being flirtatious.'

Luz flushed. 'Andrés is just being charming.' Silently adding to herself, *and it's really none of your business.*

Adalia arched a finely shaped eyebrow. 'Yes, he's very good at that, isn't he?'

Luz glanced down at her glass. 'Andrés is an ambitious, powerful man. I think charm goes with his job.'

'Oh, I'm sure.' Adalia stared at her again then her elegant lips broke into a smile. 'Our family has a substantial number of Eduardo de Salazar's artworks, you know, in our private collection. I'm sure you'd find it useful to see them for your book. You must come over to the house one day.'

Luz's eyebrows went up in surprise. 'Your private collection,' she repeated. Why had Andrés not mentioned this himself? Wasn't it a significant piece of information she should have known? No matter. Though she wasn't about to admit her embarrassing ignorance of the Herrera collection, she had to concede that this would be very useful indeed for her research.

'That would be fascinating, thank you,' she replied enthusiastically. 'The more of Eduardo's originals I can study, the better.'

Luz hardly admitted it to herself but she was also curious about Adalia. She couldn't help but be charmed by her despite her meddling tongue; she was also curious about the young socialite's relationship with Andrés. Clearly Adalia felt proprietorial over him. That could be simply the protectiveness of an old friend, almost like a sister, but somehow Luz doubted it. Her heart gave an unpleasant squeeze at the thought of the intimate bond the two clearly shared. She was being ridiculous; why did this bother her?

Luz broke out of her thoughts and met Adalia's smiling eyes. *They don't miss a trick*, she couldn't help thinking, a little uncharitably.

Adalia seemed quite genuine in her invitation, eager to have Luz visit their house: 'It's the least I can do to help. I don't know if Andrés told you but my parents were friends with Eduardo, though sadly I never met the great man himself. Our family is keen for your project to be a roaring success, too. From what Andrés tells me, with your talents we could well have a bestseller on our hands.'

Luz looked uncomfortable. 'Gosh, I don't know about that. I'm still at the research stage so it's a bit soon to be making any predictions.'

Adalia was far more subtle and agreeable than her brother, but Luz still found that she couldn't feel entirely comfortable around her. For one thing, it was hard to know how to react, other than awkwardly, to the young woman's lavish compliments. Luz was much too down-to-earth for social gush. Nonetheless, she couldn't help but feel a little guilty for having branded Andrés' friend patronizing and unfriendly. She would certainly accept Doña Adalia's invitation to view the Herrera private collection; she just hoped that Lorenzo would not be around.

Adalia seemed intent on bringing the conversation back to Andrés. This time she gazed closely at Luz for a moment, a picture of solicitude. 'You do look very tired. I hope that old tyrant isn't working you too hard, Doña Luz. You must let me take you for lunch one day. We could go shopping, give you a break from the book. And from Andrés, too,' she added, giving Luz's arm a little squeeze. Adalia leant in to whisper in her ear, her eyes dancing mischievously. 'I can tell you all about his wicked ways and how to avoid them.'

Luz thought back to the kiss on the beach and coloured a little. 'Oh, I don't think I'll need any help on that score. Andrés has been professional throughout,' she lied. 'We've already had some very productive meetings and the project's shaping up well,' she added, trying not to think about just how unnerving those encounters had been. Then, not to seem rude, she thanked Adalia warmly. 'Lunch would be nice, that sounds lovely.'

Luz took a sip of sangria and then, almost as if she couldn't help herself, she asked nonchalantly: 'Do you know much about his wicked ways?' She sensed it was probably not a great idea to gossip about her employer with one of his dearest friends, but she was curious to know more about the man.

Adalia's eyes gleamed a little more brightly as she regarded Luz. 'Oh, I like to think I have a special relationship with Andrés. I probably know him better than anyone. I've seen many women come and go, and he tires of each one sooner or later. Yes, I've learned something of his tactics by now.'

Before Luz could absorb this remark, or find out what those tactics might be, Adalia smiled an inscrutable smile and nodded over Luz's shoulder. 'Oh, look, I think those dancers are wanting you to join them, Doña Luz,' she said, watching another line of people approach the table, one of whom reached for Luz's arm.

As she was pulled from her chair and away into the crowd, Luz didn't have time to stop and watch the smile fade from Adalia's lips.

*   *   *

The week of festivities went by quickly with different activities taking place each day. There was the great San Fermín procession through the old part of Pamplona featuring a statue of the saint and the *gigantes* – huge papier-mâché puppet figures, twirling through the streets to the sound of loud traditional drumming music – sporting competitions, bullfights and fireworks every evening, all interspersed with drinking, singing, dancing and general merriment. Luz attended the parade of giants, and that of the picadors on horseback, with Alba and Carlos, and she watched the running of the bulls twice more. Whenever she got a moment to herself, she roamed the streets of Pamplona, her eyes always searching in the hope of bumping into Leandro but he was never anywhere to be seen. Their sudden meeting had taken the carefree and happy edge away from her holiday. She missed him dreadfully and ached for him every moment of the day. There was no doubt in her mind that the scales of love were tipped against her happiness. How had she managed to get herself in such a mess?

One night Carlos took Luz and Alba down to the lower part of the old city to watch the bulls for the next day's run being driven from the reception pens on the outskirts and taken to the temporary corral in the Calle Santo Domingo, where they would spend the night. Luz was not particularly enthusiastic about going but to refuse would have been impolite.

They stood in a recess of a building waiting for the bulls to pass by. It was the dead of night when they heard the muted rattle of hoofs in the distance. Suddenly, the magnificent creatures loomed out of the shadows, a picador on horseback at their head. A shaft of silver moonlight fell on their glistening skins as they hurried on past. Their panting echoed eerily in the darkness as they went, leaving in their wake a waft of animal smell that was carried on the night breeze. The *peons*, their keepers, ran beside them armed with stone slings; agile young men with long hair who reminded Luz of Leandro. There was a nobility and dignity in their physical bearing so like that of the young gypsy that she was for a moment entranced. In seconds the ghostly convoy had gone, swallowed by obscurity, the drama ended.

Lorenzo had rung several times during the week, wanting to invite Luz for a tête-a-tête lunch or dinner. She always declined sweetly but firmly. Carlos and Alba were a little bemused: they couldn't understand their friend's antipathy towards the *torero*.

'Most women would give their lives for a glance from Lorenzo, let alone the attention he's lavishing on you,' Alba noted, regarding her friend with curiosity as they both dressed in her room for dinner one evening. 'Are you just playing hard to get?'

'No, I don't play those sorts of games, Alba, you should know me better than that,' she answered tersely. 'There's something about that man I find a bit creepy. He's too smooth, too slippery. You know, like quicksilver …'

Alba gave Luz a slanting look. 'You like them rugged, the rough diamond types, do you?' she said teasingly.

Was that it? 'Maybe,' Luz murmured wistfully as she thought of her beloved gypsy, 'but I don't think so.' She pondered on that thought for a few seconds. 'No, there's something deeper than that, something I can't put my finger on, and which I find a little, well … repulsive about Don Lorenzo,' she ended with conviction.

'Luz! That's a little harsh, don't you think?' Alba looked at her indignantly for a moment but then breathed a sigh of relief. 'So, in that case, I take it that you won't mind if I make a beeline for him at his party tomorrow night?'

'Of course not, Alba, don't be silly!' Luz felt suddenly embarrassed that she hadn't attempted to hide her vehement dislike of the man. 'I had no idea … I'm so sorry. He's probably perfectly nice, just not my type,' she added hastily, unable, however, not to privately wonder at her friend's taste in men.

Alba flushed pink. 'I've been in love with him since I was eighteen and went to his first *corrida*. He's all I've ever dreamed I wanted in a man. Can you blame me? He's handsome, charming, courageous and rich. Surely, you have to admit that?'

Luz nodded, not trusting herself to comment. Luckily Alba wasn't looking for a response. The relief her friend clearly felt in unburdening herself was coming out in a flurry of chatter, the words tumbling over themselves.

'What more could a woman ask for?' she added, her eyes shining, before their expression became rueful. 'Look, it'll probably come to nothing – he's never shown much interest in me. But at least I can be honest with you now: I was afraid you liked him and were just biding your time. I'm so relieved that's not true! Mind you, I can't believe there's a woman on earth who wouldn't be flattered by his attentions.' She nudged her friend teasingly. 'Well, apart from you, clearly. Luz, you are a strange girl sometimes.'

She paused to give Luz a little hug before rattling on again. 'Anyhow, he isn't attached, as far as I know. The newspapers would have been full of it if he were.' She smiled. 'Carlos thinks I stand a chance, you know. We're quite well matched when you come to think of it. Our families have known each other for ever.' She paused again, looking earnestly into Luz's face. 'But you know, don't you, Luz, that if you were in the least bit interested, I would have stepped aside. I would never want to compete with a friend.' The side of her mouth quirked up. 'Particularly not one as ridiculously pretty as you.'

Luz was touched. 'Well, you can rest assured, Alba, I have no interest whatsoever in Don Lorenzo Herrera. I will be only too happy if you monopolize him at the party. And that is the solemn truth, I promise,' she ended firmly. 'Actually, I've half a mind to say I'm too ill to go tomorrow. Besides, I'm really not in the mood for a party.'

'Oh no, Luz! You can't, that would look really rude. Anyhow, he'd guess it's a lie. He's rung every day and you've turned down every single one of his invitations. You'll simply have to go to this one. After all, it's not as though you'll be alone with him.'

Luz sighed deeply. 'Yes, I suppose so.'

Alba eyed her friend with concern. They had been close since childhood and had seen a lot of each other, on and off, over the years. 'Anyway, what's come over you? You used to love parties.

I can tell something's the matter. You seem too quiet. It's as if you're only half-present these days.'

Luz put on a bright smile. 'Nothing's the matter, honestly. I still love parties, I'm just a little weary at the moment.'

'Something tells me there's a man behind this. Are you in love?'

Luz looked away, her throat suddenly painful. 'A man? Me, in love?' She let out a small, bitter laugh. 'Never!' she breathed with a catch in her voice, forcing the smile back to her drawn face. And then, unable to contain her grief any longer, she burst into tears and sobbed her heart out.

Alba put her arms around her. 'Hush, hush.' She smoothed Luz's hair away from her tear-stained face. 'So, it's rather more serious than I thought,' she murmured. 'Who is this scoundrel? Do I know him?'

Luz gave half a sob and shook her head. 'He isn't a scoundrel … actually, quite the reverse. He's rather decent, and no, you don't know him.'

'Is he Spanish?' Alba prompted. 'I know most people in our circle.'

Luz shook her head again. 'I don't want to talk about it, Alba, I'm sorry. It's just that the pain is too raw at the moment,' she explained haltingly, blowing her nose roughly with the tissue her friend had handed her. 'One day, maybe, when it doesn't feel so painful.'

'You'll get over it,' Alba told her with an encouraging smile. 'One always gets over it. No man is worth the heartache. Look at me, for instance. I've been pining over Lorenzo for so many years but, in the meantime, I've still managed to fall in and out of love more than once and each time I've thought it was the end of the world. Soon enough I was proved wrong, every time.' She hugged her friend. 'Mark my words, you'll get over him.'

'I don't think so,' Luz insisted in a broken voice. 'You don't understand. I've never felt this way about any man before.'

'Nonsense! Every man is different, anyway. No two experiences are the same,' Alba declared emphatically. 'If you can feel this way about one man, you can feel it for another.'

Luz smiled sadly; she could really do without all this pain and humiliation. 'I hope you're right,' she replied with a shaky sigh. 'I really do.'

*   *   *

The dashing silver car climbed and snaked its way among extensive fruit plantations as Luz, Carlos and Alba motored to Lorenzo's Navarrese home outside Pamplona. Carlos drove quickly, familiar with each bend in the road. Luz was lost in thought, looking at the countryside out of the window without seeing it, and Alba, who could not contain her excitement, made up for her friend's silence with her constant chatter.

La Fortaleza, the family home of Lorenzo and Adalia's mother, Paloma Castillo-Gomez, was an impressive hacienda set on a plateau on the banks of the River Arga in the midst of the green countryside and surrounded by mountains. Its grey walls had stood there for two centuries, grand and imposing among landscaped gardens and ancient specimen trees. The grand house had been the home of the Castillo-Gomez family uninterruptedly during all that time. Rumour had it that their wealth had its origins in smuggling, but today they were respectable traders, holding large corporations in Spain and over the border in France. The marriage of Don Felipe, Lorenzo's father, into this wealthy old family had been viewed by many as one of pure convenience and continued self-interest on the part of the Herreras. In later years, La Fortaleza had been divided by the Herrera and Castillo-Gomez families into individual large apartments to accommodate various sons and daughters and their offspring, when they came to spend their holidays there, while the main core of the house was shared by everyone for parties and other social gatherings. Tonight, Lorenzo had the run of his mother's ancestral home to entertain a cluster of handpicked guests.

Twilight was passing into darkness as they arrived. Shadows were expiring in the dusk and the pale evening star shone in the sky. The remains of a setting sun gilded the dark-grey bastion with a special but fleeting glory. At the edge of night it stood out mysteriously with its background of mountains, the essence of repose and solitude.

'It is rather grand,' noted Alba as the car turned into the long drive.

'It's eerie, that's what it is,' Luz shivered. *It suits Lorenzo's persona to a tee*, she thought, but kept that to herself. 'It should be called Castillo de los Vampiros.'

Alba was a little put out at Luz's thinly veiled slight. 'That's such an unfair thing to say,' she exclaimed. 'It's pretty impressive, if you ask me. You're biased. Just because, for some reason, you find the man insufferable ...' She gave Luz a sideways look. 'I sincerely hope you don't intend to spend this evening being the ghost at the party.'

Luz laughed. 'Well, I wouldn't be out of place, would I?' she teased, her sense of humour returning, blue eyes glittering with mischief.

As they came in sight of the ancient gateway, grey and massive, the gloom that had oppressed her all week rapidly seemed to lift and a tingling sensation of excitement swelled into a greater emotion that appeared to engulf all other feelings. She was surprised at this abrupt mood swing, and couldn't account for it, but welcomed it all the same.

Alba was right: she had always loved parties. Tonight she wanted to forget Leandro and the heartache he had caused her. With time, she would forget him. Someday she would meet someone new ... maybe it would be tonight. How she wished it would be tonight so this heartache would stop.

CHAPTER 7

Carlos parked the car in La Fortaleza's large gravel parking area and together they strolled across a quaint old bridge over the River Arga that ran through the estate. They made their way through an ancient stone horseshoe arch that interrupted a wall overgrown with ivy and into a broad courtyard planted with pollard trees that led to the house. The hacienda itself was a large pile of dark-grey granite, imposing in its magnitude but with scarcely a trace of beauty, Luz thought, as they approached the great central portal. La Fortaleza's crenellated walls and hard angles made it resemble a brooding fortress more than a home, and the heavy wooden doors stood open like the cavernous roar of a huge beast.

Everything was of gargantuan size. They were shown by a solemn major-domo into an enormous hallway, where dramatic paintings of conquistadors and bullfighters stared down at them, and then through to the magnificent reception room with its intricately decorated ceiling and dark, rich panelling, carved out of twelve sorts of wood. Very different to the houses in Andalucía, this one was built for the rugged cold and wet winters of Navarre.

A group of thirty or forty men and women in evening dress, flashing with gold and jewels, were chattering and laughing, smoking and drinking, under a gigantic glittering Baccarat crystal chandelier, brought over from the iconic salon in Paris at the turn of the century.

All eyes turned on Luz as she and her friends entered the room. She wore a long, figure-defining dress in white jersey with a plunging neckline and a large cutout at the back. The bright white material accentuated her copper tan and her irises appeared almost dark blue beneath her black lashes. The gown was accessorized with a bib necklace of hammered gold circles that lay over her décolletage; by intimating rather than exposing, the jewellery enhanced the mystery, allowing a glimpse of the curvaceous hollow between her breasts. Her hair was piled high on the crown of her head, showing off her graceful, swanlike neck, the perfect oval of her face and her delicate features. As usual, without intending to, Luz stole the show.

Lorenzo and his sister Adalia crossed the room, hurrying to greet their guests. In flounces of purple chiffon, which suited her colouring to perfection, Adalia looked more beautiful than ever. The sophisticated social butterfly par excellence, she welcomed Carlos and Alba effusively with air kisses. Luz wasn't certain but Adalia seemed to freeze for the tiniest instant as she turned to her. But if she did so, she recovered herself instantly, extending a pale hand to hold Luz's, a dazzling smile lighting up her face.

'How divine you look, Doña Luz,' Adalia breathed, still radiating her perfect hostess smile. 'I'm so glad you could come. We really must have our lunch date when all this is over.'

'Divine? Oh yes. I think Doña Luz will steal the hearts of some mortal men tonight,' Carlos joked, glancing towards his sister's friend affectionately.

'Yes, she truly is the belle of the ball.' Adalia let out a tinkling laugh that didn't quite reach her eyes. 'We'll have to hide you from all the jealous wives tonight in case you steal their husbands away.'

Luz smiled awkwardly. 'You look stunning, Doña Adalia, and I'm sure any jealous eyes will be looking in a completely different direction tonight.' She found herself wondering what Andrés might think of Adalia's beguiling appearance had he been there. Could any man resist such elegant beauty?

'Doña Luz, you're too kind,' answered Adalia, appearing gratified by the compliment though Luz still sensed something odd in the glassy depths of her eyes. 'You must let me introduce you to some of my friends later,' she continued airily. 'There must be hardly anyone you know here and we'd hate you to be bored. Besides, given half a chance my dear brother over there will monopolize you all evening and we can't have that!' Her expression seemed to brighten before she turned away and engaged Carlos and Alba in extravagantly charming conversation. Luz moved away from them, already tired of the brittle social chatter.

'You look like a dream floating in the clouds,' Lorenzo whispered as he came up to her. His voice was suave with a suggestion of hidden, provocative aims. Bending over her hand, he raised it delicately to his lips and the gesture felt to Luz as if he were branding her. As he lifted his head, his sharp gaze met hers. She had to concede he was a very handsome man but his eyes, though they attempted to look caressing, seemed cold and calculating.

'You are very gallant, *señor*,' she said graciously with only the hint of a smile.

'Please, call me Lorenzo. We should be on first-name terms. After all, we're working on the same project, are we not?' he said, taking her arm and leading her further into the room.

Her dark brows knitted together and she stopped dead. She looked up at him. 'I'm not sure I understand your meaning ...'

'Eduardo's biography,' he clarified innocently, as though he hadn't noticed the alarm and terseness in her tone.

'I wasn't aware that you were also involved in the writing of this book,' she said curtly.

'Well, only indirectly. Our family owns an extensive collection of Eduardo de Salazar's paintings, especially his earlier work.

No doubt they should be incorporated in his biography. They have never been properly archived and it only makes sense that it's part of the project. Of course, you would need to spend some time here at La Fortaleza, a prospect that would give me great pleasure,' he declared, the pressure of his fingers tightening a little on her arm.

'Our collaboration on Eduardo's life story is essential, I'd venture to suggest. And I, for one, will find the whole thing fascinating. I've made it known that I'm perfectly happy being a contributor and editor. In fact, I'd positively enjoy it.' He gazed at her dumbstruck face before adding: 'Look, I'm a little surprised Andrés hasn't mentioned this to you. I hope I haven't put my foot in it, but it has always been the plan.'

A plan on which she had obviously not been consulted. How dare they? To presume she'd work as an unpaid hand, archiving their wretched collection, and then to have this pompous creep presume to edit her work. Insufferable! Luz's eyes sparked but she managed to smother her anger, instead giving Lorenzo her most charming smile. Again, he appeared oblivious to the undercurrents as he took two glasses of sangria from a passing waiter and offered one to her.

'Señor de Calderón and I are still in the early stages of outlining the project,' Luz declared, letting the chilled wine soothe her dry throat. 'I'm sure the Herrera archives will be on the agenda the next time we speak.' She wondered what else was on Andrés' agenda that he had not yet deigned to discuss with her.

Lorenzo smiled at her over his glass as he sipped slowly. 'And when you do, I look forward to making myself available to you at La Fortaleza whenever possible.' He gave a courteous nod of his head but his gaze travelled over her in a way that made Luz recoil inwardly and look away.

Why had Andrés not told her about this? What was he playing at? First she had found out about the archives from Adalia and then Lorenzo Herrera had announced his involvement in the project ... There had certainly been no hint of her spending any time at La Fortaleza with Lorenzo, which of course was unthinkable. She was appalled at the thought of how far Andrés was trying to use her. Once again he had left her feeling wrong-footed and confused.

She caught sight of Adalia, throwing her head back and laughing conspiratorially with a group of admirers. Luz hadn't forgotten the socialite's knowing comments about Andrés. Watching her now, it seemed to Luz that Lorenzo's sister had the kind of allure and self-assurance that Andrés most likely would find captivating. Not for the first time she felt a strange pang at the thought of what their 'special relationship' entailed.

'Your sister looks very happy this evening,' she mused, groping for a change in the subject.

'Ah, yes, my sister. So she should, I suppose,' Lorenzo replied casually. 'After all, she and our friend Andrés are, I imagine, close to announcing their engagement.' He glanced at Luz and smirked. 'Though if he's ever to settle down he's going to have to give up his, how shall I put it ... democratic appreciation of the fairer sex.'

She stared ahead, not daring to speak. Why, instead of relief, did she feel a strangling lump in her throat? So there was something between them ... more than something. How many more disturbing revelations about Andrés de Calderón were there to come? Of course, she had sensed that Adalia had set her sights on him, despite her description of them as merely 'old friends'. What was strange was that her declaration about his dalliances with other women hadn't seemed to bother her in the slightest. Maybe Adalia felt such a degree of confidence in her power over Andrés that his previous history mattered not one jot to her. Luz glanced again at the beautiful blonde woman holding court. Why did her insides suddenly burn with a slightly sickening feeling? She should find Lorenzo's sister a welcome diversion in whatever game Andrés was playing, she told herself. And yet he had kissed Luz …

She blinked and swallowed uncomfortably. 'I'm sure that Señor de Calderón and Adalia will make a fine match,' she said softly.

From that moment, the evening ahead stretched uncomfortably before Luz. Her head spun with uncertainties and she badly wanted to get away from the social glitter, where suddenly everyone seemed to be playing games. She tried her hardest to steer Lorenzo in the direction of Alba, whose glances kept flicking longingly to the *torero*'s face, as if therein she might see something to stir her hope. Luz smiled and nodded, even laughed, in all the right places but Lorenzo's words were like cold fingers of dread squeezing at her heart.

She was not sure which revelation had unsettled her most. Memories of that evening she had spent with Andrés on the beach kept flashing into her mind … the way he had looked at her with those dangerously beguiling eyes and held her hand so tightly as they walked, as if he was afraid to let her go. Why had she let herself be drawn into his ridiculous charade? How did he manage to disturb her emotions with such force? He was determined to dominate her in every way, whether professionally or in private, she decided. Was this his last flirtation before settling down for good? Anger bubbled up again. What overbearing arrogance and deception! She wished she could give the man a piece of her mind right now.

Adalia's effusive cries of affectionate welcome signalled her wish had been granted rather sooner than she thought. Luz turned to find Andrés standing like Mephistopheles at the entrance to the drawing room. His dark evening suit emphasized his overpowering satanic good looks and the air of danger he carried with him like a second skin. Her mind went blank for a moment, as it was now accustomed to do whenever she saw Andrés unexpectedly, before outrage gathered in her again. Across the room his slow smile met her scowl and the battle flashing in her eyes, just before he was partially shrouded in a haze of purple chiffon.

With Adalia on his arm, he moved from one group to another, courteous, charming and ... forbidden. The aristocratic-looking socialite had claimed him and was intent on making it quite clear to everyone present.

Luz felt a pinch in her chest as the pair mingled with the small gathering. She did not stop to analyze her feelings; after all, why should she? Her opinion of Adalia had already gone down: at the very least, Lorenzo's sister had been disingenuous in Pamplona. At worst, she had sent a well-disguised warning shot over Luz's bows, while feigning friendship.

As far as Luz was concerned, Andrés was deceiving and contemptible; she would gladly have nothing more to do with him. Unfortunately they were bound together, for better or worse, on this project and there was nothing she could do about it but stand up for herself and fight for her rights. She would also be the consummate professional with Andrés de Calderón. Whatever remorseless Nemesis had loomed over Eduardo de Salazar's biography and plagued her from the very start, Luz was determined now more than ever not to let herself be beaten. However difficult and discouraging, she would see the whole thing through to the bitter end.

Lorenzo was by Luz's side again when his sister and her beau came to a halt a few steps in front of her. Adalia gave Luz a direct gaze. Was that a look of casual innocence or a flash of triumph? Luz lifted her chin, deigning to give Lorenzo's sister only the briefest glance before arching an eyebrow at Andrés. His velvet-black irises regarded her with a remote kind of amusement that was somehow challenging and insolent. Her hands clenched; she must control herself. This was neither the time nor the place to have a scene, however much she needed to get her resentment off her chest. There was an odd pause while they considered each other, then he held out his hand and his face broke into that familiar charming smile.

'Luz,' he exclaimed, 'such a pleasant surprise.' His gaze briefly swept over to Lorenzo, then back again to her. The sardonic expression in his eyes deepened into something Luz couldn't quite fathom. 'What brings you here, the festival or other interests?'

His insinuation did not pass unnoticed. How she wished she could swipe that Cheshire cat smile off his handsome face. She cursed the hot, treacherous pink that washed up her cheeks. As usual, she was letting him get to her. She glanced at Lorenzo with the brightest smile she could manage before her eyes flitted back to Andrés.

'Oh, this and that. My interests are quite wide-ranging,' she heard herself shoot back, not quite knowing why she had given him such a boldly foolish answer.

A transient spark registered in Andrés' dark irises and his demeanour stiffened imperceptibly. 'Then I wish you the best of luck in your endeavours,' he muttered coolly. The affable smile he gave her, she noted, did not quite reach his eyes.

'Andrés, *mi querido*, didn't you know?' Adalia gave a glittering smile, pulling a little more tightly on his arm. 'Lorenzo and I bumped into Doña Luz in Pamplona. As you can see, she and Lorenzo had an instant rapport and he made sure to invite her along to the party.' Her smile faltered only slightly as she turned to Luz. 'And of course I was delighted that we should have the chance to see Doña Luz again.'

Luz inwardly cursed herself once more for not keeping quiet or saying something that placed some distance between herself and Lorenzo. It had only given Adalia the opportunity she needed to encourage the misunderstanding.

'Fate is indeed a curious thing,' Andrés said, his gaze hovering briefly on Luz before he moved on, Adalia in his wake. As they walked away she cast a glance over her shoulder, her mouth twitching with satisfaction.

From then on, the evening advanced on leaden feet. Though many young men made a point of trying to engage Luz in conversation, she was distracted and felt an oppressive awareness of Andrés that she tried constantly to shake off.

Dinner seemed to take forever. Luz was seated at the far end of one of the long tables set with white tablecloths and ornate candelabra. The dining room was dramatically lit with exposed dark beams running across the vast ceiling; it was dominated by a gothic stone fireplace that would add admirable heat to the room throughout one of Navarre's bitter winters. At the other end of the table, Adalia was taking every opportunity to lean into Andrés and whisper in his ear, touching his arm and laughing.

Luz's sense of humiliation mounted. How could she have been foolish enough to trust him? Professionally, he was wrong-footing her for the second time despite his promises to 'start again'. And emotionally, why could she not smother these urges towards him that she did not want to feel? She despised Andrés for having such control over her, and she hated herself for letting him. Adalia was declaring her territorial claims and Luz fought a rising sense of irrational jealousy. She tried not to look in their direction but instead engaged her dinner partners in conversation. Every now and then irritation and curiosity got the better of her and she glanced up; on more than one occasion meeting Andrés' challenging dark gaze before he looked away.

Luz did not eat much, and drank quite a bit, so that even the light and fruity sangria began to have an effect on her senses. After her concerted efforts to ignore Lorenzo's cloying overtures, he had at last given up on her. By the looks of it, Alba seemed to have finally gained his attention and the pair were involved in an in-depth discussion opposite her. *At least one good thing has come out of tonight*, she thought, as dinner drew to a close. Carlos was flirting happily with a young socialite, who looked up at him with fluttering eyelashes and adoring eyes, while Adalia's claws were still deeply embedded in Andrés. Though it was not a particularly hot night, Luz found the place stifling; she needed some air. After picking up her evening bag, she moved on to the terrace and down into the garden where everything was still.

Under the night sky the grounds, like the house, were singularly grand and solemn, outlined only by high walls and treetops. Silence reigned and a sense of mystery hung over the whole place as she walked haphazardly along a dark avenue of giant trees. At a turning, she came out unexpectedly on to a glade and face to face with the river. The view of the house from the bank was awesome: the massive fortress stood out majestically under a waning moon, in all the light and shadow of which night is so fond. It was the perfect setting for the images of wizards and werewolves her imagination conjured up as she gazed around her. Despite the fact that it was not at all cold, she shivered.

'Lost, or strayed?' asked a deep, sonorous voice breaking the silence.

Luz turned abruptly to find Andrés leaning against a tree just a few paces behind her. Shrouded by darkness, there was nothing to distinguish him from his gypsy double. Her heart jumped wildly and the breath caught in her throat. She realized with rising alarm that the sexual tension that seemed to gather between them like a pacing animal when they were together had returned now, more potent than ever.

'What are you doing here?' she said, fighting to keep the emotion out of her voice.

'I could ask you the same thing,' came the unhurried answer.

She sensed rather than perceived the sarcastic smile and her chin rose. 'I have a bone to pick with you.'

'Yes, I thought as much. You've been sending me unfriendly vibes all evening, though I'm not sure what I've done to justify them,' he said grimly.

She regarded him with contempt. 'Is there any end to the depths you would stoop to to get what you want? *Madre de Dios! Yo no lo creo!* I don't believe it. You are the most devious, unscrupulous …'

'Spare me the tirade and get to the point. What's the problem, Luz?' he cut in, his mouth settling into a hard line.

'Don't act innocent with me, Andrés de Calderón. It's a word that's never figured in your dictionary.'

'And sensible has never figured in yours, it seems.'

She glowered at him. 'What's that supposed to mean?'

'Meaning that your impetuous nature often gets the better of you.'

'I'd rather be impetuous than deceitful,' she snapped. Andrés narrowed his eyes but the intense look he gave her was not enough to dam her gushing temper. 'Your duplicity really is staggering, in every way …'

'And what duplicity is that?' he cut in. An odd expression burned in the depths of those dark irises.

'I've had enough of this! Your games may excite the likes of Adalia and all the other women you have swooning at your feet, but not me.'

She started heading towards the trees, intent on getting away from him as quickly as possible, but he shook his head and hastened after her. 'Hey, wait a minute,' he laughed, grabbing hold of her bare arm, making her skin tingle alarmingly. 'Don't tell me you're jealous.'

'Jealous?' her cry was shrill, startling a night bird in the coppice. It flew out into the open with a great flutter of wings before settling in another tree. She yanked away from his grip, breathing faster. 'Don't flatter yourself. And don't look at me with those dark, caressing eyes of yours, I'm not a fan.'

'Yes, I suppose you can't be everyone's fan,' he said sarcastically. 'But then your interests are so wide-ranging, as you pointed out.' He was standing so close to her now, his gaze fierce and derisive.

Hate was too benign a word to describe the way she felt about him at that moment. He had hit a raw nerve that she had barely acknowledged; the reflex was simultaneous. Her eyes flashed a dangerous grey as her hand swept up to his face with a force of which neither of them had imagined her capable.

She heard his sharp intake of breath before he pulled her into his arms, eyes blazing. He held her fast against the force of his body, his hands urgently gripping her shoulders. She tried to break away, struggling furiously for release and praying for the willpower to resist, but he refused to let go, pinning her against his powerful frame. The sheer masculine energy of him pounded at her: urgent, fierce and dominating. And then they were stumbling backwards, his mouth taking hers in a most desperate, hungry kiss, as if determined to reach inside her and make her respond. And she responded. Suddenly she was against the hard surface of the tree and he was pressing against her. Something flashed like light inside her at the sheer carnality of it and she knew he felt it, too. It was as if neither could stop themselves. She was not prepared for the rapid rise of emotion nor the overwhelming desire that exploded in her as he plundered her mouth with a savage fervour, searing her lips with his fire, demolishing her resistance. Trembling, her head fell back and she closed her eyes, surrendering helplessly as her legs turned to jelly, her heart thudding loudly in her ears.

He broke off the kiss, panting, his eyes dark and hungry. 'What are you doing to me, Luz? I want you so badly, *querida*, I think I might die,' he growled with a fierce intensity that sounded almost familiar.

Finding her mouth again, his kiss deepened and she felt the pressure of his pulsing arousal, potently communicating the extent of his desire. She gave a soft moan. A mindless ferment of yearning was building up in her as his skilful hands found the swollen curves of her breasts and the taunt pink tips crying out for his touch. He tantalized and caressed them and when finally he pulled aside the top of her dress and his warm lips captured the hard peaks, her fingers grasped his hair and the ache and burning hunger for him made her cry out.

'Leandro, oh Leandro, I love you ... take me, here ... now!' she pleaded, uncontrollable tears streaming down her cheeks.

Her own voice sobered her up as it tore into the night and she realized what had happened. With a smothered gasp of anguish she pushed Andrés with both hands, tearing herself away from him, before once more raising her hand to give him a stinging blow to the cheek. She staggered backwards, covering herself again.

'Who *are* you? What do you want from me?' She was shouting almost hysterically, crossing her arms around her shoulders like a protective shield against the terrifying danger he represented.

The colour drained from his face and his features froze in a mask of utter pain. 'It's all right, Luz. *No tengas miedo, querida,*' he whispered soothingly. 'Don't be afraid, it's all right. I'm sorry, we can sort it out.' He took a few steps towards her, extending his arm.

But she was having none of it. 'Don't you dare come near me!' She backed further away from him, her cheeks still wet with tears of confusion and humiliation; his reaction as bewildering as her own shocking behaviour.

'*Maldita sea*, damn you, Andrés de Calderón!' she declared. She picked up her evening bag, which had fallen to the ground then turned on her heel and stumbled off without a backward glance.

'Wait, Luz, *déjame explicarte*, let me explain,' Andrés called out. But she was already too far away and, though she caught an almost fraught despair in his voice, she kept going.

Luz made it back to the house unsteadily. As she came up the steps of the terrace, she breathed a sigh of relief. One of the maids was clearing away glasses and ashtrays that had been left on the balustrade. After asking for the cloakroom, she freshened up as quickly as she could, smoothing back her hair and taking deep breaths.

She was a dense mass of quivering nerves, tension and confusion taking over her mind. Staring at her reflection, Luz touched her lips, which were still swollen from the fire of those kisses. In a moment of madness, her body had betrayed her. Why, when she did not trust Andrés and found him hateful, had she responded to his caresses with the same fire and uninhibited elation that engulfed her while in Leandro's arms? Was she turning into some kind of nymphomaniac? She couldn't think straight. In fact, she couldn't think at all. At this precise moment she only knew she wanted to go back home to Cádiz or to El Pavón; maybe even to her flat in Chelsea. Anywhere that was familiar and safe, and would put miles between her and the mayhem of her present life.

After putting some order back to her sorry state, she hurriedly left the cloakroom. With any luck her little escapade would have passed unnoticed. She crossed the hall and went into the brightly lit drawing room. Most of the guests were still there. Maybe she hadn't been missed but that was too much to ask: as she paused at the door Lorenzo rushed over to her and grabbed her arm proprietorially.

'Luz, where have you been? I looked for you everywhere.' He seemed more miffed than concerned.

She tried to sound casual and smiled demurely as she disengaged her arm, slowly but firmly, from his clutch. 'I needed some air and walked down to the river,' she explained.

'I only wish I had been with you. You must visit the grounds in daylight,' he said in sugary tones, his pale-blue gaze travelling all over her frame. Clearly he had decided to renew his efforts to charm her.

She nodded absentmindedly and her eyes tried to catch those of Carlos or Alba, who were standing across the room, as she searched for a reason to take leave of her hosts. The trouble was, that although it was well past one in the morning, for most of the guests the night was still young. How she longed for the privacy of her room back in Pamplona.

Presently Adalia joined them. 'You do have other guests,' she reminded her brother curtly, smiling fixedly as she did so. She turned to Luz.

'We missed you after dinner,' she noted, her piercing gaze considering the other woman shrewdly. 'Maybe in England it's the done thing to slip away for a whole hour but let me give you some friendly advice. Here in Spanish society we consider it rather rude, especially when it coincides with the absence of a male guest,' she rasped, keeping her voice low. 'You never know, people might start talking about history's nasty little habit of repeating itself,' she ended stiffly, before marching back into the middle of the room and circulating elegantly among her friends as though the incident had never occurred.

Luz was mortified. Although she now saw that Adalia's charm concealed a manipulative and barbed nature, still her own sense of shame and confusion pooled inside her like curdled milk. She wanted to hurry away but Lorenzo put a hand on her shoulder.

'Look, I must apologize for my sister,' he said, adopting a look of embarrassment. 'Don't take any notice. She's just a little upset because her fiancé-to-be had to leave sooner than she had wanted. Unforeseen business.' He gestured with his hands, as though describing the unavoidable situation. 'Apparently, Andrés is catching a plane back to Cádiz in the morning and wanted to have an early night. It's as simple as that.' He smiled unctuously. 'Please, don't give it another thought.'

Luz's scalp prickled and suddenly she wanted nothing more than to be away from this place and these people. Lorenzo either had no idea to what his sister was alluding or cared even less to explain. His affected concern and pointed remarks about Andrés made her want to slap him, but instead she took a small breath to calm herself.

'I think it's time for me to go, too,' she announced wearily. 'I'm not used to staying up so late.'

'I'll be seeing you at the *corrida* in the afternoon and maybe we can all go out and celebrate afterwards,' he responded, his eyes still boring into her.

She had no intention of either attending the *corrida* or any celebration for that matter. By the afternoon she hoped she would be well on her way back to Andalucía, if not already at El Pavón or L'Estrella – she had not yet decided which. Still, she forced herself to smile up at Lorenzo acquiescently, wanting to avoid any more scenes or pressure from him. She'd had enough for one night. The Spanish were an intense, passionate people and, from time to time, the small amount of English blood that ran through her veins cried out for peace and quiet, and a little decorum.

Thankfully, Alba came over. With one look she could see that Luz was pale and edgy. Without a word she took her friend by the arm, smiling shyly at their host, and the two women bade him goodnight. Alba steered Luz out of the room in search of Carlos, whom they found still in the company of the young woman who had captured his attention earlier that evening. He reluctantly disentangled himself with a whispered word of farewell in the ear of his admirer that left her giggling coquettishly.

Silently they drove back to Carlos's flat, the two young women huddled in their own corner of the car throughout the journey. Luz's brooding thoughts enveloped her like the darkness outside. In repose, the outline of the countryside with its mountains and plains looked solemn and mysterious; a weird aspect of nature's art, she thought, watching the leviathan shapes slip by in the distance like slumbering giants, immutable and oblivious to the petty concerns of human life. An oppressive sense of melancholy descended on her that she had never experienced before; suddenly she wished she could be swallowed up in that still, secret blackness and escape the relentless torment of her own feelings.

The car finally reached the outskirts of Pamplona, where the sight of the city's lit-up medieval churches and old stone buildings pierced the gloom of Luz's introspection. Carlos pulled up in the narrow street outside his flat and jumped out, opening the door for them both.

'Would you both like a nightcap before bed?' Carlos looked at Luz, gauging her mood before glancing at Alba, who shook her head.

'It's late, Carlos, and we've all had quite a bit of excitement this evening. We need our beds, don't we, Luz?' She linked arms with her friend as they walked inside. 'We've lost enough beauty sleep as it is tonight. We'll all go out for breakfast tomorrow as it's Luz's last day in Pamplona.'

'Very well, *buenas noches de las señoras*,' Carlos smiled, waving them off upstairs as he headed for the drinks cabinet.

'Will you please tell me what's going on?' Alba asked her friend once they were in the privacy of the bedroom.

'I don't know what you mean.' Luz continued to brush her hair energetically as though she was trying to beat the life out of it.

Alba came up to her. 'Is Andrés de Calderón the man you're pining after? Because, to put it vulgarly, he certainly has the hots for you.'

The question was blunt and made Luz pause and put down her brush. 'No, it's not Andrés de Calderón,' she said quietly.

Alba eyed her sceptically. 'I watched you both. There's definitely something going on between you two.'

'Yes, of course – we're working partners. I've told you, I'm writing his uncle's biography, nothing else.'

'Yes? And I'm the Queen of Spain! Really, Luz.'

'That is the honest truth, I promise you.' Luz frowned.

Alba lifted a quizzical eyebrow. 'Well, there's a missing link there. You can deny it as loudly as you want, but the chemistry between you was sizzling all evening. And trust me, I wasn't the only one aware of it.'

'What do you mean?'

'I mean that Adalia, who's been after him for years and to my knowledge hasn't yet landed him, was nervous as a kitten tonight. She's never felt threatened before by any contender to that very alluring catch, *el Señor* de Calderón. If looks could kill, we'd be attending your funeral in the morning.'

Luz shrugged. 'Andrés de Calderón, I'm told, is a notorious womanizer. If what you say is true, she should be used to his libertine ways by now.'

Adalia's nose had certainly been put out of joint, she reflected. Her biting remarks – obscure though some of them were – did little to conceal her animosity now.

'You both disappeared this evening at the same time,' Alba persisted. 'Are you honestly going to tell me that it was pure coincidence?'

'I was hot and went for a walk. Is that such a crime?' Luz felt on the defensive. She didn't want to think about people talking about her and Andrés together. Besides, she didn't want to think about it herself. 'Anyway, why is it so important? Why are you quizzing me?' She began braiding her hair vigorously.

'Because I feel you're in trouble and I don't want you to get hurt.'

A lump clogged Luz's throat. 'It's too late, *amiga*, that's already done!' The phrase came out huskily. The sadness that had settled in her chest since Leandro had left her that day on the beach bubbled to the surface, bringing tears to her eyes. Luz turned her face away; she wanted nothing more than to go to bed and have a good cry, alone.

Alba ran over and put her arms around her. 'Oh, Luz, you're upset. I knew there was something more to this. Isn't there anything I can do to help?' She stroked her arm tentatively.

Luz hesitated a fraction. She dearly wanted to unburden herself to her friend but explaining everything was too daunting. But she was so mixed up and confused herself, what if Alba misjudged her and disapproved of her feelings for a *gitano*? She shook her head emphatically. 'There's nothing anybody can do. I have to live with it and hope that someday I may forget.'

Alba eyed her dubiously. 'Whether it's Andrés or someone else … I don't know who this rogue, this *picaro*, is and what he's done to you. But if it's any consolation, men flow to you like bees to honey. I saw them tonight – Lorenzo being no exception, much to my chagrin,' she admitted laughingly. 'Whatever your feelings are for Andrés de Calderón, that man is head over heels in love with you. I assure you, Carlos noticed it as well.'

'Carlos? What do you mean?' Luz sounded surprised.

'I mean that *el Señor* de Calderón's eyes were glued to you all evening. Carlos was sitting near him at dinner and was not so wrapped up in his own flirtation not to notice. Even during dinner, when you were sitting at the other end of the table, Andrés was watching you quietly behind those long dark eyelashes of his. I tell you, nobody else stands a chance when you're in the room. And that must have hit home loud and clear to Adalia tonight.'

Luz was listening now with her head slightly tilted to one side. She had never lacked confidence and had always been aware of the opposite sex's interest in her, though she rarely felt inclined to return it, so why did Alba's words fill her with such reassurance? A feeling of warmth suddenly invaded her heart. Andrés always disorientated her. Even when he had seized her in that scalding kiss tonight, pressing her to him so urgently and swamping her reason and she had thought that he was toying with her again, she had not cared. Could there be something deeper behind it? The thought of it was so strange it frightened her, even more than her wanton response to him.

'Do you really think so?' she muttered, as though measuring all that it meant.

'I *know* so. He said goodbye to the Herreras as soon as you walked out of the room. That's why everybody who noticed, including me, assumed he had followed you into the garden,' she continued. 'You could have cut the air with a knife. Andrés insisted Adalia shouldn't accompany him to his car, practically ordered her to stay with her guests. Plain as daylight!'

Her friend's gossiping drew an amused smile from Luz, who was secretly enjoying these details. 'What else did your eagle eye register? It's fascinating.'

Alba beamed. 'Oh, after all that drama, everything else was dull,' she told her, a mischievous twinkle in her large brown eyes. 'So did he or did he not follow you into the garden?'

Luz shrugged, letting her friend deduce the conclusion she wanted.

'Goodnight, Alba. You're a good friend and I do appreciate your concern, but I really don't think you want to get involved in all this. Thanks for trying, though.'

Alba sighed, clearly resigned that she would receive no more information. 'Are you still intent on leaving tomorrow morning?' she asked.

'Yes,' said Luz, resolutely. 'I need to get back to work as soon as possible. And anyway, I've never been a great fan of *corridas*, you know that.'

She got up and hugged her friend affectionately.

'And twenty-four hours will make such a difference to your work?' Alba eyed her sceptically and laughed, hugging her back. 'For what it's worth, Luz, if I had a man like Andrés de Calderón in love with me, I'd grab him and never let go. He's not my type, of course – too intense, too passionate and besides, my heart lies elsewhere. But hidalgos like him are few and far between these days.'

CHAPTER 8

It was only when she was back in Cádiz that Luz began to put some order into the chaos clogging her usually clear mind. For days she trotted along the beach on Zeyna's back, lost in her own maze of conflicting emotions. Her reaction to Andrés' lovemaking in Pamplona had shaken her to the core. She resented his desire for her as much as she was ashamed of hers for him. The man was a duplicitous snake, yet when his hands explored her so hungrily, his mouth tasting her with such heat and urgency, she could not still her body's response; he had aroused the same passionate need as when Leandro had made love to her on the beach. The thought of it unnerved her.

Andrés was just as attractive and compelling as his gypsy counterpart, with the added polish and charisma of the well-bred gentleman. So much about the shrewd businessman remained a mystery, apart from the fact that he was distrustful, manipulative and underhand: a cluster of attributes she did not care much for. Nevertheless, there was something more to him beneath that calm exterior. She had been aware of it in his company but she could not put a finger on it. The other night as he held her in his arms, and when he'd called after her as she left him, she had sensed it more than ever: an anguish and a vulnerability that were unexpected in a man of his station.

What about her? In all this confusion, what was she waiting for? What did she really want, true love or simply an affair? It seemed she responded to Leandro and to Andrés with equal fire, as her body had proved to her the other night. Thus the conclusion she must draw is that she loved neither of them: it was pure unadulterated lust. After all, what did she know about sex? Leandro was her first lover. All the needs that had pulsed through her that afternoon on the beach were new. She had dated a lot, but very few of the young men made it beyond a kiss. 'You don't know what you're missing!' her friends had teased. Now she did. Still, she did not regret her previous ignorance; at least at twenty-four her senses were not jaded, unlike those of many young women of her generation. But, sadly, she would never have the chance to get to know Leandro. There was not the briefest connection between their universes.

As for Andrés, he might be a far more suitable proposition but he was already spoken for if she was to believe Lorenzo; and even if he were not attached, she was determined not to let her relationship with him go beyond the biography project. After all, he was a client and she knew to her cost that mixing work with pleasure was never a good idea. Her father had often told her to beware of making a mess in her own backyard.

Indeed, she had made an utter fool of herself the other night. Her behaviour had been outrageous. Firstly she had responded with undisguised pleasure to Andrés' lovemaking, secondly she had called him Leandro by mistake, thirdly she had slapped him across the face – twice – and finally, to cap it all, she had rushed away in hysterics as if she were the injured party. Guilt and shame wrestled together as she acknowledged the magnitude of her stupidity. Andrés must be so contemptuous of her; he was probably so disgusted that he never wanted to set eyes on her again.

He'll pull the project, she thought. There were countless people who could do the job. It would enable him to write a new contract with terms that suited him better, with someone more biddable than her. Yes, she was sure she would soon be getting her marching orders and she could not blame him for that. Her morale sank to rock bottom.

She daren't get in touch with Andrés. How could she after such appalling conduct? Surely he would make contact in due course. At least if he did, she would have something decent to present to him; if not, then maybe it would be all for the best. Luz tried her best to put her nagging anxieties behind her as she continued work on the biography each morning – it became her chief solace and distraction. And though she spent a lot of time on the beach, she never went back to the cove. Her memories of the place were still vivid and despite her determination not to think of Leandro, they hurt. But it seemed that she would not be allowed to forget the gypsy that easily.

One evening, Luz couldn't sleep. She had gone to bed early but a couple of hours later had awoken from another dream about the gypsy and his doppelgänger that had left her skin damp with heat and flagrant desire. The night was hot, the French windows flung open, making the curtains waft gently now and then in the scant sea breeze. Luz slipped out of bed and went on to the terrace, scraping her hair back with her hands, her breathing still heavy. She was increasingly convinced that her sensual impulses were spiralling out of control.

Even though it was late, she was restless now and needed to shake off this feeling. Pulling on some cut-off jeans and a white camisole vest, she left the cliff house and headed down to the beach. A long walk by the sea would clear her mind.

Light from the moon spilt on to the surface of the inky waters and dark clouds formed themselves into fantastic shapes across the indigo sky. Like the elongated figures in one of Eduardo's paintings, Luz thought as she gazed upwards. The briny smell of the sea filled her lungs, its rhythmic roar echoing the raging of her body and the ache in her heart. She felt small and insignificant against the great dark curtain of the night and yet, at that moment, she felt her emotions were powerful enough to burst and fill its infinite stretch.

She couldn't bear this constant torment. Her head was plagued with images of Andrés and Leandro. One moment she was recalling that afternoon not so long ago when Leandro's warm, hard body had pressed against hers in the cool water, his wildly intense lovemaking surging through her like a force of nature; and the next, thoughts of Andrés took hold of her as if she were possessed ... the primal erotic charge between them when his hands had seized her, sending her blood burning with that passionate kiss; her own desperate hunger to surrender to his dominion ... She shivered again just remembering. Both liaisons were doomed, she knew, but something about these two men compelled her to act in a way she couldn't understand. This new libidinous, wayward streak in her was deeply disturbing. What was she hoping for? What was she supposed to do? She didn't know.

Surely the strange resemblance between the gypsy and his gentleman double was to blame for her wanton behaviour? Somehow she had the uncomfortable feeling that the truth was a little more disturbing. They must be twins, she pondered. It was still not inconceivable for children to be kidnapped by gypsies. Perhaps the two had been separated at birth.

Besides, she and Leandro had never had the chance for real conversation; their bodies spoke the same language, but that was about it. They came from different worlds. What did they have in common except for an overpowering physical attraction that was almost certainly hormonal and would eventually fizzle out? Leandro had obviously come to that conclusion already; that was why he was refusing to take their brief relationship any further, she reasoned. Kind and unselfish, he had a conscience, too: a gypsy hidalgo. At least she knew that about him. Sometimes, when she was feeling weak, she allowed herself to daydream, imagining all the obstacles separating them were knocked down. Then he would come to her and lift her into his powerful arms; nothing else would matter but their love and passion for each other. A lamenting laugh tore from her throat, smothered by the hiss of the sea, as she felt the million pieces of her shattered dream blow away in the wind.

Wrapped up in her own thoughts, she had followed the path of the beach for a long time, further than she had ever ventured on foot, before she became aware of faint strains of music wafting on the night air. She looked towards the dunes and spotted an orange glow of fire in the distance: the music was coming from there. Following its sound, she scrambled up the dunes from the beach. Was she nearing the gypsy camp? This was a different place entirely – just a small patch of sandy hillocks, half surrounded by carob bushes and even closer to the sea.

As she climbed further, the music became more distinct, accompanied by whooping and clapping. Two guitars thrummed furiously against each other as the clapping and hollering crescendoed to its finale and then stopped, cheers and laughter breaking out. Among the shouts of exclamation in Spanish there was another language Luz didn't recognize, which wasn't *Caló*.

Luz reached the top of the sandbank and crouched down, slowly crawling forwards until she found a vantage point. Lying on her side against the hilly dune and propping herself on one arm, she peered out between the tufts of grass on to a large clearing where the ground had been trodden flat. Whiffs of roasting meat and tobacco mingled with the salty sea air.

An enormous group of men and women, perhaps a hundred or so, were assembled around three or four fires. These held rudimentary spits on which rabbits and small fowl were being turned by women with jangling bracelets on their arms, who every so often poked at the embers with long sticks. Around the largest fire a semi-circle of men were staggering, shouting and clapping, squirting wine wildly over each other's faces, while others, men and women, squatted on mats or sat on low wooden stools to the side.

Some of the men looked different from the *Calés*, as far as Luz could make out: the older ones had pointed, straggly beards and the younger men sported thin moustaches; all of them wore dark waistcoats and short brimmed hats, and many had sharper features than the other group. Similarly, there were women who looked more Eastern European or Turkish than Spanish, with red scarves tied around their heads and long plaits that fell below their waists.

These were gypsies, sure enough, thought Luz. But what kind of tribe were they and what were they doing there?

From where she was lying, Luz was only a few yards from the large fire and the *gitanos* seated around it. As she watched them talking and passing the wineskins around, she suddenly spied the black-eyed gypsy rose seller, whom she'd last encountered so memorably in the orange grove at El Pavón when she had gone looking for Leandro. Luz froze and her blood ran cold. She looked away, worried she might be discovered, even though the long seagrass provided good cover.

Yet her curiosity was by now far too aroused to leave. She took a steadying breath and turned back. The *gitana* was talking to an imposing-looking man in his fifties or early sixties, with a bushy moustache and triangular beard, wearing a slightly taller peaked hat than the other men. They were sharing a pipe and nodding.

The man then put two fingers in his mouth and let out a piercing whistle. At this, the sound of the revellers died down a little. 'Grigoras,' he called out in thickly accented Spanish, 'bring out your fiddle, you've been sitting too long. Need some brandy to whip your sluggish carcass into life!'

A young drunken *gitano* waved a bottle. 'Yes, Grigoras. *Darle un palo al burro*, give the mule a taste of the stick!' he piped up to gales of laughter from the crowd.

'Toñito, if you're mean with your wineskin, I'll conjure the Devil himself and he'll take his own stick to you,' answered another *gitano* with a thin moustache. He grinned broadly as he pulled himself up from his stool, a violin under his arm.

Toñito laughed. 'Hey, Grigoras, you may have only just arrived tonight, but if you *Tzigane* musicians aren't as good as you say, then you'd better run straight back to Transylvania before your instruments are smashed over your heads!'

More laughter erupted.

'I'd like to see that,' chuckled another man, who was strapping on his accordion. He nodded at the bearded man sitting next to the gypsy rose seller. 'Nicholae, will you dance this one?'

The bearded man, Nicholae, clearly the king of the *Tzigane* tribe, waved his hand dismissively. 'Later, József,' he grunted. 'I will keep Marujita company for now. And then she's promised to honour us with a dance.'

He turned to the gypsy rose seller next to him, who nodded.

'Nicholae, the honour will be mine.' The *gitana* gave a rasping cough before picking up a glass and necking a shot of brandy. 'I've had too much of the pipe,' she said and then gestured with a heavily braceleted arm. 'Now, *amigo*, let's have your dancing!'

Nicholae reached for the bottle at their feet and waved it at the musicians. 'Grigoras, Jószef, show these sea *Calés* how the mountain *Tziganes* get a thirst.'

At the order of his king, the gypsy Grigoras drew his bow across his fiddle and it was as if fire leapt from the strings. The melody bounced furiously along while Jószef, the accordion player, joined in, his fingers running like spiders over his instrument, tapping an impossibly fast counter-rhythm as he wailed a rousing song over the top. The whole camp broke into clapping and stomping.

The music, like the people, was free and wild. They wore their gypsy identity like a badge of honour, showing the world that they were *gitanos* with a fierce, joyful arrogance. The men got up first and danced in pairs, each one dancing around the other, jumping and stamping, then slapping his chest, thighs and feet with fast and intricate movements. They snapped their fingers rapidly to the furious, syncopated rhythms of the violin and every now and then indulged in acrobatic movements, even somersaulting, as the women clapped out a rhythm off the beat, crying out in time with the song. After a while other women came to join in, clasping their full skirts, which they moved quickly about them to the rhythm, gyrating their hips and vibrating their shoulders.

There was energy and elegance in the way they moved. They seemed to be a people who danced whether they were happy or sad, with or without an audience, to release energy or just for the pure joy of it. It was in their blood, in their bones, and was the air they breathed. They danced as if they wanted to break through the earth beneath their feet.

Luz watched, entranced, as dance led into dance, each one followed with ever-greater whoops of approval from the Spanish gypsies, who began getting up and careering about with their *Tzigane* counterparts. Guitars joined the violin and accordion as men leapt over bottles and pulled their women into spins.

It was then that she saw Leandro. Her heart jumped into her throat. He was wearing a tight white T-shirt and faded loose jeans rolled above the ankles. Firelight flickered on his bronzed skin and muscled arms as he danced barefoot in a group of *Tzigane* men, all interlinking arms across each other's shoulders. His long chestnut hair fell over his face in wild disarray as he moved in a way that made him look almost primitive.

Luz felt a visceral hunger burn in her blood at the sight of him, every nerve ending in her remembering how his body had felt to touch when he had made love to her in the sand that afternoon, and how far away he was from her now. When the music came to a halt and more cheers and shouts broke out, he accepted a swig from a wineskin, drinking deeply and wiping his hand across his mouth. Although he smiled at his fellow *gitanos* as they patted him heartily on the back, Luz noticed his body language was pent-up and restless, like that of a caged animal, as he stepped back from the small group and went to join Nicholae and the *gitana* he had called Marujita.

Luz shifted uncomfortably in the sand, watching Leandro take a seat in the ring of people that had increased around the fire. Looking down, he ran a hand through his hair. A familiar feeling of pressure formed in her chest: this was his world and she had no part in it. Did he still think of her? Could he turn off his passion so easily? A jagged pain cut through her even though she knew it was hopeless to yearn for him this way.

The feast in the gypsy camp was now in full swing. Voices rose rhythmically, shot through with shouts and the occasional report of a revolver. The moon shone in all her silver splendour, spotlighting the lone figure now central to this kaleidoscopic whirl of colour, a dancing *Tzigane* girl with piercing black eyes and long jet-black hair worn in a single braid that hung down her back like a gleaming rope. She wore voluminous, flounced multicoloured skirts, an embroidered bodice and tight basque of coloured calico.

The girl's waist was tightly cinched by a narrow belt, which further emphasized the curving lines of her very full bust and hips. Her slender arms were covered with gold bracelets, bangles and chains, and in her graceful hand she held a tambourine, which she tapped in time with the music. A gauzy veil floated on her head, which she used for posturing. Her well-shaped feet and ankles were bare. From time to time there were glimpses of silver anklets and hennaed toes and heels as her feet twinkled in and out under the long skirts. For this brief interlude she was queen of all, surrounded by a circle of men and women, now four-deep, who were beating time for her dancing by clapping hands and knees rhythmically; all the while they chanted a loud call, which rose in volume until the air throbbed with it and then diminished to a lower note before swelling higher again.

The *Tzigane* girl danced faster and faster, hesitating only when deciding on which man she would choose to join her in the dance. At each new round her gestures and postures became more provocative until she threw her veil over Leandro, who was seated in the first circle.

He looked up as the veil trailed off his face. Leaping up, he instantly seized her waist and they swung together amid the *olés* and cries of exhilaration of the excited audience in the circle, surrendering to the repetitious, stimulating beat. There was a look of something fierce on his face as he danced: an exorcism of some passionate, angry emotion that gripped him as he spun himself and the *Tzigane* girl around. Though he looked at her intently, it was as if he wasn't seeing her.

Now Leandro signalled to Marujita to join them inside the ring. The older *gitana* took up her castanets and stalked into the space, twirling her hands like proud birds. Now the true queen had taken the stage for all to see. With mesmerizing nobility the gypsy danced, her head held high, hands and arms moving with a power and beauty that were breathtaking. Every movement, while exaggerated in its twists and turns, was fluidly graceful; then she dipped and twirled aggressively like an Amazon warrior, her castanets clattering like gunfire. Marujita's black eyes shone like some terrifying goddess as her arms swooped up like wings about to take flight. Even the *Tzigane* girl fell to the side, leaving Leandro encircling Marujita, an expression of fire and reverence on his face and, if Luz was not mistaken, pain.

Luz was so transfixed that she forgot herself for a moment and raised herself up to get a better view. Suddenly she saw Marujita's head jerk towards her as if she had caught her scent, but then the gypsy turned back again and carried on with her dance. Luz dipped down and lay on her back, breathing faster. Could she have been seen? Surely she was too well hidden. Nevertheless, Luz had seen enough; she did not belong here.

It was tempting to cast a last glance back at Leandro but instead she wriggled slowly back, keeping as low as possible, hearing the explosion of shouts and *olés*, whooping and whistling as the pulsating music came to a roaring finish. Once at the edge of the dunes, Luz scrambled quickly down the bank. She skidded so fast through the sand that she half fell the last distance, grabbing on to a hard tuft of seagrass.

'Back again, looking for him?'

Luz's head snapped up, startled by the husky female voice, and her eyes met the jet-black stare of the gypsy, Marujita. She was standing with one hand on her hip, the other holding a bottle of brandy at her side. Beneath the heavy make-up her skin was even greyer than Luz remembered, making her look suddenly much older, without a trace of the beauty she must once have held. A triumphant smile curled at Marujita's lips.

'You're persistent, *hermosa jovencita*!' She took a gulp from the bottle, her charcoal eyes fixed on Luz. 'As I told you before, gypsies have long memories and I remember you. Very well.'

Luz straightened up and dusted the sand off her jeans. It unnerved her to think that the *gitana* had somehow sensed she was there, hiding among the dunes. The gypsy made her want to bolt, but she stood her ground, meeting the older woman's intense gaze.

'I was taking a walk as I couldn't sleep and stumbled across your gathering quite by chance, *señora*,' she explained truthfully.

Marujita ignored her. 'You've no business here. This is not a place for *gajos*, though I know why you've come,' she almost sneered.

Luz raised her chin, determined not to feel intimidated. 'I don't know what you mean. Besides, you don't own the beach. I have as much right to be here as you.'

The gypsy let out a rasping laugh and took a swig of her bottle. 'Oh, you're a rebellious one, aren't you? Well, you have no rights in our world. Gypsy law is gypsy law.' She gave a sly smile and tossed back her unkempt hair. 'But I could help you with the one you want, help you catch him. That's what you desire most, isn't it?'

Luz gazed at Marujita impassively, not wanting her to know how rattled she felt. The *gitana* had the most disturbing presence she had ever encountered. What did she know of Luz's feelings for Leandro? She had offered Luz a love talisman when they had first met and, if the old witch Paquita hadn't snatched it back and warned Marujita off, what would Luz have found wrapped up in that small parcel?

'How can you know what I want?' Luz said. She didn't really want to hear what Marujita had to say but part of her was intrigued.

'I know things about you just by looking into your face,' Marujita replied. Her sardonic smile seemed to harden as her black eyes roved over Luz's features as if taking them in anew. In the pale moonlight Luz could see that the gypsy's expression had assumed a deadly mask. 'Oh yes, I know you, *hermosa jovencita.*' Then abruptly she snapped, 'The one you want has other fish to fry. He doesn't want you – not in the way you dream of.'

'And what makes you think you can see into the head of every *gitano* in the camp?' Luz shot back boldly, not caring that she might be giving too much away.

'I am the queen of the *Calés.* I know everything about them, each and every one of them.' The gypsy's eyes gleamed malignantly. 'You think you *gajo* women can come along and take our men whenever you want. You can never have the one you run after. He is a *gitano,* and blood doesn't mix.' A strange look crossed her face as if the thought pained and angered her at the same time. 'Why would he look at you when there are plenty of fine gypsy girls lining up for him? He is one of us and tonight he can have the pick of any girl!'

Luz's heart constricted. The thought of Leandro in another woman's arms was almost too much to bear. She stared at the gypsy with stunned incomprehension. It was well known that *gitanos* distrusted anyone outside their own kind and on their previous encounters Luz had put Marujita's cryptic, threatening aura down to that peculiar quality that some gypsies had. But what she saw now in the *gitana*'s dark eyes was pure hatred. What was wrong with this woman? Why did she seem so determined to hurt her?

Luz breathed in and gazed at her intently. 'As I said, *señora*, I don't know what you're talking about.'

Marujita took a final drink and looked Luz up and down balefully. 'You can never escape your fate,' she hissed. And with that, still clutching her bottle, she picked up her skirts and disappeared into the dunes.

Luz stared after her for a moment, nervous anger and distress coursing through her veins. What had the *gitana* meant about fate? Hadn't that old witch Paquita warned that she would be cursed if she tried to avoid her destiny? She shuddered. In any case, whatever was in store for her, she felt powerless to fight it now. Her life was like the inexorable tide of the sea, pushing her further into a great, unknown expanse … or was she heading closer to the rocks? She wished she knew. None of this was what she'd expected when she left the cliff house that night and, as Luz made her way back along the shimmering stretch of beach, she had a sense of foreboding that descended upon her like a crouching incubus.

The silver moon bathed the shoreline in a luminous glow as streaks of dark cloud reached out towards it like long arms wanting to extinguish the light. As Luz followed the brim of the water's edge back to L'Estrella, the lone figure of a man stood at the top of the dunes staring after her. Silhouetted against the fire-lit indigo night, he watched Luz for a long time before disappearing back to the gypsy camp.

*   *   *

The next week flew by in a blur. Luz was determined to bury her turbulent emotions in work and exercise. Carmela commented on her relentless activity but Luz reassured the housekeeper that she was merely enjoying being busy. Her inner torment remained a secret only she would know.

One morning Luz had spent a good hour exercising Zeyna up and down the shore. Along the waterfront a few cotton-wool clouds seemed to bounce over the harbour and the ships' masts, with sunlight rippling on the water and reflecting the bows. Afternoon shadows threw chequered lights upon the white dune-backed beach. Windsurfers glided silently along the transparent blueness of the ocean.

Luz was splashing back through the shallows, a game she often indulged in with Zeyna, when suddenly she froze and stared, her heart lurching uncontrollably. There he was, large as life, twenty yards away, leaning casually against his motorcycle and talking to his gypsy friends. His jeans clung to his athletic thighs as he swung one leg over the bike, the black tank top moulding to his torso in a way that made her mouth go dry; his long sun-bleached hair was ruffled by the breeze with wisps across his face accentuating his rakish good looks. As he gripped the handlebars, her eyes were drawn to his muscled, tanned arms, which time and again had hauled her into their powerful embrace. How she longed for him! Had he been on his own, she would not have hesitated to jump off her horse and run to him, all resolution cast to the winds.

Instead she made Zeyna slow down and steered her into his view, wanting to catch his eye, for him to smile, wave at her or make any sign at all to acknowledge he had seen her and that, even if they were not lovers any more, they were not complete strangers either. As she neared he lifted his head and for a second her heart leapt joyously in the hope that he was going to turn towards her, but he slammed the engine into gear and rode off in a roar, kicking up a mist of thin white sand as he went.

Luz felt the sting of tears well up in her eyes as she nudged her mare to a full gallop in the direction of home. The words of the gypsy Marujita rang in her ears: 'The one you want has other fish to fry. He is a *gitano* and blood doesn't mix.' Strong gusts whipped her hair across her face as she rode, gripping the reins ever more tightly.

Like a forbidden mirage he would always appear just when she thought her love for him was waning.

*   *   *

The next day, Luz finally heard from Andrés. A note was hand-delivered from his office, but without roses this time. She was hardly surprised after the way she had behaved at La Fortaleza. With trembling hands she opened the cream envelope. His note was brief and to the point, very courteously summoning her to Caldezar Corporación, SA for a briefing session to bring him up to date. He hoped she could make the appointment he had set up and would be most grateful if she would either confirm it or make another date with his secretary if this one was inconvenient. She breathed a sigh of relief – at least she wasn't being fired.

The meeting was set up for the following morning. Luz took particular care to present a neat and professional appearance just as she had done before when she first visited Andrés' office. She wore a beige suit, which hugged her in all the right places, and put up her hair in a severe chignon, which offset her shapely cheekbones and made her sapphire eyes seem even wider. Pearl earrings, a small quilted Chanel bag and matching high heels achieved the quietly sophisticated image she was looking for. A last glance in the mirror assured her that she could not have presented herself better.

Luz was nervous. Despite the heat, her hands were ice-cold as she arrived at Caldezar Corporación, SA's grand office in Plaza de España and was taken up in the lift. Her stomach churned uncomfortably and her heart raced so hard that she thought it would leap out of her mouth at any moment. She could not bear to think about her behaviour that night at La Fortaleza. How could she face him? What excuse could she give? He had probably lost any shred of respect he'd ever held for her. Still, she must face the situation and if that meant she had to grovel a little, then so be it. After all, Andrés de Calderón was not that saintly himself and if she needed to remind him of that, she would. No, no, that was exactly what she must not do, she remonstrated. She needed to look poised and self-assured at all times. She could argue her point calmly, even firmly, but under no circumstances should she be rude, belligerent or uncontrolled – that was sure to get her into hot water again.

As she was being shown towards Andrés' office, Adalia burst out of the room. She looked flustered and her eyes were red, hardly the confident socialite Luz had seen in Pamplona. She almost knocked Luz over as she brushed past without seeing her. Was there trouble in paradise? Luz wondered.

When she entered the room, he was standing by the window looking out to sea with his back to her, one hand thrust in his pocket. His office felt cool after the heat outside. Sunlight cast lengthy, bright oblong beams through the picture window, fanning around him as though radiating from his body.

'Doña Luz de Rueda,' his assistant announced.

Andrés waited until the woman had left the room before he turned. His dark gaze settled on Luz.

'Good morning.' An imperceptible tremor of anxiety ran through her skin at the sound of his voice, which his alert eyes did not miss. 'Are you cold? Shall I have the air-conditioning turned down? It has been said that I keep my office too cold.' A faint smile touched his lips.

He was perfectly courteous, but he exuded something that turned her throat dry. Luz shook her head mutely. He stood there a moment more in the halo of sunshine surrounding him, so clearly master of the situation.

'Please, take a seat, Luz.' He watched her as he settled down in the large leather chair behind his desk. Luz forced herself to gaze back at him steadily. Her face was a little pale but otherwise she managed to maintain a cool and dispassionate exterior that belied the storminess inside her.

'What are you thinking?' he asked, breaking the silence, his intelligent eyes scanning her face intently.

She cleared her throat and tried to look composed. 'I was thinking,' she said, raising her chin a little, 'that I owe you an apology for my appalling behaviour the other evening.' Her face flamed with colour. There, she had said it. She was feeling a little easier now it was out.

There was a moment of awkwardness then, to her utter astonishment, it was not contempt she glimpsed in his steady dark eyes but a look of understanding, something almost gentle. He smiled that special muted smile, which no doubt set all women's hearts a-flutter.

'I myself was largely to blame,' he conceded in a quiet voice, 'so let's put all of it behind us and write this biography. There's much work to be done.'

Luz's eyes widened. She had not expected such a chivalrous answer. Was it simply because he was a gentleman that he chose not to embarrass her over her dreadful faux pas at La Fortaleza? Or was this another game, merely designed to encourage her to lower her guard and once more give him the upper hand? There was a slight pause as they continued to look at each other.

His unwavering scrutiny held nothing that threatened her this time, she was almost convinced of that. She tore her gaze away and, not for the first time, wondered what made the real Andrés de Calderón tick.

She smiled slowly and reached for the notes in her bag. 'Yes, let's make a start.'

The simmering nervousness inside her faded as they began to discuss the book. Her notes were considerable – at least the time she had spent buried in her work had paid off. She outlined her plan to him, the layout of chapters and the way she would tackle the development of her ideas. Following this, she gave him an in-depth view of the conclusions she had drawn about Eduardo de Salazar's personality and his fantastical art, based on facts she had gathered about his personal life and his extensive travels around the world. There were still big gaps, she told him, and she would need his assistance to fill them in.

For over an hour Andrés wore his businessman's hat and together they worked in harmony. She seemed to be talking endlessly but that did not matter. Luz was determined to explain her research meticulously and noticed that Andrés spoke very little but was attentive as she outlined her thoughts. Despite being caught up in her own fascination for the material she had unearthed about the artist, she found her attention frequently drawn to Andrés' mouth as he watched her intently, resting his elbow on the arm of his chair, a finger on those sensual lips, while she sketched out her proposal for the early chapters of the book.

He must be a brilliant poker player, she caught herself thinking, because his features were giving away nothing about what he thought of her work and the progress she had made with the project. Well, at least he was listening. He had known how to put her at her ease so he had drawn her out and she was glittering.

Luz finished her presentation. She leaned back in her chair, relieved that it was finally over. Going through her work again, she had been surprised by the amount of detail she had been able to squeeze into these first chapters. The meeting, she felt, had been a success. Was this the right moment to take the bull by the horns and tackle the subject of Lorenzo's apparent collaboration and the archiving of the Herrera collection? For almost the first time since they had met, Andrés and she were not at loggerheads. She had to admit being on good terms with him was such an agreeable feeling that she dared not jeopardize it. Still, she had to say something. It was important he understood that those terms he and Lorenzo had put in place, without prior discussion with her, were unacceptable. She wished she understood more about this man; that she knew what was going on in his head. At times she thought she must be dealing with a case of Dr Jekyll and Mr Hyde: today it was the likeable Dr Jekyll's turn to make an appearance and she had no doubt that that was when Andrés de Calderón was at his most dangerous.

Their eyes met, locked. Hers were shining, his steadfast and impassive. For a few harrowing moments she thought she had misinterpreted his silence. Her heart sank. Was what she had taken for mute appreciation in fact disappointment? She drew in a breath and waited for some sarcastic comment.

'I'm impressed, Luz. I think it's likely you have given us something important we can share together,' he said, beaming. *Us? Share? Together? What was he saying?* This was all new to her. She was more accustomed to his patronizing tone, peppered with biting sarcasm. What game was he playing this time?

He must have sensed her alarm and frowned faintly. 'What is it, Luz?'

She did not answer and his frown deepened, vertical lines furrowing his forehead. He paused as if waiting for a reply but, when none was forthcoming, his eyes narrowed. 'You really are wary of me, aren't you?' It was more of a statement than a question. Suddenly his extreme self-assurance, his aura of power evaporated. Shutters came down over the dark irises. He passed a hand wearily over his hair and sighed. 'What have I done this time to merit the silent reproach in those expressive eyes of yours?'

She could see the despair in his gaze, so unlike the confident man she was used to. Was this all part of the game, too? Had Lorenzo told him about her reaction to their plan?

She sat up, straightened her back and ran the tip of her tongue over her drying lips. Still she hesitated, reluctant to battle with Andrés and knowing they were bound to clash when she brought up the dreaded subject.

'Why did you not tell me about the Herrera collection?' she asked quietly.

He seemed a little taken aback. 'What about the Herrera collection?' He shrugged. 'It's like any other collection you're investigating,' he told her dispassionately. 'We're still in the early stages of this project, there's plenty we've not talked about. In fact, I've had my assistant compile a list of collectors whom you should meet and interview. The Herreras are on that list, of course.' He stared at her but still she could not read his mind.

'You rightly spoke about gaps that needed filling when you outlined your plan to me this morning and I've told you that I'm always here to help. I thought it a little premature to load everything on to you before now.' His eyes searched her face. 'I didn't realize the amount of information you had gathered in such a short time but I hadn't wanted to pre-empt or influence your thoughts in any way. I'm obviously biased, since Eduardo and I were extremely close, and the works held in the archives at Puesta de Sol are closest to my heart. Maybe I should have talked about other specific collections before.'

Luz swallowed hard before speaking, trying to conceal the tremor in her voice. He made it all sound so logical, simple; honest even. But there was more to this, she knew, and she felt a fresh wave of anger bubble to the surface.

'Why didn't you tell me that *archiving* the Herrera collection was part of my contract? Why didn't you also ...?'

'Hey, wait a minute,' he interrupted, leaning forward. 'Archiving the Herrera collection has never been on the cards.'

Liar! she thought, but managed to remain composed. 'Not only was I told it had all been arranged at the early stages of the project but I was also informed that Lorenzo would be an editor and contributor, and that I would have to work on site at La Fortaleza, which I'm afraid is totally unacceptable,' she stated coldly.

'You were told what?' His eyes darkened and there was a dangerous edge to his voice.

Not for the first time since the beginning of this assignment, Luz wondered what she had got herself into. Andrés seemed genuinely taken aback. She had anticipated he would find a plausible reason to enforce his decision. After all, she had to concede that even though it did not suit her, and she certainly did not relish spending any time alone with Lorenzo, the plan to archive the Herrera collection and other portfolios did make sense. Eduardo de Salazar was a prolific and diverse artist; she would have thought with such a variety of works, records and some sort of indexing would have already been set up but, if not, Andrés would surely see that this was probably the time to do so. And one could argue that Lorenzo might be helpful in the process, though not to the degree the vain *torero* imagined.

'There was never any talk of this,' Andrés continued, his dark irises glittering with fury. 'Eduardo's work in its entirety has already been catalogued. He was not only an artist but also a shrewd and meticulous businessman. There is not a stroke of his paintbrush that has not been listed, photographed and archived. Who,' he demanded, 'who told you these lies?'

Luz sat absolutely still. She stared up at him, confusion and doubt shadowing her eyes. There was an uncomfortable pause. 'Lorenzo, your friend and business partner,' she answered calmly.

Andrés acknowledged the jab and his jaw tightened. 'He made it very clear that we would be working closely together,' she added.

'*What?*' At this, Andrés swore robustly. Luz had never seen him angry; it was a fascinating revelation. His voice sounded like thunder in the otherwise silent sunlit room and his face appeared almost barbaric, eyes lethal. This was either news to him or he had passed up a very promising career with the Royal Shakespeare Company.

He pushed back his chair roughly and stood up, glaring ahead of him. Looming over his desk he looked like a fallen angel, raised from the bottomless pit to take out his wrath on mankind. A muscle jerked in his jaw and his midnight gaze moved to her face as he struggled to remain calm. He placed a hand over his heart.

'Luz, you must believe me when I tell you that I would never dream of putting you in that sort of position.' Outwardly, he might have had the finesse and charm of the sophisticated gentleman, but it struck her as an irony now that the hidalgo seemed closer to a gypsy at heart.

He strode across the room. The fabulous animal-like vitality he barely held in check was formidable. Luz's spine tingled as, reluctantly, she felt herself aroused, somewhere deep and hidden. He clenched his hands into fists to keep a lid on his anger, which was threatening to explode. In two strides he was at the door and opened it briskly. He called out to his assistant: 'Is Don Lorenzo still in his office?' His voice was cool and Luz marvelled at how quickly he had managed to regain his composure.

'No, *señor*. Don Lorenzo and Doña Adalia have just left for the day.'

Andrés nodded and came back into the room. The volcano seemed to have died down as swiftly as it had erupted. Still, his eyes burned into Luz as he stood facing her, before he settled down once again into the chair behind his desk. He paused for a moment, lost in thought, and the atmosphere changed subtly.

'Have dinner with me tonight at Puesta de Sol and I will prove to you that there's no truth in what Lorenzo told you.' His voice stroked her, his eyes were caressing. Something stirred in Luz that she did not stop to question.

'I will ensure that you can visit Eduardo's archives at my home whenever you have the need,' he said. 'I should have sorted out all this before, I realize now it was wrong of me not to have done so. Please forgive this lapse,' he said humbly. 'As for Lorenzo,' he added, the fallen-angel look flickering dangerously in his jet irises, 'I will deal with him when I see him next.'

For a moment Luz was nonplussed. Her deep-blue eyes questioned his sincerity. In the light of this revelation, she really had nothing to reproach him for – apart from the fact, of course, that he had pounced on her like a ravenous wolf that night at La Fortaleza. After her violent reaction she was quite sure he would not attempt that stunt again, or at least not for the time being. She would be safe from him, surely?

As she marshalled her thoughts, she was so tempted to believe this time that he meant what he said. Still, she had been there before and where had it got her? Humiliation at every turn. Wrestling with logic, she tried to be businesslike and put her work before her unsettled pride; but pride won. She couldn't bear to be his puppet, her string jerked by him whenever he so chose.

'I'm afraid I have a previous engagement tonight,' she heard herself say.

His jaw tightened. 'Then maybe we can make it another night,' he paused, 'at your convenience.'

Yes, that's better, she thought, adding: 'I will take a look at my diary and let you know.'

Andrés looked at her steadily, his gaze challenging, and suddenly a smile tugged at the corner of his mouth. 'I will learn to be patient,' he muttered. There was something about that dark voice that made her cheeks flush. He turned his gaze away and once again seemed lost in thought, leaving her with his beautifully etched, arrogant profile to admire. The curtain had come down, it was time for her to leave.

Luz stood up. 'I really must get on,' she said, extending her hand.

Slowly, he stood up too. His dark gaze moved back to meet hers, steady and night-like. He took her hand and held it firmly.

'Luz, I know you're wary of me,' he said and, though his tone was calm and collected, she could see his irises burned with fire. 'I realize that it has been in great part my fault. I'm not asking you to lower your guard ... I'm merely requesting a truce for the time being until we know a little more about each other. Can you do that?'

There was a brief, electric-filled second while Luz braced herself, ignoring the pounding of her heart and the warmth flooding her body. Again he was violating her senses. Why did he have to look so much like Leandro? She couldn't be sure what his true feelings were, instead she could only think of her own. The way he was looking at her sent her pulses skittering. Her defences locked into place.

'I'm here to do a job and I don't see the need for endless soul-searching,' she stated plainly.

The flames in his eyes leapt and intensified, scorching her. He shook his head sadly and gave a defeated sigh. Letting go of her hand, he raised both his in a desperate gesture.

'Remember,' he said, 'I tried to reach out to you.'

He looked hurt; she had managed to puncture his ego. Luz could see he was deflated, so why was she not basking in triumph? All she wanted to do now was get out of his office and run far away from the powerful and dangerous hold he had on her. She could feel it creeping up on her, tantalizing her, his potent sex appeal rendering her vulnerable and defenceless. These feelings were both unfamiliar and unwelcome. She shrugged.

He stared at her blankly. 'Is that really how you want it, Luz?'

'I don't want anything from you, Andrés,' she told him, her eyelids dropping so he could not see the struggling emotions behind them. There was a defensive look in her eyes when she lifted her gaze abruptly, her chin tilted in challenge. 'You took me on to write a biography, you don't need to win a popularity contest. Don't worry, I'll deliver.'

Once more the old tension had sprung up between them; the barrier that had never truly been lowered was quickly raised again. He crossed over to her swiftly and, before she could move back, lifted Luz's chin to meet her sapphire eyes.

'You're as stubborn as a mule,' he said, 'but you'll come round.' His smile was mild, at variance with his words. His face was so near that she couldn't help but stare at that perfectly sculpted mouth, remembering how it had felt on hers.

'Listen to me, Luz de Rueda. One day those two beautiful legs of yours will bring you back to me.' His mouth moved a little closer still. 'I don't want you to fight me, I want you yielding ... consenting.'

She was so disturbed by his touch that it took a few seconds for what he had just said to sink in and then the sheer thrill of it rushed through her. Her pulse leapt erratically, her head pounded painfully, the blood ran riot in her veins. Then, just as she thought he might kiss her, he let go of her, brushing the back of his hand against her cheek. She jerked her head away.

'Don't hold your breath,' she muttered, stony-faced, without looking at him.

She turned and left the room without a backward glance.

*   *   *

In the still dark, early hours before dawn, Andrés stood on his veranda at Puesta de Sol, far above the raging sea, his hands thrust deep in his pockets. Though tired and totally dispirited, he could not sleep. The more he tried to extricate himself from a situation he had mishandled from the very beginning, the deeper he was sucked into the quicksand he had created, it seemed. Anyhow, there was nothing he could do for now.

Was Luz coming round to him? He remembered the heady sensation of her against him in the garden of La Fortaleza, the taste of that sweet mouth. His body still seemed to ache from the sharp need and the passionate mutual energy she had so suddenly and so determinedly withdrawn from. And yet he could feel her struggling with herself today when they stood so close, his own frustration charging his desire. There was a shimmering heat between them that she surely couldn't deny, despite her confusion. He had ached to kiss her, to make her realize that she wanted him as much as he desired her. Still, he was not normally the kind of man to kiss a woman against her will, no matter how much he yearned to do so. For a second he had been tempted to go after her when she stormed out of his office, resolving in some primal way to bend her will to his, but more pragmatic thoughts had prevailed.

Andrés was always master of his emotions; he had to rein himself in. When Luz had told him of Lorenzo's outrageous attempt to lure her to La Fortaleza on the pretext of working together on the Herrera archives, he thought his blood would boil with the fire he so often had to keep in check, causing him to rage out of control. Even with Lorenzo, he would have to be careful for the time being. He could not do as he pleased until fate had unravelled its path and he could not be sure exactly what course that would take. It would not be easy for a man like himself. No woman had made him yearn the way Luz did, had made him burn with such exquisite pain.

All through their meeting he had found her so beautiful, with her deep-blue eyes flashing with enthusiasm; she was passionate and alive. But not only that: he admired her intelligence and the perceptive insights she'd had when discussing Eduardo. The book would not be just a bland narrative of Eduardo de Salazar's personality and work, it would be a lively explanation of his life and his art, too. He had been right to follow his heart and take her on. So he had hung on to her words in silence, interrupting her rarely, only for her to clarify a point; all the while making sure he kept a firm grip on those hormones clamouring for him to ravish her. To bide his time would be the hardest thing he had ever done but *she* had to come to *him*.

He remained there for a long while, a solitary figure; his only company a single pale star shining in the west, hanging above the trees along the cliff tops, sharp black outlines that the darkness exaggerated. Broodingly, he gazed down at the water roaring and sighing up the sand and listened to its song echoing through the night. There was a distinct sadness in its melody, as in the expanse around him, he thought, a sadness reflecting his own hollow despair.

Only when the star had gone in and the pale dawn sky looked coldly down upon him did he start back. The air was fresh, keen and bracing. He stared up at the sky, still streaked with gashes of purple, poised between night and day. Until his plan had come to its conclusion and all the players had played their part in this melancholy drama, he would not be free. Pulling up the collar of his jacket, he made his way back to the still-sleeping world.

CHAPTER 9

It was nine o'clock in the evening when Salvador, Alexandra and Luz arrived at the Cádiz Yacht Club for the Fiesta de las Rosas, a charity ball in aid of cancer research. Salvador had received an invitation to take a table from the foundation's chairman, Andrés de Calderón, and without consulting Luz had gone ahead and put together a list of guests for the gala night.

Two weeks had passed since Luz's meeting with Andrés at his office and she was still confused about the way it had ended. Everything seemed complicated as far as she was concerned, full of the kind of risk that she dared not formulate even in her own mind. The prospect of seeing him again made her nervous. She had tried to wriggle out of the event but, when her parents insisted, she capitulated without much fuss to avoid awakening their suspicions that everything was not going smoothly with her employer.

An oasis of green, white and blue, the yacht club was at its most glamorous that evening, lit by candles and flood lamps. The heat of the day was gone. Gone too were the brightly fringed umbrellas that had been a constant protection against the fierce sun. Inside the clubhouse the decor was very nautical, with ships' lanterns and lots of canvas and polished wood. Most of the guests came from a small pool of people in neighbouring towns and almost everyone knew each other. The mood was relaxed, convivial and comfortably tribal. The women wore summer evening dresses in light, delicate fabrics while the men were in dinner jackets. Tables were adorned with white tablecloths, glass candlesticks and vases of colourful, sweet-smelling flowers.

The table Salvador had reserved was outside with a prime view of the harbour. Atop it, red roses stood in a small crystal vase, some of their petals scattered on the white tablecloth.

Luz spotted Andrés as soon as she walked out on to the vast terrace. He was sitting at the table next to theirs with Lorenzo and Adalia, three other young beauties, two beaus and the elderly couple she had noticed him with in the box at the theatre. At the sight of him, her heart fluttered wildly before sinking in her chest. Their eyes met and he bowed his head gravely to her. Luz smiled back demurely. She would have preferred to have her back to him but the way her father had placed her made it inevitable that she would look straight into Andrés' eyes every time she lifted her head. It was unnerving. At this distance and in the semi-darkness she couldn't distinguish the colour of his irises and it was as though Leandro was sitting there in front of her. Andrés' proximity and the beauty of the night whipped up her memories afresh. She felt a melancholy loneliness, a deep hollowness as an overwhelming yearning to see her gypsy lover once again consumed her.

Above their heads was a sapphire-hued sky and millions of twinkling stars of all sizes lit up the night. They seemed so near to earth that Luz felt she could stretch out her hand and pick one from the dark blue canopy. The sea shimmered peacefully in the moonlight and broke and foamed in a mantle of white froth along the shore. In the harbour, a stone's throw away, there were fishing vessels riding at anchor, rocking and rolling on the incoming swell. Yachts were tied alongside the quay, pleasure craft had tucked themselves in wherever they had found a berth, and an array of coloured boats had been dragged up on slipways for hull scraping.

Salvador and Alexandra's other guests arrived just as they were settling into their seats; among them were Antonio de

Cabrera, his wife Callida and their son Romero, an architect who owned one of the largest art galleries in Seville.

Luz looked exquisite in a Grecian-inspired backless halter-neck of powder-blue silk chiffon. The simplicity of the gown and the crystal-studded belt she wore defined her shape, accenting the slenderness of her waist. Her shiny black hair was arranged in a complicated braided chignon that Agustina, who had come all the way from El Pavón for the evening, had dexterously achieved. Teamed with chandelier diamond earnings and a delicate diamond necklace, the effect was breathtaking. She exuded a goddess-like glamour that did not go unnoticed by the young architect, who set about entertaining her with animated conversation as more guests arrived.

After a while Romero leaned back in his chair, stretching his long legs out under the table. The architect was a tall, aristocratic young man with straight dark hair and honey-coloured eyes in a kind face that was expressive and quick to produce a waggish smile. 'This really is a beautiful night, equalled only in its perfection by Aphrodite sitting next to me.' He looked at Luz and grinned. 'Even the stars are jealous of those sapphire eyes of yours.'

'Romero, are you always such a shameless flirt?' Luz smiled into her glass as she sipped her sangria.

'Always – and without exception,' he replied. 'What can I say? I'm an incurable romantic. Besides, it's not every day that I have such charming company, señorita. You know, my parents often drag me to such evenings hoping to match-make me with a suitable young señorita, but usually I end up being propelled towards some tongue-tied wallflower or a girl who insists on stepping on my feet when we dance. I do hope you're not going to step on my feet later, Doña Luz?' He waggled his eyebrows comically.

Luz laughed. 'I will do my best to keep my feet to myself.' She lowered her voice conspiratorially so that she was out of earshot of her mother, seated next to her. 'And yes, parents can be pushy, I agree.'

Romero chuckled before he, too, spoke more mutedly. 'At least de Calderón doesn't have that problem. If he's caught up with *la Señorita* de Herrera, it's none of his mother's doing.'

'Really? What makes you say that?' Luz enquired in a mild tone, trying to hide her displeasure at the mention of Adalia. For want of something distracting to do, she plucked an olive from one of the little dishes dotted around the table and popped it in her mouth.

'The man does what he pleases, always has done. His mother, in particular, never seems to bat an eyelid at anything and tonight is no exception.'

Her curiosity aroused, Luz tracked his gaze to the next table, her eyes roaming between Andrés and the elderly man and woman seated on either side of him. 'You mean, those people on Señor de Calderón's table are his parents?'

'Indeed they are. Granted, they look more like his grandparents, but somehow they managed to produce de Calderón Junior along the way.' He shrugged his shoulders. 'Though I find it hard to imagine Doña Eleadora as a young woman.'

Luz glanced over at Andrés' mother and noticed that most of the time her piercing eyes seemed to stare somewhat vacantly into space. She made only the barest of conversation with those around her, even her son. Santiago de Calderón was more sociable and conversed soberly with Andrés and the other men at the table. He did not possess the same handsome features as his son but had similar dark eyes in a kindly face. Doña Eleadora, on the other hand, had a stronger look of Andrés in the high set of her cheekbones and had clearly been a beauty in her youth, despite her now wrinkled skin and empty expression.

Romero slapped the table in mock agitation. 'I must say, I could eat a horse! I hope they bring the food out soon, otherwise this wine, excellent as it is, will go straight to my feet and soon it will be you hopping out of the way when we dance,' he said, grinning at Luz and refilling her glass.

She smiled and they began talking about the other guests, Luz delighting in the shameless gossip Romero had to offer on all his clients from the gallery, half of whom were there that night.

The atmosphere was heady; the hum of friendly voices and cheery, robust laughter formed an unobtrusive background. At one point Romero made his excuses and stood to greet some acquaintances passing further along the terrace. Luz sipped at her sangria and allowed her gaze to drift towards the opposite table again. She observed the collection of people there, relieved not to be among them. Adalia was smiling faintly at the beau on her right, though her whole demeanour exuded suppressed tension. Now and again she flicked a glance at Andrés, a few seats away, then turned back to her companion, laughing too keenly at something he said, before allowing him to refill her glass.

Luz wondered if Adalia, not having been seated near Andrés, had been relegated to mere business partner for this corporate event. Whatever the reason, she was not wearing her usual self-assured mien. Lorenzo was seated furthest away from Andrés, no doubt a result of the *torero*'s recent presumption concerning the de Salazar project. She would dearly have loved to be a fly on the wall when he had been exposed to Andrés' impressive wrath.

Now, as Luz glanced at the elegant businessman facing her, deep in conversation with his father, she took in the lean jaw and slight frown marring his perfect profile. She imagined he was as magnificent as an avenging angel when in full flight of fury. Luz saw him stiffen as he noticed her looking at him. That hooded gaze was back as he lifted his glass to his mouth and drank, watching her, before slowly placing it down again. She quivered as if those sensuously sculpted lips had touched hers, though remembering they had not been so restrained when he pinned her against him at La Fortaleza. Her body tingled with memories of how it had felt to have him plunder her mouth with such savage passion, to taste the dark, delectable flavour of him; how his hands had felt on her body, making her spiral into a helpless, hungry desire. Her pulse sped dangerously as his penetrating look held her captive for a moment longer. Then she breathed deeply and turned away so she could not see him any more.

'Are you all right, darling?' The warm female voice made Luz's gaze shoot up to meet her mother's green eyes.

'Y-yes, of course, *Mamá*.' Luz tried to regain her composure, taking a sip of chilled sangria to cool her burning throat, and added quickly, 'I was just thinking what an impressive evening Don Andrés is hosting.'

'There's certainly a marvellous turnout. I must confess, I do love people watching at these events,' Alexandra said, as she surveyed the terrace.

Luz smiled fondly at her mother. 'You were right. It's a lovely evening, I'm glad I came.'

Alexandra glanced over to Romero, still standing and laughing with his friends. She squeezed her daughter's hand, her eyes twinkling. 'I thought you would like the company tonight. Don Andrés has been working you too hard. You needed a bit of diversion.'

A diversion was exactly what she needed, Luz thought, but perhaps not for the reason her mother suspected.

The aroma of sizzling dishes wafted outside as waiters moved swiftly between tables. The Cádiz Yacht Club prided itself on its excellent cuisine. A French chef had been imported and the restaurant was the envy of many of the hotels and eating places in Andalucía. After an array of tapas appeared, washed down with fine bottles of Jerez and Rioja wine, they dined handsomely on warm puff pastry filled with oysters in a whipped creamy hollandaise sauce, followed by duckling, lean and flavoursome, roasted with apples. They ended with one of the chef's signature desserts: a fluffy praline soufflé accompanied by a rich black cherry syrup.

Romero de Cabrera, seated next to Luz, once more gave her all his attention throughout dinner. He courted her in a frivolous, flirty way that was refreshing and helped restore her confidence, which had been badly bruised of late. She found him light-hearted, with a great sense of humour, and his spontaneous cheerfulness was infectious. Gradually, she allowed herself to relax and became caught up in this spirit of gaiety. Soon she had almost forgotten the ominous presence of Andrés at the opposite table.

To dance with Romero was like floating to music. She felt as light as a feather on her feet and was pleased to fulfil her promise of not treading on his. At first she was a little hesitant, but the young man was an expert leader. He guided her effortlessly around the dancefloor, through waltzes, tangos and the more intricate steps of a foxtrot and an exhibition samba. To and fro he whirled her, holding her loosely then drawing her close to him, before letting her go again. Other couples, impressed by their performance, fell away to the sides of the dancefloor. Now they found themselves the centre of the show.

For Luz the night sped by with a dream-like quality, as though she were a fictional character in one of her mother's romance stories. Andrés, she noticed, did not dance. Nor did he engage much with Adalia, despite her frequent attempts to gain his attention, a state of affairs that visibly ruffled the young woman's customary composure. He drank a lot and smoked incessantly. More than once Luz caught his sharp, hooded gaze following her for a moment. Though a part of her was always aware of him, she had become strangely detached from her own feelings as the evening rolled on.

It was close to midnight. Luz and Romero were back at the table sipping coffee, teasing each other with jokes, when all of a sudden she watched Andrés approach their table.

He headed for Alexandra first. 'Doña Alexandra,' he said, giving a slight bow as he lightly touched his lips to her raised hand. 'It's a pleasure to have you among us tonight.'

'It's a pleasure to attend such a wonderful event, Don Andrés, and for such a worthy cause, too. We've had so much fun, haven't we, Luz?'

Luz smiled graciously at her mother's words. She found it curiously difficult to look at Andrés directly as she said: 'As ever, you are the perfect host, Don Andrés.'

'I'm glad you're enjoying yourself, Doña Luz.' His gaze, dark and intense, lingered on her for an instant before he turned and nodded courteously towards the young architect seated next to her, giving him the briefest of greetings: 'Romero.' Then, turning to Salvador, he smiled, a most engaging smile that Luz had learnt to recognize. 'Thank you for your support, Don Salvador. As a well-respected philanthropist and a pillar of our society, your presence here lends weight to our foundation,' he said graciously.

'I'm always happy to endorse and aid a valuable charity,' Salvador told him before briefly introducing Andrés to his other guests.

'May I have your permission to ask Doña Luz for a dance?' Andrés enquired courteously. 'Though I don't pretend to be as good a dancer as she is, I have the temerity to think that I can hold my own on the dancefloor.' He turned his head a little to look at Luz intently.

'Permission granted but you will have to ask her personally.' Salvador gave his daughter a knowing look, amusement twitching at his mouth. 'Nowadays I hear fathers don't have the right to speak for their daughters, more's the pity,' he declared. Both men laughed heartily. Ignoring her father's quip, Luz stared at Andrés, fighting off a frown.

Alexandra's green gaze moved swiftly between Luz and Andrés. 'Thank goodness those days are gone! You certainly should ask my daughter yourself, and quickly by the looks of it before she decides to refuse you,' she laughed. To Luz's relief, both her parents turned their attention to their guests, whether by design out of consideration for her feelings, she didn't know. It was easier facing Andrés alone.

He grinned. 'Doña Luz, will you allow me the honour of this dance?' There was a note of challenge in his voice as he moved towards her and held out his hand, giving her no time to think up an excuse to refuse him.

Now that he was so close to her again, Luz's cloak of near-indifference fell away. The power that only Andrés possessed, to make her feel angry, confused and excited all at the same time, triumphed more strongly than ever. Their eyes locked: his were sparkling with mischief, hers were glowing with barely controlled turmoil.

'Andrés, *mi querido*, there you are!' The voice of Adalia suddenly broke the spell as she appeared from the crowd. Her eyes flicked uneasily from one to the other, a tight smile plastered to her face. 'I've been trying to get you to dance with me all evening and now I see you're otherwise engaged.' She fixed her pale, piercing eyes on Luz, who stared unflinchingly back. If Adalia had decided she was going to make her feel small, she was very much mistaken, Luz thought.

'Yes, Doña Luz has just promised me this dance,' Andrés explained, giving Adalia a cool smile.

'On the contrary, I had not yet agreed to dance, Señor de Calderón,' Luz told him pointedly. 'How very remiss of you to neglect Doña Adalia.' She turned to the socialite. 'Do please be my guest, I've danced enough this evening anyway.'

Adalia's smile slid into self-satisfaction as she said coolly: 'Yes, Doña Luz, you must be exhausted after your impressive performance with Don Romero earlier.'

At this remark Luz quickly glanced up at Andrés but his expression was impassive as he met her eyes. But he wasn't about to give up so easily.

'Doña Luz, I think your father would think it rather rude of me to abandon you at this point, having taken the trouble to ask you to dance,' he said, before shifting his attention to Adalia. 'Besides, I believe one of your admirers looks quite determined to claim you, Adalia.'

He nodded past her shoulder at the enthusiastic-looking young man currently making a beeline for them.

Adalia looked behind her and, before she had time to protest, Andrés pressed his hand into the small of Luz's back and gently, but resolutely, propelled her away through the crowd. Luz shivered at his touch and realized any objection was now fruitless. Sliding an arm round her, Andrés led her to the dancefloor just as the lights were dimming and the orchestra was engaging in a haunting, slow melody. The soft crooning song struck a chord with the lonely ache in her heart. She couldn't help but think of Leandro and she missed him. Even though their love was doomed, in many ways the gypsy had made her more sure of herself than she could ever imagine being with the man who had just guided her lightly through the crowd. Andrés moved his palm subtly over her satiny skin, his touch firm and warm on her bare back, searing into her and making her tremble slightly. She tensed, recognizing the familiar, instinctive stir in her body as she responded to his proximity.

They moved into the seething mass on the dancefloor and he took her in his arms, holding her tight, so she was aware of the thundering beat of his heart against her breast. His thigh brushed against hers. The surge of arousal that ran through them both as their bodies met was like an electric shock. Her nipples stiffened; a rush of blood went to her head. She didn't want to feel this way but her will had been sapped. The music was plaintive, tearing at her, and she closed her eyes, shutting out all sight and sound from her world. Once again she was in Leandro's arms, drifting in a sweet semi-conscious state, at one with him. She relaxed, melting, as undeniable warmth flooded her loins. Sensitive to her need,

Andrés drew her ever closer into his embrace, clasping her to him, feverish and possessive. A yearning sensation filled her but she was not sure where it came from now; she only knew that she was surrendering to it, and to the man holding her in his arms. He had the most sensual touch and she savoured it with wanton abandonment. His jaw was brushing against her temple and she could just make out the spicy aroma of his aftershave mingling with the familiar scent of him. It felt good; it felt right. Time stood still. Above them the stars twinkled like diamonds and the moon was warm and glowing. She wanted this moment never to end.

All of a sudden the psychedelic lights were turned back on, startling her out of her fantasy world, and the orchestra engaged in a lively twist-and-shake number reminiscent of the sixties. Reluctantly she drew away from him, a little dazed. Andrés walked her to her table, his hand still on the small of her back.

'It has been a pleasure dancing with you,' he whispered, his jet gaze settling intently on her face as they reached Luz's seat.

His caressing voice came to her through the mist that still clouded her brain. Moving his palm from her back, he took her hand in his. 'I've been meaning to call you to discuss our project further. Maybe we can meet sometime during the week.' She felt his fingers tighten their grip.

As he broke into her thoughts it was like an awakening call. She blinked and returned to the present. Her stare fixed on his face. Amusement danced in the black eyes and she knew beyond a doubt that he was all too aware of the emotions he had elicited in her, but she was beyond caring. Something undeniable had taken hold of Luz, intoxicating her with its heady essence. She nodded and gave him a brief smile. He leaned towards her and though she knew this was neither the time nor the place, she yearned for him to kiss her, every part of her eagerly expectant.

'I'll call you in the morning,' he said. Behind those words lay an emphasized intensity and the tender look in his eyes told her all she needed to know. Thereupon he bade her goodnight, took his leave of Salvador, Alexandra and their guests and walked back to his table.

Half an hour later, she and her parents were being chauffeured back to L'Estrella in Salvador's vintage Hispano-Suiza and Luz had fallen into silence. She watched her mother doze, her head leaning comfortably on her father's shoulder, and was relieved to be left to her own thoughts. Salvador had made a few comments on the way back from the Yacht Club and she was well aware that he had noticed Romero's fervent interest in her – not to mention the young architect's obvious disappointment at her departure – as well as noting Andrés' more discreet attentions. Naturally she had pooh-poohed it all when he had teased her about it, but it was obvious that both Salvador and Alexandra had been watching her all evening, weighing up the prospective suitors. Eventually, they had given up their probing, though Luz knew that she had only been let off temporarily.

That night marked the first tremors of a turning point for Luz. She was filled with an intense euphoria, coupled with a vague sense of guilt. She could not deny that while in Andrés' arms her imagination had run wild; it had been so easy to pretend that the man holding her in his embrace was Leandro. Still, tonight, just like the night at La Fortaleza in Pamplona, the magnetism between Andrés and herself had been unmistakable. Her feelings for this man had crept up on her stealthily like a predator and their very nature was alien and fascinating to her: dark, intimidating, dangerously thrilling. Something had stirred in her tonight, a tingling awareness that played with her mercilessly. Was this mere sexual excitement? Luz wasn't experienced enough in matters of the heart to know but she had no doubt the ardent fire that now devoured her equalled his. The kindling had been there from the first moment they had laid eyes on each other, just waiting to be ignited. She knew that she was on perilous ground, yet the idea of not pursuing this reckless feeling, of not seeing Andrés again, was even more disturbing to contemplate.

Perhaps it was not so odd that she should be attracted to both the hidalgo and the gypsy. Despite their different circumstances and upbringing, there were qualities they shared: in their own ways both men were charming, arrogant and manipulative; each with a force of personality impossible to ignore. If Andrés had been the one she had met first, how could she be so sure that it wouldn't have been to him that she would have lost her heart?

Nevertheless, she felt a poignant stab of disloyalty towards Leandro as she mulled these thoughts over in her mind. True, the gypsy had rejected her but she had no doubt he loved her profoundly. Had her body's response to Andrés this evening meant that she had given her love for Leandro its final farewell?

Surely Andrés' attraction to her was purely erotic, fulfilling a carnal need? After all, if she were to believe Lorenzo, her employer was engaged to be married to Adalia, though they had not exactly behaved as a couple tonight, that was for sure. Nonetheless, Luz was well aware of the Spanish traditions that ruled the women in her country. Men often had dalliances before they committed to marriage; it was widely accepted. Spanish society also demanded that a woman be a virgin on her wedding night. This truth had never really occurred to her until now and its acknowledgement came as a shock, prompting tears to her eyes. She flinched away from the thought: it hurt too much. It meant that somehow she was just as taboo to Andrés as she was to Leandro. Andrés could never commit to Luz in any serious way now, even if she wanted him to. This was not England. Her brief idyll with the gypsy was an unforgiveable indiscretion. She had broken a vital social code of conduct. Even in this day and age, it would be a very broad-minded and self-assured Spaniard who could happily do away with what her countrymen called *la honra*. Andrés may have a tremendous ego but, going by what she knew of him, she very much doubted he was free of prejudice.

Soon they were back at L'Estrella and after Luz had said goodnight to her parents she undressed slowly in her room, her mind and emotions still circling in agonizing loops that made her toss and turn on her pillow.

When she eventually got to sleep, she dreamt of Leandro; a lively, tangible, erotic dream. They were lying naked on the silvery sands, bathed in moonlight, soothed by the lulling break of small waves on the beach. He was on his side, his head leaning on one hand propped up by his elbow, while the long tanned fingers of the other drew slow, sensuous circles over the quivering skin of her stomach, inviting her desire with every stroke. His hypnotic green irises never left hers, revelling in the intimate plea that he read in her eyes. Though savouring his caresses, her hungry body demanded more and more. She passed her tongue over her dry lips, her back arched and her thighs parted as she motioned how he could please her most. She closed her eyes now. Still his caresses were butterfly-like as he traced the feminine contours of her body, roaming lower and lower until his hand brushed between her thighs, gingerly exploring, tantalizing and tormenting to heighten the final thrill.

She wanted to feel him, touch him, gratify him with a little of the pleasure that he was so generously lavishing on her. Clasping the thick silk of his hair in her fingers, she opened her eyes. A midnight gaze now held hers, burning with desire that would not let her go. She didn't care and gave herself completely to him. And as the excitement built inside her, the stimulation of his fingers grew stronger and suddenly exploded into flames that leapt through her body like quicksilver, licking her secret parts with overwhelming incandescent sensations.

She cried out so loudly that she woke with a jolt, finding herself moving, rocking to and fro and shuddering uncontrollably under the effect of her explosive climax. Then, as she gradually came back down to earth and realized that it had all been a dream, she remembered that it had been Andrés' face she had seen at the end. Leandro would never be hers and Andrés was a tormenting phantom that would never let her rest. She sobbed bitterly, tears of self-pity flooding the pillow in which she had buried her face, her nails clawing desperately, disconsolately, at the soft mattress.

*   *   *

She slept until late. When she got up, she was thankful to learn from Carmela that her parents had already returned to El Pavón. She had no desire to be submitted to their eager interrogation once more.

With the new day the effects of the dream had evaporated slightly, though she remained disturbed and in a state of confusion. She had to get used to the fact that there was no future for her with the gypsy. Never would she find peace unless she got over him. The resolution made her feel better. It stifled the ache in her heart that gripped whenever Leandro invaded her mind. But still, too often, thoughts of Andrés haunted her.

Romero had already rung, Carmela had told her, her eyes gleaming with all sorts of innuendoes which, to the housekeeper's disappointment, Luz immediately quashed. Still, Carmela would not be fobbed off so easily. Was he the *valeroso caballero*, the gallant gentleman who had sent her the red roses and from whom she had received a letter not so long ago? He seemed very nice, *y tan cortés*, so courteous and eager over the telephone. His name was well known in Andalucía, as was his gallery. Many *señoritas* must be after him. He was a *muy buen partido*, a very good match. Luz agreed that he was probably all that but she was not interested and Carmela should put the story and her hopes to bed.

She wondered when she would hear from Andrés. The energy of the previous evening had scarcely dimmed in the cold light of day, though she was still confused at the strange compulsion she felt towards him, one she couldn't wholly understand.

The sun was unforgiving by the time Luz had donned some denim shorts and a T-shirt over her bikini and had set off for the beach. It was dry and harsh, without any softness or humidity, and no cloud in sight. Even in the shade the temperature was scorching. Most of Spain was still taking its siesta at this hour, except the ubiquitous cicadas with their ceaseless grating, but Luz felt restless waiting for a sign from Andrés. So she set off with Zeyna to embrace the fury of the sun, the beach and the sea.

She was not disappointed. Beneath a sun-baked sky, the blue and silky bay and its silvery sandy shore beckoned. The stark, sweeping coastline spread before her as she cantered purposefully to her favourite spot at the end of the lengthy stretch where the bollards lay motionless, like guarding giants. The sand was deserted beneath an expanse of azure sky, sparse tufts of wild grass appearing here and there like emeralds on the rolling dunes.

Already she felt better; she had left her problems at home. She loved the quietude, the isolation and the bright Cádiz light reflecting off the water. A sense of calm came over her as her eyes feasted on the unspoilt beauty of her surroundings. The sea was in kind mood, and the rustle of wavelets on the rocks as gentle as the sound of dry leaves blowing in the breeze.

All of a sudden she was aware she was not alone. A shadow moved at the side of her. She turned abruptly. Paquita was staring at her, solemn as an owl, leaning on her stick, which she was gripping tightly with one gnarled hand while the other held some sprigs of wild herbs. She wore a scarf over her head, which partly hid her tousled, dishevelled hair, and her clothing was scarcely more than a bundle of old rags.

Luz's features tensed and a frown creased her forehead. Though the sun was hot in the heavens she shivered. She drove her eyes back to the scenery and fixed them on the frothy, lacelike edge of the shore in front of her. Maybe if she ignored her, the intruder would go away. She could gallop off on Zeyna if she wanted to but, for some unknown reason, she was compelled to remain.

Moments passed. Now Luz's focus was riveted once again by the gypsy hag. The vulture's eyes were watchful, shining like fierce furnaces in her sun-shrivelled face. She was silent, waiting.

Strangely, Luz found she had mixed feelings about Paquita. On the one hand, she feared and was a little in awe of the old woman because she was a gypsy; on the other, it was almost like being in the presence of an old friend. After all, according to Paquita, the gypsy seemed to have played some beneficial role in her parents' love story and though she spoke in riddles, which Luz did not wholly understand, she did feel that the *gitana* had her welfare at heart.

'What do you want?' Luz ventured hesitantly.

The old woman's laughter crackled and her strong features broke into a smile.

'You're not afraid of Paquita any more,' she said as she approached the mare.

'Careful,' Luz warned, 'Zeyna doesn't know you and she might buck.'

The laughter resounded again in the silence. 'Don't you know that gypsies have a special relationship with horses? We talk to them and they listen.' She shuffled closer, extended the crooked hand that held the herbs and patted the nose of the mare. The beautiful creature dipped her head, nuzzling into the newcomer's pockets, looking for some sort of reward for her sweet nature. Luz was not accustomed to Zeyna taking easily to strangers and she had to concede that Paquita must possess some magic power.

'How is Leandro?' she blurted out suddenly, wanting to swallow her words as soon as they had left her lips.

Paquita's hawk eyes rolled. 'You must not despair, child. It is written that, like your parents, you'll find true love and will enjoy a good life,' the gypsy reassured her, albeit somewhat obscurely.

Luz bent a little over her mount and stared helplessly into the unreadable eyes.

'What do you mean?' she asked, irritated.

The old hag glanced up at her face and studied it as though deciphering a map. 'Beautiful lady, love always prevails,' she declared in a hoarse voice, as though stating a non-contentious fact.

'Does that mean our love may still survive? Could we really have a normal life together?'

The witch chuckled, uncovering her ungainly jaws. A fire lit up in her watchful hawkish eyes and flickered in her parchment face. She gazed into the depths of Luz's blue irises.

'Paquita unearths the secrets of all beings. Nothing is hidden from her,' she croaked arrogantly, waving her stick in the air menacingly. 'The world is small, the legs of lies short and coincidence has a long-reaching arm.'

At this Luz felt troubled about whatever it was Paquita was trying to tell her. Flushed and more than a little apprehensive of what the gypsy would say, she still prompted: 'What do you mean? *Ay Dios!* I'm so confused. You talk about love and lies but none of it makes sense! *Por favor, ayúdame*, please help me. Can't you shed some light on everything that's happening to me?' She waited, breathless, for the answer.

But the eyes of the wizened old crone glazed over; blinds came down. Suddenly she looked as though she was making a great effort. Beads of perspiration glistened on her weathered face. As previously, her cavernous voice resounded eerily in the silence and echoed through the air as she turned her small, bowed figure and slowly hobbled away across the dunes.

'Beware of masks, blinkers and tinted glass,' she cried out. 'Remove the shield that shades your eyes. Forget the gypsy and love the man. Look beyond the veil of revenge and search your soul, it will guide you. When the mist lifts you will find the treasure that you are looking for, buried among the dust and the rubble of days gone by and memories. The glittering green jewel, the precious stone, is lying there, so clear, so pure, waiting. Don't be afraid! Reach out for it, it is a gem for you to keep.'

Luz tried to call her back but, as usual, Paquita was not listening, engrossed as she was in her trance, incoherently repeating what only made sense to her. The young woman attempted to follow her on Zeyna but the old gypsy had vanished into the dunes before Luz had time to work out in which direction she had gone. She swore under her breath. *Why did the witch have to speak in riddles? Why could she not just say things plainly?* Luz struggled to remember the words she had just heard. She wished she had something with which to write them down. By the time she got home she would have forgotten most of them anyway. Lies, coincidences, revenge and memories ... what was all this?

For a long time Luz rode Zeyna along the beach, letting her splash through the seawater before finding an outcrop of rock with some shade. The heat of the afternoon was not so relentless now. She jumped down and led the horse into the shadiest part of the sand, in the lee of the cliff, and patted the mare's flank; Zeyna needed to rest and would stay obediently for a while. They would have to return to L'Estrella in a few hours so that she could be watered but, for now, Luz had a little more time to herself.

She stripped down to her bikini and ran into the gentle waves. The water cooled her burning skin and she spent the rest of the afternoon slipping in and out of the sea, sometimes sitting next to Zeyna on the sand, letting the mare reach down and nudge her comfortingly with her muzzle every now and then, as Paquita's words continued to float through her mind. Luz arrived home to find an overexcited Carmela hovering restlessly at the entrance to L'Estrella.

'Don Andrés de Calderón is waiting to see you,' she burst out, even before Luz had come through the gates and noticed the smart convertible Ferrari parked next to the porch.

'He's been here an hour,' she said. 'I told him I didn't know how long the *señorita* would be but he insisted he would wait.' The poor woman was speaking all at once, her eyes glowing. 'I've seated him on the terrace and have offered him a café latte and *perrunillas. Lo que es un hombre guapo,* what a handsome man, *charming y tan apegados a la señorita,* and so attached to the *señorita,* too,' she declared.

'Calm down, Carmela, you did well,' Luz reassured her as they walked towards the stables. Her stomach was a-quiver with nerves at the thought of Andrés waiting for her in the house. 'I will attend to him now. I suppose I will have to ask him to stay for dinner. What have you cooked for tonight?' she enquired, trying to sound detached.

'*No te preocupes. Carmela tenderá a la comida,* Carmela will tend to the meal so you can give all your attention to the young gentleman,' the housekeeper told her with a cheeky grin.

'Don't get too excited,' Luz warned. 'He's commissioned some work and has probably come to check on its progress. I'm only asking him to dinner out of courtesy. I doubt he'll accept but we must be prepared.' She hoped she sounded convincing.

'*Por supuesto,* of course,' Carmela agreed tactfully. However, she eyed her employer with expressive dark eyes, openly indicating she had not been duped, and once more Luz felt colour tinge her cheekbones.

As Luz came on to the veranda, Andrés gathered himself out of his cane chair with the sort of languid ease that characterized all his movements. His handsome, chiselled mouth stretched into an engaging smile and the intent jet eyes fixed themselves on her face.

Her pulse, which had quickened a little even before seeing him, was now racing – would she never get used to his carbon-copy looks of Leandro?

'I'm sorry you've been kept waiting but I hadn't the faintest idea you were going to call on me,' she declared, trying to sound like a hostess casually greeting a guest. She was only too aware that after the afternoon's swimming, her damp shirt was still sticking to her body and she flushed.

He favoured her with a swift, searching look as he took her hand in his. She felt her skin quiver under its warmth and prayed that he was unaware of it.

'Waiting can only make the heart grow fonder, isn't that so?' he said, his gaze flicking mercilessly over her and then moving up to her eyes. His gentle teasing was unsettling; it made her feel vulnerable.

She swallowed hard, at a loss for words, but he made up for her silence, saying: 'I wanted to thank you in person for the truly enjoyable dance you allowed me last night and I wondered if you would do me the honour of dining with me tonight.' Still holding on to her hand he spoke fervently, his burning gaze never straying from her face.

She pulled her hand away and dropped her eyes to cover her confusion. 'Since you've come all this way,' she said, 'I think it's I who should ask you to stay for dinner.' *Had she really just asked him that?* Regaining her control, she looked up at him. A sweet smile hovered on her lips. 'I'm not sure what Carmela has in mind, but she's a good cook and I'd be more than delighted if you would share whatever she had planned for me. We can eat early.'

'I think that's a wonderful idea,' he acquiesced, giving her a dazzling, unguarded smile. 'I've already sampled some of Carmela's specialities. She looked after me very well during your absence. She and I are old friends now,' he chuckled.

Luz's smooth brow creased into a frown. *Oh dear,* she thought, wondering what the maid had been up to. You never knew what Carmela would say or do. The housekeeper's heart was in the right place but her obsession with *novios* and her eagerness that Luz should find a husband, sooner rather than later, had always meant you could not trust the impulsive wag of her tongue whenever she thought an appropriate suitor was in the vicinity.

'Will you excuse me for another twenty minutes or so?' Luz said apologetically. 'I've come straight from the beach and so I need to freshen up and change my clothes.' Her manner was a little more confident now. 'Would you like a glass of fino or Rioja while you're waiting, or maybe something a little stronger?' she offered.

'A glass of Rioja would be perfect. Take your time,' he said. 'The view of the harbour from here is spectacular. I'll have plenty to amuse myself with in anticipation ...' He left this phrase in suspension as his gaze poured devilishly into her watchful blue eyes. And as she turned away she heard him say: 'Enjoy your shower,' and there was a smile in his low, smoky voice.

The remark, innocuous though it was, made her pulse quicken and her body tingle. Why did she have the impression he sounded like a huntsman ready for the kill? Excitement simmered in her throughout her shower and as she dressed. The hot water had made her body warm in all the right places; the afternoon sun had given her skin a natural apricot hue so she needed no extra make-up on her cheekbones. Her eyes were shining more than usual, courtesy of the havoc the man waiting downstairs had created within her. A little kohl and a soupçon of mascara made them look even wider and deeper. To finish off she applied a tinge of transparent gloss to her sun-kissed lips.

She had changed into a white silk kaftan edged with narrow gold braid and delicate gold flat sandals. Oversized matching hoop earrings were her only other accessory.

Before joining Andrés she passed by the kitchen to find, to her horror, that Carmela had enlisted her mother and sister to assist her in the cooking of a banquet. The housekeeper's enthusiasm was touching but Luz did not think it appropriate to be so lavish. After all, Andrés had turned up unannounced and she had invited him out of courtesy to share her dinner. This over-the-top welcome could only be construed the wrong way. Having explained this point to Carmela and cut down on the number of dishes she was planning to provide, Luz went to rejoin the young man on the veranda.

She found that dear Carmela had already provided an array of delicious tapas, which Andrés was happily munching his way through. Small dishes of *chanquetes*, whitebait, squid in ink and morsels of tripe cooked in a thick creamy sauce lay half empty on the crowded little table; there were also Carmela's very special *riñones al Jerez*, kidneys in sherry, slices of cold tortilla and numerous other delicacies. Luz was always amazed at how quickly Carmela was able to conjure up any number of appetizers. That evening she had surpassed herself and Luz was in two minds whether to cancel the dishes she had just ordered for dinner, but her guest seemed so content that she decided to leave well alone.

Once again he rose quickly from his seat as she came on to the terrace. The way he looked at her, she just knew he was imagining her without any clothes on. Her face flamed. Silently she cursed herself for being such an open book.

He smiled his slow smile. 'Ah Luz, how beautiful you look.' His eyes were still travelling over her in a manner that made her heartbeat spike. 'Come over here and share this extraordinary selection of tapas the lovely Carmela has provided before I polish them all off,' he invited cheerfully, pulling a chair out for her next to him.

'Carmela is never so happy as when she can display her culinary skills,' Luz told him, settling down and taking the glass of wine he was offering her.

'I make it a rule never to drink alone,' he said as he filled his glass, which until then, she noticed, had been standing empty.

She helped herself to a cheese croquette and, doing her best to ignore the overpowering presence of the man sitting beside her, slid a little deeper into the soft cushions of her chair, trying to unwind a little.

'Any particular reason?' she enquired coolly.

He shrugged. 'I suppose it's a kind of protection. In our circle there's a lot of alcohol abuse – and even recreational drugs – taken as a means of relaxation. Indulging in them on one's own is treading a very dangerous path,' he said with a veiled smile.

She swung around sharply and looked up at him with a directness that seemed to stun him. Her dark-blue eyes lightened to a steel-grey.

'Do you mean to say you indulge …'

His burst of laughter interrupted her. 'No, no,' he said, raising an elegant tanned hand. 'Don't get me wrong, I've never touched any sort of drug. Cigarettes or the occasional cigar are my only weakness. I have been known to polish off a bottle of red wine or two every so often in an evening, but always in company, never alone.' He paused and smiled. 'Honestly,' he went on, raising an eyebrow, 'do I look like someone addicted to anything but my work?' He eyed her, amusement twitching at his lips.

Definitely addicted to the fairer sex, though … she mused. Intense, loveable and dangerous were the best words to describe him. Mothers, she was sure, were panic-stricken whenever he was caught lurking around their daughters. The temptation to tell him so was strong, but she thought better of it and decided to leave well alone. After all, it was only fair that he should be given the benefit of the doubt, the doubt in this case being rather strong.

It was a peaceful evening with no wind. The air was filled with the tang of the sea. The only sounds disturbing the serenity were the cooing of pigeons and the roar of white-capped waves breaking like distant thunder against the rocks at the base of the cliffs. A series of split-levels, all bowered with sweetly scented flowers, created an ambiance of privacy. The terrace, cascading with plumbago, petunias and geraniums, faced the limitless expanse of mottled blue ocean. It was shaded by the heavy, shining, palmate leaves of fig trees and led down to a refreshing, floodlit, saltwater pool. In the distance Puerto de Santa María hovered like a mirage above the Atlantic, a turquoise band, with a fringe of pine-edged shores that deepened into dark sapphire sea.

When Luz wanted, she could be a charming hostess and tonight that was what she wanted to be. So, they reacquainted over a dinner of gazpacho and an eye-catching *fideuà*, seafood paella cooked with vermicelli instead of rice. When the dessert was produced, Andrés went into raptures over the homemade *bunuelos de viento*, light-as-air fritters, filled with Carmela's pastry cream and Agustina's thick bitter marmalade made of oranges, lemons and grapefruit from El Pavón's citrus grove.

'Carmela has excelled. This food is truly superb,' enthused Andrés as he tucked into the rich dessert.

'Yes, she really has done us proud. Dearest Carmela, she's an absolute godsend,' said Luz fondly. She chuckled. 'I'm surprised you could get through it all after the tapas she produced. You must have been hungry.'

'I'm always hungry, Luz.' His eyes gleamed wickedly, causing her to take a sip of wine to moisten her dry throat. Andrés was watching her intently. 'I can see that you have a special relationship with Carmela and she's clearly devoted to you. Not everyone has such a warm and open heart that they inspire that kind of loyalty.'

Luz felt herself blush at the compliment. 'Well, given that Carmela has won your approval and worked such wonders with the meal, we could open one of my father's special bottles of wine, if you'd like?'

'No, please, keep your father's wines for another occasion, Luz. This Rioja is perfect and I wouldn't want you to deplete his undoubtedly excellent reserves on my account.' He smiled warmly at her and traced the length of the glass stem idly with his finger. As Luz watched him, muscles clenched deep in her stomach as if that same finger had reached out and was running down the base of her spine. She tried to banish such wayward thoughts.

Andrés tilted his head to one side, surveying her. 'Does your father share your love of art, Luz?'

'*Papá*?' Luz forced her attention back. 'His interest lies more with horses. *Mamá* was the one who took me to galleries when I was a child and we used to spend hours there. You, of course, must have grown up surrounded by it.'

They had spoken more about painting and sculpture at the beginning of the meal. Andrés, she realized, was highly knowledgeable. His perception and comprehension of art was deeper than hers and encompassed a wider range.

'Yes, I spent a lot of time with Eduardo when I was a child so he began training my eye and moulding my taste from when I was quite young.' Luz remembered from their conversation at Puesta de Sol that he'd had a happy if somewhat lonely childhood, without siblings, and so she knew a little of what that must have been like for him.

'Did you have many friends growing up?' she asked.

'Only a handful, but I picked them carefully. I enjoyed their company but I liked being on my own, too. My mother and father were older than most parents when I was born. My mother was just over forty and my father more than a decade older than her. Although they lavished gifts on me they were less generous with their affections or their time.' His gaze roamed thoughtfully over her face. 'I should have introduced you to them at the Yacht Club last night but never seemed to find the right moment.'

Luz remembered the emotionally charged tension between them throughout the previous evening. 'Yes, I know what you mean,' she said, a faint blush smudging her cheeks.

A smiled hovered on his lips before he swallowed a mouthful of wine and continued. 'Nowadays, my father is around more and they try to be supportive – at least, he does. My mother is often in her own world. As a child, because I saw relatively little of them, I went to see Eduardo most days and did as I pleased.'

He paused and then grinned. 'I think, perhaps as a result, I was a rather unruly child, brimming over with energy, always off on some daredevil adventure or another.'

Luz laughed; she was seeing a side to Andrés that intrigued her still more. 'Andrés de Calderón, the daredevil, now, why does that not surprise me?'

He grinned. 'Once I went off for two days when I was thirteen with three other boys. The others got their parents' consent, but mine didn't even notice I was gone.' An eyebrow arched. 'Don't look quite so shocked, Luz, I didn't care at all. I enjoyed it immensely. The freedom was exhilarating.'

'Where on earth did you go for two whole days?'

'We camped out in the ruined fort on the Isla del Trocadero. It was meant to be haunted by the ghosts of dead soldiers who were slaughtered there during the Battle of Trocadero in the early nineteenth century.'

He gave a dismissive gesture. 'I forget how the argument came about but an older boy – one I didn't much care for – dared me to stay there overnight. He said I didn't have the nerve and would never do it. So, with two friends of mine as witnesses, I did.' His eyes sparkled mischievously. 'They had to be somewhat persuaded, but the power of illicit cigarettes is an impressive thing at that age. It took us a day to get to the island and back, and we slept rough in those ruins. When we returned to Cádiz, I no longer felt like a boy.'

Suddenly, Luz began to see that the suave businessman was not so far removed from his gypsy doppelgänger after all. 'Did you see anything? Ghosts, I mean …?'

He shrugged. 'There were some pretty strange noises in the night but I'm not sure any of them were supernatural.' He polished off the last spoonful of his dessert. 'For an eleven-year-old, it was a wonderful experience. As was the satisfaction of proving the boy wrong.'

'He believed you? You could have pretended to have done it and he would never have known.'

'True, we could have.' Andrés glanced at her with an enigmatic smile. 'But one look at me and he knew I had gone there.'

Somehow, Luz did not find that hard to believe. 'I've often wondered what you must have been like when you were young.'

'You have, have you?' There was amusement in his voice as his eyes sparkled at her.

She smiled back shyly. 'I imagine that you must have got into trouble at school with behaviour like that.'

'"Reckless and headstrong," that was how my teachers described me. I'm afraid my temperament hardly fitted with the severe discipline of school. I was always getting into trouble. After a while, at Eduardo's suggestion, my parents resorted to private tutoring, a solution that suited me to perfection. Mornings were reserved for lessons and in the afternoons I could play a variety of sports. With a way to channel my energy, I began to focus on my lessons and found that I actually enjoyed the challenge of exams and passed them easily enough.'

Luz raised her eyebrows. 'So the "reckless and headstrong" boy became a successful international businessman.'

His mouth curved in a wry smile. 'After a Master's in Marketing and Business and entering the family firm a few years later – yes. I just needed the right environment. That's true of us all, don't you think?' He looked at her, his head tilted to one side.

Luz nodded pensively. 'Yes, I suppose it is.'

After dessert, they finally pushed away their empty plates and moved on to other topics. There was a new rapport between them, an ease that had not existed before, as if in mutual understanding they had decided to turn over a new leaf. Luz noticed how expressive Andrés was with his hands when he became excited by an idea and even when they disagreed, they did so with easy tolerance of the other. So engrossed were they, they missed the sunset.

They spoke about school and university in England. Andrés was interested in the boarding school system but vehemently against it. He would never send a child of his away; they needed to grow up with the tenderness of a mother, the firm hand of a father, the love of both parents and the security of a united home. Only then, he insisted, would they grow up to know themselves and be confident and stable. He spoke with an intensity that had struck her, the passion in his voice tinged with an undercurrent of bitterness bordering on anger, which puzzled her.

'Eduardo never married, I wonder if he ever regretted that?' pondered Luz, sipping the coffee Carmela had left them and helping herself to one of the housekeeper's petits fours. Luz had insisted Carmela should not wait up for her, sending her off immediately after she had cleared away dinner.

'He hinted at it a few times when I was older,' said Andrés. 'He was too dedicated to his career for marriage but he was well known for his romantic adventures. Eduardo's father disapproved of his son's love life and wanted him to be more conventional but Eduardo was looking for something, I suppose, something he never found … not completely.'

For the first time Andrés seemed lost and, for Luz, the world shifted on its axis at that moment and refocused in a different place. This was an Andrés she had never seen before.

'What was he looking for?'

'Passion, excitement – but above all love, I think.' At this, he fixed his midnight gaze so intently on her that Luz's mouth went dry. He was not playing with her at all now; there was no innuendo, no attempt to unnerve her; his eyes simply held a mournful candour that went straight to her heart and made her feel dizzy.

Hours had flown by. It was past midnight now. Andrés had lit a cigarette and was smoking silently, lending her his profile as he gazed into the darkness over the ocean. With the coming of night, the sky that had been a vivid blue all day under a scorching sun had changed to a sapphire heavy-velvet texture. As though shaken by an invisible hand, stardust was spilled about this dense canopy like specks of gold of all sizes and the moon looked over the young couple, glamorous and enchanting, touching them with her glow and turning light to silver, shadows to velour. And though Luz's mental state was soothed by the gentle rustle of leaves and by the monotonous swish of the sea, her emotions were stirred because of the man sitting beside her. In candlelight she could not distinguish the colour of his eyes and she had to constantly remind herself that the devastating, handsome man she was entertaining was Andrés and not Leandro.

'That was quite a show you gave us last night,' he said suddenly, out of the blue, watching her through his thick eyelashes. He had become more absorbed in the last hour and she sensed a subtle change in his mood that she couldn't put a finger on. 'Where did you learn to dance like that?'

Why did she get the distinct impression his tone was now slightly reproachful? She shrugged. 'Oh, I was just following my partner. He's a brilliant dancer and it was really little to do with me,' she said lightly.

One dark eyebrow rose quizzically. He cleared his voice. 'Your partner, he's the suitor your parents have chosen for you?' There was a faint question at the end of his statement.

'I'm quite capable of choosing a suitor for myself,' she said, somewhat needled.

'He must be a very broadminded suitor to allow you to entertain a gentleman on your own in the middle of the night,' he observed placidly as he lit another cigarette. She saw the narrowing of his eyes in the oscillating light of the flame.

He leaned back in his chair, his gaze fastened intently on the spiralling grey smoke rising above him. All of a sudden he had become prickly.

She laughed, aware that he had misunderstood her. Momentarily she toyed with the idea of continuing this deception as a game. 'I don't see why men should be allowed to court a number of women at the same time and women shouldn't,' she offered, still not denying Romero was any more to her than an acquaintance she had only just met.

'Is that what they taught you at boarding school?' His voice sounded almost as dark as the eyes that were surveying her over the candle.

Oh, no, she thought. The conversation was sliding down a dangerous avenue. Still, she was amused and a little lightheaded, and she wondered how far she could take this topic without marring the wonderful atmosphere that had marked the evening.

She shrugged again and assumed a noncommittal air. 'Boarding school has nothing to do with it. The rest of the continent has a much more relaxed attitude to relationships between men and women. Where sex is concerned, Spain seems still frozen in the Middle Ages.'

His face tightened into an impassive mask and his voice schooled itself to an even tone. 'Does that mean that you find it normal that a woman should indulge in casual sex?' He sounded cool, detached.

'At the end of the day it should be the woman's choice. I don't see why you, as a man, should have the sole prerogative to multiple relationships. A woman's body has just as much sexual need as a man's,' she asserted. *Something of which I am well aware*, she thought ruefully. Her own body had kept reminding her of it ever since she first laid eyes on Andrés and his irresistible twin brother.

'I don't see any logical reason why a woman shouldn't have the same right as a man to satisfy herself,' she continued.

With almost savage mockery, his charcoal eyes flew up at hers. 'So, I must take it that you were merely relieving a sexual need last night when you were reacting so vibrantly in my arms on the dancefloor? Is Romero de Cabrera not a talented lover?' He scoffed. 'Or maybe you require variety?' he ended bluntly with a twisted smile, a curious edge to his jet-black eyes.

'Variety can be stimulating, don't you think?' she parried, trying to keep a straight face. An Englishman would not have reared up so passionately and it secretly pleased her to see Andrés so fired by his Spanish temperament. She could not resist goading him a little further. 'After all, you are well placed to understand that motto,' she persisted, twisting the knife with some latent satisfaction. 'I am told that like your uncle, you're not loath to distribute the attentions of your handsome body around Andalucía,' she ended triumphantly.

His eyes blazed. 'I doubt your father, the respectable Count de Rueda, would be happy to learn his daughter has such lecherous views and desires.'

Now that hurt. The contempt in his voice made her cringe inwardly. He was hitting below the belt, though, fair enough, it was her fault for indulging in this dangerous game. She should have guessed that Andrés would be a formidable opponent and not one to be toyed with lightly. In the past, she reminded herself, he had proved himself more than once.

Her eyes took on a mysterious depth and she felt herself colouring as the thought crossed her mind that, somehow, Andrés' words were not so divorced from the truth. Had she not been fantasizing, while floating in his arms, that it was actually Leandro she was dancing with? And what about tonight? Was her heart still preoccupied by the gypsy? No – tonight was different. As the evening progressed, she had gradually seen things in Andrés that were new to her. It was not just an intoxicating physical attraction, she was aware of something deeper going on between the handsome hidalgo and herself. She really didn't want to think of how Andrés de Calderón had affected her in his own right this evening. It was too daunting, especially after the conversation they had just had. Tonight had been perfect and she was near enough to spoiling it. She must try gracefully to wriggle out of the awkward position in which she had put herself.

He was still waiting for her response, rolling his empty glass around in his fingers, his beautifully etched face hidden by the shadows of night. There was no mistaking the angry jut of his jaw or the strained stance of his body language. Around them the air was sizzling dangerously.

So she smiled at him a little sheepishly. The best way to diffuse this volatile situation was to come clean and admit that it was all of her making. 'Actually,' she said, leaning forward in her chair to look into his eyes, her own gleaming with a hint of mischief, 'yesterday was the first time I'd ever met Romero de Cabrera. His parents are friends of my parents.'

She shrugged. 'I have no idea whether *Papá* and *Mamá* envisage him as a prospective suitor, but I can assure you that he does not attract me in the least and I don't think I will meet him again except socially, of course, given that our families mix in the same circles,' she told him earnestly and hoped he would accept her word.

Although Andrés did not move, his shoulders relaxed almost imperceptibly. He stared at her in silence for a long moment, his eyes intent, so intent that she began to wonder if she had said something even more offensive to him.

She swallowed hard. 'I didn't realize at first that we were speaking at cross purposes and once I did, I … I …' she hesitated.

'You what?' he growled.

'I continued the deception for fun.' *There, it was out!* She wrinkled her nose like a naughty child. 'Sorry.'

'*Fun*? You think it's amusing to manipulate a man that way? Doña Luz María de Rueda, you should be ashamed of yourself for being so provocative,' he said, his tone severe. Luz's face crumpled in dismay. He continued to consider her with unreadable eyes and then all of a sudden his midnight irises lit up with the sunniest smile he had ever given her.

'You are almost as mischievous as I am,' he said, regarding her with a look she could not decipher. Then they both burst out laughing.

'By the way, for what it's worth, I don't believe in casual sex. That is, I mean for either a man or a woman,' she told him. The thought of Leandro stole guiltily into her mind for an instant but she waved it away.

His eyes twinkled with good humour. 'Ah, I see you're setting the grounds for another debate,' he said, his oh-so-sensuous lips breaking into a broad smile that made her pulse quicken to a dangerous rhythm. 'A serious one this time, hey?' He glanced at his watch. 'Unfortunately, it will have to wait. It's already two o'clock in the morning, far too late to indulge in any sort of discussion. I must let you get some sleep.'

He rose to his feet, steadily watching her as he slowly sauntered round to her.

She looked up at him and met the charring depths of his eyes. Her heart thundered so hard she was afraid he might hear it. The breath caught in her throat. *He's going to kiss me*, she thought, and instinctively moistened her lips with the tip of her tongue. Andrés stooped towards her, but instead of touching her gently parted lips, his burning mouth brushed the tip of her nose. He drew back and Luz's gaze collided with his, glinting with the Devil's mischief.

'Goodnight, *querida*. If I don't leave now, you will accuse me of wanting to distribute the attentions of my handsome body,' he teased, giving her the benefit of a wicked smile. 'People are terrible. They'll spread all kinds of slanderous gossip,' he added, his lips curling into a mock sullen pout. He winked at her and grinned. 'Don't you think?'

His proximity meant she was beyond thinking. All she wanted now was for him to take her in his arms and relieve the rampant desire that had been nagging at her senses all evening but he was not playing ball. For some reason he seemed to have decided tonight was not the night.

Under an enigmatic moon she walked him to his car, reluctant for the evening to end. 'Care for a moonlight swim?' he asked lightly as they passed the saltwater pool.

She glanced at him sideways. 'It would be a marvellous idea but you don't have your swimming things.'

'Who needs them?' he murmured, that daredevil, seductive smile returning. 'Have you never experienced the delight of swimming nude?'

'Sorry? What do you have in mind?' Her eyes widened. Surely he didn't mean …? She knew only too well what had happened the last time she had indulged in that sort of game.

Andrés laughed as he watched the various thoughts chasing across her expressive face. 'Don't look so embarrassed, I was only joking! Don't worry, I haven't the slightest intention of flaunting my handsome body in front of you …' he paused, his eyes gleaming with amusement, and then he leaned over.

' … tonight,' he whispered softly in her ear.

CHAPTER 10

B ack in her bedroom after Andrès had gone, Luz threw herself on the bed, elated. The evening had been perfect. For the first time she and Andrés had talked seriously, laughing freely when they found something amusing and generally enjoying each other's company. She had started off not liking him but at dinner today he had shown her more of the man than ever before and now she had to admit she had been wrong. True, he constantly reminded her of Leandro, which made it somewhat difficult to separate her feelings for him, but some unknown quality about Andrés now pressed itself insistently into her heart; something else ran like a golden thread through the shape of the emotion rising between them, an unfathomable affinity that seemed to bind them together.

Still, her heart played strange tricks and her head remained wary. What was this new feeling for Andrés? She was afraid to label it. Whatever it was, she would have to take it one step at a time. New emotions were awakening in her that she found both exhilarating and unsettling. Could such intense feelings be the beginnings of love? Luz sighed and closed her eyes. Hadn't she already thrown herself headlong into a passionate idyll she thought was love? That had only ended in a blind alley. She was beginning to understand that true love was built on a thousand small things and, unlike passion, it grew slowly and required commitment.

That her mind had strayed to the notion of love with regard to Andrés disturbed her, so she opened her eyes and shifted from the bed. After running a hot bath she soaked for nearly an hour, mulling over her scattered thoughts.

Andrés had told her he would ring soon. Maybe they could continue their discussion about Eduardo's work over lunch, or even a picnic, he had suggested. She had always been told that mixing work with pleasure was a recipe for disaster. Still, there was a large part of her that wanted to accept his courting, while the other flashed a million red lights calling for caution.

She squeezed hot soapy water over her face from her sponge, remembering Alba's words: *the tension and electricity between you was sizzling all evening.* Even then, in Pamplona, when she had believed she was madly in love with Leandro, her friend had been aware of the powerful attraction between herself and Andrés and had gone even further ... 'That man is head over heels in love with you.' Luz's heartbeat quickened at the thought, making her whole body pulsate beneath the hot water.

Yet the sobering reminder returned: Andrés was a notorious womanizer. Alba had likely been mistaken. The emotion her friend observed in him could easily have been down-to-earth lust rather than a lasting love. By encouraging the young man's advances was she not heading for disillusionment and heartbreak? On top of that, how shallow and frivolous it would be of her to jump from one brief affair to another – if that was even what she wanted. And of course, there was the rumour that he was about to get engaged to Adalia.

He never spoke about the beautiful socialite but, then again, he wouldn't, would he? Luz had noticed that he had not danced with Lorenzo's sister at the Yacht Club ball but there was certainly a tension vibrating between them. None of it made sense and she was tired of hitting brick walls whenever she tried to work her way out of this prison in which her emotions were trapped.

Outside, the night was humid and a little heavy, threatening a storm later perhaps. With only a sheet to cover her, she lay on the bed and stared up at the ceiling. She expected a sleepless night but a rare summer wind had started up. Its gentle howling through the palms and olive trees in the garden, together with the sound of the turbulent, choppy sea, lulled her into a deep and dreamless sleep. Indeed she didn't wake up until two o'clock in the afternoon when Carmela walked into the bedroom carrying a glass of fruit juice and a plate of fresh figs on a tray. Luz did not need to see her to know that the housekeeper was agitated; it was plain from the way she slammed the tray down on the table.

'Don Andrés has called on the hour since eleven,' she told her mistress, eyeing her reproachfully. 'He's really taken with you and very anxious to speak to you.' She shook her head. '*Pobre hombre*, poor man, I can't tell him you are still asleep when he telephones in an hour so I decided to wake you up. He will be ringing again at three.'

Luz opened her eyes reluctantly. 'What's the time?' She peered at her alarm clock on the bedside table. 'Heavens, I can't believe I've slept that long! Almost ten hours.' She smiled sleepily at the housekeeper. 'Don't look so cross, Carmela, *mi cielo*. I've been told it does men good not to be always available.'

She sat up and took the glass of fruit juice from Carmela's hands. 'Thank you, it must be your cooking that has made Don Andrés so keen. You outdid yourself yesterday. The meal was delicious. I must say, he's got a keen appetite. I thought it would be too much with all the tapas you provided before dinner,' she laughed, 'but he polished it all off.'

Carmela lifted her arms nonchalantly. '*El es un hombre sano*, he's a healthy man. At this age men need all their strength, especially when they are young studs like Don Andrés.' She eyed her mistress carefully. 'Their energy is quickly spent.' Luz could see the housekeeper was dying to impart all her knowledge on the subject but she forestalled her.

'Yes, Carmela, you can tell me all about that some other time.' She shot her an indulgent look. 'Now, I'm going to shower and dress and then wait obediently for Don Andrés to call.'

Carmela carried on regardless. '*El es tan guapo*, he is so handsome. You will have beautiful children, he is …'

'Enough of that, Carmela!' Luz scolded. 'I've told you before, Don Andrés and I are working on the biography of his uncle. He has employed me to do a job. That doesn't mean he's my *novio* or that either of us is even thinking along those lines so please get that through your head, once and for all.'

'Where affairs of the heart are concerned, I am never wrong,' the older woman declared as she marched to the door, looking behind to cast her parting shot. '*Créeme cuando te digo*, believe me when I tell you, this man is mad about you and wants to marry you.'

At three on the dot the phone rang: it was Andrés. He wanted to thank Luz for a most wonderful evening and asked her to Puesta de Sol for lunch the next day.

'We'll work in the morning,' he said, 'then visit the property and I'll show you Eduardo's archives. Later, we can picnic down on the beach, if you like, or on the veranda, whichever takes your fancy,' he told her.

'Bring rope-soled sandals for walking on the rocks and your swimsuit …' His tone lowered seductively, 'unless of course you would prefer to experience the thrill of bathing naked. It's very stimulating. A real aphrodisiac, trust me.'

Provocative humour danced in his voice and Luz could well imagine the familiar, devilish glint in those dark smoky irises, which told her he was intently aware of her as a woman and he wanted her to know it. Andrés de Calderón was being deliberately mischievous and it excited her.

*   *   *

It was glorious weather when Luz set off in the car the next morning for Puesta de Sol. The pair of ivory silk shorts she wore showed off her long shapely legs and perfect slim figure. She teamed them with a close-fitting shirt of the same colour and fabric. The curve of her small breasts and their taut little peaks could just be made out under the thin cloth, an arresting touch that, though she may not have admitted it to herself, she knew Andrés' keen eyes would not miss. The oversized collarless, camel linen-piquet jacket she had picked up in a boutique in Cádiz and the nude stiletto-heeled sandals adorning her delicate, perfectly groomed feet, achieved the easy glamour she was looking for.

Puesta de Sol in bright sunshine was just as striking as at twilight. On the last occasion she had driven there, the fading light had given the opulent villa a mysterious edge. This time, as her car rolled past the screen of cypress trees and the house came into view, she caught her breath again. Now she saw the place was pure theatre. It was almost as if one of Eduardo's paintings had been given real form. Like an Escher print playing with bizarre perspectives, Puesta de Sol had been designed with a mischievous delight in the dreamlike and the impossible. She parked her car on the driveway and looked up. From where she stood, the house gave the impression of a medieval village. The fantasy consisted of towers, terraces, porticos and irregular roofs, planned and executed in a clever arrangement that gave credence to the illusion. Lit by the dazzling sunbeams in a splendid fusion of elemental colour, it bloomed with trees, flowers and plants from almost every corner of the earth. Here, nature behaved like a magician with a lantern, concealing or revealing views of breathtaking beauty and creating spectacular effects.

A major-domo greeted Luz at the tall, arched wooden front door and she entered Eduardo de Salazar's harlequinesque world. Bright colours exploded throughout the hallway. Wherever she looked there was a splash of frivolity, something daring that reflected the artist's genius: stunning murals, twisting sculptures, cased figures and intriguing clockwork curiosities. Her eyes came to rest on a painting at the foot of the stairs that dominated the hall: a naked woman, with the head of a white bird and outrageous orange-and-turquoise wings sticking out behind her, was standing on a black-and-white chequered floor. She was clothed in a regal cloak of red feathers, dotted with staring green eyes, surrounded by half-human, half-bird people as if in attendance to their queen. Luz tilted her head and stepped closer to the work, then glanced up and found herself locked in the bold dark gaze of Andrés as he came down the imposing polychromatic stone staircase.

The major-domo discreetly disappeared and Andrés made a beeline for her, looking dashing in a pair of cream linen trousers and black polo shirt. He walked towards her, his sooty-black irises deep as chasms, exploring her slim body intently. His magnetism was such she could feel his eyes burning her with their ardent caress. The tantalizing, slow smile lit up his face as he reached her. Laying a hand on her waist, he stooped forward, brushing his warm soft lips to hers. The touch was feather-light, enticing and promising.

'You have a lovely mouth, you know,' he stated in a matter-of-fact way.

Her upturned face flushed with embarrassment. 'Hello, Andrés,' she said, trying to keep her tone friendly and sociable. Even though she could no longer control her body's responses to him, her sense of self-preservation still whispered caution. He mustn't realize how much her desire matched his. Oh, but he was aware of it, she could feel it; Luz had to stop herself from quivering at the thought.

He looked at her steadily then turned his attention to the room. 'So, tell me your first impression,' he said as he watched her walk slowly forward, her heels echoing on the huge flagstones, her gaze mesmerized by Eduardo's work.

'I hadn't realized the extent of the responsibility you've entrusted me with,' she said softly, overwhelmed. 'I thought that this kind of fantastic detail, this phenomenon of the large contained in the small, was only encountered in the imagination or in tales of wizardry and magic. There are no words to describe the first impression as one enters the maze of your uncle's fantasy. I feel a little like Alice propelled into the fantasy universe of Lewis Carroll, or Dorothy transported to the magical world of Oz.'

'You see why I chose you,' he murmured, coming to stand behind her, a bit too close, his hip brushing softly against her, the warmth of his breath teasing a tender place on her neck. She moved sideways and concentrated hard on the room to stop herself melting.

He followed her casually. 'You've got the breadth of knowledge and the right combination of sensitivity, imagination and creativity needed to understand Eduardo's vision. Rare and difficult qualities to come by, I assure you.'

He laid a palm on Luz's shoulder. She jumped and went rigid. 'You're wary of me,' he said in dismay. He put a finger under her chin and tilted it, holding her eyes captive as he searched them. 'Why, Luz? … Relax.' He looked hurt. He then let go of her but did not move away.

She laughed, a little nervously she thought. Though he was not that much taller than her, still she felt the power of his body dominated her. 'I'm fine,' she muttered, slightly breathless, not quite knowing whether she wanted him to move away or not. Somehow, she liked his proximity and the familiar scent of his aftershave tinged with the aroma of tobacco, and of something indefinably masculine that was simply him. But enjoying this feeling was dangerous, she knew.

'I was just lost in my own thoughts, that's all,' she explained, smiling brightly. 'I'm rather dazzled by the wealth of art in front of me and I've only just walked through the door. It's rather difficult to take it all in,' she added, hoping she sounded convincing.

'This is only the beginning. Let me show you the rest.' Andrés gestured towards the curving sweep of stairs and led the way up, into a vast room, which led into a series of smaller ones separated by arches.

The 'rest', as Andrés put it, was just as daunting: a synthesis of international decorative arts, every piece Eduardo's own creation. Rugs, wall hangings, spreads and slipcovers provided the background to a versatile world of sculpture and paintings, but his art did not stop there. A leather mat, a Surrealist tapestry, intricate mosaics, appliqués, ceramics, cotton and batik wall hangings, jute-and-wool rugs, even pieces of fanciful furniture laid witness to the variety of his skills and to his extensive travels. Large-scale abstract forms mingled with the figurative and concrete true-to-life works. Each room brimmed with its own mystery. Every item was signed, numbered, catalogued and had at least one paragraph of explanation. Luz had never seen anything like it and very much doubted that the British Museum or the Prado in Madrid had as considerable and meticulous documentation on everything they held. She was impressed.

'It's mind-blowing,' she told Andrés. 'Really, I had no idea. Nothing in my research suggested Eduardo's creative vision was so hugely productive and multi-faceted.'

'He was an extraordinary man and a brilliant artist. A handful of critics have in the past upset me because they can't understand his art and choose to misinterpret it.' His face hardened. 'It's been said that his work aimed to shock or confound.' The dark eyes flashed with disdain.

'They've got it all wrong, distorted everything he stood for. What his admirers respond to is the harmony and purity of saturated colour. Every piece is a hymn to God's creation, a celebration of nature and beauty in all its forms. Even with Eduardo's more disturbing images, there's a compelling truth in them somewhere. He knew exactly how to capture the duality of life: pleasure and pain, light and dark, truth and lies. And at the end of the day he managed to express all of this in his art, in stunning form.'

His eyes glittered as he paid homage to his uncle's genius. She had never seen Andrés speak with such passion. It was a sort of fire of which she had always been aware but which he kept rigidly in check. Only once had she witnessed it, when she had seen him lose his cool in his office, about Lorenzo's archives, but that was different: he had been angry then.

'It's obvious you were very fond of your uncle.'

'Yes.' He nodded thoughtfully. 'He was always generous with his time and taught me a lot. We were very close.' Then his gaze shifted away. There was a short pause when he tried to get a grip on the emotion that seemed to have flooded him. 'He said I reminded him of himself when he was young,' Andrés smiled ruefully. 'A kind thought, but I certainly don't have his genius.'

'He's really captured the essence of Cádiz's beauty,' Luz remarked, her attention now caught by three large paintings of the city of light, each depicting a time of day: *Dawn*, *Noon* and *Dusk*.

'Yes, he was fascinated by Cádiz's extraordinary luminosity. He used to ride his horse along our vast beaches at different times every day to catch the city's clean-swept Atlantic light, which changes from hour to hour.'

They had almost reached the end of their tour. As they went through the last arch, Luz's breath caught in her throat as she came face-to-face with a statue that stood at the centre of a smaller room. Lifesize, it was surrounded by representations on a smaller scale of the same person, in various positions and in different materials.

She turned to Andrés, who was standing in the archway, leaning against one of the pillars and watching her silently. '*La Pouliche*, am I right?'

He nodded. 'The love of his life,' he murmured. There was a small choke in his voice, which caught at Luz's heartstrings.

As their gaze held for a moment, she thought she read something there of a deep sadness, but it was gone almost as quickly as it had appeared. *It must be my imagination*, she thought, and turned her attention back to the sculptures.

'There's almost no documentation about her, but when I delved deeper in my research, I noticed the few references there were hidden away,' Luz continued, beginning to circle the statue. 'It's fascinating. She's hardly mentioned in the books written about him and I've never come across a sculpture or even a painting of her before today.'

'He uncovered this shrine to his muse only a few months before his death. No one knew anything about its existence before that.'

'She looks a great beauty and a sensual one at that. She also seems very young.' Luz observed, looking up at him. 'Who was she? Why did Eduardo not marry her?'

Andrés shrugged. 'I tell you, he was very ill when these works came to light.' His jaw was set in a grim line, eyes hooded, his expression revealing nothing.

Luz searched his face, trying to read his features. Suddenly she sensed that he resented her questions. But how was she supposed to write about his uncle if she couldn't get to grips with her subject? *La Pouliche* – it was her official name – contrary to all the information she had gathered so far, had clearly been a great part of the artist's inspiration. Luz continued to walk around the room, examining each and every one of the numerous small standing and reclining figures of *La Pouliche*, The Filly. Always in a relaxed attitude, the beautiful body of Eduardo's muse knelt, stood or reclined, arms draped about her head, each part of her alive and sensually provocative. Luz paused in front of one of the bronze busts of the model, whose head was thrown back in an arrogant taunt, her mane of hair cascading untidily behind her. She could almost see the fire seething in the large, animated eyes. Where had she seen that look before? 'Are there no paintings of *La Pouliche*?' she asked, suddenly surprised at this obvious gap in the collection.

Andrés did not answer immediately; he seemed to ponder what to say. 'There are a number of paintings but they're being cleaned prior to us archiving them,' he said finally.

'Can I have a quick look?' Luz continued, sensing he was holding back something she could not put a finger on.

His mouth twisted. 'You'd be better off viewing them once they're in a presentable condition,' he replied tightly. He was suddenly prickling with defensiveness; she could almost see his hackles rising. It was clear he wanted to be anywhere but there.

'Some of those paintings were stored in a badly ventilated cupboard,' he said, 'and have been damaged by the damp. I've kept them all together, you'll see them in due course,' he added.

But the tone was final: he obviously had no intention of showing them to her. It was no use insisting, so she let it go.

'Are we at the end of the tour, then?' she asked, smiling up at him, hoping to mellow his mood.

The brooding darkness in his eyes cleared, like stormclouds drifting away. He smiled back at her. 'Yes, for now. There are still the gardens, but they can wait until this evening before we go for that moonlight swim.'

Silence throbbed between them for a split second. His eyes, guarded before, now shone wickedly. Her pulse quickened as she stared into them. He had planned it all, and she had no doubt he had some surprises in store for her. Warmth flooded her loins in anticipation. She swallowed hard, trying to fight the heat rising within her.

'Shall we have lunch?' he asked casually. She was pleased to see that he seemed unaware of the turbulence seething inside her. 'I've told them to prepare it in the vine loggia. It's only a short stroll from here and the walk is mostly in the shade. I hope you don't mind, but I thought it would be too hot for a picnic on the beach. And the loggia has a view of the sea.'

'It all sounds lovely,' she said enthusiastically.

And so they moved from the gallery, down the stairs and out into the sunshine. They had emerged from the back of the house on to a series of paths criss-crossing a section of the garden.

The day was hot and luminous. Luz blinked, a little dazed, and her eyes took a few seconds to adjust to the light. She took her jacket off and inhaled sharply as she felt Andrés' palm come to rest in the small of her back. As he guided her towards the shadiest path beneath some tall trees, she could feel the pressure of his strong fingers through the thin material of her blouse. She liked the sensation and unconsciously leaned a little into them. He tightened his grip, his palm stretching slightly against her waist. Quietly she walked along, trying to ignore the proud thrust of her nipples straining against her bra as the warmth of his touch radiated on her skin and she felt herself melt with longing.

With great effort she managed to move away, frustrated and a little panicked at the strength of her arousal. He did not stop her; she was relieved: if he was aware of the tempest besieging her he didn't show it, merely sauntering on a few paces before turning back.

'Is anything the matter?' he asked innocently.

Damn the man. Of course he was aware of what was going on inside her and he was enjoying it.

'No, nothing at all,' she managed to say, trying to steady her erratic breathing.

'Sorry, I didn't realize, I've been walking too quickly. How very ungentlemanly of me,' he said, deliberately slowing his pace so she could keep up with him. His gaze now roamed over her slim body, slowing to linger for a few moments on her breasts. She knew he could see her nipples tighten further under his stare and the heat rushed to her cheeks as well as spreading down between her thighs. Seeing his eyes darken, Luz hurried past Andrés, sensing him pause a moment before he followed.

She turned her attention to the numerous amphorae overflowing with colourful flowers, which stood among the variegated shrubbery and exotic trees. Luz got the impression she was walking in a scene straight out of a Technicolor film, the midday sun acting as a powerful projector to illuminate the sumptuous garden.

As they came to the long stone loggia overlooking the ocean, she was overwhelmed by the bird's-eye view of the whole of the coast and, on missing the step up, she stumbled. Andrés, only a few paces behind, was quick to catch her. She fell back against him and found that he was unmistakably aroused. He wanted her.

An instant later she was swept into his arms and locked in his powerful embrace. Fire shot through her blood. She released a helpless little moan as his warm lips claimed and devoured hers with fierce and blatant hunger. She returned his kiss with equal ardour and wound her arms around his neck as her legs turned to jelly, pressing herself against him, wanting to absorb him.

Her mouth had opened hungrily, beginning to receive his darting tongue, when they were abruptly, though discreetly, called to attention by the tactful cough of a waiter bringing in lunch. They broke apart. Luz felt herself blush to the roots of her hair with mortification, even though the poker-faced retainer went about his job without batting an eyelid.

Andrés dismissed him gently. 'We'll serve ourselves,' he told him. 'Just place the food on the trolley and the wine on the table and we'll do the rest. *Gracias.*'

Dark irises gently teased the look of embarrassment on her flushed face as they crossed the loggia to the table. When the man was out of earshot, Andrés smiled at her reassuringly. 'Don't worry, he's like the three wise Japanese monkeys: "See no evil, hear no evil, speak no evil."'

Luz eyed him sceptically. 'He must be used to this sort of thing,' she observed, still a little shaken and ashamed of the awkward episode. What had got into her since her return to Spain? She had never been fast, had never exposed her feelings so blatantly and had certainly never entertained the sinful thoughts and images that assailed her now.

His smile was uncertain. He looked a little puzzled. 'Why do you say that?'

She flashed him a wry look. 'You're a notorious womanizer, Andrés. Don't try and deny it.'

He raised one dark, rakish eyebrow. 'I resent the word "womanizer". I am a lover, not a womanizer.'

'I don't see the difference.'

'Have you ever been made love to?' His voice was low, his expression soft, his gaze gently stroking her.

She stiffened. 'That is none of your business.'

'A womanizer takes a woman to satisfy his own desires, a lover gives as well as receives pleasure. With me, a woman's need is never left unfulfilled.' The dusky eyes studied her with narrow intent. 'One day, Luz, I will make love to you, and you will know what it means to be truly loved.'

Her brows lifted and, though goosebumps broke out over her skin at his words, Luz's pride couldn't help but rear up. She met his stare challengingly. 'That's a very arrogant statement. Don't you think you're overrating yourself a little?'

'I won't answer that,' he wryly drawled. Andrés merely pinned her with a bold look, his dark eyes moving over her. His sculptured, sensual mouth curved up seductively. 'As you say in English, the proof of the pudding is in the eating.' He poured them both a glass of red wine and picked up a bowl of small olives.

'Here, taste these. They come from my own olive grove,' he said, offering them to her. Chocolate-brown, they were hardly bigger than swollen raisins. She helped herself and he popped one into his own mouth. 'Their flesh is thin, but their flavour is full. They're small but potent with taste.' Luz met his glittering eyes as they regarded her over the rim of his glass, eyes as dark as sin, and she knew, without doubt, to what he was alluding.

He had fired the ignition. She felt the inevitable stir his provocative insinuations had created in her already sensitized body. He was addling her brain. Andrés did not need to touch her for her to want him: he did it with words or silently with his eyes. The man was the Devil himself. How had she ever allowed herself to become so vulnerable? She glowered at him.

Andrés saw the look on her face and laughed that low, hoarse laughter that came from deep in his throat. 'Come, Luz. You can't expect a hot-blooded man, faced with such a beautiful, sensual and desirable young woman, to remain unmoved and not be tempted to enflame her.' He winked at her, continuing the flirtatious charm. 'Come on, give me your plate, I'll serve you,' he said lazily, standing up and moving to the oversized trolley that served as a side table, where the waiter had laid the food.

'Let's eat, time is getting on and the cold lobster soufflé will melt. I don't know about you, but I'm starving.' He paused. 'In more ways than one,' he added, eyeing her with an amused glint.

Luz's deep-coloured eyes turned from blue to grey and, before she could unleash the whipping retort so clearly gathering in them, he laid down the plates and put his hands up in surrender.

'An attempt at humour, nothing else, I swear!' he said with a broad, endearing grin.

They lunched in the sheltered intimacy of the spacious loggia, which marked the edge of Puesta de Sol and its gardens. Its graceful stone columns were invaded by vines and wisteria, thick foliage creating a haven of leafy freshness and shade. The banks of roses surrounding the entrance exhaled a heady scent, enhanced by the heat of the relentless summer sun. And then there was the ocean, its dazzling iridescent tones shimmering like a dream in the early afternoon haze. Turtle doves cooed beneath the purple jacarandas to the side of them, while the breeze carried sea fragrances on its breath; down below, the lulling sound of breaking waves set a soothing tranquil pace to the afternoon.

The food and wine they enjoyed were equally wonderful as the view. They started with the soufflé, which was light, smooth and deliciously creamy, followed by chilled slices of a perfect rare beef fillet with red onion relish and a salad of roasted vegetables. They ended with a three-layered chocolate mousse cake and a terrine of red fruit in a white wine jelly, which was delightfully refreshing.

Over lunch, they spoke seriously about Eduardo de Salazar's works. Luz was fascinated by Andrés' alert, multi-faceted mind: he had inherited much of his uncle's visionary skills but they had been channelled into more practical pursuits. Both she and Andrés took great pleasure in lively debate on a variety of subjects; their minds fenced well together and their wits were a good match.

More than once Luz tried to bring up *La Pouliche* in the conversation but there was no pinning Andrés down. Each time he retreated into his shell and, though highly loquacious and helpful about everything else, he clammed up whenever the subject of The Filly was broached.

'Eduardo's muse must have been an intriguing woman for him to have kept her out of his main body of work,' Luz observed, glancing up at Andrés as she took her last spoonful of the red fruit jelly.

The spoon in Andrés' hand paused almost imperceptibly. 'Indeed, she must have been,' he answered, before it continued to his mouth.

'How frustrating it must be for you not to know her identity,' Luz tried again.

'I've come to terms with it.'

'Have you never tried to find out?'

He fixed her with an inscrutable look. 'Eduardo was careful to keep her a secret and I, along with the rest of the world, knew nothing about her.' He smiled. 'And do you know what makes *you* such an intriguing woman, Luz?'

She found herself smiling, too, into those melted-chocolate eyes that gleamed spiritedly. 'No, Andrés, but I know you're dying to tell me.'

'Your tenacity,' he laughed. 'Just one of the reasons, anyhow. It's also why you're the perfect writer for this book.' He cocked an eyebrow. 'Now, I think I'll have one more helping of this rather good dessert.'

Luz knew that it was no use pushing further. Andrés had yet again manoeuvred the discussion away. She was convinced he was lying when he said he knew nothing about the model, but that only spurred her curiosity and she promised herself that she would elucidate the mystery of *La Pouliche* as soon as possible. Eduardo's muse had almost certainly been a married woman moving in the high ranks of society, afraid of scandal. All this secrecy was to preserve her reputation. Still, she seemed rather young to be already married but, then again, girls married early in Spain.

Time passed at a staggering pace. It was now well into the afternoon and they were still sitting in the seclusion of the loggia. Andrés had ordered more coffee and some little cakes, which they went through as they chatted, discussed, argued and planned the way to move forward on the book. They worked well together, as they had done in their previous planning meeting.

As the day progressed Luz found she was falling deeper and deeper into the abyss of helpless attraction. As she fought with all her might to keep her emotions in check she hoped that, despite his extensive knowledge of the female psyche, he was unaware of what was happening to her. His command over the expressions of his face and his enigmatic eyes meant that, more often than not, she was left in the dark about his own feelings. Sometimes he let her glimpse what was going on under that impassive surface, but she knew it occurred only when he wanted it to.

At six o'clock Luz glanced at her watch. 'I've been here almost all day, I'd better get going,' she said, secretly hoping he would ask her to stay, though fearing the consequences if she were to do so.

He grinned as though he had read her mind. 'I thought you'd kept the whole day for me, or have you forgotten I promised you a moonlight swim?'

She smiled back and shook her head. 'I hadn't forgotten.'

'But perhaps you thought I had.' He raised an eyebrow, still amused.

Luz scrambled for something to say. This would be another step forward on already dangerous territory. 'I just wasn't sure if it was still on,' she heard herself answer, before she could think properly.

'You bet it's still on. Do you think I would willingly pass up the opportunity to be near your beautiful naked body under the shimmering moonlight?' The blunt avowal of his intention penetrated her brain. Luz paled as she met the wicked glint in Andrés' eyes, mixed with something deeper and unrecognizable. His soft voice not only caressed her ears but the whole length of her, arousing her with its bold request. Before she could find a suitable answer to quash him, he leant across the table towards her.

'I promise not to touch,' he murmured, his face set in feigned melodramatic secretiveness. 'I'll just admire from afar. Except, of course, if you want it otherwise.' Was he teasing her gently – or mocking her?

Luz felt trapped. Thoughts of escape entered her head but that was the wise part of her mind. She knew exactly what she must do if she listened to reason but she was not in a sensible mood; nor had she been for days, weeks, months. First it had been Leandro, and now Andrés. She could not escape what she felt when she was around him; all rational judgement disintegrated. Even more than the gypsy, he had awakened a whole array of complex feelings about which she was ignorant. She had lived quite happily before this in proverbial bliss – or had she? Andrés would argue that she had been missing out on one of the most enjoyable essentials of life.

Luz's expression was clearly anxious enough for a momentary look of shocked surprise to cross his face.

'Don't look so worried. I didn't mean to alarm you. You've nothing to fear from me,' he said, lifting his hand and brushing the back of it against her cheek. 'I will never ever ask you to do anything you don't want.'

'And I would never do anything I didn't want to either,' she answered quietly. Yet at that moment Luz was sure of what she wanted; she just didn't know if it was wise.

Andrés scrutinized her for a moment; his eyes were serious, his tone grave when he spoke again. 'You're still very innocent and I find it refreshing to be around you. Forgive me if sometimes I forget myself and embarrass you, Luz. I never knew there were women like you in the world. Your reactions are so unusual, so heightened that, like a naughty child, I find myself wanting to provoke them.'

He seemed truthful enough and she believed him; still, she was lucid enough to realize it would not take much for her resistance to melt.

'I keep a small dinghy on my beach. Would you like to go sailing?' he asked, still leaning forward a little to scrutinize her face. 'The sun is not so hot now and there's a slight breeze. Besides, the scenery is magical at this hour.'

Her lips curled into a smile. 'Thank you, I'd like that very much,' she said quietly.

'You'll need your swimsuit if we do decide to have a dip in the water,' Andrés suggested carefully, his lips hinting at a smile. 'Don't worry, I'll spare your blushes and not insist you swim naked.' His mouth broke into a broad grin, as if reading her thoughts. For a fleeting moment it made him seem so like his gypsy double that she blinked. 'I already have mine on, but there's an alcove with a seat further down where you can change,' he continued, nodding to a place behind her where the loggia was part divided by a wall. 'I promise I'll stay over here,' he added, still grinning.

Luz shot him a wry look: 'How very gallant of you.' For an instant she saw his eyes flicker with something before it was gone. Picking up her bag she walked away from him, letting out a deep breath. Why was he so ridiculously attractive? And why was her pulse racing like a schoolgirl's on her first date? She quickly changed into her bikini, put her clothes back on over the top and returned to the other side of the terrace.

The shade under the trees devoured them, lovely, dark and cool. They walked down to the beach, conversing lightly and casually as they went, accompanied by a mild breeze that carried the soapy scent of Spanish fern and that of the roses crowding the garden. On the beach, colour blazed across their retinas. The sky was azure and serene; it was still warm and the sun-splashed sea was alive with phosphorescence. The crystal-clear quality of the water was such that, five hundred yards from the shore, they could see every rock and pebble on the ocean floor.

The fourteen-foot white sailing boat with its blue sails lay on its side on the sand. 'We'll leave our clothes on the beach,' Andrés suggested as he tugged his polo shirt over his head and took off his trousers. His tall, lithe and broad-shouldered body appeared to Luz in all its golden glory, with only a slim black apology for swimming trunks, which barely covered the well-endowed bulge between his thighs. The shadow of chestnut hair covering his muscled chest arrowed pointedly to his waist and disappeared beneath the waistband of the minimalist garment.

Luz's insides melted as she watched him. *Calm down, old girl,* she remonstrated as she dragged her eyes away from the godlike physique before her, *he's only a man ...* Yes, but what a man! He was so like Leandro in his stance and build that she couldn't help but think once more of the gypsy and wonder if they were blood brothers somehow, though the thought was swiftly driven from her mind by the awe-inspiring sight of Andrés and the impact of his overwhelming presence.

'Your turn,' he grinned, teeth gleaming white against his swarthy tan.

With rather unsteady hands Luz rid herself of her clothes and kicked off her sandals. Damn it, she was blushing. *What's happening to me?* she asked herself despairingly. She was in the habit of wearing a bikini, so why the sudden coy reaction?

Andrés, with the considerate attention of the perfect gentleman, despite his earlier quip, had carefully averted his eyes and was busy pulling the sailing boat into the water.

Donned in a sheer kaftan, which she had slipped over her marigold-yellow, twist-front bandeau bikini, she walked to the side of the boat, which was tossing about in the shallows. Water swirled round her feet; it felt good. Before she could protest Andrés had turned swiftly and swept her up in his powerful arms, drawing a gasp from her lips. He had caught her off-guard; his hands were cool but his torso was hot against her already quivering skin and her unprepared body responded immediately to this sudden contact. She knew no seductive movements; she had no need. The faint suggestion of her silhouette beneath the thin material of her kaftan was alluring enough to turn Andrés' irises into a molten inferno. She could hear the pumping of his heart as her cheek brushed against his chest.

His grip on her body tightened a little as he pressed her against him for a moment. Then he set her down gently in the boat.

'You look beautiful, Luz,' he whispered. 'A dream creature in the sun.'

She smiled up at him and coloured under the intensity of his gaze. The erotic sensations his body had left imprinted on hers were deeply distracting.

'I've not sailed much before, but show me what to do and I'm sure I'll get the hang of it,' she told him, a little breathlessly.

'Are you ready then?' Andrés gave her a wolfish grin.

Luz nodded, trying to ignore the butterflies in her stomach.

Andrés looked around him to check everything before putting on his sunglasses. He asked Luz to take the tiller while he hoisted the mainsail and away they went, out into the sun-dappled open sea, to meet the golden sunset, which was not far off. When the sail was well filled with wind, the rope attached to it entwined around his long fingers, Andrés came and sat beside Luz. He showed her how to tack into the wind and explained how she should move over to the other side of the boat each time he called 'ready about', ducking under the boom to sit with him on the side as the boat shifted to an almost vertical tilt. As they worked together to manoeuvre the dinghy, Luz felt exhilarated. At one point Andrés crossed over again to sit next to her and covered her hand resting on the tiller with his palm. Their eyes locked intensely but neither spoke. The ocean was deserted; it appeared to be all theirs. Trapped momentarily in the amber of time, they sailed silently under the huge arc of sky.

Luz watched Andrés as he tightened the sheet of the mainsail in its cleat. The sun threw a splash of gold over him and she found herself studying those features that, after Leandro, now seemed doubly familiar to her. He was so handsome it was unfair. She had never seen such devastatingly attractive brooding eyes, with long thick dark lashes women would die for; their colour was simply a detail. Andrés' dark irises that were now hidden behind the screen of his sunglasses were just as arresting and compelling as Leandro's green ones. It was the passion, the mischief, the soul behind them that counted. She was discovering each man was as wild, exciting and lovable as the other. The longer-than-average shock of chestnut hair, bleached by the sun in places, was equally arresting whether worn swept back in a tidy ponytail or tousled, naturally curling over a broad forehead, framing the face like a halo.

But at that moment she knew she was falling in love with Andrés. He had been a nebulous, mysterious figure in her thoughts while Leandro had had all her heart and had been forever in her mind. Now Andrés appeared larger than life and the image of the gypsy seemed to have receded, though a part of her mourned him still. However, Andrés was still an enigma to her. Though they had talked a lot, he had volunteered relatively little about himself and she got the impression there was a whole side of him she still did not know.

'Mind your head!' Andrés shouted suddenly, jolting her out of her thoughts. She ducked beneath the boom just in time as it swung over with a shudder.

They were on another tack, sailing into the freshening wind. It had not been strong when they had set out, but it had increased in the last half-hour. She could see Andrés was a practised sailor. He manoeuvred his boat adroitly, changing tack swiftly and efficiently.

After some time Andrés bent forward to speak: 'We'll be sailing with the wind now and we'll be able to stay on the same course all the way to shore.' He pulled up the centreboard and moved opposite her to balance the boat. 'Running with the wind will feel surprisingly smooth and quiet after tacking, but the boat's actually going much faster.' Relaxed, he settled back, his arm stretched along the side.

'Have you been sailing long?' she asked.

'Yes, Eduardo bought me my first dinghy when I was thirteen. Whenever I had a quarrel with my parents or was upset, I used to sail out to sea. All the anger seemed to disappear magically. The sea's so huge, the sky so immense, it felt like somehow nothing else mattered.' He had taken off his glasses and Luz saw a look of sadness had crept into his eyes. She wondered what it was that haunted him.

They spoke of the wind and the sea, but were conscious of each other. Once or twice, Luz looked up at Andrés and their gazes fused: his, intense and ablaze like the great orb descending towards the horizon; hers, blue and deep as the vast ocean they were sailing.

On the way back, the boat hugged the coast until they reached the secluded beach in the cove of Puesta de Sol. Afloat in twilit waters, sliding across the setting sun, they watched an orange sunset flow like molten gold behind the cliffs, while along the bay the lights of Cádiz twinkled on. Dazzling colours filled the sky. Lonely white clouds turned into flaming swords, deep orange and red marking the west; the peak of the many rocky hills rose like church steeples, shooting forth tongues of flame from the reflecting sundown. In the distance the sinking orb gilded the houses of Cádiz with a special fleeting glory, their windows winking and flashing in the fading sun. Small vessels and steamers were moored alongside the quays; work was over for the day, everything still and tranquil. Soul stirring, the scene was all poetry and romance, depth and mystery.

As the small boat approached the shallow waters of the beach, the shadows were dying out in the twilight and the pale evening star shone in the sky. Wave upon wave broke in showers of spray against the immense cliffs that rose to the left and right of the secret place. Andrés jumped out first and helped Luz climb down on to the sand. They secured the boat, tying it to a stake with the mooring rope. As they came round the other side of an outcrop of rock, she was surprised to see that a canvas gazebo had been set up on the beach a few yards away from them. Slowing her pace,

Luz's enquiring eyes looked silently up at Andrés: this seemed much more than just a place to swim.

He grinned. 'The night is still young,' he said mildly as he shot her a sideways glance.

She looked doubtful, the voice of wisdom in her head whispering to her again. 'I think I should be getting home.'

He walked ahead and turned. The smoky eyes settled on her. 'Don't think, Luz, just enjoy.'

That would suit you to perfection, she thought, and in that precise moment, she had to admit, it suited her, too. She stared at the man standing before her in the lambent light, a man women would die for, a man the mere touch of whom sent her body, her senses, her mind and her soul into exquisite chaos. There was no use struggling against it; one way or another, she knew deep down that fate would deliver her into Andrés' arms.

'Why not?' she breathed enticingly on a little rush of laughter.

'That's the spirit,' he said and promptly popped open the bottle of champagne that lay waiting for them in a bucket on the table.

Everything had been set for a candlelit dinner for two. Andrés had planned it all down to the smallest detail, which in this case was a not-so-small blow-up sofa that stood in the shelter of the gazebo on the sand. He followed her eyes. Now it was her turn to glance at him sideways. He gave her a sheepish smile.

'Just in case …'

'Yes?' she prompted, eyeing him quizzically. She wanted him, but she was not going to allow herself to be pushed into it. Not that she needed to be. Still, he had to understand that.

Andrés shrugged. 'Oh, I don't know, Luz. Juan or one of the staff probably thought they were doing right. You know, making the place more homely.'

'So long as you don't expect me to …'

His face grew serious at her slightly clipped tone and he gently cupped her chin with his hand, his thumb momentarily skimming her lips. 'Have I not told you before that I will never do anything you don't want?'

Luz nodded, locked in his gaze. As he took his hand away, her mouth tingled where he had touched her.

'I stand by my word,' Andrés said, and Luz knew he meant what he said. There was a sense of offended pride radiating from him that made her believe whatever happened would be entirely of her choosing. A warm smile replaced his frown. 'And now, shall we drink to that resolution and enjoy our dinner?'

Luz smiled back and nodded. 'Actually, I think I could manage something to eat, yes.'

They laughed and sat down at the table, laden with exquisite silver and fine china, printed with details of delicate red-gloved hands tangled in a twisting pattern of green leaves and branches, which he explained had been designed by Eduardo.

As they sipped the cold champagne and savoured a large bowl of lobster, artichoke, potato and chive salad, both took care to keep the conversation light, never once verging on the deeply personal. They talked about their hobbies, their work, travels … anything, in fact, but what was on their minds.

Long after the sun had gone down to light other worlds, a small breeze started up; the night was cool now. Andrés slipped on a red cashmere sweater and offered Luz a blue one. At first she refused, but the camel-coloured jacket she had brought with her proved cumbersome and so she graciously accepted. Dressed in a garment that was his, impregnated with the familiar medley of aromas so obviously him, it was as if she were wrapped up in his arms. The disguised intimacy conjured up all sorts of images and sensations that made her head swim. Candlelight rendered the dark planes of his narrow face, his elegant features and those sensual curved lips even more dramatic. She found it difficult to look into his eyes: they were now too readable, mirroring her own thoughts, sending her into further chaos.

The stars had come out in the dark canopy of the sky, large and flashing as they gazed warmly down upon them. The silver crescent of the first moon was just visible as it competed shyly with the brightness of the other celestial bodies; the sea a plum black and darkly aloof. They were together in this lonely place, highly aware of each other, the world lost to them, eaten up and absorbed into the cavern of night.

'A glass of Manzana Verde or Licor 43?' Andrés asked. 'Or maybe you would prefer a Cognac, my favourite?'

'I'll have a very small Licor 43, please,' Luz heard herself say against her better judgement. She had drunk more than she usually did and knew another glass would only reduce her already dulled inhibitions but she felt reckless tonight. It had been such a perfect day all round and she did not want it to end. Secretly, she was waiting, no, *hoping* that he would take her in his arms; his feigned aloofness – she was well aware that he was holding back – was killing her. Andrés was trying to prove that he was quite capable of letting her leave tonight without laying a finger on her.

He poured a shot of Licor 43 for her, two fingers of Cognac for himself and lit a cigarette. Then he stood at the entrance to the gazebo, sipping his drink quietly, his profile to her, looking up at the sky. He was still in his skimpy swimming briefs but the soft red sweater covered his hips. Not for the first time her eyes took in his broad shoulders and the strong muscles of his thighs; it took some effort to keep up a bit of meaningless conversation.

'How nice to have your own beach.'

'Yes, it is … nice.' He looked back at her, his eyes glowing with amusement.

'You must enjoy the privacy.'

'Yes, particularly tonight.' Seeing his mouth curve up, she sipped her drink again.

'The meal was perfect and I must make a note of Eduardo's china.'

But the light cross talk seemed foolish. The air around them quivered with the wild emotion that was taking possession of them and clamoured for some outward expression.

'Come here,' he whispered suddenly, looking up at the night sky again. 'It's a first moon.' The faint possessive note in his voice and the way her mind and body reacted to it brought Luz a new awareness of her vulnerability. Now was the time to leave if ever she wanted to save herself from this man. For the first time in her life, she regretted her limited experience of men. She said nothing and remained seated. He turned to rest his eyes on her candlelit face. Fascinated by the burning look in his dark, dark irises, which galvanized to the surface an answering emotion within her, Luz waited breathlessly. His stare was full of so many emotions she could not read. After what seemed an eternity, he held out his hand to her. The devouring flames of his gaze engulfed her and once again she was lost.

She went to him, heart pounding tumultuously. Tomorrow she might regret what was about to happen, but tonight she did not want to think about the future: she would live for the moment and embrace wholeheartedly the night's promise. She turned her face up to him and they gazed at each other.

'Look up at the new moon, make a wish and it will come true within a year,' he told her, his eyes never leaving hers. She glanced upwards and stared wistfully at the silver crescent. Would the Queen of the Night really grant her heart's desire?

Andrés put his arm around her, drawing her close against the length of his body. 'I can't resist any more, it's too much to ask of a man.' His voice was hoarse and suddenly edged with a raw emotion that made Luz quiver.

Their mouths were inches apart and she knew that she should pull away but she could not. Suddenly she she was unable to remember why she had been keeping Andrés at arm's length.

'Tell me you don't want me to touch you,' he whispered in her ear. 'Tell me you don't want me to taste you all over, that you don't want me to pleasure you.' His breath against her ear was warm, his voice as dark as the desires he aroused, his hands febrile as he stroked her back, sending tingling shocks up and down her spine. Luz did not need more to feel the ache of her need surge up with unbearable urgency. She leaned into him with a little moan, her eyes closed.

Scooping her up, he carried her to the sofa. He helped her pull off the sweater and very slowly peeled away the top and the bottom of her bikini, the last hindrance to what he had been waiting for: she was finally there, lying naked. For a long moment Andrés looked down at her, his eyes burning. They rested lovingly on her face and moved down to her throat, where a telltale vein throbbed steadfastly, then slowly to the taut pink nipples of her firm round breasts and fleetingly over her tight flat stomach, to finally come to rest on the small dark triangle between her thighs.

'*Dios mio*, you are beautiful, Luz. Your body would drive a saint to drink,' he murmured. The throbbing of his most intimate part bore blatant witness to his own fiery need.

Her eyes grew wider, their sapphire colour almost black with longing as she devoured his statuesque tanned and muscled body. She held her arms out to him, her irises dilated, flesh quivering.

He moved slowly and rested his lithe strong frame on his side next to her, propping himself up on his elbow, looking down at her. Uncontrolled tremors shook her as his warmth came into contact with her skin. Wet heat throbbed between her legs and her eyelids fluttered down. He had barely started and she was ready for him.

'Tell me it's me that you want,' he said, his mouth near her ear again.

'Andrés …?' she breathed, her body moving restlessly, craving him to touch her.

'Tell me you want me, Luz,' he rasped deeply.

What was he saying? Could he not see how much she wanted him? There was an expression in his eyes of uncaged desire, of hunger, and a need borne of something else altogether. And then she realized that he wanted her to admit her desire for him, to say it out loud.

'Yes, Andrés, Yes, I want you. Please ... take me now.'

She was so close to the edge he would not need to touch her to bring her to climax. His look, his words alone, had the power do so.

Despite the hunger burning inside her, Luz's heart filled with gratitude, banishing the last fragments of her reservation. 'I'm not a virgin,' she murmured. 'You wouldn't be compromising me.'

She was mesmerized by him and as his head came down, his mouth finally claimed hers in a profound, caressing kiss. Then lifting it once again, he looked deep into her eyes. 'Virgin or not, *querida*,' he muttered in a soft voice, 'you are pure and innocent, *una paloma blanca* ... and I love you.'

Her gaze flew to his, her heart fit to burst. 'But you don't understand, you don't know. I ...' she continued, deciding to be truthful. She did not want to deceive him, even if it meant ... she ached for him so much, she could not bear to think of the consequences of her confession.

He silenced her with his hot demanding kiss. 'Shush, *querida*,' he murmured feverishly. 'Let me please you and love you the way I want to. No woman has ever inflamed my senses so much, I'm obsessed by you. I live and breathe only you.' He began dropping butterfly kisses down her cheek to her neck.

'Just give yourself up to me and I'll take you to stratospheres you have never dreamed of,' he whispered against her burning skin. 'Let me kiss you, stroke you, taste you. Let me satisfy your body and your soul with sweetness beyond your imagination.'

She was breathing faster, his words threatening to push her over the edge; she could feel the waves coming, trembling at the edge of the cliff. Helplessly she closed her eyes and surrendered to him.

'You are made to be desired and loved. Look into my eyes and relax; don't touch me, just enjoy what I'm going to do to you,' he ordered huskily. 'If you want me to stop, if I'm not pleasing you, just say the word and I will.'

She heard the emotion in his voice and saw it in the glowing fires of his irises as his large hand began its sensual journey over her skin. It moved over her breasts, his touch light, just brushing at first, then as they firmed, his expert fingers drew a circle around the little pink peaks, toying with them briefly until they lifted proudly, eager to be stroked; then his palm moved downwards, lingering on the warm flesh of her bare stomach.

She gasped and stiffened, her eyes glazing over as he found the silky dark triangle of her Mount of Venus. She felt him stop and trembled violently with the urgency of her need, her thighs parting imperceptibly in anticipation. His eyes were still watching her as he slid his fingers down, gently stroking. She licked her dry lips with the tip of her tongue. He found her other lips with his expert fingers and fondled the silky warm damp folds of her femininity. She ached for him to touch the little swollen bud buried deep in the secret part of her, but he left it behind. As she cried out his name, desperately trying to guide him where she wanted him most, he stilled his hand, tormenting her with agonizing pleasure.

Now he claimed her mouth, plundering it as he sought her tongue with his, then probing deeper and deeper, kindling her flame into a roaring fire. His kisses remained hot as his lips found her breasts and devoured them with his mouth. This time there was no holding back as he nipped, licked and suckled the firm mounds that had surged at his touch and their tight, quivering pink peaks. She was desperately aroused and her sinuous body moved gracefully as she moaned her pleasure. As he grew harder, his deep breath was audible as he slowed himself down, obviously fearing to lose control. His head dipped further. The curve of his lips lingered on her navel; he knew just how much pressure to use as he stroked and licked in slow, sensuous moves, causing every nerve in her body to vibrate, passion grasping her in its relentless fold.

He turned his attention to the secret part of her waiting for him, moist, swollen and throbbing with desire. She cried out when he gently peeled away the silky-smooth petals protecting her mystery. He took the fevered rosy bud in his mouth, sucking, teasing with the tip of his tongue, stroking slowly at first, then faster and faster, harder and harder, stimulated by her cries of encouragement. She never wanted this delicious torment to end. Each moan, each cry she let out seemed to illicit a growl of pleasure from him as she opened up and yielded still further under his touch. She knew she was intensifying his need and felt the almost primitive erotic fire burning them both. Her blood was thundering now; every limb, every nerve, every inch of flesh of her taut body crying out for release. Whimpering, pleading, she was almost sobbing her need for him to fill the void inside her.

His gaze never leaving her, he finally eased himself back up and claimed her open lips with all the tenderness of his love. Lifting her slightly, he cupped the cheeks of her bottom to draw her closer. Instinctively she parted her thighs to receive him. He eased himself into her using his fingers first to make sure he did not hurt her. Holding her hips, he began thrusting into her soft, silken moisture, firmly and deeply, as her muscles tightened avidly around him, gripping and caressing him.

Now they were moving rhythmically together, luxuriating in each other's pleasure. Tongues of fire lashed at them. The swirling kaleidoscope of sensations that rushed through them was more than they could bear. Her nails dug into his shoulder as she moaned his name again and again, telling him how she loved him and how he was pleasing her. Her frenzy was driving him deeper into ecstasy, his hunger for her naked and unconcealed, blazing like a roaring fire.

Their passion had escalated to a raging ache that was begging to be released. As he gradually gave up control, his kisses became wilder, his embrace ever tighter, melding their bodies into one. He thrust deeper and deeper into the moist core of her, gradually increasing the tempo. Breast to chest, thigh to thigh, they were rocking to each other's hungry cries, savouring every shade, every tone of pleasure, until this crescendo broke into an almighty storm of lightning, the sensual waves engulfing them both and exploding in final release, dragging them, united, deep into the ocean of ecstatic bliss.

Their climax was long and powerful. When they finally surfaced into this world, they smiled against each other's lips, hearts still beating frantically in unison. As he lay on top of her, Andrés smoothed Luz's hair back and kissed her forehead. He grinned.

'*Dime querida*,' he whispered tenderly, his eyes intent on hers, 'do you still think I'm a womanizer?'

She gave a happy little chuckle. '*No, usted es el hombre que amo*, you are the man I love.'

He stared at her, his eyes clouding with intensity before his lips brushed the tip of her nose and he rolled off her. Spent and satiated, they drifted off to sleep, wrapped in each other's arms.

CHAPTER 11

Luz returned to L'Estrella before dawn. It was one thing to get back in the small hours and quite another to stay out all night. After tucking into the scented juicy flesh of a large white peach and making herself a cup of thick hot chocolate, she showered and was still floating on cloud nine when she went to bed.

Lying awake, she marvelled at the way her feelings for Andrés had made a complete U-turn in the past two days. She knew she had fallen in love with him yet how could she transfer her passion so easily from one man to another? She had never been promiscuous. How could this be happening? Tonight it was Andrés, not Leandro who had captivated her body so entirely and made her emotions soar to new heights. Her newfound recklessness would surely end in tears. A warning voice whispered inside her head: *had she not learnt her lesson with the gypsy?*

Still, there was no escaping the force that pulled her and Andrés together like magnets, compelling, powerful and irrepressible. Leaving aside his evident skills in lovemaking, in the past two days they had spent together he had given her a glimpse of the man behind the arrogant mask: the overwhelming male self-confidence she had so despised when they first met had fallen away to reveal thoughtful complexity, his haughty impudence replaced by irresistible mischievousness. Time had evaporated while they were together.

Yet Luz had a nagging feeling that he was holding back something and that made her uncomfortable. At times he was moody and secretive and, in those moments, those silences, she felt completely isolated from him. She could not follow the strange currents of his mind that took him away into his own world, of which she was not part. It unsettled her that he never allowed her to probe further than a certain point in his life. Even when she was able to push a little further in the hope of catching him off-guard, she always came up with a blank.

From time to time she had noticed a harrowed look in his eyes, which pulled at her heartstrings. Was it sadness or fear? Doubtless he had lied about Eduardo's paintings of *La Pouliche* – but why? She had the heady sense that she had stumbled on to something vital and was determined to find out more about those paintings and their mysterious model.

Eventually, she drifted off into a dreamless sleep and was awakened a few hours later by the chorus of birdsong. The sunbeams entering her room summoned her to enjoy the freshness of the hour.

It was a fine and glowing day. She went on to the flower-filled veranda outside her bedroom, where she sat in her rocking chair, looking out to sea. The light was white far into the distance, where Puerto de Santa María still lay sleeping in the morning haze, abutting on the exquisite emerald of the ocean. She listened to the buzzing of cicadas in the branches of nearby trees, the chirruping crickets and the soft murmur of the sea in the distance. It filled her with a sort of intoxication, which made her feel drowsy again. The garden at this hour was streaked with broad lakes of shade; the colours were beautiful. Nature was moist with dew, glittering with a strange luminosity. Apart from the humming stir of insects it was a benign and tranquil sort of morning, though the telltale haze announced a hot day. She could hear the clicking of a watermill in the distance. Butterflies hovered around her, busy sipping honey from the flowers; lizards crawled over the ballustrade or lay very still on the walls, basking in the sun.

She watched a hawk swoop not so far away into the bay, which lay blue and silky under the burnished sky. And there, out of sight, somewhere behind the cliffs on her right, slept the lonely little beach that had witnessed her night of love. Strange how it had also been on a beach that she had given herself to Leandro. But she didn't want to think about Leandro now; it made her feel uncomfortable. It was almost as though the twins were competing with each other and she found the ambiguity of her situation unnerving. Of course she had no proof they were twins – the idea was so far-fetched, even absurd. Most probably they were unaware of each other's existence. One certainty remained in her mind, though: no man had awakened her senses in the way they had and she was sure she would never again encounter such compatibility with anyone.

The discovery of this sensuous, rather wanton facet to her personality frightened her; she deeply resented being so uninhibited. She still blushed at the thought of how she had revelled in Andrés' intimate caresses and how quickly she had surrendered to him, unable to control herself. Years of self-discipline simply disintegrated into thin air. Like a flower to which he had shown the sun, she had bloomed but it somewhat went against the grain: the English part of her shrank from that sort of exhibitionism, finding it distasteful.

Thinking of Andrés flooded her body with a languid longing. She would be meeting him later on, down at the beach. They were going snorkelling.

'I will take you places you've never dreamed of,' he had told her with a wicked twinkle in his eyes and that suggestive intonation in his voice she was beginning to recognize. Only too aware of his skills of initiation, she tried to suppress the rush of euphoria that invaded her as graphic images of the 'places' to which he was proposing to introduce her clamoured in her mind. She was looking forward to a long, leisurely day of exploring.

And so she showered quickly, dressed in a pair of figure-hugging shorts and went down to the kitchen. She was relieved it was market day; she wouldn't have to bump into Carmela and be confronted with her endless questions. After ransacking the housekeeper's larder to pack up a picnic, she set off.

The haze was dispersing; the sun was up and hot. The ocean, intense blue skies, the clean-swept Atlantic light and salty air, the rambling beach and Andrés were all waiting for her. She noticed him as soon as she had traipsed over one of the high dunes: a somewhat lonely figure silhouetted against the vast immensity. He had brought his boat ashore and was sitting on the side of it, arms folded against his muscled bronze chest, watching her approach. As Luz moved towards him, he never took his eyes off her and she, in turn, was transfixed at the sight of him, bare-footed in his sailing shorts, his naked torso like that of some god in mortal form. An unbearable yearning for him coursed through her. So this is what real desire felt like. She hailed him and he waved back.

Luz had barely reached him when he was beside her, encircling her waist and scooping her up in his athletic arms. He twirled with her once, twice, holding her in a close embrace. Caught off-guard, she let go of her bag and her hands went up to his bare shoulders. His skin felt hot beneath her cool palms and Luz caught his slight intake of breath and the tensing of muscles as she touched him. He wore sunglasses so she could scarcely make out his eyes behind the dark screens but she knew from the tautness of his body that they were wild with desire. He lowered her to the sand, dragging her down slowly so she brushed against the length of his frame, feeling his unmistakable arousal against the apex of her thighs. Andrés stilled, obviously trying to control the same violent need that Luz already felt engulfing her.

'I think we ought to go, don't you?' he whispered. 'The boat is ready. We're lucky, we have perfect conditions today.'

The impatience in his voice was evident, she noted with satisfaction: he had missed her.

The wind was blowing onshore, which would make it tricky to sail away from the beach, she realized, but Andrés worked quickly. He had already placed their belongings in the dinghy and the mainsail was ready to hoist as soon as they were aboard. Luz helped him drag the dinghy out into the water and, once it was floating clear of the breaking waves, they scrambled aboard and headed out of the cove, the sail canvas beating heavily through the roar of the wind.

They were sailing parallel to the beautiful coastline now, away from Cádiz, heading south. Luz had never come this way before. The landscape was quite different, the shore backed by pinewoods often spliced by great, blond sweeps of beach, and the skyline ringed by cloud-dappled mountains.

From time to time Andrés withdrew his gaze from the horizon and turned towards Luz. Though she could not see the expression in his eyes, she knew he was studying her. They hardly spoke but anticipation swirled around them, outdoing the vigorous gusts of wind.

The sailboat had gathered momentum and Andrés warned that he would be moving into a tack. 'We're practically there,' he announced as he turned the rudder sharply. *He's going to capsize, the wind will flip the sail,* Luz thought, ducking under the boom as the boat jibed, but Andrés proved an expert sailor and, as with everything else, he was in total control of his boat.

He smiled. 'Worried?' he asked as though he had read her mind.

'That was a bit close, don't you think? We almost capsized!'

His smile grew broader and more roguish. 'No faith, Luz, that's your problem. I'm in charge, I'm always in charge. Haven't you learnt that yet?'

He had certainly been in charge yesterday night. Did this man never say anything without double entendre?

'How can I forget?' she parried, her eyes glittering with the same mischief she knew filled his. He laughed out loud, and she thought how often he did that now compared to when they first met. It made her smile.

They were approaching what looked like a secluded, curving beach. The view was pure poetry. Distant citadels of cliffs and flying stone buttresses rose above the dark silk water, topped with deep-green cicada-singing pines, gnarled olive trees and wild carobs. On one side was a pretty town, dazzling white in the sunshine, hugging the hill midway; on the other gently rolling and rising vineyards.

Like a bronze sculpture, Andrés stood at the tiller, aiming the boat at a given spot on the beach. As they neared the shore there was a grating sound as the underside of the boat met the shingle. He jumped out of the dinghy and gripped the gunwale.

'Stay where you are,' he ordered. 'I'll come and get you in a minute.' He began tugging the craft up the beach, all in one long movement, so the curling waves would not swamp her as they broke along the shore.

As he extended a hand to help Luz out of the dinghy, watching her face as he did so, he said: 'I can't decide upon the exact blue of your eyes. Last night, when I held you, they were such a dark cobalt blue, they seemed almost black. Today, they're more azure, like a cloudless sky on a midsummer's day.'

There was a flash of genuine amusement on her face as she climbed out of the boat. 'Thank you, Andrés, very poetic,' she smiled. 'Unfortunately, while you hide behind those sunglasses, I can't repay the compliment.'

He turned his head and looked out to sea, his mouth falling into an impassive line. Was that the hint of a frown she glimpsed? She could see only part of his profile. But his next words were ordinary enough. 'The glare hurts my eyes, especially when I'm out at sea,' he explained, facing her again with a faint smile and removing his sunglasses.

Perhaps she had been wrong; there was nothing troubled about his look now. His jet-black stare fixed on her intensely, in a sensuous, enigmatic way that sent her falling into its depths. Suddenly she felt shy and nervous as if they had just met for the first time.

'The perfect spot to spend an idle and delicious day,' she said, dragging her eyes away from him to survey her surroundings properly. She looked back at the enamelled sea, the colour of pure cobalt, bathed in the exhilarating white light refracted from the rocks and the talcum powder sand. What a jewel! This was an unadulterated place, undiscovered and almost wild, where the only occupants were the sea creatures and birds.

'I discovered this beach one afternoon when I was a teenager,' Andrés explained, with a distant, dreamy look as his gaze moved beyond her. 'At the time I was deeply troubled and needed to clear the confused thoughts in my head. Ever since then, whenever I have a problem, I come here to think. To my knowledge it's never been explored and has remained secluded and immune to the demands of the world.' He smiled ruefully, lifting their things from the boat. 'When I return home, after a few hours spent in this place, I'm calm and have usually found an answer to my problem.'

'Yes, I can see why,' said Luz, smiling. 'It's stunning, like a natural sanctuary. Is that a cabin?' she continued, noticing a tiny thatched hut as she wandered up the beach. Tucked away in a far corner, it was shaded by a few bedraggled palms.

'Yes, I built it. Sometimes it's quite cold out here in winter. The wind is sharp and the sea gets quite choppy.'

Luz felt an uncomfortable wrench in the pit of her stomach. He didn't just come here to clear his mind, she thought. This was the perfect love nest for his mischievous games. Was she the first to come here or had there been others? Andrés caught her eye. She was convinced once again he had read her mind. Damn her expressive, transparent face! It gave away her feelings every time, without fail.

Andrés watched the light blush rise and fade in her cheeks.

'Relax,' he said, the familiar flicker of humour twinkling in his dark irises. He dropped their bags on the sand and came closer. Lifting her face up, his gaze bore into her troubled eyes. He viewed her gravely.

'This is my secret place. I've been jealous of it and have never wanted to share it with anyone,' he whispered, his low voice charged with meaning; he paused a little and then his mouth moved slightly into a wry smile, 'until today.'

Once again Luz was captive of his will and her lips parted imperceptibly, inviting the kiss she had craved since they had separated the night before.

'I don't want any other,' he murmured softly, tracing butterfly kisses slowly down the curve of her cheek to her throat. 'From now on, there will be only you *mi tierno amor. Solo tú, para la vida y para siempre.*' His mouth trailed back up, securing her lips and sealing his words with a kiss that was everything she had yearned for.

Finally, they pulled apart and he stroked her cheek with his finger.

'Are you hungry, Luz?'

She looked up at him. 'For food?'

'Señorita de Rueda, that is not something you should say to an alleged womanizer,' he murmured, his eyes darkening.

She raised an eyebrow, watching his mouth, which was still only inches from her own, the same mouth that had been all over her body only the night before.

'I know, Senor de Calderón, you're clearly a bad influence on me.' It was true, she didn't know where these wanton feelings were coming from but she was beginning to enjoy them.

He grinned. 'We should eat. You'll need your energy. Besides, difficult as it is for me not to have my way with you right here, delayed gratification will make dessert all the sweeter.' His molten, dark eyes gazed down at her and so much longing flooded her that Luz thought her legs would turn to jelly.

'Come, let's get under the shade,' he said and led her to the palms overhanging the hut. They dropped down on to the sand, listening to the swish of the seawater washing against the rocks and the quarrelsome cries of gulls fighting overhead.

It was a wild beach, like no other she had seen in Spain, with soft dunes to lie in and umpteen coloured shells to collect. Nothing could disturb this spot, its sequestered beauty and its magic. She could quite understand why Andrés had chosen it for his secret den.

'Wild oyster beds and sea urchins lie everywhere around here, tangled on the rocks of these little creeks and inlets,' Andrés told her. 'I grew up near the sea. Oyster gathering, crabbing and beachcombing were a great part of my life. A lonely but very rewarding pursuit.' He grinned. 'I'll go and get some for our lunch,' he said, jumping up with one athletic movement, his joints as agile and supple as those of a feline.

'I've brought a picnic,' she said, smiling up at him.

'Excellent! We'll supplement it with whatever I'm able to gather.'

'Shall I come with you?'

'It'll be quicker if I'm on my own. Besides, the sun is already hot and I'd feel guilty if you caught sunstroke.'

He produced a knife and a child's brightly coloured pail from the canvas bag he had brought with him. Her eyes widened as the steel blade, catching a sunbeam, flashed dangerously. 'My tools – I've had them since Eduardo bought me the boat. I never went out without them,' he explained, his eyes softening as he thought back to obviously happy memories. 'Wait here. I won't be long. I'll be just over there, see?' He pointed to a rocky spot a little further down the beach.

As he went off she turned over on her side, resting on her elbow, and dug her fingers idly into the fine sand, scooping up handfuls, which she poured swiftly between her fingers back on to the beach. She watched him move away, graceful and lithe as a panther, muscles rippling under his skin, his strong back tapering to a lean waist. Leandro … all Andrés' movements reminded her of the gypsy. At times like this, as her eyes followed the distant golden figure scrambling nimbly over the rocks, the similarity edged on the uncanny. She sighed. Would she never be able to put her Romany lover out of her mind?

Andrés was soon back, his bucket brimming over with spiky brown urchins and small wild oysters. He resembled a god of the deep, his long, wet chestnut hair glistening with droplets of seawater, which picked up the sun's rays. Passing a tanned hand over it, he squeezed the water out of his ponytail and smiled.

'There are drawbacks to long hair, don't you think?'

But she could not think, spellbound as she was by the statuesque perfection of the man looking down at her, his heavily lashed dark eyes equally mesmerized as he took in every detail of her body.

'Here you are, *mi princesa*,' he said, laying down the pail at her feet. He sprawled across the sand beside her and linked his hands behind his head, his brown muscular body stretched out to catch every sunbeam, his limbs hard, smooth-skinned and the golden colour of polished oak. 'We'll have lunch in the hut, don't you think?' he suggested, then grinned. 'That way we won't get sand in our butter.'

The interior of the hut was very primitive. A couple of tree stumps served as seats and a large flat rock as a table. Hurricane lamps, a small stove and candles stood on the windowsill with a box of matches and a pack of cigarettes. A large shelf, of some sort of dark iron, held a kettle and a few pots and pans while an earthenware urn, which he explained that he filled with cool water from a nearby stream, lived next to the door with a pile of wood and kindling. Deep-sea fishing and snorkelling gear were piled up in one corner. Still, the plain layered bedding made out of straw that lay in the opposite corner did not go unnoticed. He gave her an oblique look.

'Sometimes, when the winds have come up suddenly and the sea is rough, I've spent the night here,' he said, answering her unuttered question. He paused and smiled rakishly. 'Alone, I swear,' he added, lifting his hand to his heart.

They lunched in the comfort and shade of the little thatched cabin, seated on the low tree stumps, and augmented their picnic of wine, bread and butter, dried meats, hard-boiled eggs and salad with the sea urchins and oysters that Andrés had gathered from the rocks. He split them using the edge of his knife. With bread, butter and a squeeze of lemon they were delicious.

They talked and laughed a lot – easily, lazily, because the wine was velvety and sensuous. Tasting it, their moods mellowed in anticipation of the next few hours they would spend in each other's company. All the while their bodies ripe for pleasure as they savoured this tantalizing awareness.

Luz tipped another citrusy oyster into her mouth and, without thinking, licked the salty liquid from her lips. She glanced up and found Andrés watching her intently. If he had chosen oysters as an aphrodisiac, she mused, it was unnecessary. The electricity between them had been palpable from the moment they had met on the beach. 'Have you been outside Spain much?' she asked, mesmerized by his steady gaze.

'Yes, a lot. I travelled all over the world in my early twenties after I left university. I was still looking for adventure, I suppose.' He broke off some bread, smearing it with butter and biting into it.

'And did you find it?'

Andrés chewed quickly then grinned. 'Invariably. I studied anthropology, including tribal differentiations. That took me to Peru, to reservations in North America, aboriginal grounds in Australia. I spent some time with the Maoris in New Zealand. Papua was particularly interesting. I found myself among the Kombai clan. I was a *kwai*, which means spirit or ghost but it's also a term used to describe an outsider. So I was regarded with suspicion for a while, until I was befriended by the chief's son.' He saw the question in her eyes and glanced away, reaching for his glass to take in a gulp of wine. 'But that's a story for another time. Suffice to say I was finally accepted into that clan, but not before one of them accused me of being a *Khakhua-Kuma*.'

Luz was intrigued. 'What on earth is that?'

'A man who practises witchcraft.'

She tried not to laugh but couldn't help it. 'It seems the Kombai are a very good judge of character,' she added, smiling.

He grinned and took a knife to one of the oysters. 'Cannibalism was still carried out by the Kombai as a form of tribal punishment for male witches. If the chief's son hadn't defended me I could have been eaten.'

Luz stilled. 'Goodness, Andrés, are you serious?'

'Absolutely.' He eyed her mischievously. 'Though I'm glad I escaped the pot, I think my flesh would have been rather delicious, don't you?'

She shuddered. 'I don't even want to think about it.'

He laughed out loud, prising open the oyster shell. 'You don't want to think about my delicious flesh? I'm mortified, Doña Luz.'

'You know what I mean.' She shot him a wry look but as he raised his head to tip the oyster into his mouth her eyes dropped to the tanned, muscled, naked thigh so near to her. Yes, his flesh certainly did look delicious. She cleared her throat softly, adding: 'Where else did you travel to?'

'I managed to make it to the Naga Hills in north-east India, a beautiful land of hills covered by flowers but full of precipitous ravines. I stayed with the secluded hilltop tribes there for a while. That was fascinating. They may have stopped practising headhunting now but in most respects they still live in a hidden world of ancient traditions that haven't changed in hundreds of years. It was an incredible experience.'

He looked younger and carefree when he spoke of his globetrotting exploits, quite a different man to the one who spoke of his childhood and his family life. Not so brooding, Luz thought. She looked at him quizzically, a little awestruck.

'And you actually lived with all these native people?'

'Yes, of course. I had to in order to study their ways.' He smiled a dazzling smile.

'Apart from being rather dangerous, by the sound of things, it must have been so, well … basic.'

He shrugged. 'Once you get used to it, you just accept that aspect. Human beings only need the basics, Luz,' he added softly, with a sensual undertone. She felt her skin heat as her eyes were once again drawn to his perfectly formed mouth, which curved into a slow, lazy smile. 'Then it's just a question of following that society's rules.'

'Yes, and I suppose some are just more complicated than others,' Luz murmured. She sipped her wine, wondering at the kind of unwelcome judgements she must be inviting, with her recent behaviour and now just being with Andrés.

'We're all tribal,' he continued. 'Nations, families, blood ties, class … You yourself returned to your own tribe when you came back to Spain, wouldn't you say?'

She had never thought of it that way. 'It does feel like that. I was never truly comfortable until I was back home with my family. But I've never had adventures like yours. I wish I had travelled more and seen the world. It sounds so exciting, seeing other cultures, being able to reinvent yourself wherever you go.'

A hint of a frown creased his brow. 'It's liberating, yes. But most paths lead full circle, and everyone's journey is different.'

'A woman's journey is more restricted,' she answered ruefully.

Andrés nodded. 'Granted, in Spain there are certain expectations for a woman. I can see that England must have suited your mind and your spirit in many ways.' His expression became fervent as he regarded her. 'And now you feel Spain coursing through your blood again, letting free a part of you that's new and frightening.'

Her eyes widened. *How did he know so accurately what she had been feeling?* 'You seem to know me remarkably well already,' she observed.

His seductive smile appeared and he cocked his head to one side. 'I've been paying attention, Luz.'

Her desire for him at the moment struck her deep down and she yearned for him to take her in his arms. But she wasn't confident in the art of seduction and so she followed his lead, holding back, waiting for him to reach out to her first, but he seemed intent on drawing out the torture.

Comfortable with each other, they worked their way through the rest of lunch, managing to stay on stimulating, though less provocative, topics of conversation. They shared their thoughts about Spain and what it meant to them. Both were passionate and restless individuals, they had that in common, as well as having individualistic ideas that sometimes clashed, but neither fell back into scoring points in the way they had in the beginning. It was easy and fluid, though a powerful sexual awareness still charged the air between them.

At four o'clock, when the weather was cooler, they went back on to the beach. The sun was still hot. 'Shall we go snorkelling?' Andrés suggested, his gaze intense and lingering. 'The sea is lovely and warm by this time in the afternoon. I know a beautiful cave off the rocks near the place where I lifted those oysters. The water there is crystal-clear.' As they walked, their arms brushed, sending Luz's pulse skipping frantically. His mouth curved seductively into a smile. 'It's one of the rare surviving sea gardens, a well-kept secret, teeming with all sorts of marine creatures and strange vegetation,' he added invitingly.

'A well-kept secret? I've a feeling I'm going to like it,' said Luz, returning his smile.

He stared at her for a moment with some unfathomable emotion before looking up at the sun. 'I hope so,' he murmured.

Equipped with masks and snorkels they headed to the rocks. The sand was searing hot and scorched the sensitive soles of Luz's feet. She gasped. In a flash Andrés gathered her up. The surge of blood in her veins was instantaneous as she was overtaken by the torrent of erotic feelings that had been simmering for so long. He held her tightly, his arm resting around her waist, the light down feathering his chest brushing sensuously against her skin. Swiftly and smoothly he walked across the blazing beach to the rocks beyond.

'Be careful not to step on those spiky black sea urchins,' he cautioned as he put her down gently.

His arms were still around her as Luz's feet came into contact with the crisp, cool waves that licked the lava rocks and the frothy foam that gathered around her slim ankles. Her toes sank into the soft sand beneath the shallow water. 'Mmm, that feels good,' she murmured.

A tremor ran through Andrés' body and their eyes locked. Luz's little moan of pleasure, innocent as it had sounded, blew on the already hot embers quietly burning in them both since their lovemaking the night before. He tensed, his eyes glinting, and she could tell his control had finally snapped. She saw the desire burning fiercely in his gaze. The flames that raged through her now were like nothing she had experienced before.

'Does it feel as good as this?' Grasping her by the shoulders, he pulled her forcefully to him, searing her lips with the passionate demand of his mouth. He hooked his thumbs under the straps of her bikini and slid them down, his searching hands freeing the firm curves of her naked breasts; then he reached behind to unfasten her skimpy top and flip it away. His strong fingers were exquisite on her skin as he kneaded her breasts gently and teased the pink peaks that responded before he had even touched them.

Luz arched her back, aching for him with every heartbeat. She felt his hardness brush against her stomach and her hand flew down, slipping through the black swimming brief that covered the part of him that she knew hungered for her. She curled her palm around his burning shaft and teased the velvety tip with her long fingers. He hissed out a breath, holding her against him with one arm, staring into the deep blue of her eyes that had grown dark with desire. Momentarily he released her to rid himself of the obtrusive garment, throwing it on to the rocks. She followed suit, discarding the remainder of her bikini. And so, free from any hindrance to their lovemaking, he scooped her up into his arms, seawater dripping from her toes on to his skin.

Never taking his eyes away from hers, his hands cupped the twin mounds of her small round bottom. Instinctively she wrapped her legs around his waist, her thighs hugging him, and felt the powerful muscles of his shoulders beneath her hands. Her body arched, opening up to his raging need, guiding him with its movements to where she wanted him most. She threw her arms around his neck as, without waiting, he thrust urgently into the moist core of her being; her inner muscles closed around his hardness, imprisoning him as she pressed him on. His mouth found hers; he plundered it insatiably, and she returned his kisses with as much fervour and equal savage passion.

'You're so soft, moist and delicious, *mi amor*,' he rasped. 'You're driving me insane.'

Then he began to plunge into her and withdraw, deeper and deeper, making her cry out his name again and again and again. She could feel his breathing grow faster as a moan growled deep in his throat; she knew he was building up to his release. The head of his erection was now so deep that her climax was also mounting in wild anticipation. She arched her spine, throwing her head back, drawing him deeper inside her, linking herself to him as close as possible, wanting to be at one with the man she loved. Then suddenly he withdrew and the agony she felt at his retreat broke from her throat in a gasp. They were both hovering on the tip of the mountain, poised on the edge of ...

He plunged back in, his thrust this time almost savage. It felt so good she nearly screamed aloud. Their breathing accelerated, their hearts thundered on, their senses caught up in a storm that would break any second now. He moved deeper into her, almost reaching the edge of her limits. Crying out each other's name, they tumbled into space, fireworks exploding through every sense and nerve ending. One explosion came after another, shattering in their intensity; spasms of pleasure took over not only their bodies but their minds and their souls, too. Trembling with ecstatic delight and clinging to each other, they spiralled down through layers of erotic delirium, lost in a mist of hedonistic sensations that were taking their time to fade away. When finally they came down to earth, they held on to each other hard and strong, in the firm knowledge that what they had just shared was real, everlasting love.

* * *

Over the next few days they whiled away the hours by going for long walks along the numerous beaches of the Costa de la Luz, relishing in the feel of the sun-warmed sand, so soft and fine beneath their feet, combing the seashore for colourful shells and drinking in the delicious fresh sea air. Together they swam in cliff-shaded waters so clear that they could see the sea floor, thirty feet below, and in and out of sheltered coves within sight of the villages and towns. They snorkelled and played in the deep, among the fishes and the coral reefs.

One day he took her fishing in his uncle's old fishing boat. They anchored at a place where the sea twitched with the movement of fish and came back to Andrés' hut to cook their catch over a wood fire on the beach under the moon. Often they simply sat for a while beneath the palms in calm seclusion, listening to the wind and the roar of the sea. They did not need to talk to enjoy each other's company; they just basked in the joy of new-found love.

Sometimes Luz and Andrés would explore places inland. They would find a deserted plain at the top of a cliff and lie in the sun, watching sea birds fly in formation out to the reefs, or dragonflies, butterflies and lizards dart among the wildflowers, plumbago and the sweet-smelling herbs. Everything they chose to do together exhilarated them and made them feel light-hearted and alive. Andrés kissed her, caressed her, loved her until, satiated, she would cry out for him to stop. Every so often she would take the initiative to please him while she watched his body shake with wracking spasms and listened to him groan his ecstasy, revelling in the heady control she had over him in those moments, and how much she was learning about this new sensual power.

She was happy. Women stared at Andrés whenever they went anywhere public together and she was proud to be the one he had chosen. Aside from his undoubted masculine beauty, he was warm and funny, too. There was a combination of gentleness and pure primitive passion in his character that never failed to surprise her. Still, occasionally he would go silent, a distant look clouding his dark eyes. At those times he seemed so divorced from her that she thought she must be in the company of a complete stranger. In the back of her mind was the unwelcome notion that it might be something to do with Adalia; she thought she perceived momentary flashes of guilt in his eyes but couldn't be sure. Luz had never asked Andrés about Lorenzo's sister, too fearful perhaps of what his answer might be. She didn't want to face the prospect that, however much he cared for her, she might be destined to be merely his mistress and nothing more; after all, it was what many Spanish men took for granted while they were formally betrothed, and even after marriage. Yet she could not believe this of Andrés, not now she knew him better. Was there another reason for his brooding silences?

At one point she had mustered up the courage to ask him outright what was wrong. But he shook his head stubbornly and whispered as though to himself: 'Not now, not yet.'

She had been insistent. 'But Andrés, I know something's wrong. Why won't you talk to me? Perhaps I can help.'

His jaw had set, his eyes narrowed. 'Don't pry, Luz. It's no use your asking me, no matter how prettily.' The hardness behind those words had chilled her, but she hadn't dwelt on it. Most of the time he was such a wonderful companion, so why should she complain?

Now and again he left on business. On those days and nights she missed him, oddly bereft, as though the rapture of the past days could never be recaptured. Life was flat without him. She thought of him most of her waking hours and, even while she was asleep, he would come to her in her dreams: strong, virile and loving. But he soon came back and would swiftly take her in his arms and smother her with kisses when all her misery and fears would evaporate. And time drifted all too easily away.

There were blue skies and the deep blue sea; the days were hot with the golden sun and the nights were romantic with the silver moon; on and on they shared their passion through a succession of rising and setting, waxing and waning. The rose of each dawning day and the starlit indigo of every night impressed themselves on Luz's mind as the euphoria of her own new love, a colourful existence of red or silver shot with blue. She was enveloped in him, and he in her, their world perfect like a glass ball suspended on the edge of paradise.

*   *   *

There was nothing to warn Luz that life would soon turn in such an adverse direction for her, with events rapidly taking on a nightmarish quality, one that would require all her inner strength to cope. Fate was waiting just around the corner, with its unpredictability and harsh blows. And it came one afternoon in the form of Adalia Herrera.

Andrés had been away that week. It would not be long now; he was coming back the next day and they were planning to spend a quiet evening at L'Estrella. Luz was lying in a hammock under a jacaranda tree just outside her terrace, watching the cotton clouds slowly float over the ocean beyond, dreaming of her new-found love.

Carmela bustled into view. The housekeeper had been surprisingly discreet about Luz's comings and goings over the past few days as if she sensed the young woman's need for privacy; even Carmela knew when to leave well alone if matters of the heart were to flourish. Now her protective antennae were quivering.

'Doña Luz, you have a visitor,' she announced with raised eyebrows and an audible tut, her arms folded.

Puzzled, Luz prized herself from her comfortable vantage point, a little irritated to be disturbed from her solitude. She wondered who could be calling on her at this hour. The sun was shining like brass and most people in Spain would be taking their siesta. But she did not need to wonder for long.

Adalia had not waited; instead she had followed hard on Carmela's heels. Luz winced and took a deep breath as she watched her sway gracefully up the path on perilously high heels, dressed in a perfectly cut ivory summer suit, rings flashing rainbows on her fingers. She had not seen Lorenzo's sister since the party at La Fortaleza, nor had she forgotten her unnecessary rudeness or the perfectly unfounded insinuations. Now things were even more complicated. The sight of Adalia made Luz freeze and inside she was burning with dread. Her instincts had told her this day would come; that she and Andrés could not remain in their secluded romantic idyll forever. However unwelcome she might be, Adalia was still a guest in Luz's home and she would receive the young woman with the courtesy she had been taught to bestow. She forced a smile on her face.

'Good afternoon, Doña Adalia,' she said, moving towards the newcomer with an outstretched hand. 'What brings you here on such a hot afternoon?' Then, turning to Carmela: 'We'll have some cold lemonade on the terrace and some of those newly picked cherries from the garden, *por favor.*'

But Adalia looked down her extremely pretty nose at Luz and lifted a hand. 'No, thank you,' she said with a humourless smile. 'I'm not here to make a social call, just to clear up a few things … in private.' She looked at Carmela pointedly before turning back to face Luz.

Luz got the hint. 'Thank you, Carmela – if we need anything, I'll call.'

Carmela stood her ground a moment longer, a feeling of protectiveness making her pause, before disappearing back into the house.

Luz and Adalia walked down to a spot in the garden that wasn't one of Luz's regular haunts, partly because it did not have a view of the sea but also because it was more formal, with closely woven cedar hedges, clipped in pointed arches, leading to a multicoloured rose garden planted in even squares. It was her mother's favourite part of the garden, though, and Salvador had commissioned a gazebo to be erected in the centre of it. The structure was an exact replica of the one at El Pavón, where Alexandra had spent many days writing during that long-ago year when she had stayed at the family home before she was married. It was still somewhere Luz's parents sequestered themselves whenever they came down to L'Estrella, often enjoying romantic tête-à-tête dinners in perfect seclusion.

'I hope this is a private enough place for you,' Luz said, lifting a dark eyebrow, her voice gently mocking.

As Adalia paused on the steps leading up to the gazebo, the glance she gave Luz was certainly wintry.

'Look, what I have to say has no bearing on the reputation of either my family or myself. Sadly, I cannot say the same for yours, so you'd better thank me that I've chosen to speak to you alone, away from eavesdroppers. We all know what servants are like.'

Luz turned to look at Adalia, an elegant figure with the afternoon breeze blowing through her long ash-blonde hair, and met her icy-blue eyes, which were surveying her hostess with cool disdain. Everything about her was Madonna-like until one looked into those razor-sharp steel irises. 'I'm sorry, Adalia, but I consider Carmela and the people who work in our household to be part of the family,' she retorted.

Adalia shrugged and huffed in a less than angelic fashion. 'I'm hardly surprised, I suppose. After all, your family have generally made a point of treating the lowest of the low as one of themselves, getting cosy with the servant classes, thinking it will excuse a number of sins. But that is not why I'm here today …' Her voice was steady and unhurried.

Luz made a great effort to bite her tongue. Whatever Adalia had to say, this was clearly not going to be an easy conversation. At the party at La Fortaleza and again at the Yacht Club, Lorenzo's sister had given up any pretence of friendship or even civility, but now it was becoming increasingly apparent that her animosity for some reason extended to the de Ruedas in general.

They went into the summerhouse. Adalia pulled out a chair from under the wrought-iron table. It screeched noisily on the stone tiles and a pigeon flew out of a tree above with a great flutter of wings, obviously displeased to have been disturbed on such a sleepy afternoon. Adalia sat down and crossed her beautiful alabaster legs.

A puzzled look remained in Luz's eyes as she sat in the chair opposite, waiting for Adalia to explain herself. 'Please enlighten me as to the purpose of your visit,' she said finally.

Adalia, taking her time, lit a cigarette before answering. 'Don't worry,' she said in a husky, cat-like purr, 'this won't take long.' She lifted a perfectly manicured hand and drew on her cigarette, pausing to watch the cloudy blue swirls rise to the ceiling.

'I mentioned your family's habit of being overly familiar with servants,' she added disdainfully. 'Another much more serious trait is stealing other people's lovers.'

Luz stiffened as a sudden surge of anger rose inside of her. Outraged, she half rose from her chair. 'Who do you think you are—?'

'Please let me finish.' Again the look of contempt crept into Adalia's eyes as she lifted a peremptory hand to cut Luz short.

'I have said it to you before, and I'm saying it again – with some people history has a habit of repeating itself. In this case, in a highly unpleasant way.' Her diamond-sharp gaze settled on her opponent and she inhaled deeply on her cigarette before continuing.

'Years ago, when Doña Alexandra came to Spain in search of her fortune, Don Salvador was seeing my aunt, Doña Isabel. Unlike in your mother's country, here in Spain a real gentleman always honours the promise of marriage, even when rings have not been exchanged. Your mother weaselled herself into your father's life very cleverly and his attachment to my aunt became a thing of the past. Doña Isabel, being the proud lady she is, quietly withdrew, leaving the way clear for your mother. She was not about to degrade herself by getting into some cheap tug of war.'

Adalia paused again and glanced at the tip of her cigarette before extinguishing it in the glass ashtray on the table. 'Because of some unsavoury story involving gypsies, Don Salvador could not marry your mother immediately. So, not content to have wrecked my aunt's life, she then set about seducing my father, Don Felipe, whom she literally dumped on the night he was going to announce their engagement at a party in her honour. She ran off to meet Don Salvador and they were literally caught red-handed in the throes of passion at the bottom of the garden minutes before my father was to make his announcement.'

Luz, who had sat quietly during this venomous tirade, released the breath she had been holding. Now she really was seething, though she tried to seem cool. Her deep sapphire-blue eyes turned to silver, glittering dangerously.

'How dare you come into my house and accuse my parents of such things! This is nothing but vicious lies designed to smear their good name. I'm surprised you would stoop so low, even if your family holds a grudge against my mother.'

Adalia's eyes narrowed. 'My dear, I am not inventing anything,' she said silkily. 'This story is common knowledge. At the time it made the rounds of Spanish drawing rooms for months.' Her voice dripped with scorn. 'There's nothing like a good scandal to entertain society.' She paused and lit another cigarette. 'If you don't believe me, why don't you ask your parents?'

Aghast, Luz tried her hardest to appear unruffled although she wasn't completely successful. Two bright spots had appeared on her cheeks. 'I fail to see why you're bringing up this unpleasant piece of calumny now,' she quietly observed.

Adalia laughed. '*Please*, don't put on that naïve, innocent-little-woman look for me! Andrés may be gullible enough to be fooled by it, but I'm not. I see women like you drifting in and out of my brother's bed every day.'

Taking this unpleasant blow on the chin, Luz drew in a deep breath, all the while battling with the urge to let loose her rage. Allowing her emotions to run wild only meant Adalia would win and so she wasn't about to do that. 'I don't see what my personal life has to do with you,' she declared evenly.

Arctic eyes, cutting like ice picks, settled on her face. 'Andrés and I were supposed to be engaged almost a year ago,' Adalia explained. 'My father died unexpectedly and we had to postpone our engagement. I think my brother Lorenzo must have mentioned this to you when you came to La Fortaleza last month.' Her icy gaze did not waver.

'I know that you are Andrés' mistress, the whole of Andalucía is talking about your affair. Like Lorenzo, Andrés has had a string of women like you. He's a virile man and it's perfectly normal, of course – a man like him needs to sow his wild oats before he settles down, I understand. Every well-bred Spanish woman accepts that sort of thing during the courting years. But the liaison he's having with you is more flagrant. You're flaunting yourselves like common gypsies and it's harming his reputation, and mine.' She arched an imperious eyebrow.

'On that note, as you probably know, it is Andrés' birthday this weekend and I'm throwing a party for him at El Ecrin. It has been arranged for months, long before you came on the scene, and I would rather you didn't embarrass us all by turning up.'

For a few moments Luz couldn't speak, so flabbergasted was she by such virulent animosity. Trying to control the tremor in her voice, she kept her tone low, hoping to sound cool and detached. 'I think I've heard enough already. I'm not prepared to discuss the ties that bind Andrés and me together. I'm afraid you have exceeded your welcome here and I would be grateful if you left now.'

But Adalia had not finished; the death blow was still to come. 'Don't kid yourself, darling. Andrés might be the modern international businessman but he's also deeply wedded to the traditions and customs of our country. He would never marry a woman who is not a virgin on her wedding night.' She continued her taunts relentlessly, her tone rising a fraction.

'*La honra* is very important to him. Have you never heard of *la honra*? No, I suppose not – how would you?' she spat out scornfully. And with that, Adalia got up, slung her bag over her shoulder and prepared to leave. Looking her rival up and down, she sneered before dropping the final bombshell: 'After all, there's a saying in Spanish, *como madre tanto hija*, like mother like daughter. And *your* mother is one of the biggest tramps there is!'

At this, Luz gasped as if she had been struck. The anger gradually welling up in her since the elegant socialite had arrived now reached its peak. In a paroxysm of rage she leapt from her chair. The slap she administered to Adalia echoed in the empty room with a resonance that equalled the one her opponent dealt her almost in the same breath. Then, without turning a hair, as if nothing had happened Adalia calmly straightened her suit.

'Unfortunately,' she hissed haughtily, 'when dealing with the gutter one must sometimes dirty one's hands.' As she marched to the door of the summerhouse, her head held high, she spat, 'Don't bother to show me out, I know the way.'

There was a slight ringing in Luz's ears. For a long while a kind of vertigo stole over her senses and she closed her eyes, unable to think clearly. What was all this mud Adalia had churned up? Was any of it true? Was this the reason her parents had been so cagey about the past and suspicious of gypsies?

And what about the present? Andrés … had it all been a pretence, some sort of sick game he had been playing in which she had been the victim? She knew that her reckless, wanton behaviour had hurtled her down a dangerous path and now perhaps she would have to pay for it. Why hadn't she listened to her head and controlled her visceral urges? It would have been so much simpler had she questioned Andrés about his relationship with Adalia. It seemed she had discovered the truth about what had been bothering him. Luz opened her eyes, dark now with pain and shock. Her dream, her beautiful love, her whole world trembled precariously beneath her feet.

She would confront her parents immediately and Andrés tomorrow.

*   *   *

Luz arrived at El Pavón in the early evening to find that her parents had gone away to Granada for a week. Her nerves raw and quivering, she went straight upstairs to her bedroom to lick her wounds in private. With her parents away the whole place was hushed. El Pavón, an austere house at the best of times, seemed to her even more lugubrious than usual. The dark corridors that had once unnerved her mother had pretty much the same effect on Luz.

Agustina had been advised of Luz's arrival by Sarita, the maid – it was not Luz's habit to turn up without notice, especially when she had been away for a long time. She hadn't been back to El Pavón since the masked ball and now, when the housekeeper entered Luz's room, she was unusually tight-lipped, an expression that quickly softened when she saw how unhappy the young woman looked. Usually so open and bubbly, this evening she had no enthusiastic welcome for the beloved old servant.

'You're as pale as a spectre,' Agustina told her. 'Look at those shadows under your eyes. What have you been up to, child?'

Luz got off her bed and wandered out on to the veranda without answering. She was shivering, despite the balmy night. At this hour the rays of the dying sun only half illuminated the trees and drew lines over the grass, giving grotesque effects of light and shade and mysterious corners full of soft tones and shifting colours. Such a peaceful view, but such chaotic thoughts!

Agustina followed Luz, the frown between her brows deepening by the second as she noticed the young woman's withdrawn manner and the secretive look in her eyes.

'What is upsetting you? You know you can talk to me,' the old retainer said in a low, coaxing tone.

Instinctively, Luz's hand shot to her throat as she tried her best to suppress the choked-up feeling that was preventing her from answering. Her eyes welled with the tears she had been holding back since Adalia's visit. Muttering the worst curse she could think of, she then turned to the *duenna*, whose eyes had widened in surprise.

'Chickens always come home to roost, don't they, Agustina?'

'What are we talking about here?' the old woman asked, guardedly.

Luz hesitated. Should she unburden herself to Agustina? She had no doubt the old housekeeper knew all the answers: after all, she had been in service at El Pavón long before the events Adalia had been talking about and had been the trusted confidante not only of Doña María Dolores, her great grandmother, but also of Alexandra. She gazed blindly out into the penumbras of the garden, biting thoughtfully on her bottom lip.

A warm breeze ruffled her hair. She passed her fingertips through it, pondering. Andrés was returning tomorrow; she needed to know today. If Adalia had fabricated the story about Luz's parents, then there was a good chance she had also lied about her involvement with Andrés. Women often mistook their dreams for reality. Similarly, had Luz herself been a victim? Panic struck her as the idea crept into her mind, even as she did her best to fight it.

She sighed. 'I wish I could see into the future,' she whispered, and then, covering her face with her hands, she burst into tears.

Agustina waited tactfully for the sobbing to cease. Eventually Luz relaxed enough to pour out her heart to the trusted retainer, including what had happened on Adalia's visit.

'I've got to open up to someone or I'll go crazy,' she murmured. 'You have been the wise confidante of our family for years.' A spasm of emotion passed over her face. 'Please be frank with me, Agustina. It isn't just idle curiosity on my part, it's important. I wouldn't go rummaging in my parents' past if I wasn't feeling so desperate.'

The housekeeper nodded and sighed. It appeared that the time for frankness had come. 'You know, Luz, when a bird flies blind, it imagines it is flying straight, though, to the onlooker, it is flying to disaster. In your parents' case, an unhappy sequence of events led to much misunderstanding and pain.'

'Is it true that my father was engaged to Doña Isabel Herrera and that my mother *stole* him from her?'

'Yes, your father was indeed engaged to Doña Isabel but that was long before your mother came to El Pavón. A few months before their wedding, Don Salvador had an accident and doctors said he would never walk again. In no time Doña Isabel had found herself a new, titled and rich suitor, much older than herself, who died shortly after the wedding. She didn't even have the decency to break off her engagement officially before her marriage to the Marquis de Aguila was announced in the press. Your mother had nothing to do with all that, she had not yet come to Spain.'

Good, that was one issue out of the way. Adalia had lied and Luz's heart sang with joy. 'And is it true that my mother was about to get engaged to Doña Isabel's brother when she was caught misbehaving with my father, minutes before the engagement was announced?'

Agustina winced slightly, remembering the turbulence of those far-off days. 'We come back to the bird that flies blind. Your mother got caught up in a situation where her youth, her naïvety and maybe a lack of self-preservation made her overlook certain dangers. She was also a young Englishwoman used to different ways.

'Don Felipe was a notorious womanizer: handsome, charming and manipulative. He offered his friendship and she accepted it quite innocently. She walked into his trap, like prey into a spider's web, and she did not know how to escape once she was entangled in it. Although she never accepted his proposal, she did not turn him down immediately either because she did not want to jeopardize the important *corrida* he was preparing for. If he had had an accident in the ring, she would never have been able to forgive herself. Anyway, she was postponing her answer until after the bullfight. Unfortunately, events overtook her. If anything, your mother was only guilty of a small error in judgement. Of course, tongues wagged at the time, but we all know what society is like at the least sniff of a scandal.'

'Since my father and mother loved each other so passionately, why did they not marry immediately? I was always told that it was my great grandmother's dearest wish.' Luz paused and quickly glanced up at the old woman whose serene face was not giving anything away. So she pushed a little further. 'Adalia mentioned an unsavoury story with gypsies ...'

At this, Agustina shifted uncomfortably in her chair and Luz sensed a certain reluctance; clearly she was not keen to take the lid off what must be a Pandora's box.

'Please, Agustina, I need to know!' Luz persisted. 'I've met Paquita the gypsy several times. She's spoken to me in riddles that I don't understand. Maybe if you told me what happened in the past I would be able to make sense of her strange words.'

She then told the housekeeper more about Leandro and Andrés and their uncanny resemblance, without mentioning the extent to which she had been involved with the gypsy, though she could tell by looking at Agustina that the *duenna* doubted Luz was telling her the whole truth where he was concerned. She didn't seem comfortable with what she was hearing; her dark eyes, more serious than Luz had ever seen them, were fixed on the young woman's face. Luz ran her fingers impatiently through her hair and searched Agustina's troubled gaze once more.

'Is it as bad as all that, that you can't bring yourself to tell me what happened so many years ago?'

The *duenna* was quiet for a moment more and then said slowly: 'Sometimes the truth takes on an ugly face if misinterpreted. After all, it is not my secret that I will be divulging. I would be betraying a confidence.' She shook her head. 'It goes against the grain.'

But Luz was determined to get to the bottom of all this mystery. Deep down, she was sure that many answers to her present uncertainties lay in a convoluted past. She scowled. 'I'm sure that my parents would forgive what you see as an indiscretion and I see as a necessary cleaning away of cobwebs, ones which are affecting *my* life,' she retorted. 'Because of my ignorance of the facts, I couldn't defend myself properly against Adalia's unpleasant accusations today. It's a terrible position to be in, can't you see? For goodness sake, Agustina, let me have the truth!'

Agustina closed her eyes in resignation. 'As I mentioned earlier, your father had a bad accident that left him paralysed from the waist downwards. The general prognosis was that he would never walk again. The *Duquesa* was heartbroken. Specialists were brought over at great expense from all over the world but the opinion remained unanimous. Doña María Dolores had lost hope.'

There was a pause, during which Agustina drew breath. She shifted in her seat and folded her hands in her lap, clearly uncomfortable, before continuing. 'One November morning – I will never forget it because it was one of those rare overcast days – a gypsywoman, looking like a fox stealing into the henhouse, came to the front door at El Pavón and asked to speak to the *Duquesa*. José, who at the time was the major-domo, tried to turn her away, but she whined and cajoled, even invoked the Blessed Madonna, insisting her daughter Marujita possessed the *gracia de mano*, the power to heal. She had come to offer her services to the young Count and would not be turned away until she had spoken to the *Duquesa*. At this point Her Grace was prepared to try anything and she allowed Consuelo and her daughter the chance to cure your father.'

Agustina paused. Luz could see that she found dredging up those unhappy memories difficult and thoroughly distasteful. A shadow passed over the servant's usually serene face.

'At the time Don Salvador was miserable and vulnerable. Marujita was a real beauty. At eighteen, she was already a *lumiasca*, a harlot, well informed in the ways of the world and of men, having sold herself since her early teens. She took advantage of your father's defenceless situation and soon possessed his naked soul. Miraculously, she did seem to aid in his physical recovery and, feeling that he owed his life to Marujita, he found himself truly enslaved. Only the great love he avowed for your mother cured him of that evil creature.' Agustina sighed.

'It was a sordid affair and I will spare you the ugly details, but for Marujita it ended badly. Months after she left El Pavón she helped her brother, *El Mono*, the monkey, steal the *Duquesa*'s jewels but Don Salvador caught them before they could escape. In the struggle your father was knifed, the police were called and Marujita and her brother were both sentenced to a few years' imprisonment. *El Mono* died of pneumonia before his time was up. As for Marujita, we never heard of her again.'

Luz stared at Agustina, trying to take in all this information that was completely new to her. 'No wonder *Mamá* gets so nervous whenever the subject of gypsies crops up. *Papá* is much cooler about it.' Her expression then changed and she huffed irritably.

'I don't understand why they made such an issue about keeping this from me all those years. I was bound to find out some day. Things like these don't get buried forever, especially if they made a bit of a rumpus at the time. On the contrary, brushed under the carpet they just get magnified beyond belief. Wouldn't it have been simpler to talk about them frankly? Why complicate life? I might have learnt a thing or two in the past and not been at such a loss today,' she said resentfully.

Agustina's answer was, as usual, gentle and wise. 'Knowing your parents as I do, I'm sure they had good reasons for acting as they did. Gypsies have long memories, it's said that they never forget. Who knows what your parents think they are protecting you from?'

'But it still isn't clear why they delayed getting married for so long. It seems to me unbelievably foolish,' said Luz, frowning.

'Don't be so quick to judge,' Agustina remonstrated crossly. 'It's because of the gypsies and their *venganza de Calés* culture, that's why. Revenge and the gypsies go hand in hand. Even though your parents fell in love at first sight, your father did not venture to court your mother while she was in Spain. For many months he fought his love for her in order to protect her. For an onlooker, one who could read between the lines, there was no doubt he loved her to distraction. But put yourself in your mother's shoes: what was she supposed to think? She was still very innocent for her age, with little knowledge of what makes a man tick. The future must have been one gigantic question mark. A very traumatic experience, my child! Thankfully their lucky star was looking over them. As it turned out, the fairy-tale romance had a happy ending. However, it could well have ended in disaster.'

Luz fell silent: she knew what it felt like to have your future as one gigantic question mark. Her mother's experience had parallels with her own, she thought ruefully. But at least now she had some of the answers. One day, she would try to talk to her mother carefully about the past and show her that she understood what she had been through.

Adalia had completely distorted the truth and given her a fabricated version of what really happened more than thirty years ago. In other words, she had told a pack of lies about her parents, so why should it be any different where Andrés was concerned? There might have been a time when Andrés had dated the young socialite but, somehow, Luz very much doubted that he had proposed to her. Adalia just wanted to warn her off in the hope of creating a misunderstanding between herself and Andrés. Luz had already known about Andrés' birthday party, too, and he had not seemed uncomfortable about her being there, though it would no doubt suit Adalia if Luz felt too awkward to attend now. Still, she would confront him the next day when he came over to L'Estrella for dinner.

Some of the weight had lifted from her mind, but she would not feel completely at ease until she had clarified matters with the man she loved.

CHAPTER 12

While Luz was having a heart-to-heart with Agustina, she was far from suspecting that, at the far end of the El Pavón estate, just a few hundred yards away, Leandro was mourning the loss of his mother.

The tribe was also grieving. For them, a powerful member of its people had been lost. Though wilful and riotous in her youth, breaking every code of behaviour in the *Calés* book of rules, Marujita had ripened into a strong *gitana* with a commanding presence, someone others would follow. The harsh years spent behind bars had changed her. Tough and unforgiving, so different from the nimble libertine she had been in her youth, she had become a she-thug during and after her prison years, as well as a warrior matriarch, respected and feared by all. Despite her wild and disreputable past, not to mention her involvement with a *gajo*, the gypsies of Andalucía had elected her their queen. That evening they were arriving in droves, advancing in straggling bands from every corner of that sun-kissed region to pay their last respects and see their queen off to her final home.

The orb of day had sunk and the rocks had turned an indigo tinge in the dusk. A full moon high in the sky cast a blue haze, an almost ethereal light, on to the camp. Here, the world was frozen in deathly silence, full of mystery. Soon the place would erupt, first into lamentation and then into jollification but, for the moment, human, beast and nature itself seemed to wait in solemn and reverential hush.

Marujita's coffin had been moved out in front of a cave, lit by candlelight. There she lay, washed and coiffed, on a bed of red roses and wearing her best finery, hands crossed over her chest. Her favourite mandolin and a pair of ornate castanets had been placed next to her. In her youth she had been a great Flamenco singer and dancer and, over the past few months, even sickness had not prevented her from performing under the stars for her people.

A six-metre-long table had been stocked as for a banquet with cold meats, cheeses and a good deal of wine and brandy to keep the mourners going through the long hours of the wake.

The *gitana*'s two younger sons, Toñito and Diego, stood at the entrance to the cave with a few other gypsies, keeping their distance, while Leandro, Marujita's beloved eldest son, sat beside her, his face buried in the long, tapered fingers of his hands. His heart was cold and heavy. He had loved his mother with the strange hungry passion of a starved child and she, in turn, had worshipped him. Leandro had never been blind to her faults, quite the reverse. He saw only too clearly that she had been a hard, spiteful and bitter woman who had harboured a lifetime's hatred for the people she thought had wronged her. She had always been relentless in her thirst for revenge. Prison had hardened her heart to everyone and everything, except where her eldest son was concerned. He had been the apple of her eye and she had lavished her tenderness on him exclusively. In return, he would do anything for her ... and had already done so.

After that fateful night when Marujita had called for vengence on Luz and her family, and Leandro had turned his back on her and walked away, his mother had been implacable. Initially, Leandro had met with hostile silence. Then she began hectoring him at every opportunity. It was only when the doctors had given her six months at most that he had finally softened, loath to let her down. Had she not been riddled with cancer he would never have danced to her tune. Surely he owed her some indulgence?

Leandro was so attuned to the conflicts that fought within her breast, the fierce, wild emotions that stirred her to thoughts of hateful revenge. He could see what had made her this way, but it pained him to think how much of her shadow had been cast upon him. Conflicting loyalties tore at his heart but the very thought of hurting Luz was abhorrent to him.

When he had appeared to Luz at the El Pavón ball dressed in Tuareg costume, it had started out as a simple, mischievous game. He had kissed her because the budding attraction between them had been overwhelming; an attraction that began long before he had known anything about the role her parents had played in his mother's life. He had tried to stay away from her but it had proved impossible: fate kept throwing them together. He had never planned to take her as he did on the beach that afternoon but their mutual passion had defeated his self-control. Yet he was aware that nothing could exonerate his act, none of the hundred-and-one excuses he could dream up would ever work to alleviate his guilty conscience. Deliberately or not, he had followed Marijita's plan, causing Luz pain in the process.

But he loved Luz to distraction. Now he couldn't wait to take her in his arms again but would she ever forgive his deception? He shuddered at the thought of losing her. Surely, now that Marujita was gone, there must be some way he could make it up to her … that was, if she still wanted him after knowing the whole truth?

He could not have spoken before now; he felt he owed it to his mother to make her last months as comfortable as possible, telling himself it would not be long. If he at least appeared to see her plan through then he could endeavour to make amends later. But he knew he had been playing a dangerous game, and one in which he and Luz might both end up being the losers.

There was so much explaining to do and the longer he left it, the worse it would be. Luz would condemn him for playing his mother's game until the end, which in some ways was true. There was only one thing for it: he had to put his trust in the kindness of the young woman's heart and in the love she held for him. Because if there was one thing he was certain of, it was Luz's unremitting love.

Lamentations had begun in earnest now, drawing Leandro from his dark reverie. Men, women and children lined up in an orderly fashion, uncharacteristic for such an unruly people. They all held candles, the ends of which were wrapped in paper, and were now circling the open coffin where their queen lay in peace, her eyes closed to the world. As they circled the corpse, they chanted and then joined hands for the *Abejorro*, the bees' dance, which they performed, all the while imitating the insect's sound.

Suddenly, Juanillo moved out of the circle. Leandro's uncle began to loudly engage in the age-old ritual of confession and absolution, claiming the sins of his sister as his own, then challenging Marujita in a loud, powerful voice for all to hear: 'Take your mandolin, dear sister, and play. Hold your castanets and dance. If by these actions I have done wrong, may your music strike me deaf. But if you find I have not sinned, then stay quiet, do not move and do not play, so I may receive absolution.' A few moments of quietude followed and then, turning to the crowd, he cried out: 'Let the festivities begin!'

His invitation was received by a great number of *Olés!* The driving thrum of a guitar sounded, taken up by the fast yet mournful accompaniment of a violin, the notes of its melody spilling out furiously like an infernal call to the dead. Men, women and children began their frenzied singing, clapping and leaping about. Food and drink were devoured in no time; even the animals joined in, waiting for morsels to fall from the table.

Leandro knew that the merrymaking and revelry would go on well into the night and probably till dawn. He joined in, allowing himself to be pulled into the crowd in their bacchanalian requiem for his mother, but his heart was not in it: he was still thinking of Luz and how he would earn her forgiveness. Having hurt her once, he would have to do so again before things could come right between them. He would have to tell her some things she would not want to hear.

After a round of dancing, he stumbled back from the circle as a wineskin was thrust roughly against his chest. He looked up to see Toñito rocking slightly before him. As Leandro grasped the wineskin, he studied his brother's face, lit by the vivid moon. The young *gitano*'s eyes were red, whether from crying or too much brandy he wasn't sure, but he saw the mixture of anguish and animosity that burned in them.

'So our mother's finally gone. Now, you will drink with me, brother.' There was nothing familial or welcoming in the harshness of Toñito's voice.

Leandro paused before lifting the wineskin, taking a long gulp of brandy and then wiping his mouth with his sleeve. 'You're right, Toñito. Our mother is gone, our people have lost their queen and so now it falls to us to carry on in her place. We're family, Marujita's family. Everyone will be looking to us for leadership. You have a duty, same as me, to be part of what keeps our people together now.' He handed the wineskin back to his brother. 'That's what we should drink to.'

Toñito's gaze wandered blearily to the ground. 'Family. Blood. Duty. That's all *she* ever talked about!'

'And she would want us to stand together,' said Leandro.

Toñito's eyes filled with scorn as they swooped to meet Leandro's. 'Is that what you think, brother? Stand together? You stand alone, like you've always done.' He gestured to the crowd of gypsies who were cavorting wildly to the galloping music. 'You think you can look after our people? And I am to be the lapdog at your heels?' He shook his head. 'We may share her blood, but we will never be what she wanted us to be.'

'Is there anything left of that brandy for your Uncle Juanillo?' came a rasping voice from behind them as the older gypsy sauntered towards them. 'My belly needs warming on this dark day.' He grasped Toñito's head in his large hands as they touched foreheads in a gruff embrace of mutually acknowledged grief.

'It's yours, *Tío*,' said Toñito, slapping the wineskin into Juanillo's hand. He glanced back at Leandro, his face a sullen mask. 'I'll find another one.'

They had been standing next to a jumble of upturned crates and Leandro sank wearily on to the nearest one as he watched the hunched figure of his brother disappear into the throng. Men and women were now falling over one another, casting long shadows in the light of the candles that still burned around Marujita's coffin. Some had even leapt on to the banquet table and were stamping and clapping to the music that raged on.

Juanillo took a deep swig of brandy and lit up a cigar, setting his carbon-black gaze on his nephew. 'I've been watching you, *sobrino*. You should honour your mother's memory with more fire in your gut.'

Leandro simply stared ahead. 'I honour her memory well enough. Though if I need absolution, I need only ask her to rise up and play her mandolin till I go deaf.' He glanced up sharply and held Juanillo's hard gaze.

'Even when my sister is laid in the ground, she can still do harm to the living if it's her will,' noted Juanillo, the cool edge of menace in his voice. 'As fast as a man runs, he can't outpace a ghost in a shroud. A curse of the dead will reach him, however far he wanders the earth. In case you have forgotten, it's still your duty to carry out vengeance against Marujita's enemies. Revenge is justice, *sobrino*.' Juanillo chewed on his cigar and threw the wineskin at his nephew's feet. 'Drink and be a man.' With that, he walked off to join the whooping mourners.

Leandro kicked the wineskin away and, though he had not taken a swig, he wiped the back of his hand across his mouth, his face impassive in the spectral moonlight.

*   *   *

Luz sat on the veranda at L'Estrella looking bleakly out to sea. The light of the day had faded into a hazy apricot glow while the sea, darkened to a smoky blue, murmured against the sand. On the opposite shore, Puerto de Santa María and its marina of boats was already a mosaic of beckoning lights as the town prepared for approaching dusk. It seemed as if she had been watching the seascape for hours.

Early that morning she had left El Pavón to return to Cádiz, wanting to spend the day at home before Andrés met her for dinner at L'Estrella. She had not slept much at her parents' house, disturbed by nightmares and the noise that came from the far end of the grounds, where the gypsies seemed to be having some sort of wild party. Moreover, she had been increasingly on edge since Adalia's visit and her conversation with Agustina. She had thought a lot about Adalia and her unpleasant accusations. Agustina might have convinced her that the socialite had been lying about everything for the sake of her own agenda, but Luz did not like the sense of shame that swamped her every time the young woman's venomous words came to mind. The housekeeper's explanations had not really alleviated that feeling.

Her parents' love affair had obviously been a salacious topic of conversation at the time and disapproving tongues would have wagged and accusatory fingers pointed. However, were she to be honest with herself, it was not her parents' threatened idyll that niggled away at her for they had risen above such defamatory gossip and survived it with consummate dignity, their true friends still loyal and loving. No, something else in Adalia's diatribe gnawed at Luz far more persistently: *He would never marry a woman who is not a virgin on her wedding night. La honra is very important to him …*

But Andrés had not seemed unduly concerned by thoughts of *la honra* at the time and nor had she, lost as they were in the throes of passion. Adalia's words had somehow managed to taint something that had seemed so pure, so natural, and Luz now blushed at the thought of her wantonness during those days and nights she and Andrés had spent together. No, a woman who had sacrificed her virginity – and to another man at that – was probably not what a Spanish hidalgo looked for in the woman he chose to be the mother of his children. The thought brought with it such anxiety that the feeling was more akin to pain.

Children. That was something else that had lurked at the corner of her mind as they rushed headlong into passion. *What if she were pregnant?* They had never been careful, never given a thought to the repercussions of their involvement. Luz stared at the darkening sky. She must get a grip on herself and shake off these alarming feelings before Andrés' arrival.

The day had seemed never ending, even though she had busied herself with cooking, preparing succulent dishes of tapas in anticipation of her dinner with Andrés. She had given a disappointed Carmela the whole day and night off in order that she might be alone with him. Luz wanted it to be some sort of celebration. She had not seen Andrés for ten days; he had never been away for so long and she had missed him terribly.

Luz had spent hours in her bath, washing her hair and buffing her body, rubbing deliciously scented oils and creams into it to make her skin even silkier than it already was. Andrés had once commented that she had such pretty feet, so she had gone out and bought a new pair of gold lamé sandals, which she was wearing tonight. She wore a soft, lightweight, summer mini-dress with with an all-over design of vibrant, abstract swirls, a heavy ruffle hem and low-scooped bodice and back. The wide peacock-coloured cuff encircling her slender wrist was eye-catching, though of no great value.

She tried to rehearse what she would say, anticipating his answers, playing various scenarios over in her mind. What if Andrés admitted that he was actually engaged to Adalia, that what he and Luz had shared in the past few weeks was a casual affair that would have to end once he had pronounced his marriage vows? She could not bear to think of the misery it would cause her. Never had she known such happiness as in those times they had spent together. Life without him was inconceivable.

Still, where was he tonight? Luz glanced at her watch. He was never late. It was past eight o'clock; he had been invited for seven-thirty. She went to the front door and opened it. Maybe she had not heard the bell ring. She walked to the gate. Her eyes pierced the distance, looking for his convertible. Maybe he'd forgotten they were meeting? Unease began to rise. Should she ring him? Pride killed that idea; she would not cheapen herself by running after him. Adalia's spiteful words had poisoned her mind and all sorts of misgivings had crept into it.

Time marched on. She was getting edgier by the second. Maybe he had been held up by traffic or work? Surely he would have called, though? He was very particular about such things and punctuality was important to him. She smiled as she remembered his comment the day of her first interview. Maybe he had fallen asleep in his bath. Maybe, maybe, maybe … maybe he was not coming.

The clock struck ten; the phone rang. Luz ran to answer it, nearly tripping over in her mad rush, but it was her mother telling her they had finished their work in Granada somewhat earlier than planned and would be coming down to Cádiz the next day. Alexandra didn't mention Agustina nor the fact that she was aware of Luz's visit to El Pavón, but Luz knew the old housekeeper and her parents only too well. She had no doubt the *duenna* had been in touch with them and that they, the loving parents they had always been, were now rushing to be by their daughter's side.

Night had fallen. The nearly full moon shone in a broad silver path across the calm sea. Across the water Puerto de Santa María, with its twinkling windows and lit church steeple, now lay fully luminous in the streaking shadows of clouds, like a silent poem of colour and light in the deep brooding darkness. Luz often found it a captivating sight at this hour but, this evening, the town's nocturnal magic merely seemed distant and excluding. She found herself pacing up and down the moon-flooded garden in the soft night air, from the iron gate to the front door, on to the terrace and back again. Her hands were clenched at her sides, her ears subconsciously straining to catch the sound of his car or the telephone ringing.

At one o'clock in the morning Luz had to accept that Andrés was neither coming nor was he going to call her. Sapped of energy, she went to her room, undressed slowly and crept into bed. In spite of the cool breeze that came through the window she felt stifled, hemmed in, too weary to sleep and too numb to feel anger or any other emotion. Perhaps she had always been waiting for something to punish her for her reckless desires and disprove the truth of her happiness.

Now that hovering dread eased its cold fingers into her soul, she gave herself up to her deepest fears, raking over the past months. Had Andrés ever truly loved her? He had only said the words while making love to her. Maybe they didn't count. He had neither made any promises nor had he asked her to commit to anything. They had enjoyed a day-to-day, carefree relationship. Had all the dreams, the plans she dared to make about him during the past weeks, been one-sided? She questioned everything miserably but it all seemed confused and unreal. What a mess; her head ached. How could she have walked twice into the same trap? She was full of vain regrets for Leandro and overwhelmed with longing for Andrés. Both had used her and then swept her aside without a second thought.

A lump rose in her throat and her eyes misted with a sudden rush of tears that she fought back. It was useless to cry now. Even though there was so much she still did not understand, she must forsake all those naïve dreams and look to her future instead. Perhaps it was inevitable that she and Andrés would have to part for good. She shuddered at the thought. Despite Adalia's put-down she had still planned to be with him at his party at El Ecrin. Now she could not see herself turning up at his home for the first time, not knowing if he wanted her or not, with the added possibility that she might be humiliated among all those people, including Adalia. Finally, her mind exhausted and her body weary from tossing and turning, she fell into a dreamless deep sleep.

*   *   *

Luz woke very late with a headache. Memories of the previous day flooded back, with all their attendant pain and hurt. Frustration at her own stupidity overwhelmed her. She rolled over, hid her face in her pillow and sobbed bitterly. After a few moments the door opened slowly. Luz looked up through a haze of tears to see her mother entering the room with a cup of steaming chocolate, which she placed on the bedside table. Alexandra perched on the side of the bed, took one look at her daughter and held out her arms. Luz leaned into her mother's embrace, hugging her tightly, her tears now spent.

'Agustina telephoned us, and your father and I arrived in the early hours of this morning,' Alexandra explained, gently offering her daughter a handkerchief to dry her tears, 'before Carmela had a chance to clear the table,' she added pointedly.

Luz glanced at her mother, whose expression of grave concern was mixed with the tender patience of maternal curiosity. Her parents, having noticed the table still laid with candles for a romantic dinner, wine standing in the cooler, the food lying in the kitchen, untouched, would have known what conclusions to draw.

Salvador appeared in the doorway and came over to his daughter. Leaning down, he cradled her face in his hands and kissed her forehead.

'*Niña*, how are you?'

She smiled weakly. 'I'm fine, *Papá*, really. I'm glad you're both here.'

'So who has made my little girl so unhappy?' Salvador asked, settling himself in a chair as he gave his wife a meaningful glance, which didn't escape Luz's notice.

'How much have you guessed?' she asked with a sigh, leaning back against the pillows and eyeing them both apprehensively.

Alexandra placed a comforting hand on Luz's knee. 'We guessed that you've been seeing Don Andrés since the charity ball at the Yacht Club. You seemed happier than we've ever seen you, and then we got this call from Agustina and knew that something had happened ...' She glanced at her husband. 'And we know that Adalia Herrera set about to create mischief between you both.'

Luz stared at her mother, not knowing where to begin. 'She said so many things about Andrés and me ... and about you and *Papá*. I know it was all hideous lies,' she added quickly as she saw her mother's face darken with anxiety.

'Luz, we will explain everything to you, I promise,' said Alexandra, intent eyes never leaving her daughter's face, 'We had our reasons for not talking about certain things in the past.'

Salvador nodded. 'Your mother's right, but there's plenty of time later to deal with all that. For now, what is more important is finding out what has caused you such distress.'

Just having her parents there cheered Luz immensely and she felt a weight lift from her chest, no longer having to keep secrets from them. She drank her hot chocolate and slowly told them about Adalia's visit. They both listened without interrupting until she had finished.

'Are you sure you love this man?' Salvador asked when there was obviously nothing more for her to tell.

'Yes, *Papá*,' she whispered. 'I've never felt like this about anyone before.'

'And he loves you?'

'He obviously doesn't, judging by his cavalier treatment of me. He didn't even have the courtesy to ring and apologize.'

'Umm … not necessarily true.' Salvador scratched his chin as he got up and paced the room. 'If the lion bares his teeth, don't assume he is smiling. Things are not always what they seem, you must know that, *querida*.'

Alexandra sighed. Luz could see her mother was deeply upset. 'If this woman is as wicked as her aunt, then God preserve us!'

Salvador frowned and looked at his wife. 'Simple,' he said. 'If Luz loves him, she must confront him.'

Luz, however, did not seem convinced. 'What about my pride? I'm not going to run after him,' she said grimly.

Salvador shrugged. 'Pride … pride … What about your pride, *niña*? Either you want this man or you don't, there are no two ways about it.' He looked at his wife. 'Don't you think, *querida*?'

'Don't look at me. I'm the last one to give advice on that front,' Alexandra said, shaking her head. 'I made such a mess of things and nearly lost you with my foolishness. If it hadn't been for the kindness of Doña Inez, you would have never known the truth and I'd be still in England, pining for you.'

Salvador slanted a mischievous smile at Alexandra before turning to his daughter. 'You see? Your mother admits that her

English pride nearly got the better of her. There is no sense in anyone staying in bed and crying for love,' he told her, an inflexion of indulgent humour in his voice as he gazed at her anxious face. 'You agree, *niña*?'

Luz nodded and smiled up at her father. 'I guess so, but I'm not quite sure how to go about it.'

'Have you rung his office?' Alexandra enquired softly. 'He might still be away.'

Luz looked a little sheepish and caught her lower lip between her teeth. 'No, not yet,' she admitted. 'I've never rung him at work before. I feel a little awkward doing it, especially with the situation being what it is.'

'He seemed a perfectly reasonable young man with excellent manners. I can't imagine him behaving so discourteously, even if he doesn't want to see you any more. I don't think you should cross your bridges before you come to them,' Alexandra told her daughter.

'Listen to the voice of wisdom, *niña*. As usual, your mother sees the sensible way forward.' He gestured with his head towards Alexandra and made a show of lowering his voice. 'Well, at least now that she's grown out of her young "foolishness".' He grinned broadly at his wife, who merely cocked an amused eyebrow. 'Your words, *querida*, not mine.'

But Luz had no time to reply as there was a knock at the door. 'Come in,' she called out. It was Carmela bearing a huge bunch of flowers. 'Oh, red roses,' Luz gasped as she leapt out of bed and ran to take them from the housekeeper. The last time she had received some, they had been from Andrés.

'I'm sorry, Doña Luz,' said Carmela, her hand resting contritely on her ample bosom. '*Madre de Dios!* I gave the delivery boy a clip round the ear. These are a day late,' she explained. 'That boy has the face of an angel but the brain of an ass,' she muttered as she hurried off in the direction of the kitchen.

With trembling hands, Luz unfastened the small envelope attached to the cellophane and impatiently tore it open. The typewritten note was brief and to the point: 'So sorry – I will have to miss dinner tonight. I have been unavoidably held up. I'll see you at my birthday party at El Ecrin on Saturday night. With my best regards.' It was signed Andrés de Calderón. Luz was a little disappointed. He had obviously not written it himself, no doubt leaving it to his secretary to send this rather formal note on his behalf. Still, the flowers came as a huge relief and now she would be able to attend the party on Saturday without being dogged by the fear that he had somehow cast her off without a word of explanation.

Nonetheless Luz still felt uneasiness in her bones; she sensed something was not quite right. Why had he not rung her instead of sending her this bland note? It seemed the obvious thing to do. When she aired her misgivings, Alexandra was sanguine.

'"Absence carries its reasons," goes the Moorish saying,' she said. 'Don't jump to conclusions, it's one of Agustina's favourite sayings.' She laughed lightly. 'Those endless proverbs used to irritate me but some of them are very wise. Your Andrés may have a perfectly good reason and he will tell it to you in due course.'

Luz gave the roses another thoughtful sniff. 'What do you think, *Papá*?'

Salvador smiled indulgently at his daughter, shook his head and left it at that.

'*Papá!*' Luz prompted.

'Do as your mother tells you, give the man a chance to explain. If the explanation doesn't convince you, then we'll rethink.'

*   *   *

The few days between then and Saturday stretched uncomfortably for Luz; she half expected Andrés to appear at the front door at every moment. Why should he not? After all, he owed her an explanation and this silence was unnatural. The roses, the note, had only gone a small way to allay her fears. He was forever in her mind, her emotions on a constant seesaw. Treacherous voices whispered and hinted, infiltrating her heart with unpleasant doubts. She swayed from being elated, on the one hand, in anticipation of seeing him again, to melancholy on the other. It was the thought of Adalia's place in his life that kept creeping insidiously into her mind. Clearly they had a business relationship; after all, he had introduced her and Lorenzo as his partners. But so much suggested that their bond did not end there: the way he had let himself be monopolized by her at La Fortaleza and all those other little private, personal signs more eloquent than words. But if they had been intimately involved in the past, were they still? In Andrés' mind, was Adalia the future wife and Luz some sort of stop-gap mistress, as the socialite had implied?

As she dressed for his birthday party, it suddenly occurred to Luz again that this was the first time Andrés had invited her to El Ecrin, his home. Always before they had met either at L'Estrella or at Puesta de Sol, his uncle's house. She had never questioned it, never found it strange. But now the thought hit her out of the blue and it threw ice water on any excitement she felt at the idea of seeing him again. She drew a breath. Her naïvety beggared belief; things were adding up. It was only now that she understood how unrealistic she had been. With an effort, she cast those negative thoughts aside. No matter what the harsh truth might be, she would keep her chin up and concentrate on the task at hand, which was to look her best tonight.

'*Te ves divina*, you look divine,' her father exclaimed as she walked out on to the terrace. 'An ode to romantic glamour!'

Luz burst out laughing; her father could always bring a smile to her face even at the most miserable of times. 'No wonder *Mamá* fell head over heels for you. You do say the most beautiful things,' she said, putting her arms around his neck and kissing him.

Salvador and Alexandra surveyed the understated elegance of their daughter. She did indeed look divine in her floor-skimming periwinkle chiffon bustier gown. The sophisticated look lay in the perfect cut of the garment: the bodice was tight fitting, ruched at the top of the heart-shaped décolleté, while the skirt flowed gently to the ground in draped panels, slightly shorter at the front. Sparkling, dainty high-heeled strappy sandals adorned her feet, her pretty painted toenails peeping out of them like little pearly enamelled shells. Luz held herself like a queen. She had her mother to thank for that, Alexandra having insisted her daughter took ballet lessons as a child, hence her perfect posture.

'I haven't seen that necklace before,' Salvador commented on noticing the delicate strands of pearls, diamonds and amethysts adorning Luz's slender neck. 'It's quite lovely.' She had lifted her heavy, lustrous raven-black hair up on to the crown of her head and the necklace set off the pure line of her swan-like throat, drawing attention to the perfect curves of her bust and beautifully smooth, tanned shoulders.

'Aunt Geraldine gave it to me with these earrings when I graduated. It has a matching bangle and ring, which would have been too much for tonight,' she told him. 'I probably showed them to you in their box at the time, but I have never had the occasion to wear them. Purple isn't usually my first choice of colour.'

'But it really does suit you,' Alexandra declared. 'It gives your eyes an interesting violet tint.' She went over to Luz and cupped her cheek tenderly. 'You are so beautiful, my lovely daughter. I simply refuse to believe that Andrés would prefer that dreadful woman to you. She is handsome, I grant you that, but so are statues and that is not what usually moves men.'

Luz kissed her mother affectionately and gave her an indulgent smile. 'You are biased, *Mamá*,' she told her lightly. 'I'm your only daughter and Adalia has not only been beastly to me, but she is the offspring of someone who hurt you and *Papá* rather badly.' She gave a little self-deprecating laugh. 'Says it all, doesn't it?'

'None of that tonight,' her father reprimanded softly. 'Go off and show them all what an elegant, sophisticated, ravishing young woman Luz María Cervantes de Rueda is. I guarantee, men will be falling over themselves to dance with you.'

Luz smiled bleakly. She did not care about all the other men in the world: for her the only one who counted was Andrés.

*   *   *

The party was in full swing when Luz arrived at the striking hacienda that was El Ecrin. Already there were several other cars in the car park. At the ornately panelled oak front door, a major-domo took her through the hall to the tall open French windows that led outdoors. The furniture was minimalist. She had just time to notice a very large painting of a beautiful fair-haired woman, given pride of place at the top of the wrought-iron staircase, before she was ushered outside.

A crowd of guests had congregated on the lawn of the garden overlooking the sea. The house was not as big as Luz had anticipated, neither was the garden. As far as she could make out, the building had been skilfully carved out of an enormous cliff, all of its rooms facing the Atlantic. Painted white all over, it lay like an exquisite fragile treasure of lace-like ironwork and gilded outside decoration, with terraces of greenery surrounding it: a jewel box made out of rock. Everything about it was of a sophisticated simplicity, quite different to the complicated fantastical creation of Puesta de Sol. Here, the genius of a visionary was just as much present as it was in Eduardo de Salazar's hacienda. The airy feel and lightness emanating from it was due to the artful contrivances of the builder, some skilled engineering and, most of all, the splendid artistic touch of the architect who had dreamt it up. Pure romance.

Though the night was still young, a dancefloor had been set up on the emerald lawn of one of the terraces overlooking the ocean and the dancing was in full swing. A golden full moon rode in a sapphire sky, studded so brightly with stars that they shone like lights in the heavens. Its vibrant rays gleamed on black, oily waters and on the white sandy beach dotted with dark shapes of boulders lying at the edge of the shore.

Luz immediately spotted the small group where Andrés was holding court, standing tall and distinguished. Her heart sank when she saw Adalia at his side. As usual she looked stunning in a lightweight maxi dress that was golden-beige and skin tight. It was a one-shoulder design with a twist strap and ruched detail on the bodice but the clinching factor that made it unique and so provocative was the thigh-high split on one side, which showed off the length of her shapely legs when she moved.

A tight fist squeezed Luz's heart. *He's mine*, she cried out silently. Still, how could she compete with that?

'He's not yours to have,' someone whispered in her ear.

She turned sharply to find Lorenzo standing behind her, an ugly smirk on his handsome face. His eyes met hers with a gleam she found intensely offensive. She moved away without answering, but he caught her arm.

'Why don't you try me instead?' he suggested in sickening, sugared tones. 'I'm faithful, generous, famous and much richer than he is.'

'Would you please leave me alone,' said Luz, desperately trying to control the tight knot of apprehension growing inside her. Her fists clenched so hard that she could feel her nails biting into the flesh of her palms.

Lorenzo released her, but not before letting his hand stroke caressingly down the satiny naked flesh of her arm.

Her stormy eyes withered him with their glance. '*Don't!*' she snapped.

The smile on the *torero*'s face faded rapidly and he immediately drew away, taking a couple of steps backwards. 'The tigress has claws,' he sneered.

Luz moved quickly towards the little group where Andrés was standing, trying to place as much distance as possible between herself and Lorenzo. When she was a few feet away Andrés noticed her and excused himself from his guests.

'Luz,' he whispered as he reached her. 'Luz,' he repeated, 'it's wonderful to see you.' He bent over and brushed his lips to one cheek and then to the other. She saw that his face was pale and drawn as his gaze settled intently on her. The usually glittering black eyes were dull and reddened as if he had known sleepless nights. He had lost weight, too.

'Happy birthday, Andrés,' she said, her brows coming together, concern for the man she loved replacing any previous misgivings. 'What have you been up to? You don't look at all well.'

But he had no time to answer her before Adalia walked over to join them. The socialite shot a silent look of condescending appraisal at Luz before pouting prettily at Andrés.

'You really mustn't neglect your other guests, *querido*, especially Señor Luis Alvarez and his wife. They've just arrived, all the way from Toledo. Remember, we need him to sign that contract.' Without waiting for a reply, she slung an arm around Andrés' waist, all the while gazing up at him adoringly. As she proceeded to steer him away she managed to turn her back on Luz entirely, completely shunning her. Andrés at least had the good grace to look uncomfortable, but it didn't prevent Luz's cheeks from flaming red.

'Yes, yes, you're right, of course,' he muttered distractedly. His voice was hoarse, his expression almost dazed. For a moment he managed to extricate himself from Adalia's clutches and then turned to Luz, his eyes full of a confusing mixture of emotions that she found undecipherable.

'I'll see you later,' he murmured. 'Duty calls.' He smiled at her lamely, a wretched shadow of a smile, before following Adalia back into the crowd.

Would he see her later? When would he explain himself? She knew it was ridiculous, but she could feel the tears stinging the back of her eyes as she watched the pair move off, Adalia's long elegant silhouette fitting perfectly against his lean masculine frame. Once more, it baffled her that Andrés seemed prepared to collude with Adalia's territorial antics, which were hardly subtle. Luz swallowed hard and gritted her teeth, blinking as her vision blurred. She must not cry, not now, not here.

I won't give that woman the satisfaction, she told herself through gritted teeth.

'I told you he is already spoken for,' she heard the loathsome voice snigger behind her.

A tide of pink rushed to her face. 'And *I* told you to leave me alone!' she hissed without turning. 'You're harassing me and, if you don't want me to make a scene in public, you'd better get off my back.' Luz was so beside herself with anger she could hardly control the urge to turn round and knock the Cheshire cat grin off Lorenzo's face with the flat of her hand.

He came closer; she could feel the heat radiating from his body as he brushed against her bare back, but this time he did not touch her. 'Why the venom, *señorita*? I'm only trying to stop you from wasting your time and making a fool of yourself, of course. You haven't a chance against Adalia,' he persisted scathingly.

At this, Luz broke into a run until she reached the house. *This must be how a hunted creature feels,* she thought as she leant, sagging a little, against a wall opposite the staircase. She was trembling and panting now, her lips parched, her hands clammy. The room was spinning a little, too.

The major-domo, who had shown her in and was still standing by the front door, came up to her. 'Is everything all right, *señorita*? Can I get you a glass of water?' he enquired.

'Yes, please,' she replied with a grateful smile. 'That would be very nice, thank you.'

She relaxed, feeling a little better now. The portrait of the lady at the top of the stairs gazed down at her enigmatically. She was very beautiful. Actually, she looked very much like Andrés but a much fairer version, with golden hair and expressively coloured eyes that smiled mischievously at her. Andrés has inherited his mother's magnetism, she thought. She moved closer to the painting, fascinated.

'Doña Eleadora, Don Eduardo's sister,' the major-domo volunteered as he handed her a glass of water.

Luz thanked him. She thought back to the sunken elderly woman she had seen at the Yacht Club ball. How very different Doña Eleadora had been when this picture was painted, so much more alive than in the flesh today.

'She's beautiful. Don Andrés looks very much like his mother,' she noted.

The major-domo smiled a polite inscrutable smile then silently moved back to his place at the front door.

Luz was in two minds whether to go home or return to the party. Many of the older guests were undoubtedly acquaintances of her parents – she knew a few of them – but she had been away for so many years, on and off, and had only a small number of friends among the younger generation. Still, having taken such care with her appearance, it seemed a waste to leave the gathering so early. Besides, it was rude; she couldn't do that to Andrés, though she wondered if he would even notice her absence. The distant look that enveloped him was like nothing she'd seen before; he looked almost wraithlike. Perhaps it was guilt eating away at him at the prospect of having to extricate himself from his relationship with her and the conversation he would have to have with her later.

Once again she stared up at the painting of Doña Eleadora, whose smile now seemed more mysterious than ever. She shook her head at her own mounting paranoia. There must be another explanation – she had to believe that for her own sanity. Whatever the reason, no doubt Adalia was capitalizing on Andrés' distracted state, clamping herself to him like a limpet at every opportunity. She took a deep breath, braced herself and went back into the garden in a new mood of resolution.

Luz circulated stiffly among the guests, stopping from time to time to shake hands or answer a question about her parents' health and whereabouts. She was hoping to find her good friends Alba and Carlos but they were probably away on holiday at this time of year. Her face ached from the artificial smile she had plastered on it and her throat was dry from the empty platitudes she forced from it in an attempt at conversation. Luz was unaware that Andrés' eyes were on her continually; that wherever she went, he manoeuvred himself so that he was only a few yards away, never taking his eyes off her. She was just about to lose all hope of meeting anybody she knew when she ran into Romero de Cabrera.

'Luz, how lovely to see you again,' he said, his eyes crinkling in that open smile that had immediately made her feel at ease when they first met at the Yacht Club. 'Where have you been? I noticed you earlier this evening and then I lost sight of you among the crowd. There are quite a lot of people tonight. It's all rather impressive, don't you think?'

'I'm so glad to see you, Romero,' she told him, smiling properly for the first time that evening. He'd be surprised if he knew how much of a relief it was to bump into him, she thought wryly. After all, she hardly knew him. But it felt like she had never before felt such an acute need for a friendly face, someone she was sure liked her; someone who was on her side.

'It was a superb evening I had at the Yacht Club ball that night and you're such a wonderful dancer.' His honey-coloured eyes twinkled with fun as he leaned his head conspiratorially towards her. 'I'm looking forward to showing off our skills again tonight on the dancefloor.' His tone was rather more intimate than the occasion warranted, but Luz liked the young man's blithe spirit and what she recognized as a perfectly healthy bit of playfulness.

'I'm game if you are,' she said cheerfully, her self-confidence growing by the second. It occurred to her that it would do no harm to try and forget her complicated situation with Andrés for the moment and she had to admit that an insecure part of her also needed him to see that he was not the only man interested in her.

Together they strolled around, talking and laughing lightly. Luz could feel herself gradually starting to thaw. She had forgotten what a pleasant companion Romero was. Maybe, after all, she would be able to enjoy herself tonight. From time to time she caught sight of Andrés and Adalia. Although he seemed hardly aware of the socialite possessively hanging on to his arm at every opportunity, still seemingly distracted, brow furrowed, the sight of them nevertheless managed to make Luz's heart bleed.

Thank heavens for Romero, she told herself. With him by her side she could make a decent stab at ignoring them and concentrating on the moment.

The guests were now being directed to a marquee where buffet tables had been set with food and drink to delight the appreciative eye of an artist, as well as please the knowledgeable taste buds of a gourmet. Giant iced bowls overflowed with striking displays of shellfish, surrounded by plated intricate morsels of every colour and variety, and tiers of sumptuous desserts. The sound of clinking cutlery mingled with loud conversation and laughter as the assembled throng tucked into the delectable feast with enthusiasm.

After dinner Luz and Romero strolled down towards the parapet at the edge of the garden separating the property from the sea. On either side of them, orange blossom bloomed among dark green foliage, interspersed with huge palm trees and sweet-smelling jasmine in flower. A light wind had started up and the sea looked rather choppy, Luz thought, as she peered over the edge into the deep, dark waters. Huge slabs of broken rock, piled one on the other in some sort of ruthless confusion with the turbulent waves smashing relentlessly against them, were somewhat suggestive of how she felt each time she caught a glimpse of Andrés and Adalia.

She and Romero talked of many things, Luz standing with her back to the sea, her companion facing her. Once or twice he tried to slant the conversation towards love and Luz ignored him, but he did not seem to mind. They flirted happily, gently laughing and teasing. Every now and again she sensed him picking up on her slight air of unease and each time he gently tried to coax her out of it. He was quick-witted, his repartee sharp and always humorous. Once more she thanked Romero inwardly, and a little ruefully, for being there. Not only was he good company but he was a gentleman, too.

Suddenly Luz stiffened. She could see a man and woman standing near the top of the lawn by the gazebo: Andrés and Adalia. Though she could not hear what they were saying, by their stance she could tell they were having a heated exchange. For once the cool blonde socialite seemed agitated, gesticulating wildly as she spoke. Andrés, Luz could see, appeared calm and unruffled.

She was now only half listening to Romero's anecdotes, completely captive to the scene she was witnessing. He gave her a wry smile. 'Doña Luz, I believe you're not listening to a word I say,' he said cheerfully. 'What's happening behind my back that's so intensely interesting?' He turned just in time to witness the slap Adalia dealt Andrés before running off towards the house.

Luz's heart leapt with joy. From where she stood, she could not see Andrés' face and dearly wished he would turn around. Instead he just stood there for a few moments, legs slightly apart. His hands were deep in his pockets, his gaze turned towards the ground. Then he slowly walked off to join a small group of guests who were laughing noisily in the middle of the lawn.

Romero let out a small whistle. 'Trouble in the nest, I think, don't you?' He raised a wicked eyebrow at Luz. 'Their relationship has been a game of chase for years,' he added in a theatrical whisper. 'I wonder which one will end up winning. Adalia Herrera has been trying to get her claws into him for I don't know how long and it seems that Don Andrés is having nothing of it. Still, there's a French saying that goes: *ce que femme veut Dieu veut*, what women want, God wants. So I would imagine the jury's still out.' He paused reflectively. 'Though some say he will never marry, you know. He's an odd one, Don Andrés. A very dark horse.'

'Have you known him long?' Luz asked casually, trying not to sound overly interested.

'Yes, didn't I tell you? We went to the same university, though we attended different classes. Since then we've met socially but I can't really say I know him well. Of course, there's been a lot of gossip floating around about him. You know how fast drawing room tittle-tattle travels. His uncle was even more of a centre of gossip. In his day, a vast amount of ink was expended speculating uselessly about his personal life.'

Slowly they walked back to the house. Luz was dying to ask more questions about Andrés but she was afraid her interest would be too conspicuous; she really did not wish to be an item in Cádiz society's rumour mill and, though she knew Romero to be a kind man, she could tell he would never be able to resist dining out on a good story. She felt a little heartened, however, that he clearly had no idea about her relationship with Andrés despite Adalia having intimated that the whole of Cádiz was talking about it.

She glanced at her watch. 'I think I should be getting home. It's late.'

'But we haven't had that dance you promised me,' he said, a little crestfallen.

'Maybe some other time,' she told him with a hurried smile.

Suddenly, she wanted to get away. The evening had had its highs and its lows and, after her brief conversation with Romero, she felt she was back to square one: as unclear as she ever was about the relationship that bound Andrés and Adalia. The scene she had witnessed earlier might be interpreted in more ways than one; it could have been just a tiff between lovers. After all, Andrés had spent most of his time at the party with Adalia and hadn't been exactly attentive to Luz. Wasn't that tantamount to signalling he didn't care? Still, she tried desperately to reassure herself, during the few moments they had been together, albeit with Adalia hanging on his arm, he had seemed glad to see her. Maybe he had missed her even. Luz gave a shaky sigh. There was something impalpable about the whole evening, like the heaviness of the atmosphere before a storm.

'Perhaps I'll see you again soon,' said Romero, cutting into her thoughts.

'Yes, perhaps,' replied Luz.

The young architect paused, looking at her thoughtfully, and then his mouth curved in a charming smile, almost in resignation. He inclined his head. 'So until we meet again, Doña Luz. It's good to have a new friend in Cádiz.'

She returned his smile warmly, her eyes silently communicating her relief and thanks that he understood the way things truly were between them. 'Yes, indeed. Goodnight, Romero.'

After she took her leave of Romero, Luz went looking for Andrés to say goodbye. The party was still in full flow. He was nowhere to be seen outside so she went into the house. The major-domo had abandoned his post at the door so now the hall was empty, except for the mute portrait of Doña Eleadora presiding over the place, an enigmatic smile behind her magnificent eyes. Luz looked up at her: 'Where is your son? Where is Andrés?' she murmured and her voice echoed in the empty space.

'Just behind you, *querida*.'

Luz's heart missed a beat; she turned sharply. 'Andrés, Andrés, where have you been?' she cried out, her tone slightly reproachful but her gaze brimming with love.

He came towards her, eyes shuttered, and took her in his arms. 'Shush, *querida*. Tomorrow we'll go to our secret place and everything will be all right.' He kissed her tenderly on the lips first and then on the forehead. 'The nightmare is nearly over,' he whispered, so low she barely heard him. She wondered what he meant by that; he was acting so strangely tonight. He cupped her face in his hands.

'Go home now, I'll call you in the morning,' he told her.

She gave him an uncertain look. 'You will ring, won't you?'

He sighed and nodded. '*Si, si querida*, don't worry. I promise I'll call you then.' He stroked her face and brushed her lips again with the tenderest of kisses.

Andrés escorted her to her car, where he hugged her tightly before drawing apart to kiss her again. He seemed so very sad. There was something desperate in his whole manner tonight that she could not fathom, a bittersweet note to his embraces. Luz hesitated with her hand on the door of the two-seater, looking up at him with questioning eyes, but he simply shook his head and pushed her gently inside.

She drove off slowly, her heart a little heavy. As she turned towards the gates, she glanced up. Andrés stood under the dusky luminous moon and the stars, a bleak, lonely figure. She could still see him in her mirror, unmoving, as she disappeared into the night.

CHAPTER 13

They met on the beach, as they had often done in the past. The sun shone brilliantly on the mirror of the sea and there was a crystalline, razor-edged beauty to the day.

Luz walked through the dunes towards Andrés. In the strong sunlight, he appeared stark against a backdrop of deep-blue sky and roaring ocean in his white T-shirt and shorts, his chestnut hair tied back as usual. His shoulders seemed more hunched than normal, she thought as she drew nearer. His mouth was a thin, unreadable line and she wondered what expression lay behind his opaque sunglasses as he watched her approach. A new surge of foreboding flooded her heart and her eyes clouded at the thought of losing him.

She was standing very close to him now. He dipped his head and kissed her lightly on the lips but he did not take her in his arms as he had invariably done in the past. Luz gave him an uncertain look, trying to decipher his feelings, conscious that he was hurting. He looked gaunt, his cheeks hollowed. With every nerve in her body she wanted to comfort him. Silently she put her arms around him, drawing him to her, hugging him with all the love of which she was capable. She felt a quiver run through his frame but he eased apart, the strain gathering in his face.

'Let's go, *querida*,' he whispered, stretching out his hand to take hers and lead her to the boat.

'What's wrong, Andrés?' she murmured, looking up at him. Her deep-sapphire eyes reflected the desperate confusion and longing that overwhelmed her. 'I love you.'

His jaw clenched as his hand went to her face but then dropped again. 'I love you too,' he replied in a choked voice and then quickly, as though not trusting himself to speak another word, he turned his head away. He helped her into the boat and then climbed in himself.

Already the sun was strong and hot. The glare was blinding, with a clean white brightness about everything. The beautiful blue sea stretched to the horizon, wide and shimmering, as they sailed into the sunshine.

Luz finally broke the awkward silence. 'Are you all right?'

He smiled, but she sensed he had changed. At the party, too, she had noticed that there was an odd look about his face, as though it was not easy for him to smile. He was so near, yet she sensed he was a great distance from her. Though she knew he loved her, somehow his still, silent face confounded her and she was afraid. Was he going to tell her that, even though his feelings for her were deep and he did not love Adalia, he had made a promise to her, which as a man of honour he could not break? *Please, let it not be that.* Luz felt the wind on her face and tasted salt spray on her lips. It could have been a wonderful day if not for the fear that gnawed at her heart.

Slowly they sailed towards their favourite beach. Despite the brightness of the day, melancholy wrapped them in silence. The wind had changed direction and was blowing much stronger now. Here, the open sea was quite choppy, breakers rising and falling in soft swells. Very soon, the boat began to pitch, water splashing in at its sides. Andrés pushed the tiller over, bringing the dinghy round on a new tack. Luz moved forward, half-standing, to tighten the sheet of the jib, the way he had shown her. Just as she did so, a powerful gust made the boat jibe, the mainsail swinging round violently. The boom hit her a glancing blow on the head, just enough to make her lose her balance.

'Andrés!'

Her shocked cry rent the air as she was catapulted into the turbulent blue waters.

Andrés reacted swiftly, immediately taking command. Releasing the sheets of the sails from their cleats, he steered the boat into the wind to halt its progress. Without hesitation, leaving the boat unmanned, its sails flapping wildly, he dived into the water.

Luz's head was tilted back, nearly covered by the waves, and every time she went under she swallowed seawater. Gasping for air, she choked, her arms frantically flailing about to no avail. She couldn't seem to use her legs. Whenever she tried to take in a breath and swim in a particular direction, she made no headway.

'Hang on, Luz!' Andrés called out, swimming towards her, his voice sounding thin over the space of the sea. *He'll never reach me! He's too late*, she screamed inwardly. And then the water closed over her head, shutting off the world above. Blind fear gripped her now; her legs wouldn't, couldn't, hold her up. They were paralyzed as if in a cramp, the muscles knotted in pain. She felt herself sink vertically into the deep.

Then, in one swift motion, powerful arms dragged her up to the surface and Andrés was there, supporting her head and limp body against the strength of his frame. She was helpless and heavy, but he managed to float her on the surface and swim back to the boat. Luz didn't know how he managed to haul her aboard the pitching dinghy. It was as if he had superhuman strength but, at last, they were both inside. Luz huddled in the bottom of the boat and, with one hand, Andrés grabbed a towel to wrap around her, while, with the other, he took the tiller. He must have adjusted their course, bringing the craft round to run with the wind because they were on an even keel now, but Luz was barely conscious of anything. Andrés bent over her with concern, water dripping from his hair, his clothes clinging to his body.

Luz was as white as a sheet and cold. He rolled her gently on to her side so that she could cough up the water from her lungs.

She lay there, pale and shivering, while Andrés returned them to calmer waters. After some time she became aware of the hull hitting the sand and being hauled on to the shore. Her head hurt. Andrés lifted her gently from the dinghy and wrapped her in a large Guernsey sweater he retrieved from a canvas bag. Now he was massaging her legs with his strong fingers as he attempted to relieve her cramped muscles. She felt warmth and life return to her body with the friction and pressure of his hands. Her lungs, though, still strained to draw in any breath.

'Luz, are you all right?' His words sounded anxious as he leaned over her.

She moved her head and whimpered his name. Through the mist of her benumbed state she could hear him calling her. She coughed up more water. Then her eyelids fluttered and opened.

Blankly she gazed up at her rescuer's concerned face. She blinked once, twice, in disbelief as she met a pair of piercing green eyes: Leandro's eyes. Her confusion wouldn't clear. Surely it was Andrés she had called for, but where were his velvet black eyes? Why was Leandro now peering down at her, his long hair loose and wet around his face? She had left Cádiz with Andrés, on his boat, she was sure of that. They had been in the middle of the ocean. What was going on? Andrés and Leandro couldn't be there at the same time, unless …

And then Luz froze for a few seconds as her hazy mind grasped the reality staring down at her. 'Leandro? Andrés? … Who are you?' she cried out in horror. She struggled to sit up on the sand. Her head was in a vice, clamped at her temples. As panic gripped her, her stomach heaved. She retched once, then again. *How could he? … Why?* She was not so much shocked by the truth as shattered by the deceit. But it all made sense now. It was almost as if some part of her had always sensed that Leandro and Andrés were one. Wasn't that why she had responded so passionately to Andrés' touch without feeling real guilt towards Leandro?

Andrés attempted to calm her down. He started to pull her back into his arms. 'Hush, *querida*, let me explain, I …'

But Luz wanted none of it. 'Don't touch me! I don't want to hear a word,' she said, pushing him away and trembling now, less with cold but more with anger at her own credulity. She did not glance in his direction, but kept her eyes focused on the encircling headland. He had got them here, to their beach.

'Take me back now,' she told him. Her voice was flat, ice-cold. 'I have no idea what sick game you've been playing but I can't stand the sight of you!'

Luz was no longer sure if she loved this man in front of her or hated him, in fact, she was no longer convinced of anything except the desire to go home and be alone in her room. She thought she knew him intimately but now he was two men – or wasn't he merely one stranger?

Andrés gazed warily at her as if at any moment she might jump up and run, just to be free of him. After a moment of silence between them, he knelt back on his heels.

'I know what I've done is unforgivable,' he said bleakly. 'I was planning to tell you the truth today. I do have an explanation, I promise, Luz. And as flimsy as it may appear to you now, I want you to hear me out before you judge me.'

There was cold disdain in the look she finally gave him and the smouldering anger in her heart blazed up. 'Nothing can excuse such despicable deceit,' she told him, her voice shaking. 'You deliberately set me up. How *could* you have acted the way you did? *Why? Why? Why?*' she cried out, reproach and hurt filling her eyes.

He ran his hands through his wet hair. 'I would have saved you this entire nightmare if I could, Luz,' he said in a low voice. 'But circumstances were stronger than both of us. And I needed to protect you, as much as anything. Let me explain,' he pleaded again.

'Oh, please! Andrés? Leandro? I don't even know what to call you any more,' she said with a laugh, full of self-derision. 'Spare me the doleful hero act.' She struggled to raise herself from the ground but he put a hand out to gently stop her.

'Don't hate me, Luz. My name is really Andrés Leandro. I am half-gypsy and half-*gajo*, and that's the truth,' he explained softly.

'I don't want to know,' Luz cut in harshly, flinching away from his touch. Inside, she was torn apart by his betrayal. 'Andrés, Leandro … they have both ceased to exist for me.' She looked up into the green irises that still managed to hold her captive for a moment, her heart beating faster. But her eyes were swimming with tears. She spoke quietly and the words were fraught with meaning: 'As long as I live, I will never forgive you. Whatever happens, in my heart I will always hate you.'

Andrés looked as though Luz had struck him physically. His eyes, so green and penetrating, seemed to fill with shock, then hopelessness, before taking on a steely edge.

'That's fine, absolutely fine,' he said, getting slowly to his feet.

And in the numbness of her pain, the edge to his voice sounded to Luz like indifference.

*   *   *

Luz sat on her veranda watching the day being swallowed up by the hot darkness of night. She could not believe how gullible she had been. Andrés had deliberately set her up from day one. All the time she had been mystified, he had been watching her. It was a twisted game he had played but, to the best of her knowledge, he was not that sort of man. How could she have been so mistaken? Of course he had been very cunning, planning the subterfuge down to the smallest detail. From the gypsy accent and wild, carefree attitude to what must have been lenses that changed the colour of his eyes; it had all been masterfully calculated – but why? And to what end? The reason for him going to such lengths to deceive her still escaped her.

Looking at it with this new-found knowledge, she found many things now made much more sense. She had never understood her sudden powerful attraction to Andrés after she had thought herself so deeply in love with Leandro; it was so unlike her. She had always felt uncomfortable, as though she was being disloyal to her gypsy lover, even though he had been the one who had abandoned her.

Still she came back to the same question: *Why?* What had Andrés to gain in staging such a cruel charade? From what she had ascertained about him during the few months they had been lovers, he was well thought of and loved by his friends. It was true that she too had found him kind, thoughtful and generous whether gypsy or hidalgo. Could she have been fooled to such an extent? Of course the logical way to find out why he'd done this to her would have been to hear his explanation, but the first thing in her head had been to get away from him. Even looking at him and listening to his voice had hurt her, like holding fire to her skin. She'd had to be alone so that she could lick her wounds in private and nurse her shattered heart.

The lights of the ships were now dots of gold, fading gradually into the mists above the ocean, and the palms in the garden shivered and clattered in the breeze. Luz watched the great orange moon rise majestically from the sea on the far horizon as if a child's hand had suddenly decided to paste it to a scenery card in a myriorama. She sighed and went indoors, tears streaming down her cheeks. There was nowhere for her to turn. Sheeting waves of pain clutched at her heart. How would she be able to forget the man every nerve in her body ached for?

She retired to bed, longing for sleep. It eluded her, but she dozed languidly in a semi-consciousness state as scene after scene of her recent life in Spain unrolled like a film in her mind's eye.

Much later, when the curtain moved, she was barely aware of the shadowy figure entering stealthily through the doors of the open French windows, blocking out the moonlight spilling into the room and padding with a velvet tread towards the bed where she lay.

Luz opened her eyes and gasped as she recognized the man who had been haunting her days and nights during all these months. As she sat up and scrambled over to the middle of the bed, her hands moved to her mouth to smother her cry. She could see his eyes taking in the curves of her body, just visible beneath the transparent fabric of her flimsy nightdress.

'What are you doing here?' she asked in a strangled voice, reaching for the sheet and instinctively pulling it over herself in an attempt at modesty.

The green irises glinted in the dark like a cat's eyes, as though her surprise, her annoyance and her sudden shyness amused him.

'Don't be afraid, Luz. I've come to apologize. To explain myself,' he murmured calmly.

At first she looked at him in silence, making out in the shadows the lean, tanned frame of the man whose body she knew almost as well as her own, but whose eyes remained to her as impenetrable as a moonless night.

'Did I not make myself clear when I told you I didn't want to have anything more to do with you?' she said coldly, trying to sound convincing, although her voice quivered a little. 'Please go.'

His jaw contracted. 'Hear me out and then decide. Even a criminal is given a chance to defend himself.'

He had caused her more than her fair share of pain so how could she be sure she could trust him to tell the truth? With an effort she hardened her heart.

'I'm not interested in what you have to say. You've told me lie after lie, so why should I believe anything you say now?'

His eyes gleamed again, but this time with something like panic. He reached out and skimmed her cheek with his fingers. Luz's reaction was instant. She pulled away from him as though his touch had scorched her, as indeed it had, with so many feelings she could not begin to describe, but she remained silent so he could not detect the emotions his proximity had unleashed.

'Luz, give me the chance to explain,' he pleaded softly, his voice infinitely sad.

'Why should I?' she uttered hoarsely. She glared up at him, though her heart compressed painfully. 'So you can hurt me again? So you can use me while you prepare for your wedding with Doña Adalia Herrera?'

'What are you talking about?' In the shadows she could almost discern his frown. 'There's no wedding, Luz. Adalia and I have known each other since childhood. She's a partner in my company and, though she can be difficult sometimes, I still value her as a friend. My interest in her stops there.'

Luz let out a low, bitter laugh. All previous rational thought had given way to her chaotic emotions now. She shook her head. 'Still lying, still trying to pull the wool over my eyes, even now. You are really incorrigible.'

'I give you my word of honour …'

'What honour?' she retorted derisively, wanting to lash out at him and hurt him as much as he had hurt her with his duplicity.

Andrés pressed his lips together in a thin line but ignored her barbed insinuation. 'Adalia is nothing more to me than I've just told you. We dated once, many years ago, but it wasn't right and to be honest, I've known she's had designs on me, on and off, since then,' he explained. 'But believe me, Luz, her feelings are one sided.'

'Is that so?' She didn't bother to hide the sarcasm in her voice. 'Anyone seeing you together would think you were a couple.

You've not exactly gone out of your way to discourage her. Did you ever think how humiliating it must have been for me at your party, barely acknowledged by my own lover, whose attention was entirely taken up by that creature hanging on his arm?'

He sighed. 'I know, and I'm sorry. But try to look at it from my perspective, Luz. As I said, as well as a friend of the family, Adalia is my business partner, and a good one at that. She helped organize the party and I was grateful to her.' He raised his hand to prevent Luz from interrupting.

'Yes, I know, I've probably indulged her more than I should. I stuck my head in the sand, I suppose, to preserve the status quo. There would have been repercussions for our families and the business had I rejected her outright. Anyhow, I finally told her, in no uncertain terms, that I would never marry her, which is all she's interested in. I'm sure that in the next few days I will receive a letter asking me to dissolve our partnership and buy both Adalia and Lorenzo out.'

Luz's pulse quickened faintly. She stared at him. *Could she dare hope?* A soul-destroying voice told her to be reckless and give herself up to her need, her passion and her love. But she had to smother it before it vanquished her pride.

'Please go,' came her low, gutteral reply.

But Andrés knew her too well; he had always been able to read her. Even now, as they spoke in moonlit shadows, he had no need to see her features to detect the emotions that threatened to overwhelm her or her ache for him. She could sense it quivering in the air between them. He sat on the side of the bed, almost close enough for her to feel the heat of his body, and she swallowed as he leaned towards her.

'*Querida*, hear me out. Whether Leandro or Andrés, my love for you has always been true. It has never wavered. Think back, I have always been there. Does that count for nothing in your book?' he whispered.

A shaft of moonlight fell on his face. He looked distraught, his green eyes shining with emotion. 'I'm not asking you to give yourself up to me and trust me immediately. All I want is for you to listen to what I have to say and then maybe you'll give me another chance.'

He was not hiding his vulnerability from her and she could feel herself weakening. The knowledge of just how easy it would be to succumb to those woeful eyes sent a shiver of exquisite anticipation rushing up her spine. She knew she still loved him, still needed him; still wanted him. She must be crazy; had she forgotten all the reasons she had for hating him?

'What possible story could you invent to exonerate you from those months of deceit? And why should I believe you?' she went on inexorably, twisting the knife.

'The facts are sad and complicated. Some aspects of them are not so good but, at the time, they seemed justifiable because I had every intention of making up for them. You're a warm, generous woman, Luz, and I just had to trust to that.'

'Flattery will get you nowhere.'

Andrés sighed. He stared at her, his expression pained. 'I love you, Luz,' he said softly. His body was taut; she could see he had difficulty in keeping it in check.

'Look me in the eye and tell me you don't love me and I will not press you any more. I'll walk out of your life,' he said, cupping her face gently in his palm and turning it to face him.

His hand was warm, the feel of him as electrifying as she remembered. And the magic was working for she was mesmerized by his compelling eyes, the softness in his voice, the tenderness of his touch. He was subtly different, the gypsy and hidalgo both present before her in a strange combination of passion and self-control. Emotions were spiralling swiftly out of control inside her. Oh, how she had missed him! Remembering the first time she had set eyes on him, she hastily tossed out a question that had been niggling her since his identity had been revealed.

'That first day, when I fell off Zeyna, had you set out to attract my attention?' she said, inside reproaching herself for asking.

'Yes, but it was not with the intention of distracting you. Unfortunately, fate intervened on that day and reshuffled the cards,' he replied easily.

Luz was unconvinced. 'So when did you decide I was prey worth hunting?' she asked shakily.

'It wasn't like that,' he told her as he heaved a painful sigh. He paused and stood up, moving out of the moonlight to retreat into the shadows against the wall. 'I will answer your question, but let me first put it in context.'

Her laugh was sarcastic. 'Oh, please do,' she scoffed. 'I'm dying to know what made you go to such lengths to set up that ingenious piece of theatre on the beach.'

She got out of bed abruptly and wrapped herself in her silk kimono. 'It's stifling in here,' she said. 'Let's sit outside.'

They moved on to the veranda. Under the moonlight the ocean shone in cool, dazzling splendour like an enormous heaving carpet of shimmering silver. Twinkling stars seemed very close to earth. A big liner at anchor in the bay sat like a dark pencil across the length of the horizon, its lights burning steadily, while a few fishing boats moved slowly over the water towards the open sea. Luz felt the nostalgic quality of the atmosphere.

Andrés took up the seat next to her, where he had sat so many times in the past month, but tonight was different. Tonight, though he was near her, the man she loved had never felt so far away, forbidden to her now by his own betrayal. For her pride's sake, and to remain sane, she must not let herself be tempted.

They stayed silent, avoiding each other's gaze, looking out to sea, listening to the quiet breath of the wind. Luz tried to appear remote and aloof. Andrés lit a cigarette and puffed on it for a while. Neither wanted to speak, spellbound by the beauty of the night, savouring this temporary moment of truce.

When Andrés spoke at last his voice was hoarse and low, revealing bitterness long suppressed.

'I am the lovechild of *La Pouliche*, a *gitana*, and of Eduardo de Salazar. I was born in a prison in Jerez, where my mother was serving a sentence for theft. I was only a few hours old when I was taken from her and brought to Cádiz. My father could not keep me but he loved my mother and so he arranged for me to be adopted by his sister, Eleadora, and her husband, who had no children. I grew up ignorant of this until a few weeks before my sixteenth birthday when Eduardo, who was dying, called me to his bedside. He told me the truth and I went looking for my natural mother. She had made the enormous sacrifice never to approach me, though she had followed every step in my life since I was adopted by my aunt and uncle.

'Eduardo's solicitor sent her a report on my progress every month, with the latest photographs, and an annuity so she could live comfortably. She could have taken a house on her own but she chose to live with her people, the gypsies. Because I am her son and because they respected her, despite having a *gajo*'s child, they received me with open arms. Among them, I discovered a part of myself that had always puzzled me. Before then, I had always been wild and restless, wanting something so different from the life I knew.'

His lips curved in a gentle smile. 'My mother lavished on me the love I had never had from Eleadora. Some of my gypsy family resented it, but she was the queen of our people and her word was law.' A shadow passed over his face. 'At first, I visited once a month and slowly I began to spend more time with them until it became a way of life. Ten days a month at the gypsy camp, the remaining days among the people I grew up with. My mother had given me the name Leandro, Eduardo chose the name Andrés and I was baptized Andrés Leandro.'

He stubbed out his cigarette and gazed out over the gently rolling waves. 'I went to university, went travelling, still struggling with my identity. When I returned to Cádiz in my mid-twenties, I became a successful businessman, dabbling in the latest technologies. Transformation of any kind fascinated me – I suppose that's why I played around with coloured contact lenses when they came on the market. Another early innovation I couldn't resist. Once I tried them, the buzz I got from splitting my personality was exhilarating. I could be the wild, dishevelled green-eyed gypsy, Leandro, one day, and then slip back into the persona of Andrés the next: both were me and neither were me. I already had a reputation for a degree of eccentricity so everyone got used to the brown-eyed Andrés de Calderón quickly enough. Over the past few years it's given me great satisfaction to lead a double life, to keep those sides of myself separate.' He sighed heavily and turned his head towards her. 'Until now.'

Luz surveyed him a moment, taking in the features she knew by heart: the strong jaw, the curve of his lips, the hollows in his cheeks that were a little deeper tonight. The pain on his face and the haunted look in his eyes tore her apart.

She took a deep breath. 'Why didn't you tell me?' she asked. 'Why the lies? Why the deceit? I still don't understand,' she said desperately, tears running uncontrollably down her cheeks.

He sighed deeply, closing his eyes briefly as though to shut out a nightmare. 'I wish I didn't have to tell you this and hurt you even more,' he whispered. 'Fate has played a cruel part in both our lives …' He hesitated.

Luz wiped her face with her hand. 'Anything is better than not knowing,' she told him resolutely.

'My mother's name was Marujita, she was the gypsy your father sent to prison more than thirty years ago with her brother, who died there of pneumonia,' he stated flatly, lifting his gaze to face her.

Luz sucked in a deep breath. Her head was spinning painfully; the puzzle was fitting together and she could almost guess what he would say next. She stared at him.

'Yes, my father sent them to prison,' she said eventually. 'Were you never taught right from wrong? They were thieves and, correct me if I'm wrong, but your mother's brother drew a knife on my father and stabbed him. What was he supposed to do? Give them his blessing and let them go?' She was trembling with anger.

'I was only stating facts, not defending their actions,' he told her gently.

'How could you want to be part of those people? How can you live among such immorality and violence?'

'Those people are my blood but I'm not proud of what they did, Luz.' Andrés leaned forward, his elbows on his knees. 'Gypsies live by the *navaja* but so do many of the poor. It's only part of who the *gitanos* are.' He smiled a sardonic smile. 'I cannot change the fact that my mother's blood runs in my veins but it doesn't matter what I say or do, you're determined to paint me black as black, is that not so, Luz?'

In her shock at his revelation, part of her knew she was being unfair to him in laying the past crimes of his family at his door, but it was too much to take in. Yet another layer of this man was being exposed that disturbed her beyond anything else he had said. His family had hurt her own, and presumably hated them still, and he had concealed his true identity from her since the first day they had met. There could only be one reason for that. But as Luz looked at him, she knew that the trembling she felt was modified by a different kind of passion, one that had always consumed her, and always would.

His green gaze moved over her, holding her eyes captive. She felt it burn on her skin. Her pulse was going crazy, her senses ablaze with the need of him; he was sitting far too close for comfort. Guilt and confusion washed over her. Desire fought with fear and she turned her face away so as not to succumb.

She was tired of fighting. 'Please go away,' she uttered thickly.

'Why? You want me as much as I want you.'

'That's beside the point,' she said angrily, staring straight ahead, concentrating determinedly on the dappled dark skies in front of her.

'I love you, Luz. I can't live without you. I want to marry you,' he whispered miserably.

'What sort of love can you base on deceit?' she retorted hotly, turning back to face him, the sapphire blue of her eyes now a stormy grey.

'I need to tell you everything before I can go.' His voice was shaky and he was trembling. 'Don't think this confession is easy for me. God knows how much I have been dreading this moment of truth. And there's more.'

'Don't bother explaining, I can guess,' she sneered. 'You were taking your revenge for what my father did to your mother. Right?'

There was a silence. 'It was not quite like that,' he told her carefully. 'My mother wanted me to make you fall in love with me and then leave you, in the same way your father left her. I went along with her game because I knew that you would be mine anyway. She had no idea I had met you already, or that we were seeing each other and had fallen in love.' He was still watching her face. 'I made sure that Leandro moved into the shadows very early on and Andrés took over.'

Luz's eyes widened. 'You must be really proud of yourself,' she declared quietly. 'Not only did you manage to deceive me but you've also hoodwinked your own mother. What will she say when you tell her you want to marry me? Or are you planning to lie about that, too?' Her savage stare hit him head-on and he started painfully.

'My mother's dead, Luz,' he explained in a strained voice. 'She was dying of cancer and didn't have long when she demanded I carry out her vengeance. She died a few days ago – that's why I wasn't able to keep our date and why I was unreachable.'

For a few seconds Luz was nonplussed, not knowing what to say. *Absence carries its reasons*, that's what her own mother had said. It seemed she was right. Luz's features finally relaxed.

'I'm sorry, that must be hard for you,' she uttered softly. Forgetting herself, she covered his hand with her palm.

Within seconds he had pulled her to him and his mouth was on hers, fiercely coaxing. She had no time to breathe, to think, to resist. Temptation fuelled her already stirred senses, her own unabashed desire overwhelming the sense of betrayal that still gashed her heart. With a catch of her breath that merged into a sob, she felt her body yield to his touch, pliable as a liana, the better to feel him. She kissed him back hungrily, releasing all the love, the pent-up fever that had tortured her days and nights since they had last been together.

Still kissing her, Andrés moved her on to his lap and his hand slid inside her nightwear. His deft fingers found the swollen curve of one breast. Luz cried out as she felt the heat of his fingers on her skin. She was aware of how badly he wanted her when he pulled her closer and his hardness throbbed against her, begging for relief.

Tears rained inside her as a part of her wept for the vain hope of their love. She tried to remind herself of why she must put any thought of Andrés out of her mind; of what she would be letting herself in for if she submitted to the urge threatening to overtake her. But she had no future with Andrés. She loved him more than life itself, every inch of her craved him, but how could she build a future with someone who had betrayed her so profoundly?

Still, she was weak. She had no will when he kissed and stroked her the way he was doing now. Damned either way, she was drowning in the flood of sensations his caresses were creating; the dampness between her thighs and the ache of her flesh told her she was defeated. Her desire for him to take her, fill her, make her his own possessed her to the exclusion of everything else – so what use was fighting?

Would she ever be able to let her hands roam wantonly over another man as they were now doing with Andrés? She could feel him quiver with pleasure under her exploring fingers in the knowledge that she held as much power over him as he did over her. Would she ever again know the erotic excitement of experiencing her love so freely, so sensuously? There were no secrets now, no inhibitions as her mouth moved over his. They were attuned to each other, discovering hidden places that aroused them both to fever pitch, giving and taking with equal hunger and urgency. There was an almost hopeless desperation in the way she touched his face and curled her fingers tightly in his hair. How she loved the feel of his skin, the smell of him … every part of him.

'I love you, *quérida*,' he murmured between drinking in the sweetness of her kisses. 'We'll get married, and all this will be behind us for ever.'

She pulled back abruptly, and looked at him in a daze before half-falling off his lap and taking a few steps away. A slight breeze came up from the sea; the atmosphere was warm and scented. Across the garden, beyond the trees and shrubs, the Atlantic glistened. The tall lighthouse of Cádiz harbour vied with the moon and stars in lighting up the night. There was a long line of ships tied together and anchored at the entrance to the port. Tiny launches lit with paper lanterns scuttled over the water, looking like children's boats. The Puerto de Cádiz was busy tonight.

She felt as if she were being dragged into an abyss, clinging to the edge of bittersweet memories before being swallowed whole.

'No, Andrés,' she told him, 'tonight I will give myself to you for the last time. There's no future for us, I could never trust you again. I love you but part of me hates you, too. I don't think I could live with that.' Her voice was flat, completely devoid of emotion; it was so strangely unfamiliar to her, she did not recognize the sound of it as she spoke, looking straight out to sea. It might tear her apart but this could be her only way of saying goodbye, just one last time.

She heard him catch his breath as if smothering a gasp. Her heart was breaking for him, for her, for their beautiful love that now could never be. Marujita had won; the *gitana* had found her revenge.

There was a hushed silence. 'Hate is an ugly word, *quérida*,' Andrés said, slowly and stiffly now. 'There is nothing more I want, Luz, than to make you mine, now and forever, but if you won't marry me then I can't take what is not, and never will be, my right to take.'

She turned back to face him, anger rising swiftly again, spurred on by his rejection. 'You've made love to hundreds of women. You took me before. Not once, but so many times,' she jeered. 'What's the difference?'

He was standing now, his face distraught. 'Before I met you my heart was closed, so I didn't know any different. You opened it up with your innocence, your spontaneity and generosity. When we made love I was confident of your love, I had no reason to believe that one day we would not be together forever. Love doesn't judge. Love forgives unconditionally. For me now, *quérida*, the act of love is not only a union of two bodies but the communion of two souls. I don't want your body without your heart.'

A small voice inside pleaded with her to think again before it was too late but the hurt was still too raw and too great for her to listen. In rejecting her, he had just poured oil on the fire that already blazed within her. *Sanctimonious hypocrite*, she thought. His words only served to humiliate her and make her feel cheap. How dare he insinuate that she was wanton and lustful? How dare he turn the tables so as to lay the failure of their relationship at her door!

For a long moment no words came, just the storm fermenting deep inside Luz. Her mind was in a whirl and her heart began to thump in her breast. She had given him all that she had, and he had broken her. Only one need hung in the air now, to the exclusion of all else, and that was for him to disappear from her life. All the smouldering anger blazed up.

'Get out! *Go!*' she ordered, as though speaking to the most despicable creature she had ever seen, 'and I hope I never set eyes on you again!'

Andrés' green eyes darkened fractionally. He regarded her silently for what seemed an age, tortured pain written on his face, reflecting her own agony inside, and then he went without a word.

Numbly, Luz looked up at the tranquil starlit sky and then at the less tranquil but beautiful sea, shimmering like some live silver sheet under the caressing light of a misty moon. There were the passing ships, with lights twinkling from their mastheads and cabins, moving slowly out to sea, escaping towards new horizons.

The very foundation of her world had been cracked wide open; it lay shattered around her and she had no idea how to mend it. She envied those ships. For her the horizon was all fogged up. What new life could she escape to? How could she trust and love again after Andrés?

She leant against the balustrade, head in her hands. Oh, what had she done? Twisted pride and oversensitivity had wrecked her love, and her life, and now only the relics of joyful bygone days were left for her to dwell on. Tears flooded her. She sobbed for her lost love for she knew that she had truly burnt her bridges now and there was no turning back. Grief and bitter disillusionment, not least in herself, seeped through every pore. Andrés had accepted that she never wanted to see him again. She could not bear the thought that he was forever lost to her. If only she could claw back her words. Her hands clenched hopelessly into fists.

'Andrés, I love you,' she cried with all her might into the darkness but he was already too far away to hear.

*   *   *

The following afternoon Alexandra and Salvador sat opposite their daughter in the comfortable living room of L'Estrella, listening intently as Luz told them most of what had happened over the past few days. Her parents had arrived for a flying visit on their way to see some old friends in Cádiz, who had procured a few horses and wanted Salvador's advice, though Luz realized that their main agenda was to check in to see if she was all right. As soon as she saw them, she knew she would have to tell them the truth, no matter what their reaction. They were expecting to hear why Andrés had stood her up for dinner; they would never in a million years guess the terrible story behind it. Now, Luz sat cross-legged on the high-backed sofa, nervously playing with the cushion in her lap.

It took her a while to unburden herself of the whole chain of events: how Andrés had seemed at his birthday party, his argument with Adalia, then the sailing trip the following day when he had rescued her from the water. Salvador and Alexandra spoke little throughout, their expressions ranging from curious to concerned. With a faltering voice, Luz told them how Andrés had revealed his double identity as Leandro, the gypsy with whom she had first fallen in love; and then she watched their horrified faces as they heard that he was the son of Eduardo de Salazar and the gypsy Marujita, who had given birth to him in prison and was now dead.

When Luz reached the part about Marujita's plan of revenge, Alexandra gasped. She clutched Salvador's hand before rushing over to Luz and taking their daughter into her arms. Salvador cursed under his breath; frowning, he went over to the side cabinet to pour himself a drink.

Alexandra's instinctive gesture was Luz's undoing and at this she finally burst into tears. 'It's all such a mess. I just don't know what to do now,' she sobbed quietly against her mother's shoulder.

'My poor *niña*! To think that you went through all this alone,' said Alexandra softly, as she stroked Luz's satiny hair soothingly. After a few moments she pulled away slightly and held Luz's shoulders, looking at her intently.

'Can you see now why we were so over-protective of you? We always distrusted the gypsies, even though Marujita's family had left the camp at El Pavón.' Alexandra paused. It seemed to pain her to use the *gitana*'s name.

'We never knew where she'd gone after she left prison but we didn't want what happened with her all those years ago to come back on you somehow.' Her face contorted with anxiety and regret. 'And look what happened, even after all our efforts to keep you safe.'

Salvador gazed at his wife and daughter and came over to kiss the top of Luz's head. His face had been thunderous at the notion that anyone would have tried to threaten his family. Now, more than anything else, there was sadness in his eyes.

'She can't hurt you or any of us any more, God rest her troubled soul. There was so much hate in Marujita, even when she was young,' he said, swallowing a mouthful of manzanilla. He glanced at his wife and a look of understanding passed between them.

'The man I saw her dance with in Jerez years ago, the one I told you about, *querido*,' Alexandra said, looking up at her husband, 'he was an hidalgo, not a gypsy. That must have been Eduardo de Salazar …' She paused. 'It was the only time I ever saw real love in her eyes.'

'I remember,' he murmured. 'The moment I first saw him I knew she would be gone. It was the first time I could see a way of untying myself from her. I didn't know who he was at the time but I hoped she would find happiness with him. Perhaps she did, for a while.'

'So, Don Andrés was at least the product of true love,' Alexandra quietly stated.

Salvador sank back down into his chair, seeming to grapple with his thoughts. He then asked Luz: 'Did he always know he was half-gypsy?'

After wiping her eyes with a tissue, Luz shook her head. 'Not until he was sixteen. He lived as Eduardo's nephew, not his son, until Eduardo died.'

She then related what Andrés had told her, about how he had been adopted by his aunt and uncle as their own and had found out the facts of his birth from Eduardo on the artist's deathbed. Afterwards he had sought out Marujita and it was then that his gypsy roots had taken hold and he began to live a double life.

Salvador raised his eyebrows. 'It can't have been easy, finding out you're not who you think you are. And half-*gitano*, too.'

'He always seemed like a complicated young man but this is beyond what I ever imagined,' Alexandra said, gazing at Luz with wide eyes. 'All those years and no one ever knew. How could he be *her* son?' she added, as if to herself.

'I know, *Mamá*. I thought the same.'

Salvador glanced at his watch. 'Sorry, I ought to call the Belmontes. We're going to be later than we thought. In fact, perhaps we should postpone until tomorrow and stay with you tonight, *niña*? You've been through a lot.'

Luz smiled at the thoughtfulness of her father but shook her head. 'No, it's fine, *Papá*. You can stay for a while and still be with them for dinner. I think some time on my own is what I need to clear my head. Then maybe I'll come and spend a few days at El Pavón.'

'If you're sure, then all right.' He put down his glass and went into the next room to make the call.

Alexandra watched as Salvador closed the door behind him. 'I still can't believe that Don Andrés could have lived a double life for so long,' she mused. 'Apart from anything else, it must have been so confusing.'

Luz nodded and curled both feet up on the sofa. 'I could never understand his mood swings or the secretive air he always had, but now it all makes sense.'

'You know, most men are moody to some degree or other. Your father was just the same when we met,' Alexandra sighed. 'I couldn't work out what he was thinking half the time and it drove me crazy. But as it turned out, he was keeping things from me only because he was trapped in a difficult situation that he couldn't get out of and so he was protecting me. He loved me and didn't want to hurt me. Marujita and the gypsies had him backed into a corner. I know that now, but at the time I was filled with anger and jealousy.'

'Yes, I know that feeling, too.'

'Oh, how I wish you didn't, *niña*!' Alexandra smiled sadly at Luz and touched her cheek lightly. 'I won't pretend I'm not shocked to hear that Don Andrés is the son of Marujita. She was manipulative and vicious even then. No doubt prison made her worse, but your father was almost killed when her brother stabbed him.' As if reliving the memory, she shuddered.

'Doña María Dolores had no choice but to call the police and it was she who insisted on pressing charges, not your father. In many ways Salvador had an affinity with the gypsies that I didn't understand. I simply felt threatened by them.'

'Because of Marujita?' Luz offered tentatively. She didn't want to dredge up more painful memories but she had never heard her mother speak so openly before.

'Perhaps,' Alexandra sighed. 'There was that old witch Paquita too, always in the background with her strange, cryptic warnings. As soon I set foot in Spain, she was there, grabbing my hand, trying to tell my fortune. The dark magic that seems to surround them, it frightened me – it still does.'

Luz gazed at her mother.

'I suspected as much.'

She wondered how much power the old gypsy truly had. If Paquita's predictions for her mother had come true, maybe she knew Luz's destiny, too.

'What did she say to you? Did she predict that you and *Papá* would find happiness?'

'She predicted a number of things,' said Alexandra. 'For one, your father's accident before I met him and then the obstacles I would have to overcome … but yes, she saw that we would finally be together. Not that I wanted to listen to any of it, of course. At the time I didn't know if she was trying to help me or scare me.' Her gaze filled with apprehension. 'What has Paquita said to you, Luz?'

Luz paused, thinking back to the old *gitana*'s words. 'She told me that my destiny lies with someone called Gemini, that I mustn't try to avoid it or I'll be cursed. But then she said something about a curse of hatred that will never be broken unless it's erased by love. Andrés, Leandro, he must be Gemini … and the evil she talked about that surrounded me might have been his mother's attempts to use him for her revenge against you and *Papá*.'

At this Alexandra looked at her pensively and reached out to smooth a stray tendril of hair away from Luz's face. 'If Don Andrés has truly been accepted by the gypsies, he must have been willing to sacrifice everything so as not to carry out Marujita's wishes. The code of the gypsies is unforgiving … A curse of hatred erased by love,' she mused.

Emotion swam in Luz's eyes. 'But what if I've ruined any chance of happiness by pushing him away? What if it's too late for love?'

Alexandra's green eyes were still the hue of an emerald ocean and now they fixed on her daughter with deep understanding. 'It's never too late for love, darling,' she said.

Salvador re-entered the room and resumed his seat, having refilled his glass. 'So we are back to the question of love? That's what this all boils down to.' His eyes darkened, focusing on Luz keenly. 'Do you still love this man, even though he has lied to you and hurt you?' he asked, his face grave.

'Yes, *Papá*, I do.'

'And you believe that he's a good man?'

Luz sighed. She knew the truth in her heart now. It lay immutable like a bright, enduring light within her, even after all the furious arguments that had wrestled for supremacy in her mind.

'Yes. I don't think he would have carried out his mother's wishes, even if she had lived. He was just tangled up in two worlds. I believe he truly loves me but I drove him away.'

'So, in that case, he will come back to you.'

Luz hugged a cushion to her chest. 'Oh, *Papá*, I said some terrible things to him. I felt betrayed and wanted to punish him. I thought that if he was the son of someone as evil as Marujita, perhaps her nature had tainted him, too.'

Salvador nodded and clasped his fingers together. 'He's his own man, Luz. Andrés de Calderón has a good reputation in the community and that takes hard work and a strong character to build. Besides, I've looked him in the eye and seen what kind of man he is.' He picked up his drink and gazed into its depths.

'I know what it is to become dragged down by circumstances, no matter how hard you struggle.' He glanced at his wife. 'Your mother and I both do.'

Alexandra smiled ruefully. 'Your father's right. Don Andrés may have made mistakes, and there's no doubt his background makes life more complicated, but from what I've seen he's an honourable man, and one who has lost much. The past is done with, we should all bury it now.' She reached out and squeezed her daughter's hand. 'You must hold out for love, if you're certain you've found it, Luz.'

'The world is changing,' added Salvador. 'No matter what happens, if Andrés is somehow to keep his ties with the gypsy community, then we are all going to have to become more tolerant.' His eyes settled on his daughter. 'Think about what you truly want, that's all you need to do, *niña*.'

*   *   *

It was a rare stormy day. Since the night of Andrés' visit, Luz had taken to jogging every day on the beach to her favourite place where she had twice met Paquita in the past; somehow it helped clear the cobwebs that misted up her brain. The words of the old gypsy made sense to her now. Deep in her subconscious, she wished the gitana would appear again and perhaps tell her a way to rekindle her lost love and save her happiness, even though the sands of time may have already run out. Often she came across gypsy youths loitering on the beach, but Andrés was never among them. Whenever she passed the gitanos, she could feel them sniggering behind her back and wondered how much they knew.

At the beginning, after her parents had left, she had tried to put all thoughts of Andrés out of her mind, needing to empty herself of him and find some peace, just for a while. But she could not escape him in her dreams: green eyes burned through her and then turned to smouldering black. She was haunted by his caresses, the sound of his voice calling her name. Despite her father's advice she did not know what she wanted; pride still made her emotional wounds hurt, and she hoped that fate would somehow intervene to light the path ahead.

As the days went by and the shock wore off, she knew that however painful his revelations had been, she would always love him. Nothing could alter that. She felt lost, incomplete, without him. Something was missing in everything she did. She had been a fool to think she could stop loving him because he had a different name, or because he had deceived her. How would she have reacted had he told her the truth from the start? Would she ever have got to know the real Andrés? He was right: love forgave all, love did not judge.

Many times she had gone by his office building, hoping to bump into him, but he remained invisible. The notes for Eduardo's biography lay untouched on her desk. How could she continue with the project now, given all that had happened?

The weather was cooler. Consequently, the beach was quite crowded when Luz, dressed in white shorts and a vest, went down for her daily jog. Here and there seaweed was piled up on the shore, brought in by the rough sea. There were barking dogs, running backwards and forwards to their owners with a piece of wood or a small ball in their mouths; children were flying their kites, their shrill shouts mingling with the screeching of seagulls and other birds of prey fighting for titbits of litter. The ocean was teeming with traffic, going into or leaving the port. A collier, deeply laden, with a thread of black smoke steaming from the funnel, was coming down the channel with the tide. The gypsy lads were on motorbikes today; one of them said something as Luz jogged past, causing them all to burst out into raucous laughter.

The sun was vanishing; clouds were gathering. Luz ran faster, the squelch of wet sand under her feet echoing in the silence, the fresh wind whistling in her hair, tossing wisps of it across her eyes. The long, drawn-out sound of a foghorn being blown out at sea tore the air. Seabirds were screaming, swooping and diving. As she reached her favourite place, she glanced at her stopwatch: she had beaten her personal best. For a brief moment she was happy, her eyes starry. She was panting a little, still flushed; her hair had come adrift from her headband and was blowing across her face.

The sea was choppy, rhythmically heaving. She climbed on to a boulder. Waves broke with savage force on the brown rocks along the shore. They dashed with a loud bang and a shower of spray as they hit sloppily against the jagged cliffs, the water spuming back among the inlets between the rocks. A chill breeze brushed against her. Luz stared up at the sky. Sweeps of cloud feathered the normally clear blue heavens and the air was close. *I'd better go*, she thought for she did not like the look of it. She would rest only a short while before starting back home; it wouldn't be good to get caught up in the storm.

Suddenly Luz was aware of a man's figure standing not too far away, beside a boulder. He was tall with dark skin and, though his long, tousled hair was peppered with grey, as were his side-whiskers, he looked strongly built. Scored down one side of his face was a scar, above which piercing jet eyes stared at her. She had noticed him among the gypsies loitering on the beach several times in the past few days. Because the weather was grim, giving her thoughts a melancholy turn, she could only think that the menacing gypsy was an ill omen. Perhaps he wanted money. She turned her head away and fixed her attention on the frothy, relentless waves bubbling with foam as they broke along the shore below her. Perhaps if she remained aloof, he would simply go away.

Oddly enough, the aloofness did not put the man off, instead seeming to act as a spur to draw him on. Silently he moved closer and, when she withdrew her gaze from the sea, deciding to make a move, she found him standing almost next to her, barring her way. She glanced around; the part of the beach where she had ended up was deserted. In a rasping voice, the gypsy said something in *Caló*, which she did not understand, but she could still read the sneer. Luz stood rigid, rooted to the spot, as though paralyzed by a snake bite. Terror crept up on her as she met the vicious black eyes looking at her with such hatred, his mouth a cruel, ugly line. Staring into her face, he said something else to her in *Caló*, which she still could not make out.

'*No entiendo*, I don't understand,' she whispered.

He spat at her and then, as she tried to run, he lunged towards her suddenly and gripped her wrist fiercely. She jerked back so abruptly that she fell sprawling on to the wet sand with a cry. 'Please, I have no money on me, but take this ring … it's worth a lot of money. It's gold,' she gasped, sick fear curling in her stomach as he advanced towards her.

'I don't want your gold, you bitch!' he snarled contemptuously. His glittering eagle eyes moved over her openly, taking in her satiny skin, her long raven-black hair, her soft mouth and the slender curves of her body. 'I want to dirty you, the way your father dirtied my sister and killed my older brother. I want to finish the half-baked job that wimp of a nephew of mine started.'

He was now on top of her, his mouth searching roughly for hers, while she fought like a wild cat, her head moving frantically from side to side in desperate fear to avoid his coarse lips. Now crying uncontrollably, she was pleading with him to let go. She could smell the sweat on his oily skin and the mixture of garlic and alcohol on his warm breath. His body felt hard, hot and heavy as he pressed into her weaker frame, his calloused fingers pushing at her vest sleeves and lingering hungrily around her bare shoulders. Despite all her kicking, heaving and wrestling, he was far too strong for her and she couldn't throw him off. All her limbs were trembling with the effort of fighting. She tried once more to get away from under him but he pinned her down with one hand, while the other held her wrists tightly captive. He was just about to swoop down on to her mouth like a bird of prey when he was jostled from behind and jerked back by two powerful hands.

'*Bastardo!* Take your hands off her!' Luz heard Andrés cry as he raised his fist and punched her aggressor full in the face.

The sun had vanished. Now the two men were scuffling on the sand. A chill wind swept across their backs. Luz watched, her eyes wide and anxious. Andrés was wiry and muscled; he moved with speed and was lighter on his feet. Built like a bull, her assailant moved less quickly but was more cunning in the way he fought, ducking and weaving to tire his opponent, his keen eyes never wavering from Andrés' face.

Thunder stabbed the stillness of the atmosphere, pounding and rolling in magnificent peals that seemed to shake the world. A blinding fork of lightning tore the sky and Luz's eyes filled with terror as they fell on the scintillating reflection of the blade caught in the flash of light.

'Andrés, he's got a knife,' she cried out. But it was too late: the sharp edge of the weapon slashed out, slicing his arm. He stumbled. The gypsy lifted his hand to strike again; once more the knife came down, this time catching him just behind the collarbone, missing his neck by a few inches, just as Andrés leapt forward with his fist balled and struck his opponent between the eyes. The *gitano*'s head was flung violently back; he lost his balance, staggered and collapsed to the ground, hitting his head against a rock as he did so. He lay inert.

Meanwhile Andrés had blacked out and was sprawled on the sand semi-conscious, unable to move or open his eyes. Blood was gushing profusely from his wounds. Luz ran to him, her heart thumping furiously, tears streaming down her face.

'Andrés, Andrés, my love, answer me!' She was sobbing. 'Oh God, please make him all right.' Dropping to the ground beside him, her arms moving to encircle him, she lifted his head on to her lap, cradling it against her bosom. He looked as if he wanted to speak but his body was still, except for the shuddering of his lips.

People had gathered at the scene by now; onlookers who had witnessed the start of the fight but not wished to interfere and others who had been alerted to the scene.

'We've called an ambulance,' said one.

'The *gitano*, he's dead,' added another.

'Hold on in there, my love,' Luz was whispering in Andrés' ear. 'Help is on its way. Please don't leave me,' she begged, her face so

close to his that her tears fell on his pale cheeks. 'Forgive me …
I've been a fool … I love you. I love you so much. Stay with me!'
Almost hysterical now, she was sobbing her heart out.

The ambulance arrived and so did the police. She wanted to
accompany Andrés in the ambulance to the hospital but *la policia*
refused to let her go. According to them, she was a key witness to
the incident and they needed her statement. Luz watched helplessly
as Andrés was taken away on a stretcher and the ambulance was
driven off, bells blazing.

The storm had passed and the sun had come out. Now the
police interrogated everyone present. Two English women, who
had witnessed the whole incident from the very beginning, told
their version of the story. The young woman had been attacked,
Andrés had tried to save her; he carried no weapon. Yes, the
gypsy man had been armed with a knife. He'd struck twice and
wounded Andrés both times before the young man lashed out in
self-defence. The aggressor fell to the ground, knocking his head
against a rock. Other people, who had arrived halfway through
the quarrel, corroborated Luz's and the two English women's
statements. It was obviously a case of self-defence.

Later, when Luz visited the hospital to ask after Andrés and to
try to see him, her heart sank as she spied a familiar figure sitting
outside his room: Adalia. At the sight of Luz, the other woman's
eyes narrowed.

Adalia stood up briskly on her approach. 'Leave him alone,'
the socialite coldly warned her. 'Haven't you done enough
damage? Like your parents, you're just bad luck. He doesn't want
to see you, he doesn't need this kind of drama in his life. If you
persist in hounding him, he will file a complaint of harassment
against you. He will get a restraining order forbidding you to
ever go near him again.' Adalia delivered this lethal threat in one
short burst, her voice low, and her glare pierced her rival with
diamond-cutting sharpness.

'And now go,' she said, taking hold of Luz's arm forcefully, trying to lead her away, 'before I call security to throw you out.'

Luz wrenched her arm from Adalia's grasp. She was trembling with anger inside but her face, except for its sudden pallor, remained impassive.

'Don't touch me. And don't tell me what Andrés needs either. You should already know by now that it isn't you.'

Adalia blinked, her pale eyes wide with surprise.

But Luz was not going to make any more of a scene in the hospital. She walked off silently, determined to find a way to speak to Andrés without the presence of his vicious watchdog.

*   *   *

Alexandra and Salvador had flown to Luz's side as soon as they had heard about her attack on the beach. They insisted on staying with her at L'Estrella and, still deeply shaken by the incident, she was glad of their love and attention; though after a few days she insisted she was fine and they should return to El Pavón. She would come and stay soon, she reassured them. Reluctantly, they agreed, leaving her in the capable hands of the trusted Carmela. The housekeeper's shocked response to Luz's ordeal had illicited an angry tirade against all gitanos, followed by a flurry of extra cooking and fussing around the young woman. However, throughout everything, it was Andrés that Luz was more concerned about. She couldn't stop thinking about him and how seriously he had been injured.

During the following weeks Luz rang his office twice a day, religiously enquiring about his health, each time giving a false name. A month had passed before she was told that he was completely recovered and would be at his office the following day.

Luz pondered whether to get in touch with him at his home, El Ecrin, at Puesta de Sol or at his office. She came to the conclusion that all three places were a bad idea. Adalia and her brother would be vigilant, taking every precaution in their bid to prevent her from seeing Andrés. No doubt they had umpteen ways of stopping her and she did not want to awaken their suspicions. Adalia had likely seen this as another opportunity to ensnare Andrés, despite his previous refusal to marry her, and was busy trying to insinuate herself back into his affections while he was vulnerable.

Luz slept badly that night. Nightmares assailed her, making her relive the gypsy's attack again and again, turning her fear of Andrés' death into reality as she watched his inert body sprawled on the beach, bathed in blood, while the gypsy laughed loudly, his face an ugly mask of cruelty. She woke with beads of perspiration on her brow and, though it was not yet morning, she got up, took a cold shower and dressed.

To ease her nerves, she sat out on her veranda but her mind went round in circles as she deliberated how she might get to see Andrés, dreaming up scenarios in which she would bump into him, or where he came to her. Indeed Andrés filled her every waking and sleeping thought. He had not called, nor had she expected him to: why would he do so when she had emphatically told him that she never wanted to see him again? She must find a way of getting in touch with him, of talking to him and asking his forgiveness.

Finally dawn broke in the east and morning came. It came with a hush and a blinding whitening of the sky so special to Cádiz, extinguishing the lights of the stars in the canopy above her. Blood-red streaks and a breathtaking array of colour followed closely afterwards across the horizon. Even though the sky was a glorious expanse that stretched infinitely now into the light of day, Luz felt hemmed in: she needed to get away. She decided to visit the little cove to which she had not returned since her break-up with Andrés.

After donning a bikini and shorts she went down to the beach. As she boarded her boat and motored towards her destination some strong and insistent feeling compelled her to go in the opposite direction, back to Andrés' secret place. Would she find him there? Her eyes filled with tears. She had missed the lonely beach where their love had bloomed and blossomed, all those happy days before tragedy struck.

She had never travelled so far in her boat, and she hoped that she would find the place easily enough. Up came the sun behind her, gilding everything with a special glow. The sun touched the luminous town of Cádiz with a blaze of gold and crimson, window upon window seemingly on fire. As she went, Luz marvelled at its beauty. Wherever the warm rays caught the water, myriad jewels flashed and flamed. The air was sparkling-clean and light, exhilarating. Her heart was filled with a crazy euphoria, coupled with a vague apprehension, but also with hope. In the quiet of this early hour, before the sun followed its natural course, everything seemed pure, untainted. She loved this time of day.

Luz had no difficulty in finding the cove but she entered it through a different opening, where she knew there were fewer rocks, and then anchored her boat at the entrance to the bay.

On the beach, as she rounded one of the boulders, her eyes widened and she caught her breath in disbelief. The place was deserted – almost. *Was she still dreaming?*

He was sitting on a rock, looking out to sea.

Luz's heart was pounding; the blood that resounded in her ears was deafening.

He turned his head and looked at her. She stared wonderingly at him for a moment and then she ran to him, her long limbs sprinting gracefully along the shoreline.

Still, he did not move, his eyes ensnared by her approaching figure. Dressed only in Bermuda shorts, his chestnut hair was loose, blowing away from his tanned face in the soft breeze, golden strands shining in the morning sunshine. And here was the sensuous, generous mouth with those perfect, sculpted lips, the smooth, tanned skin of his torso and the potent sexuality emanating from his whole being. In that moment she recalled the strong tenderness of him and her sheer abandonment when in his arms. The surge of passion overwhelmed her, bringing tears to her eyes. Her throat tightened as she fought to choke them back. It was his eyes that told her what she yearned to know: he could not suppress the fire that burned in his green irises as she reached him and she knew beyond doubt that he loved her and had forgiven her.

She was flushed, her vision filmed with tears, as she threw her arms around him, almost knocking him over. He winced as his gaze rested on her wistful face. She was trembling.

Still sitting on the rock as she stood beside him, he lifted a hand and brushed his thumb against her cheek.

'You're here,' was all she said.

'Where else would I be?'

She looked down at his shoulder and then to his arm. Her fingers gently trailed along the pink scars before she met his gaze again.

'I couldn't see you at the hospital. Then I looked for you everywhere … but I was afraid.'

His eyes travelled over her face; he nodded his understanding. 'I thought you hadn't come, so I came here instead.'

Her heart was bursting with too many unspoken words, too overwhelming to voice.

'Don't look at me like that, *querida*,' he murmured softly and then he bent his head and took her parted lips with his hungry mouth. It was enough to set every bone in her body melting; she was on fire.

Suddenly, his powerful arms lifted her, his hands encircling her tiny waist. He pulled her up with a latent strength that took her breath away. She was now straddling him, her firm breasts pressed against his muscular chest, aware of the furious pounding of his heart echoing the reckless beat of her pulse. With her thighs pressing against his hard hip, she could feel the aggressive potency of his arousal, brushing the swollen pearl in the centre of her femininity, sending each nerve end of her senses into wild havoc. A molten dampness flooded her. Clothes were in the way. She fumbled for the zip of his shorts and pulled it down. Still holding on to her, he lifted himself so he was standing and with one sleek movement rid himself of his garment. He peeled away the top of her bikini before sliding his palms underneath her and removing the skimpy piece of material that covered her.

As flesh met flesh, they both gasped. Their skin was alive, feverish with desire. First, they made love with their eyes, their mouths, their hands, tantalizing, stroking, fondling, kissing and savouring; sensitive to each other's needs, stimulating and revelling in each other's pleasure. She was Eve, he was Adam; he gave, she responded; she offered and he took; a hedonistic game of exploration that knew no bounds and over and over brought them to the brink. But they held back, floating on a sweet wave of sensual abandonment, both wanting to prolong the exquisite torture in the knowledge that their final coupling would enthrall all the more.

Then, as they hovered for the umpteenth time on the edge of the cliff, his palms cupped the curves of her small, firm bottom. He lifted her a fraction, drawing her closer to his need, parting her thighs a little more. As the heat of his arousal brushed against the moist ripeness of her, fire spread through her veins like molten honey and she opened up for him, willing and pliant.

He slid into her smoothly. She felt his potency grow as he filled her softness and the silky liquid of her desire eased him deeper and deeper into her. Now he was trembling violently, shudders rippling through him, his breathing harsh as he tried to control his mounting need for release. She wrapped her thighs more intimately around him, arching her back; her arms encircled his neck so she could draw closer and experience the vigour of his masculinity in her core. He cupped her firm swollen breasts, the tips of his fingers teasing their taunt pink peaks, making her quiver and moan, pleading for sweet deliverance.

Made for each other, they knitted together perfectly. The fit, the movement, the rhythm, the breath were one. With a last wild thrust he drove harder and further inside her. And suddenly all restraint was unlocked and they were moving up and down and rocking as one. Their tempo quickened. She held her breath; her eyes glazed over. The gratifying sensation came in a succession of spasms rushing through her, wave upon delicious wave until she was awash with a shattering ecstasy. Her body, her mind, her voice cried out his name; her head thrown back, nails digging into his shoulders. Buried deep inside her he was submerged in the ocean of her pleasure and his control abandoned him. His gasps became gradually sharper as his need grew faster, his chest rising and falling urgently. All thought ceased, surrendered to visceral pleasure. His groan was wild, primitive and long as he exploded in her depths and was catapulted over the abyss, shuddering and delirious with passion. Gradually they floated down on a cloud of exquisite sensation, each joining the other in a dream world where light, erotic possibilities and contentment were king.

For a long time they remained silent, locked in each other's arms, body and soul satiated and at peace, drinking in the blueness of the ocean, secure in the knowledge that nothing would ever threaten their love again.

Later, much later, they lay on the beach under the stars, cloaked by the darkness of night.

Luz gazed up anxiously into her gypsy lover's green eyes.

'Andrés …'

His smile was languid and loving. 'Umm, *Luz de mi vida, mi amor, mi dulci amor?*'

'I love you,' she whispered.

'*Y te adoro*, and I adore you.'

'Do you forgive me for all the terrible things I said to you?'

Andrés gazed down intently into her sapphire eyes. His lips brushed softly against hers. He grinned and tightened his embrace, drawing her closer. 'What terrible things, *querida*? A great philosopher once said that forgiving implies remembering and I only remember beautiful things about you.'

At this he nuzzled his chin against her hair, inhaling its sweet scent, and closed his eyes. Luz settled deeper into his embrace, curving her body into his. Her heart gave a flutter of pure joy as she recognized the strong and unconcealed tremor of passion that coursed through him again: the sign of a hunger only she could assuage. Tenderly he stroked her hair and her cheek, her throat, her shoulder and then finally her breast. She moved sensuously under his touch and lifted her flushed face so he could read in her eyes the love and the need that mirrored his own.

'*Dios Mio, que te quiero,*' he whispered against her parted lips and then let his body say the rest.

About the author:

Q AND A
WITH HANNAH FIELDING

Viva España

What inspired you to write a Spanish trilogy?

When I first started to write *Indiscretion*, I had no idea that this first book in the trilogy would be the beginning of a long romance with Spain. As I visited that beautiful, flamboyant country and met its passionate, life-loving people, I immersed myself in the literature and culture, the architecture and history, and immediately realized I had a deep affinity with the Spaniards.

In my early draft of *Indiscretion*, the book was set in the seventies but, by the time I'd reached the middle of the book, I realized that it would be difficult for me to become involved with another country for my next novel – I had learnt so much about Spain that I was deeply in love with the country and with everything Spanish. That is when the seed of the next book, *Masquerade*, began to germinate in my mind.

General Franco's regime was in full swing in Spain during the fifties and, for *Indiscretion*'s heroine, Alexandra, who arrives in Andalucía at the beginning of that decade, Spanish society seems to be frozen in the Dark Ages.

Masquerade is set in the second half of the seventies. Franco is dead. Now that the tyrant is gone, the nation is reborn; Spain has opened its borders to outsiders and is preparing to enter what is now the European Union. Consequently Luz, Alexandra's daughter and the heroine of *Masquerade*, has a much more emancipated attitude to life, as do her parents and the book's hero.

In *Legacy*, the final book, the story takes place in the present day and Spain has changed out of all recognition. It is a much more liberal country now, where old prejudices and narrow-minded concepts are almost a thing of the past. However, the problems our hero and heroine have to face, the hurdles they must overcome, are of a more complex nature and are almost more challenging.

My Andalucían Nights Trilogy is a journey through Spain's different historical periods and focuses on how my heroes and heroines confront the issues facing their respective generations – that is what I found fascinating to write.

What differences did you want to convey in this heroine, Luz, compared with Alexandra in *Indiscretion*?
In *Indiscretion*, Alexandra is escaping the stifling background of post-war England. She is a successful author in her own right but has been brought up by a strait-laced aunt. Intelligent, sensitive and curious but most of all a romantic, she embarks on a journey to Andalucía to meet her estranged Spanish family. Although she is faced with even more stifling traditions and rules at El Pavón than she was back home, Alexandra, being proud and a staunch individualist, recklessly follows her own naïve star and, in view of the place and the times, almost ruins her life.

More than twenty years later, in *Masquerade*, Alexandra's passionate daughter, Luz, decides to return to Spain after an English education, wanting to embrace her Spanish nature. She is intelligent, energetic and flamboyant. Like her mother, she has a romantic view of the world and her strong independent streak makes her even more rebellious than Alexandra but, in the post-sexual-revolution seventies, the more lenient rules of Spain and the more modern attitude of her parents make for an easier confrontation with Spanish society. Adventurous and daring, she gets herself mixed up in a delicate and risky situation where her pride and trust will come up against her love. Will she recognize the dictate of her heart?

What gave you the idea for the Gemini theme?
I have always been interested in astrology but, most of all, by the sign of Gemini, which symbolizes the psyche of the human race – the duality in our personalities. We all have two sides to us: good and evil, Dr Jekyll and Mr Hyde. In Chinese philosophy, *yin* and *yang* describe how opposite or contrary forces are actually complementary – two halves that together complete the whole. For one reason or another, we all wear masks concealing our inner thoughts and feelings, our 'other side'.

The idea of 'the mask' hugely appeals to me because it spells mystery, adventure, excitement and, most of all, romance. Romance novels have frequently used disguised identity to enhance a story. Often the birth of a great hero is shrouded in mystery or he has a hidden past that has led him to separate himself from the present. For example, Sir Gawain is shrouded by typical Arthurian ambiguities and Sir Percy Blakeney dons an outlandish disguise to become the Scarlet Pimpernel. Byron created a model for the romantic hero in his long poem, *Childe Harold's Pilgrimage*, which is still compelling today. The 'Byronic hero', possessed of so many different characteristics, is sophisticated, slightly dangerous but, most of all, mysterious.

Both heroes in *Masquerade* have some of those Byronic aspects and are shrouded in mystery, confusing Luz. On one hand, Leandro the fun-loving gypsy comes from a world of danger, darkness and violence; on the other, the ambiguous, tenebrous Andrés is born with a silver spoon in his mouth, affording him a good education, wealth and an enviable place in society. With their striking physical resemblance but such fundamentally different characters, they embody the two faces of Gemini. Both are attracted to Luz: so whom will her heart finally choose, the gypsy or the hidalgo?

What do you find most attractive about your heroes, Leandro and Andrés?

Leandro the gypsy and Andrés the gentleman are each in their own way handsome, charismatic and charming and, just like Luz, I was in love with them both while writing *Masquerade*.

Leandro is passionate, mischievous and impetuous, with a smile that mesmerizes and a devil-may-care attitude. He is proud and also kind, compassionate and loving.

Andrés has a darker personality. A sophisticated, successful businessman, he tends to be arrogant and is often enigmatic and taciturn. He is a real gentleman and sensitive, with feelings that run deep, keeping his passionate nature on a tight leash. Courageous and gallant, if he were the hero of a Medieval romance he would not hesitate to run to the rescue of his lady at his own peril.

What is your favourite scene in *Masquerade*?

The masked ball at El Pavón, the de Falla family home, of course. Ever since I can remember, I have been fascinated by masked balls and so, in each of the books in the Andalucían Nights Trilogy, my main characters end up at such an event. What better protection can you have than to hide behind a mask in order to court, mystify, to be yourself, uninhibited and incognito, and to indulge in acts you wouldn't do otherwise? Oscar Wilde said: 'Man is least himself when he talks in his own person. Give him a mask, and he will tell you the truth.'

Packing Up My Suitcase

Mountain/desert/jungle/ocean – which are you?

Definitely ocean. I have lived most of my life next to the sea. I grew up in a house in Alexandria, Egypt, where my bedroom had three windows looking over the Mediterranean. Later, when I came to England, my husband and I bought a house only ten minutes from the sea. And in France, where we live for half the year, our house and its gardens overlook a beautiful bay that is so blue in summer it can be hard to tell where the sea ends and the sky begins.

What is your guilty travel pleasure?
Shopping for unusual items at the local *marché aux puces* (flea market) near my home in France. I'm especially drawn to glassware; it's an exciting day if I spot a vase by Lalique, Baccarat, Daum or Schneider sparkling in the sun.

Who is your ideal travelling companion?
My husband, of course. If he is not available then my younger sister – we've had wonderful times and great laughs over the years.

Best meal on the road? And your worst?
Surprisingly enough, the best meal I've had was at the Restaurant de la Gare at Geneva train station. It was my father – who was a great gourmet – who tipped me off about this restaurant. They make the best steak tartare in the world.

Worst? In a café off the motorway in the former Yugoslavia in 1979, where I was presented with some sort of evil-smelling stew.

A Writer's Life

What was the first life-changing book you read and why?
I have my governess and the French nuns, my teachers, at Notre Dame de Sion to thank for my love of books. Balzac, Stendhal, Théophile Gautier and Victor Hugo were my introduction to beautifully written romantic stories, which were, to some extent, a part of the curriculum but which I also used to devour in my spare time. *Le Père Goriot*, *Le Rouge et le Noir* and *Notre Dame de Paris* are all wonderfully romantic tales that I have read

again and again. I then graduated to the works of Dostoyevsky, Tolstoy, the Brontë sisters and Jane Austen. Their stories all had fascinating heroes and heroines, wonderful yarns and settings, and the descriptions were so amazing I felt I was living and breathing the story.

How do you start writing?

I only start when I am totally satisfied with the plan of my novel. Having researched my facts thoroughly (through my travels, the internet, books, films, documentaries), I plan my novel down to the smallest detail. The muse is happy as long as I have a thesaurus to hand. I used to spend hours reading a thesaurus, totally engrossed in the nuances of words. Even now, when I'm looking up a word, I sometimes find myself absorbed in the subtle shadings of words – and time just flies by.

How do you finish?

I finish when I am absolutely sure that I have nothing more to say, being careful not to gild the lily.

Any good suggestions for overcoming writer's block?

One of my favourite quotes about writer's block is this, by Sir Philip Sydney: 'Biting my truant pen, beating myself for spite: "Fool!" said my muse to me, "look in thy heart, and write."'

I have two ways of dealing with writer's block. The first is patience. If you sit there in front of a blank page – and I've done that, sometimes for as much as a couple of hours – the muse eventually takes pity on you and visits.

The second is to get into my car and drive to a place that has inspired me in the past. That also usually works. It might be a garden overlooking the sea, a meadow carpeted with wild flowers if I'm searching for a setting for a love scene, or a café bustling with people where I can find the description for one of my characters.